D1357247

INSIDE TRACK

INSIDE TRACK

John Francome

headline

First published in 2002
by HEADLINE BOOK PUBLISHING

10 9 8 7 6 5 4 3 2 1

Cataloguing in Publication Data is available from the British Library

ISBN 0 7553 0060 2 (hardback)
ISBN 0 7553 0061 0 (trade paperback)

Typeset in Times by Avon Dataset Ltd, Bidford-on-Avon, Warks

Printed and bound in Great Britain by
Mackays of Chatham plc, Chatham, Kent

HEADLINE BOOK PUBLISHING
A division of Hodder Headline
338 Euston Road
London NW1 3BH

www.headline.co.uk
www.hodderheadline.com

Acknowledgements

With thanks to Nick Oldham, Gary Nutting (www.harrythe horse.net), Scarlett Shackleton, Debbie Wicks of Carlisle Racecourse and, in particular, John Hoskison, author of *Inside: one man's experience of prison.*

Prologue

5 November, 2001

While he waited, Malcolm Priest watched the fireworks from the top of the hill. It seemed an appropriate activity. He had more than time to kill tonight. The thought amused him. If ever there were a good night to plot murder and arson it was surely November the fifth.

He had parked in a lay-by popular with dog-walkers, ramblers and courting couples, though on this bitter night he had it to himself. On a clear day you could admire Pendle Hill and the Lancashire Fells to the west. More to the point you could look directly down into the village of Staithley laid out at your feet. It was a pretty place, if you ignored the petrol station on the road leading north and the video store thirty yards up from the church. In the lanes behind the High Street stood substantial suburban dwellings with luxury cars in the driveways, and spacious gardens where the bonfires now dwindled and the occasional banger still popped.

Malcolm had no interest in the fancy houses. His eye was on a small cottage with a tatty thatched roof at the end of the lane behind the church. Through his new binoculars – a recent present to himself after he'd lost sight of a grey filly in the mist at Ripon – he had a good view of the front of the cottage. A light had just been switched on upstairs – in the bedroom, he guessed. Nearly time to go. Thank God for that. He was getting stiff after sitting still for so long. A hot drink wouldn't go amiss. He found a stick of chewing gum in the glove compartment and folded it into his mouth.

More lights came on upstairs. He had a brief glimpse of a figure at the window – blonde hair, scarlet sweater – then the curtains were drawn. Mandy was going to bed. Soon to be joined, no doubt, by her boyfriend Pete – the slimeball who'd shaken him down for the money.

Go on, you dozy twerp, get upstairs and give her one.

But the light remained on downstairs. Druggies weren't renowned for their high sex-drive, Malcolm reflected. In which case it was a mystery why Mandy had fallen for Pete. During his own short fling with the stable girl, Mandy had been a fast little filly in every respect.

Malcolm got out of the car and stretched his limbs. The night was crisp, the stars brilliant in the black velvet sky. He took a deep breath and held the air in his lungs, then slowly exhaled. He had to keep his excitement under control.

It was a ten-minute walk down the road to the cottage below. Time to get cracking.

The cottage was barely visible from the lane, so overgrown was the hedge that bordered the front garden. Malcolm pushed boldly through the squeaking gate and strode up the bumpy gravel path. He wasn't bothered if his approach was overheard.

A light still shone from the downstairs window, spilling onto the unweeded flowerbed through a gap in the curtains. Malcolm peered through the crack. He could make out a shabby chintz sofa and a pair of legs – scuffed denims, bony black-stockinged feet – resting on a low-slung coffee-table.

Malcolm tapped on the window. There was no response from the figure on the sofa, just a muffled burst of studio jollity from a hidden television. He tapped louder.

The legs slid off the table and the figure leant forward, head turned towards the window. Lank chin-length hair framed a long pale face. Pete.

Malcolm moved back from the circle of light falling from the window as the curtains were pulled to one side. 'Who's that?' called Pete over the sound of the TV show.

Now he had Pete's attention Malcolm stepped into the porch and rapped on the front door. Eventually there were noises from inside, the sound of footsteps scuffling in the hall. The door opened uncertainly. Just six inches – but that was all Malcolm needed.

'Yeah?'

Malcolm shouldered through the gap, his fourteen stone of muscular bulk wedging the door wide. One gloved hand seized Pete's scrawny throat, pinning him against the wall.

'Sorry to barge in on you like this,' said Malcolm softly, leaning on Pete so he hadn't room to swing a fist or kick out. With his free hand he shut the door behind him. He was in and there was no going back now.

'Jesus, Malcolm,' the other man spluttered as Malcolm relaxed his grip. 'What the hell do you think you're playing at?'

Just the sound of his plummy voice irritated Malcolm. It reminded him of a boy at school, an arrogant little smartarse whose leg he'd enjoyed breaking in a rugger scrum. Even if Pete hadn't blackmailed him to the tune of thirty grand, Malcolm would have relished hurting him.

But not just yet.

'Listen – is Mandy upstairs?'

Pete nodded.

Their heads were so close it was a moment of intimacy. Pete's hair was in his face. It smelt of tobacco.

'Best if we don't disturb her, eh? We'll have a little talk in your front room.'

Pete stared into his eyes, unseeing. It struck Malcolm that he was scared witless. He had reason, after all.

'Don't worry,' he said soothingly. 'A short chat. Clear up one or two things.'

'Then you'll just go?'

What a weight of meaning there was in that one word 'just'.

Malcolm smiled pleasantly. 'Sure.'

Pete looked doubtful – he wasn't a fool after all – but he led the way into the front room.

It was a scruffy tip, stuffy from the heat of the open fire glowing in the hearth.

Malcolm shut the door behind him and hit Pete in the pit of the stomach with all his weight. The thin man doubled over onto the floor clutching himself, jerking his knees up into his chest. He was too winded to cry out.

Malcolm yanked the TV plug out of the wall. Bloody irritating racket. Pete was starting to whinge, breath rattling in his throat as he took in pathetic little gulps of air. It didn't sound good. Being an A-class doper his lungs were probably buggered.

The big man took careful aim and kicked the twitching figure just below the buttocks, in the unprotected vee of his bony thighs. Pete writhed in pain, trying to scuttle, crab-like, across the floor and away from his assailant. His squeals could be heard now, a high-pitched keening like an animal in pain. It was pathetic.

Shrugging off his coat – it was bloody hot work – but retaining his gloves, Malcolm took out the cord he'd brought with him. It would have been amusing to boot Pete some more but he had a plan and intended to stick to it.

The door opened as he was tying the last knot.

'Pete?'

He'd not seen Mandy for two years and the change in her was marked. Her buxom glow had faded. Her cotton nightdress revealed skinny legs. He remembered them hooked around his waist once as he'd had her in an empty stall, her thighs strong yet butter-soft. Not any more.

'Hello, Mandy.'

She stared at him, surprise and alarm in her pale grey eyes. Then she saw Pete, trussed up on the floor, and ran for it.

Malcolm caught her before she could get out of the front door, grabbing her squirming frame from behind. He clapped a hand over her mouth to stop her screaming. She bit him, her teeth sharp even through the thin leather of the glove. He slammed her head against the wall, catching the edge of a framed poster and knocking it to the floor. He could see her pupils contract in pain as he yanked her round to face him.

'Shut up or I'll really hurt you,' he hissed.

She glared at him. There was more fight in her than in that useless streak of piss lying next door. But she nodded her head – she'd be quiet. He took his hand from her mouth slowly. He didn't trust her an inch.

'Inside,' he ordered.

Pete lay just as he'd left him, snivelling into the threadbare rug. Mandy dropped to her knees beside him and cradled his head.

'You didn't have to hurt him, you bastard.'

Malcolm ignored the remark. Given the circumstances he'd been rather lenient. Not that he'd finished yet.

He took more cord from his coat. 'I've got to tie you up, Mandy.'

'No.'

'Just for a bit. Then I'll let you go.'

She was on her feet now, backing away from him. He could overpower her, of course, but he'd rather avoid a fight. If she scratched

4

his face he'd have some explaining to do. Fortunately, there was an easy way round the problem.

He kicked Pete in the stomach. The bound man yelped in a most satisfying manner.

'Stop it!' Mandy cried.

Malcolm stamped on Pete's ankle. A crunching sound preceded the howl of pain from his victim.

That settled the issue.

'You disgust me,' spat Mandy as Malcolm lashed her arms and ankles together. 'How could you do this?'

He pulled the cord tight. 'You lied to me. You said you'd never ask for money again. You should have kept your word.'

He dumped her on the floor next to Pete. Her nightdress had ridden up over her thin hips, revealing a pale belly and a fuzz of brown hair. Once the sight would have aroused him. Funny how desire for someone could just vanish. He pulled the nightdress down to cover her. She didn't appear to have noticed.

Now she changed tack. 'We only asked for what the newspapers would pay. It's over now, honestly, Malcolm. We won't ask for anything ever again.'

He squatted next to her. Time to get on. 'Where's the photo?'

'Pete gave it to you.'

'What about the negative?'

'It's lost.'

'Did you lose it before or after you made copies?'

'I can't find it, I swear.'

Malcolm paused. This was what he had expected, more or less. She'd have the negative, all right, but it might not be here.

'Where do you keep your other photos?'

'In the sideboard.' She indicated across the room with her head. 'Over there.'

He pulled out a tin box stuffed full of snapshots, together with their envelopes and strips of negatives. He pawed through them – holidays, horses, schoolgirl stuff – all Mandy's from the look of them. He found a batch from her days at Ridgemoor and shuffled through them carefully. There were pictures of stable lads and lasses, scenes on the gallops, even photos of himself, sharing a joke with his brother in the ring at Newmarket. Not what he was looking for.

'Is this all of them? None hidden anywhere else?'

'Honestly, Malcolm, no.'

'Why should I trust you? You lied to me before.'

'No!'

'It's OK, Mandy. I'd have done the same in your shoes.'

He poked the fading embers of the fire and threw a photograph into the grate. It flared after a few seconds and curls of orange soon reduced it to feathery grey ash. He tossed on more photos.

'What are you doing?' cried Mandy.

He ignored her. Flames were licking upwards now and he added coal. He thrust the poker into the heart of the blaze and left it there. He picked up more photographs and a shiny brown strip of negatives.

'Don't burn them, Malcolm, please.'

'It's all digital technology now,' he said, adding to the fire. 'Planning to get one, were you?'

She looked puzzled. 'What?'

'You can buy a top quality digital camera with thirty thousand pounds.'

She said nothing.

'And, of course, you'd have a little left over. Smart holidays, new car, deposit on a house maybe?' He left the fire and leaned over her. 'Or, of course, you could just blow it all on smack. What a great way to invest my money. Stick it all in junkie Pete's veins. Yours, too, from the look of you.'

'Sod off, you pig.'

'Where have you put the money?'

'It's nothing to do with me.'

Malcolm laughed. He admired her nerve.

'Where is it?'

She turned her head away but he took her small pointed chin between thumb and forefinger and yanked her head round. 'Tell me,' he said softly.

'I don't know.'

She was lying, he could tell. He'd handed the cash over to Pete in York at six and seen him get on a trans-Pennine train. He'd have had no time to get it to a bank or building society, even if he'd been so inclined. The cash must be here or nearby, Malcolm was sure of it.

He took the poker from the fire and inspected it. The end glowed a deep and threatening orange, turning to white at the very tip.

'Come on, Mandy, don't make it worse than it is. Where's the money?'

She shook her head wildly. He could see she was petrified. Good.

He raised the poker. The whiteness at the tip was fading but it was still hot enough to sear and burn and scar. He pointed it at her pale drawn face.

'Where is it?' he asked gently.

A voice burst into the silence. Malcolm had discounted Pete, curled in a heap of self-pity on the floor. Suddenly he shouted out, 'Don't tell him, Mandy! Don't tell the bastard anything!'

Malcolm needed no excuse. He pressed the end of the poker across Pete's thigh.

The reaction was delayed as the heat penetrated the denim of Pete's jeans. Then his body convulsed and threshed as he tried to escape. Malcolm pushed the poker down hard and the smell of burning fabric filled the room.

Mandy was shouting at him but he couldn't make out her words over the sound of Pete's screams. He lifted the poker and rammed a cushion over the squealing man's face, lowering the volume a fraction. How he despised the gutless fool wriggling in agony at his feet.

Mandy was weeping and a string of snot swung from her nose. How on earth could he ever have found her attractive?

'It's upstairs in the toilet,' she moaned. 'In the cistern.'

'Why didn't you say so in the first place?' he said as he tossed the poker into the coal scuttle.

The toilet was an old-fashioned ball-and-chain monstrosity and he had to stand on the pedestal to reach the cistern. He laid the heavy lid on the floor then removed his right glove and rolled up his sleeve before plunging his arm into the icy water.

Thirty thousand pounds in banknotes made a reasonable parcel, especially wrapped in plastic bags and bound with tape to keep out the wet. He yanked it out and tore open a corner of the plastic with his teeth, just to check. It was his money all right. Malcolm smiled as he wormed his damp hand back into his glove and made for the stairs.

He got downstairs just in time. Though her wrists were lashed together Mandy was picking at the knots that bound her feet. He yanked her arms away.

She saw the parcel with the money in his other hand.

'Just go,' she hissed. 'You've got what you came for.'

He put the money on the table. This was a two-hand job.

'Please don't hurt me,' she cried as she saw the look in his eye.

'Sorry, Mandy,' he said as he put his big gloved hands round her slender neck. And he really was.

He held her down for a long time after she'd ceased to thrash around. Five, ten minutes – he wasn't sure. Just to make sure she was dead. Him squatting astride her body, fingers on her throat, their loins pressed together. It was almost like old times.

The air was thick with feathery dust from the smouldering photographs and the fire still crackled in the grate. There was another sound too, a snuffling, whimpering noise like an animal in pain.

He looked away from Mandy's lifeless face into the bulging, terrified eyes of Pete. He had wedged his body behind the armchair and was trying to back further into the tiny space, as if he could somehow disappear from view.

Earlier in the evening, as he had waited on the hillside and contemplated Pete's treachery, Malcolm had looked forward to this moment – when he would put an end to the blackmailer's threat permanently. But now the time had come it was just a chore that had to be seen to.

'Let's get it over with, shall we?' he said as he stepped towards his cowering victim.

He put his coat on in the hall and turned off the light, before slipping out of the front door. At the front gate he paused and watched the orange light dance and flicker behind the curtain. The fire was catching hold. With luck it would destroy the bodies though he had no illusions that it would conceal the act of murder. Just as long as no one could pin it on him.

And they couldn't – he was sure of that.

A gust of icy wind knifed into him, bringing him down from the high that had gripped him. Suddenly he felt weary. He spat out the lifeless cud of gum that he had chewed throughout the whole operation. Flames were racing up the curtain now.

Time to go.

Chapter One

Pippa Sullivan eyed her brother surreptitiously as she drove west. He was unnaturally pale, the skin drawn tight over the bones of his face. His thick coffee-coloured hair had been clumsily shorn, making him appear even younger than his twenty-one years – until you looked into his eyes. His once-open gaze was guarded, the hazel light dimmed by recent painful experience. To Pippa, Jamie looked washed-out and weak – like a plant that's been shut up in a cupboard and forgotten. But what could you expect after eighteen months in prison?

She had not exactly thrived herself since Jamie had been locked away. She had ticked off every day of his sentence on a calendar and now the day of his release had arrived she was surprised how nervous she felt. Things had changed since he'd been inside and she wasn't sure how he was going to react.

Jamie caught her looking at him. He managed a smile but it didn't reach his eyes.

'Not going too fast for you, am I?' she said.

Almost the first thing he'd remarked on as they'd driven away from Her Majesty's Prison Garstone was the speed of the car. 'Slow down, Pippa,' he'd gasped and she'd pointed out they were only doing thirty.

'Is that all? It seems like twice that.'

'Just wait till you get back on a quick horse,' she'd said, laughing, but he'd not joined in and she'd let it go. She'd eased off the gas, too, and driven like a granny for the next few miles.

The road was winding. Puddles were still holding at the edges

9

courtesy of the overnight rain. So far it had been a typically damp November day.

Now, Jamie said, 'Bet you're glad you don't have to make this journey again.'

Was she ever. Racehorse trainers were used to crossing the country day and night to get to meetings. Pippa's base in North Yorkshire was a fair distance from the big Flat tracks of the south and she logged many miles every year without complaint. But the fortnightly trip down the motorway and the long slog east below the Wash to Garstone was as gloomy a journey as she'd ever made. It would have been different in other circumstances, of course. But the anticipation of seeing her brother, the anxiety she felt at the state she might find him in and the depression of the return always left her drained. She didn't want to live through that again, or travel on the road that reminded her of it. Not that she would dream of saying so to Jamie.

'It wasn't that bad. Handy for Newmarket.' It was what she always said.

He smiled at her properly this time. 'Bloody liar.'

Newmarket was many miles from Garstone. Everywhere was miles from Garstone. Pippa often wondered how visitors without a car managed. They must spend hours on trains and a fortune on the local taxis. It wasn't just the men serving time who were being punished.

She slowed at the approaching junction and kept heading west, avoiding the turn which led north to the motorway.

He looked at her in surprise. 'Where are we going?'

'Somewhere you can see the sky and fill your lungs with fresh air.' She waited a beat. 'But first we're going to Wolverhampton.'

The joke fell flat.

'Pippa, you're not taking me racing, are you?'

She said nothing, just concentrated on the road.

'It's too soon. I can't face anyone yet.'

'But you said you were going to help me out at the yard. You haven't changed your mind, have you?'

'No.'

'Then you're coming racing. Lonsdale Heights runs in the third. The sooner you put a few faces to names the better.'

He made no further protest but she could tell from the set of his jaw that he wasn't happy.

Tough. Though she loved her brother and had bottomless sympathy for his recent ordeal, he couldn't be allowed to duck out of things any more. As a child he'd got away with murder. Their mother had always let her little boy off the hook. Pippa, on the other hand, had always had to pay the price. She was the elder, she should know better, Jamie was 'only a kid'.

This indulgence hadn't done him any favours. Leeds Crown Court hadn't considered him a kid when he'd pleaded guilty on a drink-driving charge, and all his success as a jockey had counted for nothing. Though the death of fifteen-year-old Alan Kirkstall was not deemed to be murder, this was one accident whose consequences the 'kid' could not avoid. Jamie had been sentenced to three years, which had come down to a year and a half on remission.

Pippa's resentment about the whole business still burned – she couldn't help it. Throughout his sentence she'd been the one on the outside trying to be a rock, keeping Jamie's morale up while ushering their mother through the swift and hideous progress of lung cancer.

Now her rancour touched on the one topic she had sworn to herself she would not raise on this supposedly joyful journey to freedom.

'So,' she asked her brother, 'have you got your memory back then?'

'What?'

Maybe he was startled by the question or by her tone, which was sharp, pitched higher than she had intended. The accusing tone of the aggrieved elder sister.

'Do you still not remember the accident?'

She had not raised the issue in any of her prison visits. It would have been impossible in that crowded and undignified room. But she'd assumed he'd come to terms with his crime during his year and a half inside. For God's sake, he'd pleaded guilty! He must have owned up to himself.

He was a long time responding, as if he was searching within himself for the right answer. Or maybe he was just trying to think of the right way of putting it. 'No, Pippa,' he said at last. 'I feel shame and remorse and regret. But the truth is, I can't remember what actually happened.'

She still didn't believe him.

Though regarded as one of the least attractive in the country, Jamie had a soft spot for Wolverhampton racecourse. He'd had his first winner there as a green apprentice of sixteen, squeezing home by a neck in a sprint on a summer evening. He'd been so nervous beforehand that he'd spent most of the time in the toilet. He'd gone down to the start dazzled by the floodlights, his head in a spin. It was a miracle he'd even started, let alone finished. But once his mount was settled in the starting stalls, drawn on a lucky low number, he'd tuned out all his problems. He'd gunned up the inner like a speeding bullet and never saw another horse until he looked over his shoulder when he was past the post.

So, all things being equal, he'd have been happy to spend his first day of freedom at this urban track with its multi-tiered panoramic restaurant and all-weather surface that so offended the purists. But this course, like all the others where he'd once performed so successfully, belonged to a past now closed to him. Though it would surprise many, including Pippa without a doubt, he had not planned his return to racing while serving his time. The accident had changed everything. He'd not ridden in anger since the crash and he wondered if he still could. Racing had been the best thing in his life but maybe he deserved to lose it. A boy had died because of him. He couldn't just climb back into the saddle and carry on riding winners as if that had never happened.

But he was young. He had to do something with his life – that's what everyone told him. And he didn't know much else apart from horses.

His mind was in turmoil as Pippa parked the car and he followed her towards the stands. At least they weren't heading to the weighing room. He wasn't looking forward to meeting his former colleagues. They'd showered him with letters after the trial and he'd not replied to one. Some guys had asked if they could visit him and he'd said no. Maybe now they'd forgotten him. He hoped so – it was no less than he deserved.

It was early, there was nearly an hour to go before the first race, but the lunchtime clientèle were beginning to gather in the restaurant, eager to get the eating out of the way before the serious business of the day.

'Where are we going?' he said to Pippa as they walked down a corridor and stopped in front of a chipped wooden door.

She didn't reply but opened it and ushered him ahead.

The surprise was total. The small room was jammed with familiar faces, all smiling. Jockeys, stable staff, journalists. A cheer went up at the sight of him. Champagne corks popped. He'd have run if he could but Pippa was right behind him, blocking his escape.

She must have known what he was thinking. 'Out of my hands, I'm afraid,' she whispered in his ear as a sandy-haired giant gripped him by the shoulders and shouted, 'Welcome back, you little rascal!' and crushed him in a bear hug.

Jamie found himself grinning. He'd not seen his brother-in-law for some months and he'd missed him. Somehow Malcolm made him feel that everything was going to be all right after all.

The celebration didn't go on for long. These were working people and most had a busy afternoon ahead. The riders in the opening race were the first to leave. Among them was Malcolm's brother – half-brother, in fact – who bore a striking resemblance to him: hair the colour of toast, square dimpled jaw and pale blue eyes. Richard, however, was built to a different scale, being almost a foot shorter. When Jamie and Richard had started riding, Malcolm was well known through his bloodstock agency, and the other jockeys had christened Richard 'Little Mal'. Jamie knew how much Richard had hated it but he'd smiled and put up with it. It wasn't in his nature to seek conflict. Since Jamie had been off the scene Richard had established himself as one of the top jockeys in the country. In the past year he'd won the Two Thousand Guineas, the Coronation Cup and over a hundred other winners. Jamie doubted that anyone referred to Richard as 'Little Mal' these days.

Richard shook his hand energetically. 'Are you OK?' he asked. 'This must seem a bit strange.'

'Yeah.' What else could he say? It was weird to be surrounded by so many people from his previous life. Jamie forced himself to smile – he was out of the habit. Where he'd spent the last eighteen months it was asking for trouble if you went around with a grin on your face.

'You've been missed, you know. When are we going to see you back in the weighing-room?'

Jamie shrugged. 'I'm not sure what I'm going to do, Rich. I don't know that I can still ride. I think I've forgotten.'

Richard laughed. 'No one forgets – especially not you.' He turned towards the door. 'I'll see you later. I want to introduce you to my fiancée.'

That was news. 'Congratulations,' he called after Richard as he left the room.

'You didn't tell me Rich was getting married,' he said to Pippa ten minutes later as they made their way to the saddling boxes.

'Sorry. I thought I had.'

'So who is she?'

'Some thin blonde girl with a rich daddy.'

'And?' She was striding ahead athletically, her thick dark curls obscuring her face. 'Come on, Pippa, what's her name?'

She stopped abruptly and fixed him with her coal-black eyes. He read irritation there and concern.

'It's Vanessa Hartley.'

Bloody hell. The silky-voiced siren who'd come gunning for him on the day that changed his life. Vanessa. The last woman he'd slept with.

Now he understood why Pippa hadn't told him.

He lurched out of the shower at the sound of the phone. His way to the bedside table led across a minefield of tangled bedding, plates of leftover food and empty bottles. The place was a pigsty. But that's why you paid through the nose to stay in posh hotels – you could make as much mess as you liked.

Naked and still dripping, he snatched up the receiver. It was the porter on the front desk.

'Just to let you know that your wife is on her way up to your room, Mr Sullivan.'

'My wife?'

'That's what she said, sir.' The porter sounded amused, as if he knew full well that Jamie didn't have a wife.

Jamie replaced the phone without responding. It was hard to think clearly through the thump of his hangover.

He peered around the room. Maybe the girl who'd stayed over last night – Lorraine – had left something behind when she'd scuttled out at first light and had returned to retrieve it. Or maybe she was after a bit more action, in which case she'd be out of luck. He'd given her more than she deserved already. He was knackered.

He stumbled back to the bathroom and yanked a towel off the rail.

Or maybe – a new thought surfaced – this was some tabloid trick, sending a reporter up to try and catch him out. They'd become pretty sneaky since he'd been photographed in an Epsom Jacuzzi with another jockey's wife. These days he wasn't just news on the racing pages.

He chucked an empty wine bottle in the bin and pushed a cluttered food tray out of sight behind the TV stand. Token gestures.

He ignored the first soft knock on the door but tucked the towel firmly around his waist. At the second summons he opened the door just a crack. He recognised his visitor at once. Suddenly he felt a lot better.

A tall slim girl lounged in the doorway, all legs and tousled blonde locks. 'Hi, Jamie,' she said. 'Don't mind if I come in, do you?'

He stepped aside as she glided past, apparently unconcerned by his near nakedness.

Jamie had only met Vanessa Hartley once, three days previously on the gallops above Ridgemoor. She'd accompanied her father as Jamie had put Morwenstow, a classy three-year-old, through his paces. Officially, Desmond Hartley was running the rule over his most promising sprinter ahead of the lucrative Diadem Stakes. Unofficially it was a chance for Hartley to check Jamie out as a replacement for champion jockey Kevin O'Connor, the unlucky recipient of a three-day ban which ruled him out of the race.

Whatever the background politics, both Jamie and Morwenstow had made a good impression. So too had Hartley's daughter, who'd traded innocent small talk with Jamie in a low-pitched drawl. A spoilt Sloane, he thought at first. But as her cornflower-blue eyes probed his, he'd revised his judgement. A super-sexy Sloane, he decided, who might just be interested in less innocent discussions.

She made no comment on the state of the room but strolled to the window and pushed it wide open.

'I'm meeting Daddy here before the races so I've got a bit of time to kill,' she offered. 'I thought we might have coffee or something.'

Jamie pretended to treat the suggestion at face value. He had expected to be obliged to chase Vanessa. To have her turn up on a plate, so to speak, was astounding.

'Something sounds like a good idea.' He opened the fridge which, fortunately, still contained a bottle of champagne.

Her blue eyes flashed. 'Do you think we should? I mean, are you allowed to before a race?'

He jerked the cork out of the bottle with a satisfying pop. 'No one's going to breathalyse me charging past the post on Morwenstow, if that's what you mean.'

'OK.' She accepted the glass he held out and drank languidly. She was standing with her back to the window with the sun lighting up the wheat-yellow tumble of her hair.

'Why did you say you were my wife?'

She shrugged, causing her pastel-blue summer dress to skim the tops of her bronzed thighs. It occurred to him that she probably wasn't wearing much more than he was.

'How did you get that?' she said.

'What?'

'That scar.' She placed the tip of her long painted forefinger on his sternum and traced it along the knotted ridge of tissue over his ribs.

As he told her about the fall at York a year previously, his mind was elsewhere, wondering how long it would be before the towel ceased to conceal his excitement. To think only a few minutes before, he'd considered himself completely shagged out, yet all it took was a wicked-looking blonde to pitch up and he was straining at the leash.

Go for it, mate. You deserve it.

His heart was beating fast. He placed his hand over hers and pressed it to his chest. 'Feel what you're doing to me.'

'I know.' Her full pink lips gaped open. She didn't pull away.

Everything he touched these days seemed to turn to gold.

Jamie liked the look of Lonsdale Heights, a chocolate-brown four-year-old with a splash of white across his chest. He regarded Jamie from gleaming mahogany eyes as he made a dart for his jacket pocket. Jamie allowed himself to be expertly frisked for goodies and regretted he had nothing to share.

'I'm awfully sorry,' said Jill, Pippa's travelling head lass. 'Lonnie's a terrible thief.'

Jamie scratched the horse's neck. 'I'm used to it. Plenty of those where I've just been.'

The girl's plump cheek flushed, obviously afraid she'd put her foot in it. 'I'm really glad you're coming to work with us,' she stammered. 'You used to be a wonderful jockey.'

'Thank you.'

'I mean,' she was becoming more flustered, 'I'm sure you still are. I don't suppose you've had the chance to ride in – that is, since . . .'

Pippa laughed out loud and looked up from tightening the surcingle. 'You've dug yourself a nice little hole there, Jill. If I were you I'd stop digging.'

'He looks a picture,' Jamie said, taking in the immaculately plaited mane and gleaming coat. 'You've done a good job.'

'Thanks.' Jill was still blushing. 'He's going to win today, I'm sure of it.'

Jamie knew Pippa thought so too. She'd briefed him in the car. 'Lonnie's been off for the summer with a strained tendon but he's sound now and working well on the gallops. He was third last time out at Southwell but finished really strongly. This race is a bit longer and I reckon he'll be hard to beat.'

He hoped she was right. It would be great for the yard to have a winner on his first day of freedom. A good omen.

Pippa made Jamie accompany her into the ring ahead of the third race. 'The sooner you show your face the better,' she said. 'Let the papers take their photos and be done with it.'

He'd protested that he looked awful but she insisted. 'It's important that you're seen here. It's a statement. It says you're back in business.'

Privately she thought he did indeed look awful. She'd brought him some clothes from home but they no longer fitted snugly, she noticed. The trousers were too short and the jacket was tight across his shoulders. Despite the deficiencies of the prison diet, could he have grown in the past year and a half? She supposed it was possible.

She kept an eagle eye on Lonsdale Heights' connections as she introduced her brother, but if they knew Jamie's history they didn't let on.

'Pleased to meet you, old boy,' said Geoffrey Lane, the horse's owner. 'Best trainer in the country, your sister.'

Pippa shot him a sharp glance; she didn't like having the mickey taken out of her.

Geoffrey, a podgy mid-sixties antiques-dealer, added, 'Best-looking, anyway,' at which everybody laughed, even Jamie. Then they all moved on to discuss Lonsdale Heights' prospects in the race and it was time for Pippa to do her stuff.

It was apparent that nothing less than a victory would satisfy the Lane party.

'Uncle Geoff says you've laid him out specially for this race,' said a clean-cut young business type.

'I've had it in mind since Southwell. The longer distance should suit him.'

'What's he up against? You used to train Black Knight, didn't you?'

'Lonny's the better horse. He'll gallop the legs off Black Knight any day.'

Lane's nephew grinned as he pulled a mobile from his mackintosh pocket. A lock of hair fell over his forehead. It struck Pippa that he was a bit of a dish.

'Time to get the money on then,' he murmured

'Don't get carried away,' she said quickly.

She realised, however, that she shared his expectations. This was just the type of race that should suit her horse – a test of guts and stamina over a mile and seven furlongs – and the opposition didn't look that hot. She supposed she must have said as much to the owner in recent conversations. It was difficult sometimes to keep her enthusiasm to herself.

By the time she'd finished answering Geoffrey's endless questions, calmed Mrs Lane's nerves and briefed the jockey, she'd lost touch with Jamie.

Like an anxious mother hen she looked round the ring for him, chastising herself as she did so. He was a grown man tasting freedom for the first time in more than a year. He could go where he liked.

She could see him now talking to a tall distinguished-looking figure in a cashmere overcoat whom she knew well. Her father-in-law, Toby Priest.

Pippa didn't rush over to join them. Related though she was to Toby by marriage, there was too much rivalry between them for her to be easy in his company. Toby was the doyen of northern trainers, the master of Ridgemoor stables which saddled some three hundred runners in a Flat season – one in four of which reached the winning post ahead of the competition. And he'd been competing at this level for twenty-five years.

Pippa didn't like to admit she was intimidated by anyone, but Toby, the senior of the extensive Priest clan, walked over most people in his path, including his sons and his wives – so far there had been three. Being related to Toby Priest certainly didn't guarantee an easy ride.

With relief she saw Jamie and Toby part in friendly fashion, the trainer pumping Jamie's hand energetically and gripping his forearm with his free hand. All was well there, then. And so it should be, Pippa reflected. Jamie had made his name at Ridgemoor and piloted a string of winners for Toby and his owners.

'Offered you your old job back, has he?' she said as they made their way to the stand for the race.

'He was only sounding off. He doesn't need me now Rich is riding so well.'

'Suppose he wasn't – would you consider it?' She couldn't resist.

He played the question with a straight bat. 'Of course not,' he said. 'I'm working for you, aren't I?'

She manoeuvred him into the trainers' and owners' stand and he hesitated at the crush ahead, his eyes darting suspiciously around. Pippa felt a pang of guilt at subjecting him to this public ordeal so soon after his incarceration. She suppressed it quickly. The sooner her brother adjusted to normality the better. No one here wished him any harm – quite the contrary.

'So, how did it go?'

Richard took his time replying. He avoided Malcolm's probing glance, pretending to adjust his chin strap as they walked across the parade ring.

Malcolm stopped him before they reached the knot of people surrounding Black Knight, Richard's mount.

'I'm concerned about you, Rich. You were in a bit of a twitch the other night.'

Richard didn't want to have this conversation, not here at any rate. But no one was close enough to hear and, anyway, they were all preoccupied.

'It went fine. He thinks I'm chuffed to see him back.'

'Excellent.' Malcolm grinned and slapped him on the back. The touch contained an extra ounce of force that said Do as I say. His elder brother had been thumping him like that for as long as Richard could remember. 'Just keep it up,' was Malcolm's parting shot as Richard strode away from him, preparing to face Black Knight's owner and utter a few cheerful platitudes.

How he wished he was a better liar. But not as much as he wished his friend and former racing companion Jamie Sullivan had never come back.

Pippa found them a spot beneath the glass window that fronted the bar with a good sightline to the large TV screen. His back safely wedged against the glass, Jamie appeared to relax a little.

'The Colonel says you used to look after his runner.' Everyone at the Ridgemoor yard referred to Toby Priest in this way. Even his sons called their father 'Colonel' while on the premises, lest anyone should forget who was in charge. It was a far cry from the way Pippa ran things.

She nodded in response to Jamie's remark. The SIS camera picked out Black Knight, the Ridgemoor entry, on his way down to the start of the race. Until recently he'd been one of the horses under her care. It was a sore point.

She explained the history as the horses were loaded into the starting stalls. Three weeks previously, one of her longstanding owners, Arabella Childs, had announced that she was removing her two horses, Black Knight and White Sands. Pippa had been sorry about it in one respect – the banker's widow was a prompt payer. On the other hand, she was a demanding woman, always on the phone at inconvenient times, and her horses had done nothing in two years despite Pippa's best efforts. She'd been surprised, however, to get a call from Toby Priest saying that Mrs Childs had approached him to train the pair at Ridgemoor. Did she have any objection?

Pippa had none and said so. 'The best of luck, Toby. They didn't set the world on fire with me.'

Her father-in-law had chuckled. 'Suits me, my darling. I like a challenge.'

The remark had irritated her no end as she'd told Malcolm when recounting the conversation. As usual, he'd sided with his father. 'The old man's got a heck of a reputation with bad horses, Pippa. He's been turning them round for years.'

That had really put her back up. She reckoned she had a better track record with difficult horses than Toby Priest. After all, as a rule he got the cream.

So she'd got a degree of satisfaction two days previously when White Sands had performed up to his usual dismal standard at Southwell. Now Black Knight was lined up against Lonsdale Heights and she had every expectation of another pleasing dollop of revenge.

She said as much to Jamie. 'Lonny's not as pretty as Black Knight but he's got real character. He'll die on his feet rather than give up. Black Knight's just a poseur.'

'He doesn't even look that well,' her brother said as the horses broke from the stalls and the pack settled into a steady rhythm. Black Knight, with Richard Priest wearing Arabella Childs' emerald green silks, was clearly visible at the head of the pack.

'He won't stay.'

As the runners passed the stands, Pippa could feel her stomach begin to knot. She wanted Lonsdale Heights to win so badly but, more than that, she wanted Black Knight to get beaten.

The race unwound – almost two complete circuits of the tight, left-hand oval of sandy-coloured track – much as Pippa expected. Down the back straight for the second time, Black Knight began to struggle as the pace increased. A few horses, including her own, were starting to crowd around him.

'That's it, he'll go backwards now,' Pippa said, without looking up from her binoculars.

Richard gave the horse a couple of sharp cracks. It didn't appear to make him run any faster but he wasn't going any slower either. He had the advantage of the inside and stuck his neck out to keep it. For the first time in his competitive life Black Knight looked as though he wanted to battle. As they raced past the mile-and-a-half pole, stamina began to play its part. Suddenly the race concerned only a handful of runners and, as they turned into the straight, three of those had faltered.

On board Lonsdale Heights, Billy Quinn, Pippa's jockey, looked over his shoulder for non-existent dangers. Black Knight was the only horse in front of him and he'd soon realise that Lonnie had him beat.

Pippa knew both horses so well, and she could predict what would happen next. In her mind's eye she could already see Black Knight tying up and his challenge faltering, while Lonny, hurting just as much, breath short and legs unsteady, bustled past and drove himself to the line in first place.

21

'There he goes!' Pippa cried, grabbing Jamie's arm as Lonsdale Heights quickened and surged past Black Knight. She knew she was hopping up and down with excitement, like a little kid, unable to play it cool. She couldn't be purely professional about her business. In terms of thrills, of long-term satisfaction, of wanting to do it all over again, nothing beat seeing one of her horses win a race. Not even sex. (Sorry, Malcolm.)

Billy Quinn had pulled a length clear but Black Knight, with Richard still hard at work, refused to concede.

Pippa froze in mid-hope. Suspended in disbelief. And despair.

Black Knight wasn't finished. He was coming back at her horse in the last furlong, Richard tucked in tight, urging him on with hands and knees, with no need of the whip to harness the relentless surge beneath him.

Pippa wouldn't have believed it if she hadn't witnessed it for herself. Black Knight had never contested a finish. Yet here he was, galloping right to the line for the first time in his racing career.

How on earth had Toby Priest managed that?

Jamie felt for his sister as she strode into the unsaddling enclosure to greet the disappointed connections of Lonsdale Heights. She held her head high and wore a sympathetic smile as she proffered her hand to Geoffrey Lane.

'Bad luck, Billy,' he heard her call out to the jockey.

The rider patted his mount affectionately on the neck. 'He gave me everything he had. You couldn't ask more of the feller.'

Jamie thought some of the Lane party looked less than convinced.

He turned in the direction of the winners' enclosure where a knot of admirers led by a thin middle-aged woman with an orange tan – Mrs Childs, he assumed – were making a fuss of Black Knight and his victorious jockey. He waited till the congratulations were over before making for Richard.

'You've come on a bit since I last saw you,' he said. 'Great finish.'

Richard grinned. 'Anyone could ride a horse like that.'

'So modest, isn't he?' Jamie heard the voice before he saw the speaker but the recognition was instant. That low-pitched murmur, like water on gravel.

'Congratulations, darling.' A blonde figure in a fake fur coat and leather trousers wrapped her arms round Richard and kissed him on the mouth. She was half a head taller than him.

The jockey did not rush to extricate himself, though when he finally emerged he began an unnecessary introduction.

'Jamie, meet my fiancée, Vanessa. Sweetheart, this is Mal's brother-in-law.'

She turned to face Jamie and bathed him in the light of her brilliant blue eyes. They held not a trace of recognition. 'Pleased to meet you,' she said formally and held out an elegant hand. Her fingers were cool.

'Jamie's ridden for your dad,' said Richard.

'Oh?' Her interest was polite.

'Yeah. He was on Morwenstow when he won the Diadem two years ago. You must remember that.'

She shrugged. 'Aren't you in the next race? You'll be late.'

Richard obediently trotted off and Jamie rather expected Vanessa to depart as well. But she didn't. She looked at him critically.

'You look terrible,' she said.

He would have liked to say the same about her but it would have been far from the truth. She was less coltish and fuller in the face, with a determined set to her jaw he did not remember. But she was undeniably more beautiful. A woman now, no longer just a pretty girl.

'Well, say something,' she snapped.

'Do you really not remember me?'

'Of course I bloody well do but I don't want Richard to know, do I?'

'Why not?'

'He's a bit funny about old boyfriends. So I'd rather our little fling remained a secret. I mean, it's not as if it meant anything.'

Obviously not. 'If that's how you want it, Vanessa.'

'Thanks, darling.' She beamed and tucked her arm into his, leading him towards the stand. 'You can buy me some champagne now.'

'I'd love to, but I don't have any money.'

'Well, I'll buy it then and you can tell me war stories of your time in chokey.'

'I'll stick to orange juice, thanks, and I won't discuss prison.'

'Oh, for God's sake,' she hissed as they entered the smoky bar, 'don't tell me you've turned into a bore. At least before they locked you up you were good fun. Here.' She shoved a banknote into his hand. 'Get a bottle of bubbly and two glasses.'

He looked at the note – fifty pounds, more money than he'd seen in a long time. She was giving him the full benefit of her sexy smile.

He elbowed his way to the bar.

Pippa hung back in the crowd until Toby Priest had managed to offload Arabella Childs. She couldn't bear to face Black Knight's triumphant owner. The only consolation in this sorry sequence of events was that she no longer had to. Regrettably she still had to be polite to members of the Lane party with whom she had just spent an uncomfortable ten minutes. Geoffrey, of course, had taken the reversal like the gentleman he was.

'I'm just happy Lonnie was part of such a cracking race,' he'd said to her. 'That's what it's all about. A finish to be proud of.'

His wife was less convinced. 'It's all very well being noble, Geoffrey, but I'd rather the horse had won.'

Lane's nephew had made no bones about his sentiments. He'd steered Pippa to one side and subjected her to a grilling. 'You told us Black Knight hadn't a prayer.'

'I didn't say that exactly.'

'You said you'd trained the horses side by side and Lonsdale Heights was far superior.'

Had she been that emphatic? Probably.

'That was my honest opinion. Frankly, I'm amazed at Black Knight's performance.'

'So you can't explain it?' He was leaning close, pushing his face into hers, his cheeks red. He didn't look so dishy now.

'I can't explain anything,' she said. 'Horses aren't machines. You can never predict how they'll run.'

'How convenient.' He stepped back a pace, making a conscious effort, it seemed, to keep his temper. She wondered how much money he'd lost. When he spoke again his voice was cold. 'It's obvious to me that Black Knight has benefited from a change of trainer. My uncle is a loyal man but he's no fool. I shall be speaking to him about his horse's future arrangements. I wouldn't blame him if he also wanted a change.'

The worst thing about all this was that Pippa couldn't even account to herself for the improvement in Black Knight. She reckoned she knew her horses inside out but she'd never, at any stage, seen in Black

Knight the quality he'd shown today. Uncomfortable as it was to admit, privately she conceded that Geoff's nephew had a point. If he decided to move Lonsdale Heights to Toby Priest, she couldn't blame him.

But that didn't mean she was resigned to defeat. Her next stop was Priest himself.

'Toby,' she called as Mrs Childs disappeared into the crowd. He turned towards her, a lazy smile on his patrician face. 'Congratulations,' she said.

'You're too kind, Ms Sullivan.' He used her professional name with a touch of irony. His often-stated surprise that she hadn't changed it after her marriage was another thing that rankled. To her mind there were already too many trainers in the book called Priest.

But she wasn't here to spar over trivialities.

'What on earth have you done to Black Knight? He's never run like that in his life.'

Toby nodded graciously. 'Just a change of scenery, I suppose.'

'That's the first time I've seen him finish his race.'

'I told you I enjoy a challenge.'

'Yes, but how did you do it?' Pippa hated to beg but this was eating her up. 'Please tell me, Toby.'

He laughed and slipped an arm around her waist beneath the short fleece she wore over her jeans. 'I love you dearly, Pippa, but you must realise that an old dog like me can't be giving away his tricks. Not even to his favourite daughter-in-law.'

He squeezed her bottom proprietorially and winked.

Bastard.

The silence that filled the car as they crawled through the traffic surrounding the course suited Jamie. It gave him time to reflect on events that seemed to be flashing ahead too fast for him to keep up. Already Garstone Prison seemed to belong to another life, and thank God for that. The afternoon at the races, the taste of it again, seemed to make another chance of a career in the saddle more possible. And the half hour spent with Vanessa, even though she herself was plainly off-limits, made other prospects seem thrillingly available. Of course he'd thought of women inside, but they'd existed in fantasy form only – a drink with an old flame had changed all that.

'Christ, you must be gagging for it after a year and a half,' Vanessa had said.

'It's longer than that. I was too smashed up in the accident to deal with women before the trial. You were my last, if you must know.'

'Ooh. How delicious.' Her eyes had lit up wickedly. 'It's a pity I can't get you up and running again.'

'I expect you've got your hands full with Rich.'

'Actually, I'm keeping him dangling a bit but it amounts to the same thing. But don't worry, I've plenty of friends. I'll soon fix you up.'

Jamie had declined, laughing, but the interchange had made him feel better about himself. Twenty-four hours ago he could never have imagined it taking place.

And then there was the racing itself. He'd been fearful of how he would react, but seeing Richard bring Black Knight home in a stormer had given him a real thrill. He'd watched him closely over the last furlong, knowing how the jockey was feeling and what he was looking for from his mount. And when he'd hit the front Jamie had been with him in spirit, pouring on the gas and riding a finish to the line. Once he'd been a far better rider than Richard. Given the chance, he now wondered if he could be again.

After just a few hours of freedom it seemed everything was possible.

Pippa broke into his thoughts. 'You've got to help me, Jamie.'

He knew she'd been shattered by Lonsdale Heights' loss. 'Of course,' he said. 'Just ask.'

'I'm missing something. I thought I was a good trainer but after today I'm not so sure.'

'Believe me, Pippa. You're one of the best.'

'So how come Toby's just taken one of my horses and improved it a stone in three weeks?'

'That's only one race. It's a fluke.'

She didn't reply for a bit, just concentrated on the road and the heavy traffic flow around her. It would be a long slog up to Yorkshire at this rate. Jamie wished he could help but he wouldn't be driving for a long while, since a five-year ban had accompanied his prison sentence. This was the first occasion on which it had seemed significant.

'Look,' she said, 'you're coming to the yard with a fresh eye. You've always had a great instinct for horses. Just watch what I'm doing. I don't believe I've turned into a lousy trainer overnight.'

He laughed out loud. 'Don't be daft, Pippa.'

'I'm serious. Many more days like today and I'm packing it in. Perhaps we should accept the offer on the land.'

A local developer had been after the house and surrounding acres that Pippa and Jamie had inherited from their mother. He'd recently put in a revised bid with a breathtaking number of noughts on the end and they'd discussed it on her last visit to Jamie in prison. But neither of them wanted to sell. The land was where they had grown up.

Jamie squeezed her shoulder and she managed a reluctant grin.

'That's not all,' she added. 'That lecherous old sod Toby pinched my bum.'

This time both of them laughed.

Chapter Two

Marie Kirkstall cycled wearily up the rutted lane towards the row of houses on the edge of Ridgemoor village. The low sun picked out the slopes and planes of the moor above. On the track halfway up the hill she could see two figures in custard-yellow anoraks heading up towards the treeline. That's what she should be doing, making the most of the bright winter weather and enjoying the spectacular countryside that lay right there on her own doorstep.

But there were two good reasons why she would not be joining the hikers up ahead. The first was purely practical. She'd been on the early shift, cleaning offices in town, and she was hungry, dirty and tired. By the time she'd had lunch and a bath, the best of the day would be gone. All she'd be fit for was curling up on the front-room sofa and pretending to revise for her A-level resit. Some hope. She'd be asleep before she'd read a page of notes.

The second reason was less easy to explain, even to herself. Alan had been dead for over two years now so it was about time she got back to normal. Normal as in using her brain and enjoying those things that used to give her pleasure, like hiking the hills and riding horses. Her friends had given up nagging her about it. They respected how she felt but she knew they didn't really understand – not that she was entirely clear herself. She'd scarcely been on the moor since Alan's accident. The hillside behind the house had been their playground as children, and every beck and hollow reminded her of her brother. Even though they'd spent as much time fighting as having fun they'd always gone on long walks together, sometimes in gangs of other kids, sometimes just the two of them. So it made a kind of superstitious sense that she steered clear of the hills these days. They just made her sad.

Horses were different. Unlike Alan, she'd been good in the saddle. Rugby and cricket had been his games, horses were just for a laugh. She had this terrible feeling that if he'd been a better horseman he could have avoided the car that killed him. If she, Marie, had been on Misty, their little grey mare, she knew she could have skipped off the road somehow or done something to get out of the way. It was ironic it turned out to be a jockey driving. Very funny, I don't think.

She parked her bike carelessly round the side of the house and entered through the back door into the kitchen. Aunt Joyce was at the sink, her big red arms viciously scrubbing a pan.

'You're late today,' she said, without turning round. Marie could tell from the set of her shoulders that she was fed up about something. Aunt Joyce often was.

She dumped a frying pan on the draining board with a clang. As she turned to Marie her pink jowly face softened. 'Sit down, love. I've got your dinner ready.'

'Don't you want to get away? Aren't you meeting Pam?' Her aunt usually had lunch with a friend on Thursdays.

Joyce shook her head; the jowls wobbled. 'I rang and put her off.'

'Why?'

'There's something up with your dad.'

Marie's mind went blank. She watched a drip swell on the spout of the tap and fall with a plink into the washing-up water. Another one began to form and she couldn't tear her eyes away. 'Have you called Dr Gooding?' she heard herself say.

Joyce put a rough hand on her shoulder. 'It's nothing physical, love, but I know something's up. He's stopped talking again.'

Clem Kirkstall had not spoken a word for three months following his son's death. Dr Gooding had put it down to shock and said it had nothing to do with his on-going emphysema. 'Everyone has their own way of grieving,' he'd said. Clem's, sympathetic though everyone had been to his suffering, had been hell on those around him.

'When I took his tray up he was fine,' Joyce told her. 'Said it was a great day for going up Piecrust Hill and would I give him a piggyback. I said if we both lost four stone there'd be no problem.'

'And?'

'I sorted the washing and put some whites on. But when I went back up for the tray, he was just lying there. Didn't turn his head to say hello, didn't reply when I asked him why he'd let his breakfast go cold. Three best back rashers and two fried eggs and he hadn't touched them. He hasn't got up, he's just lying there and I can't get a word out of him. I don't know what's up with the old fool.'

There was a note of indignation in her voice and her jaw was set firm, but her big pale eyes were misty with emotion. It wouldn't take much to set her aunt crying. More than anyone, she had borne the brunt of the recent misfortunes that had come their way. Marie squeezed her hand.

'I'll go up and see him.'

'I've just been. He's asleep, thank the Lord. You take your coat off and have a bite to eat.'

'OK.' Her appetite had vanished but she knew better than to resist her aunt.

Joyce quickly laid the kitchen table and produced trays and pans from the oven, loading a plate high with meat pie and vegetables. Marie had given up the battle to persuade her aunt to serve lighter meals and smaller portions. She wouldn't eat again today.

Marie chewed mechanically and stared through the window. Shadows of clouds chased across the hillside, turning the patchwork of vivid greens and rich browns into a uniform grey. The day was fading already.

Her eye fell on the tray resting on top of the microwave. It had been cleared of dishes but one item still lay on it.

'Is that Dad's paper?'

Clem Kirkstall, a devoted racing man, took the *Racing Beacon* every day. It was his essential companion to afternoons spent in front of the television.

'He didn't want it.'

'I thought you said he wasn't talking to you?'

'I left it on his pillow but he chucked it after me. Waved his arm like he wanted to thump me.'

Marie stared at her aunt. It didn't sound like her father at all.

'I know,' said Joyce. 'He's got me all of a bother.'

Marie reached for the paper and laid it face up in front of her. As a rule her father read it from cover to cover, folding and turning down pages as he went. It was clear that this edition had not even been opened. But, as Marie's eye fell on the photograph on the front page, the reason for her father's strange behaviour became obvious. It showed two men in a parade ring at a racecourse, one middle-aged and laughing, the other much younger with a drawn and serious face. Toby Priest, the leading trainer in the district, was shaking hands with Jamie Sullivan, the rider who'd killed her brother. The caption beneath the photo read 'Welcome back'.

No wonder Clem Kirkstall was out of sorts.

Shelley farmhouse had been rearranged since Jamie had been away. The big rambling building had remained unchanged since his Uncle Bob had bought it in the early 1970s. Now, after Jamie's mother's death, Pippa and Mal had built a conservatory, knocked down a couple of internal walls and added an en suite bathroom to Laura Sullivan's old room to turn it into a master bedroom. Pippa had asked Jamie during a prison visit for his permission to proceed with the alterations.

'Go ahead and do what you like,' he'd said, though he'd instinctively resisted the thought of any change. He didn't like the idea of life moving on without him. 'I trust you.'

Now, as he made himself at home in the top far corner of the house in the converted loft space, he was pleased with the result. Even though his surroundings were familiar, it seemed as if he was making a new start.

'You don't have to hide away up here, you know.' Malcolm was standing in the doorway. 'We were expecting you to take your old room.'

Jamie hadn't fancied it. They'd left it pretty much alone, down to the football posters on the wall, which dated things all too clearly. He'd slept in there since he was eight; it was time for a change.

'I used to crawl up into this loft when I was a kid,' he said. 'I like it.'

He'd worried about moving in with Pippa and her husband. They'd got married before the trial and had set up home in Malcolm's bachelor flat. But once Jamie had been sent to prison and their mother took a turn for the worse, it made sense for Pippa to move back. Naturally, Malcolm had come too.

Jamie had taken a bit of persuading to return to the family home.

'Where else are you going to go?' Pippa had asked.

'Hong Kong,' Jamie had said. A jockey could make a good living there, he knew. 'Or Australia.'

'I could use you in the yard.'

He hadn't really wanted to come back to Yorkshire. The shame of what he'd done was too much. His entire body went cold at the thought of meeting any of the Kirkstall family. Finally Pippa had convinced him of the futility of running away. 'Run now and you'll be running for ever,' she'd said and he'd realised she was right.

Shortly afterwards he'd discovered he wouldn't be allowed to travel abroad immediately after getting out; he'd have a probation officer to report to once a fortnight instead. So he'd agreed to come back – to start with, anyway. He told himself he was better off than most ex-cons – at least he had a place to begin putting his life back together.

Malcolm stepped into the room. 'I see you haven't lost the old touch,' he said. 'I watched you ride out on Noddy.'

Pippa had told Jamie to lie in that morning but he'd woken at six as usual. It had been strange lying there in the dark listening to the well-remembered creak of the old house as the wind blew from off the moor. It was quite a contrast to the constant noise of Garstone where even in the dead of night, when the last ghetto-blasters had been turned off, the snores, farts and screams of 500 men reminded him he was not alone.

He'd found some old shorts and a vest and gone for a run up the hill in the early morning light. He'd discovered running in prison – not that there was anywhere to go, but running on the spot in his cell burned up his energy and kept him fit. It was a treat to stride out across the rough grass and fill his lungs with clean air.

From up on the ridge he'd watched Pippa's first lot of a dozen horses wind their way up to the gallops. They set off in single file, doing a good strong canter between the bright orange markers. Today was an easy day. Jamie knew they wouldn't be doing anything too strenuous but, just by watching the cloud of each horse's breath condense in the cool winter air he could tell which were the fittest.

His sister had asked for his advice on what she was doing with her string. He suspected this was partly to make him feel needed but he'd shared her anguish at seeing Black Knight win and he was keen to help if he could. The fact was, there were dozens of ways of training a horse to fitness and as many dietary regimes that could be imposed to aid performance. But, in the end, if the horse didn't have an engine there was little that could be done. In Jamie's opinion, the most important thing was to keep the horses happy. If horses are content they will eat and can be trained. Then it's just a question of finding the right race for the animal in question. Easy. Except Jamie had never been a trainer.

Later, after he had savoured a long, hot bath and a full breakfast, he had wandered out into the yard and found his sister in the office on the phone.

'Do me a favour,' she'd said, interrupting her conversation for a moment. 'We're short of a lad for second lot. Fetch your helmet and jump on Noddy, will you?'

'Which one's Noddy?' he'd asked a freckle-faced girl in the tack room. She led him to a box containing a sleek chestnut colt.

'Real name's Norwegian Wood,' she said. 'Basically, he's a lazy sod and won't work. Put him on a racecourse though and he's a flyer. Won at Chester off ninety-three.'

'Yeah?' Jamie was intrigued. Ninety-three was the handicapper's rating. The ratings ranged from 0 to 150, with 30 about the lowest for a very poor Selling Plater. The best were rarely above 140. The 1965 Derby winner Sea Bird had been rated 145. The average on the Flat was around 75, so Noddy was more than useful.

'That was back in May though. He's been taking it easy ever since.'

The girl – Rosie – had been saddling the horse while she talked. She unclipped the head collar and led Noddy outside.

'Thanks,' he said as she gave him a leg up into the saddle. It was the first time he'd sat on a horse in a year and a half. Did she know that? he wondered as he fell in behind the other horses circling in front of the yard.

When thinking about this moment – his first time back on a horse – one of his many worries had been that he wouldn't remember what to do, that he'd panic or fall or, more realistically, find his instincts blunted by misuse. But the moment he was in the saddle everything felt right – it was as if he'd never been away. He wasn't racing fit by any means and his legs might protest later, but his senses were spot on.

'Come on then, Noddy,' he muttered to the horse. 'Let's see if you're capable of some proper work.'

It had turned out to be a bit of a battle. At the start of the gallop Noddy had whipped around to his left and stuck his head between his legs. It seemed he had every intention of getting Jamie on the floor. There had been no time to think and Jamie had responded instinctively, like a boxer swaying out of the way of a punch. He pulled his whip through and gave the horse a sharp crack down one shoulder. Then, as Noddy ducked back in the opposite direction, he gave him an even harder smack on the other side. That had settled it. Noddy had found out who was boss and hadn't put a foot wrong for the rest of the ride.

Jamie returned Malcolm's grin. 'I thought the little beggar was going to drop me to start with. I guess that was Pippa's idea of a joke.'

Malcolm nodded. 'Have you heard from Bertie?'

Before the accident Bertie Brooks had been Jamie's agent, booking him with top trainers around the country when he wasn't required for Ridgemoor horses. At the time Bertie, an ex-jock, had just been starting out at the game. Now he was one of the top boys, representing the cream of the weighing-room.

'He sent me a postcard from Barbados while I was in the nick.' Talk about rubbing it in. 'I think he's got a bit stratospheric for me.'

Malcolm looked thoughtful. 'I promised the old man I'd keep an eye on how you were doing. He'll give you some rides.'

'No thanks, Mal.'

'Why not?'

Jamie wondered whether to tell him about the decision he'd made just that morning. He'd been going to mention it first to Pippa but talking to Malcolm was pretty much the same thing. He was family too.

'To tell the truth, I don't think I'm going to be riding for either Pippa or the Colonel. I can't do the weight.'

Malcolm's broad brow furrowed as he looked closely at Jamie. 'I suppose you have grown a bit but you don't look fat.'

'I'm not but it's more than two years since I last rode a race. I've had eight months getting over that smash-up and a year and a half sitting on my arse in jail. I've got bigger.'

'I thought they didn't feed you inside.'

'The food was crap but I've changed all the same. My old clothes don't fit and I just weighed myself on your bathroom scales. I'm over ten stone.'

'You could get it off, couldn't you?'

Jamie shook his head. 'There's not a picking on me. I've grown. Lester Piggott said that if he hadn't begun racing at the age of twelve he'd never have been a jockey at all. Once you let yourself grow, that's it. And I've not spent all that time eating prison slop to come out and starve myself. But I don't know what I'm going to do.'

'Let's not get too gloomy,' Malcolm said. 'You've just got your freedom back. We'll think of something. Here –' He held out his hand, which contained a folded slip of paper. 'This is why I came up. Thought it might come in handy.'

Jamie took it without thinking and was startled to see it was a cheque, made out to him for the sum of five thousand pounds.

'Jesus, Malcolm,' was all he managed to say.

'Bung that in your bank account. You're bound to be a bit short.'

'I can't take this.'

'Why the hell not? Have you got some nest egg tucked away?'

Jamie shook his head. What he'd earned before the crash he'd spent, faster than a good few of his mounts.

'Things cost in the big wide world, you know,' Malcolm continued. 'I doubt if Pippa's paying you much.'

In fact, Jamie had not discussed money with his sister. He'd assumed he'd be owing her, rather than the other way round.

'Does Pippa know about this?' he asked.

'Why should she? Just between us guys, eh? Pay me back when you can.'

Jamie looked doubtful but there was no denying the money would help, even if he only spent a few hundred on clothes. And taxis. With his car ban stretching into the foreseeable future he'd need to get around. This money would at least give him some independence.

'Thanks,' he said at last, pocketing the cheque.

'Good man. And not a word to Pippa.' His brother-in-law's broad face creased as he gave Jamie an exaggerated wink.

Jamie nodded, overcome by the big man's generosity. He and his sister didn't always see eye to eye, but there was no doubt she'd done the right thing in marrying Malcolm Priest.

'Dad?'

There was no reply from the large mound of blankets on the bed where her father lay. But from the fresh cloud of tobacco smoke which hung in the air Marie knew her father was awake.

The room was in semi-darkness but she could make out the grey moon of his face against the whiteness of the pillow. A small disc of orange glowed in the shadow as he placed a cigarette between his lips.

'Oh Dad,' she moaned, unable to keep the disapproval out of her voice. It was two months since he'd promised her earnestly that he'd given up for good – not for the first time, of course. In the last couple of weeks she'd allowed herself to believe that this time he'd stick to it. She wondered where the old man had got his supply. Aunt Joyce's handbag, she suspected. Wherever it was, she could see by the overflowing ashtray on the bedside table that this most recent resolution had been utterly abandoned.

He had managed to give up properly just once, for a year. He'd started again the day of Alan's funeral.

His unhappy eyes gazed at her in reproach as she snatched the cigarette from his hand and removed the ashtray. She bustled to the window and flung it open. The cold breeze gusted into the fuggy room, dispersing the smoke.

'Auntie Joyce says you've gone back to not speaking. She's upset and so am I.'

She paused to allow him to reply but only the rasp of his heavy, tortured breathing came from his throat.

'You're not putting us through the silent treatment again, Dad. I'm not having it.'

She knew she sounded like her mother, her sharp tone an echo of the long-dead woman. Her father hadn't behaved like this when *she* died, Marie thought angrily.

She pulled his bulk into a sitting position and thumped the pillows with venom. It made her feel better – though not much.

'I shouldn't have to do this,' she spat. 'I shouldn't have messed up my exams. I shouldn't be up half the night doing some horrible job. And you shouldn't be sitting up here trying to kill yourself.'

A callused, fleshy hand closed over hers and stopped her in the act of rearranging his bedclothes. He was a big man, still strong in the arms. He'd once owned a garage and spent long hours battling with recalcitrant engines, breathing exhaust fumes in a closed workshop and ruining his lungs in the cause of the family fortunes. His grip was unbreakable.

She ran on at the mouth. It was hard to stop once she had started.

'So what if Jamie Sullivan's out of prison? He's nothing to us. We've got our own lives to live and he's mucked us up enough already. And you've got to stop smoking, Dad. Like you promised.'

She dried up, suddenly ashamed. She'd never shouted at her father in quite this way before. Not out of adolescent pique but as the responsible one – like a parent. It didn't seem right.

He appeared to know what she was thinking because his big, round head nodded and his lips stretched into a smile. He tugged at her wrist and she found herself sitting on the bed by his side. He slipped an arm around her shoulder.

She allowed herself to be pulled against him and snuggled next to his solid, familiar warmth, ignoring the smell of cigarettes and the prickle of his unshaven chin. His great chest rose and fell, the breath wheezing in his throat. Her anger subsided, to be replaced by her everyday fear. How much longer would she be able to cuddle up to him like this? How much longer did he have?

'You're a good girl, Marie,' he said at last, his voice a whisper.

She shivered and huddled closer to him. She should get up and close the window. It was almost dark.

In response to his sister's shout Jamie went downstairs for supper. The kitchen was reassuringly familiar: the old wooden dresser weighed down with the same china, the Rayburn with a row of tea towels hanging on the rail above the oven, the ledge of plants behind the big double sink.

The scrubbed pine table was laid with wooden place mats that had once seen duty as the sides of wine crates – a trick of his Uncle Bob's – and the hand-painted salad bowl was a memento of a long-distant family holiday in Portugal.

It was like a scene from his childhood.

Pippa swept past Jamie and dumped a casserole dish on the table. 'Sit down,' she ordered. 'Stop hovering around like a guest, for God's sake.'

'Sorry,' he muttered and jumped to pour her a glass of wine. He knew he would soon take all this for granted, but right now the sudden transition from jail to cosy domesticity was weird.

'Where's Malcolm?' he asked, only now realising the table was just laid for two.

'Working.' She began ladling food onto his plate. 'Having dinner with some travel agent who wants to buy a horse. He's always off with someone or other who's thinking of going into racing. Most of the time it's just an excuse for a night out, if you ask me.'

'How's his business doing?' Jamie had always been intrigued by what Malcolm got up to. Bloodstock agent sounded pretty fancy but, as far as he knew, it was a term that covered a multitude of sins. Basically, Malcolm bought horses with other people's money.

'He's doing well,' Pippa said. 'At least I think he is. But, to be honest, I don't think he'd tell me if he wasn't.'

Jamie could understand that. Everything came the same to Malcolm. He treated good news and bad with the same cheery optimism. He'd been a rock to Jamie in those grim months between the accident and the trial – which was more than could be said for Malc's brother Richard. The latter seemed embarrassed by Jamie's misfortunes and had steered well clear.

'Has Malcolm still got an office at Ridgemoor?' When Jamie had gone to prison, Malcolm had been running his business out of his father's yard.

Pippa nodded. 'I said he could work from here but Toby's got more space. Anyway, Toby trains some of Malcolm's horses so it suits him.'

One of an agent's functions was to liaise between a horse's owner and trainer, especially if the trainer happened to be part of the original deal. Jamie guessed that would be the case with the Ridgemoor animals.

'Don't you have some of Mal's horses too?'

She looked taken aback. 'Certainly not. If things go wrong – like they usually do with horses – it's best I'm not involved.'

Why not? thought Jamie. If it was OK for Malcolm to rope in his dad, why not his wife? But he kept his thoughts to himself and changed the subject.

'Did you hear anything from Geoff Lane today?'

Pippa looked sombre. 'No, but I'm sure it's just a question of time.'

Jamie knew she meant it wouldn't be long before Lonsdale Heights' owner decided to remove the horse from Pippa's care. Doubtless Lane's nephew, not to mention his wife, would have put the boot in after the spectacular reverse at Wolverhampton.

His sister was looking glummer as the evening wore on. He knew her well: she was what shrinks called a catastrophist – someone who anticipated a disaster round every corner.

'Look, Pippa, I've been thinking about what you asked me – about your training.'

'Yes?' She perked up.

'Have you ever thought about talking to an athletics coach?'

She gave him a long look. 'No. Why?'

'It just strikes me that there may be some things that work with athletes that might work on horses too.'

She poured herself another glass of wine. 'Such as?' she asked drily.

'Well, I don't know.'

She sipped and said nothing, just stared at him.

'But I know a man who does.'

Barney Beaufort was a fellow who liked the sound of his own voice and, as a consequence, made sure he heard plenty of it. That was Malcolm's conclusion, at any rate, as his client's voice echoed round the hotel restaurant. Fortunately their table was in a rear alcove some distance from the white-haired pianist tinkling his way through 1950s standards. There were few other diners, it being past the bedtime of the hotel's clientele. This was not a venue that Malcolm would have chosen.

On the other hand there were many compensations, namely the wine – the restaurant's cellar was as old as its patrons and all the better for it – the sympathetic presence of Beaufort's colleague, Beverley Harris, and the reason for the celebration: Malcolm's acquisition of a four-year-old jumper on behalf of the travel agent.

After a touch-and-go infancy and a skin-of-the-teeth childhood, Beaufort Holidays had grown to sturdy manhood in the past couple of years and now a rich maturity beckoned – according to Barney. All it needed now was a determined push to 'grow' the business from its north-east power base. As part of his strategy to establish the Beaufort 'brand', Barney was looking for creative ways of getting the company name 'out there'.

'So he wants to buy a horse?' Malcolm had been sceptical on his first visit to Beverley Harris's office.

'He doesn't yet,' she'd told him and got up from behind her desk to stand over him as he slouched on a shapeless office sofa, trying not to spill his coffee.

At first sight she cut an imposing figure: raven-black hair surrounded an unreadable face of sharp planes and high cheekbones further obscured by heavy-frame spectacles. She wore a mannish business suit modestly cut to the knee. But, as she leant back to perch her bottom on the edge of her desk and the skirt crept upwards an inch or two, Malcolm began to revise his first impressions. Her eyes, magnified by the lenses of her glasses, were the milky blue of a heat-hazed sky and the thin line of her mouth now extended itself into a sinuous smile.

'Mr Beaufort is looking for creative ways of putting the company name in the public eye. I thought of a horse.'

Malcolm put his coffee cup down on the low-lying table that stood between them. He wasn't sure where this was going but, as he contemplated the firm black-stockinged calves in front of him, she had his full attention.

'Am I right in thinking you can buy a racehorse and call it anything you want?' she asked.

'Provided it hasn't run before. There's a few rules, of course. The name can't be too long or obscene or already listed. That kind of thing.'

'But we could call it Beaufort Holiday or something like that, if we wanted?'

'Sure.'

'And suppose we bought one today, how soon could it race?'

Malcolm laughed out loud. 'Steady on, there's a few other things to bear in mind. It depends on what kind of animal we're talking about.'

'We're talking about one that will be running on a racecourse in our next financial year, i.e. next January. Otherwise there's no budget for it.'

'How big a budget were you thinking of?'

'A hundred grand. Including running costs.' The milky blue eyes bored into his. 'Can it be done?'

He hadn't hesitated. 'No problem.'

That office meeting had been swiftly followed by another, at lunchtime in a city wine bar. Beverly still wore the suit and the specs but, armed with a glass of Chardonnay, she'd allowed herself to relax just a little further. She'd leant forward across the table towards him as she'd outlined her progress.

'Mr Beaufort likes the idea. He never misses the Grand National, so he sees this as "an innovative use of resources". I quote.'

'Hang on. I can't produce a Grand National entry just like that. You could buy a four-year-old jump horse and call him what you like but he wouldn't be eligible for the National until he was six. And he'd still be far too young for a race like that.'

She laughed and the thin silver link of her necklace caught his eye as it twinkled on the creamy skin below her throat. When they'd first met, hadn't her blouse been buttoned to her neck?

'I'm not saying it's impossible,' he added hastily. 'We'd need a bit of time and a lot of luck but for that money I can find you an exciting prospect.'

She draped her jacket over the back of her chair and refilled their glasses. He caught a hint of her scent, some kind of herby aroma he couldn't place, elusive and subtle. 'That sounds good, Malcolm,' she said, emphasising this first use of his Christian name with the touch of a finger on his arm. 'But what's really important is that it runs often. To maximise the marketing potential.'

'So you're just looking to have an entry? Get the name on the racecard and throw a corporate jolly at the meeting?'

She flashed him one of those slow-burning smiles. 'Provided the Beaufort name gets bandied about – that's the important point.'

'And you don't care if the horse doesn't win?'

She shrugged. That blouse was deceptively well cut – expensive, no doubt. The no-nonsense businesswoman turned out to have a heck of a figure.

'That would be nice, of course. But I've heard that some of these horses can be right prima donnas. We don't want one that cries off if it's got a runny nose.'

Malcolm had left the meeting puzzled but intrigued. Beverley couldn't be more than twenty-five yet she treated him like an errant schoolboy. And the headmistress had an agenda, which she eked out over a series of increasingly lavish lunch meetings, paid for with a company charge card. Here was a woman who enjoyed playing the powerful business operator and Malcolm enjoyed watching her. As a rule, with women, he liked to hold the whip hand. But the females he mixed with weren't corporate thrusters with company money to flash around; not even Pippa came into that category. So he played second fiddle to Beverley Harris and was content to watch the show.

He considered the deal she was proposing. He supposed it made sense from a corporate point of view. It also had some interesting aspects from his own, and he ran the situation by his father.

'They know naff-all about racing but they're prepared to blow the best part of a hundred grand on an animal, provided he runs regularly.'

Toby saw the potential at once. 'I imagine you think you're required to employ the whole budget.'

'I'd be failing in my duty otherwise, Dad.'

The trainer shook his head in mock disapproval. 'You're a bad boy, Malcolm.'

How true that was. Even his father didn't know how bad. There were limits, Malcolm imagined, even to parental support.

He grinned at the older man. 'Are you going to help me or not?'

Toby pondered the question. 'I suggest you buy them a horse overseas.'

'I was thinking of Ireland.'

Toby shook his head. 'Germany would be better. I can put you in touch with someone, if you like.'

The contact had not come for free, as Malcolm had known it wouldn't, but the result was still satisfactory. With his father's assistance he had spent a pleasant couple of days in Bavaria in the company of a dealer called Hans-Jurgen Bach. By the time he left he had acquired a horse for the Euro equivalent of £8000, a value subsequently entered in the Beaufort Holidays account for £80,000 and Little Miss Four Eyes never had an inkling that she'd been so generous. Of course, Malcolm had had to hand half the proceeds to Toby, who had also agreed to stable and train the animal. Nevertheless it was possibly the sweetest deal Malcolm had ever done – especially considering the perks.

By then those perks – Beverly's twin perks, as he thought of them slyly – had been eased from their expensive, well-cut covering and thoroughly explored, along with the rest of her, in bed at her cottage on the River Branch. So now, as he sat in the Walnut Room restaurant of the Fountain Hotel and listened to the self-important drone of Barney Beaufort, Malcolm was able to take a prurient pleasure in the pressure of a certain Marketing Director's foot as it rested on his beneath the table.

In fact the only fly in the ointment was that it would not be him who escorted Beverley upstairs at the end of the evening. She'd already told Malcolm that Mr Beaufort stayed in town overnight after business dinners and that she was expected to join him for a nightcap.

'Suppose I get a room too?' he'd suggested. 'When you've finished tucking the old boy in you can pop down the hall and see me.'

The milky blues turned to ice. 'Mr Beaufort's not a fool, you know. Besides, won't your wife be waiting up for you?'

There was no answer to that and Malcolm had let it rest.

'Right then, lads and lasses,' announced Barney Beaufort in the tone of voice that clearly said the shutter was coming down on the evening's hospitality. 'I think we've all got our marching orders.'

Malcolm recognised his cue. 'Absolutely,' he said, and picked up the sheet of paper that the travel agent had painstakingly prepared – a design for the racing colours of his new acquisition, Beaufort Bonanza. 'I'll talk to my father and arrange for you to visit Ridgemoor as soon as possible.'

His hand still tingling from Beaufort's bone-crushing goodbye handshake, Malcolm headed for his taxi. At the door he looked back and caught a glimpse of Barney steering Beverley into the lift. The pair of them were laughing. A surge of anger swept through Malcolm. What right did that old goat have to a woman thirty years his junior? For two pins he'd turn round and take Beverley off him.

But he didn't. Control, that was the important thing. Emotions had to be controlled. Malcolm was well aware of his profound talent for destruction and how to channel it to his advantage – as some people could testify. If they were still alive, that is.

Pippa wasn't happy about the idea, Jamie could see that. 'What's his name again?'

'Dave Prescott.'

'And I'm supposed to have heard of him?'

They were lolling on the sofa in the living room, watching the flames of the fire dance on the ceiling, chewing things over.

'He was a champion middle-distance runner about fifteen years ago. The next generation after Coe and Cram.'

'So what happened to him?'

'He got a bad injury before the Barcelona Olympics. It finished his career.'

Pippa prodded him with her bare foot. 'What I meant was, how did he end up inside?'

For six weeks Dave Prescott, the man Jamie was suggesting as an adviser to Pippa on her training methods, had occupied a cell on the same landing at Garstone.

'Drugs.'

Pippa looked appalled. 'I'm not having him here then, Jamie.'

'It wasn't heroin or anything really heavy,' he protested.

'Heavy enough to have him locked up.'

In truth Jamie wasn't sure of the details. He'd listened to many how-I-ended-up-in-here stories in Garstone and they all had a degree of similarity. Someone had let someone else down. It was a stitch-up. The jury had been swayed by circumstance. It always sounded like special pleading.

In Dave's case, his brother ran a gym in London's East End where body-building drugs frequently changed hands. The police had caught Dave in possession of two packages, one containing steroids, the other a hot handgun. Dave had told Jamie he was just minding the parcels at the request of his brother. Of course.

Jamie decided not to mention the gun. 'He's OK, honestly. And he has been a top-class athlete.'

The two of them had bonded over the running. On his first morning on the wing, Prescott had stood in the doorway of Jamie's cell and watched him run on the spot, his feet pounding on the stone floor until sweat poured down his face. Dave had thought it was hilarious. Then he'd joined in, jogging alongside. At first Jamie had thought he was simply making fun of him and asked him politely – always prudent in Garstone – to go away. Dave had ignored him and then effortlessly outlasted him. Only later did Jamie find out who the new boy was.

Over the next few weeks they'd played badminton whenever they could get on the one court in the beaten-up old gym. Jamie didn't have as good a technique as his opponent but he hated to lose and threw himself around like a lunatic. Dave had laughed at that too. Jamie had been sorry when the runner was released.

Pippa got up to stoke the fire. When she returned to her seat he could tell from her face that she'd come to a decision.

'All right. Get him along – on one condition.'

Jamie knew what was coming. Malcolm had reported to her their earlier conversation and she'd been on at him already about his future. He'd repeated to Pippa his decision to give up riding and, when she'd come up with a counter-proposal, he'd rejected it. But she wasn't a woman who gave up easily.

'I'll talk to your Dave Prescott if you see Ros Bradey.'

Ros was a former show-jumper who ran a nearby schooling yard, where she put horses of all sorts through their paces over jumps. She also visited yards and held schooling sessions for trainers who didn't have the time or inclination to do it themselves. Jamie knew from his sister that Toby Priest had his eye on Ros – in every sense – and she'd been making regular trips to school horses at Ridgemoor.

Pippa's suggestion was that Jamie switch to riding over jumps, where his increased weight would not be a factor.

'I told you, Pippa, I don't like the idea.'

'So what else are you going to do with your life? Riding horses is the only thing you're any good at.'

Jamie took a deep breath and bit back the angry response that sprang to mind. Controlling his emotions was one thing he'd learnt inside. If you blew your top in Garstone you were liable to end up with half a face.

Pippa showed no such restraint. She leant closer to twist the knife.

'What's the problem? You're not afraid of getting hurt, are you?'

He exhaled slowly, trying to sort out his precise objections in his mind. Riding Flat horses had always seemed to him the ultimate racing experience. Competing for the top prizes on the most stylish race-courses. Riding in the legendary races – the Guineas, the King George, the Arc and the rest. Here was speed and elegance and big money combined. And what did National Hunt have to offer? A scrum called Cheltenham, best watched on a sofa at home away from the booze-filled punters from over the water. Mostly it was flogging lumbering steeple-chasers through the mud at gaff tracks for lousy prize money. Compared to the Formula One glamour of the Flat, racing over the sticks was a minor-league drag race.

And, there was no getting away from it, you were much more likely to do yourself serious damage.

On the other hand, what *was* he going to do? Pippa was right – being a jockey was his only skill.

He returned his sister's steely gaze. 'OK then.'

'So we've got a deal?'

'I'll give it a try, Pippa. I promise.'

Jamie glanced anxiously round the crematorium chapel. As expected, it was full of people he knew. It was possibly the last place he'd wanted to be so soon after his release but he could hardly opt out on the basis that he might find it embarrassing. He'd not known Mandy Parkin that well but he had a clear memory of an animated, pretty girl, smothering her horses with affection. It was hard to believe that she was lying in the coffin at the front of the hall. The murder had taken place a month ago but the police had only just released the body.

These circumstances put his own problems into perspective. And no one here was going to be concerned about him when their minds were concentrated on the unhappy fate of a girl who had recently been one of their own. Jamie had been puzzled to hear that the fun-loving, horse-mad Mandy had fallen for a druggie – and now look what had happened to her. But he shouldn't be entirely surprised. He'd seen for himself in Garstone just what drugs could do.

By his side Richard looked sombre. Jamie tried to catch his eye as the jockey pushed a lick of sandy hair off his forehead in a familiar, nervous gesture. But Richard avoided his glance. He wasn't enjoying this any more than Jamie.

On the other side of Richard, looming over him, Malcolm gave Jamie an imperceptible wink. Buck up, mate, was the message. He'd urged Jamie to accompany them, saying it would be a good opportunity to see a load of familiar faces and let them know he was back in circulation. 'Kill two birds with one stone,' was how he'd put it – which wasn't exactly tactful, given the circumstances. But Jamie had laughed all the same, he couldn't help himself.

Malcolm was used to the sensation of looking over the heads of his fellows. When you're six foot three and spend most of your life in the company of jockeys, it's a familiar feeling. Right now, as he came out of the chapel, he found himself gazing into a face on a level with his own. The fellow had wide-spaced eyes, gelled black hair and a bruiser's nose. Sudden excitement gripped him. He'd never seen the man before but he knew who he must be. It had spread like wildfire among the congregation that the detective investigating Mandy's murder was in attendance.

Malcolm couldn't resist. He smiled ruefully at the policeman. 'A bad business,' he said. 'She was a great girl.'

The other took the bait – well, he would, wouldn't he? Why else was he there?

'She seems to have been very popular.' A Welsh accent – that was interesting. Malcolm thought the Welsh were thick.

'Didn't you know her?' Malcolm injected surprise into his voice. 'I thought you must be family.'

The other man shook his head. 'DCI Leighton Jones. I'm looking into the circumstances of Miss Parkin's death.'

'Oh, you're the police.' More surprise. 'Malcolm Priest. Mandy used to work at my father's yard.'

Jones's eyes lit up. 'Would that be Toby Priest?' Malcolm nodded and the detective became animated. 'Your dad's earned me a few bob in his time. Gregory's Cottage in the Thousand Guineas a couple of years back was one of his, wasn't he?'

So the copper followed the horses. Maybe he'd come along to pick up some racing tips. The thought tickled Malcolm – he could give the police some real tips.

'I'm puzzled why you're here, Inspector. Is it like in the movies, when the detective attends the funeral looking for clues?'

Jones looked momentarily affronted. 'I'm attending at the request of the family. Just paying my respects.'

'That's a relief. For a moment I thought we might all be under suspicion.'

A small patronising grin crept across the detective's face. 'Hardly. It's no secret that our enquiries are leading us in another direction. In my opinion, if young Amanda had kept to the company of you racing people, she'd be with us still.'

For a mad moment Malcolm was tempted to wipe that smug expression off the other man's face and tell him the truth. Instead he murmured a polite goodbye and moved on. Only as he walked towards Jamie and his brother waiting for him by the car did he realise that sweat was rolling down his back. Talking to the plod had been some rush. And very satisfactory. The stupid sod was barking up completely the wrong tree.

Chapter Three

With unspoken reluctance Jamie allowed Pippa to give him a lift to Ros Bradey's yard. To fulfil his part of the bargain, he'd spent the morning on the phone trying to track down Dave Prescott. He'd not seen the runner for six months, not since Dave had vanished out of Garstone overnight, transferred to another institution by some quirk of the system. They'd had no time to say goodbye and he'd not heard from Dave since. Prison was like that. You could spend years living almost literally in another man's pocket, then you'd wake up and find him gone for good. Sometimes, of course, that was a blessing.

All Jamie knew about Dave was that he had less than two months to serve before his release date, provided he didn't lose his time off for good behaviour. That was always a possibility. All it took was for some headcase to wind you up – push ahead of you in the phone queue or nick your bog roll – and then if you fought back everything you'd worked for could be lost. But Dave was a smart guy, more alert to these kind of pitfalls than Jamie had been. He'd saved the jockey's bacon more than once.

Jamie began by ringing Garstone, which had been a waste of time. Maybe they were just being bloody-minded but they refused to pass on any information about inmates, past or present. Jamie cursed himself for not pretending to be a longlost relative, though he doubted if he would have learned much more. The prison authorities were bloody-minded by reflex. It wasn't exactly like ringing the old school.

He then thought of searching the internet – there were bound to be old boys' networks, athletics clubs and chat rooms and message boards for followers of the sport. If he sowed a few seeds surely he'd reap a reward in due course.

When he told Pippa why he wanted to get on her computer she said, 'That sounds like hard work. Why don't you try calling that gym of his brother's?'

Jamie wondered why that hadn't occurred to him. It was probably the thought of the gun that had put him off. And Dave had sworn he was not going anywhere near his brother when he got out. But it made sense.

Half an hour on the net and a few phone calls yielded a list of gyms and health facilities in south-east London. Some he could obviously discount, like the big health chains, full no doubt of gently perspiring yuppies. Dave's brother's place would be some kind of macho-man sweat tank where no one bothered to mop up the blood. A bit like Garstone.

He rang round, asking first for Dave's brother who he remembered was called Christopher. He got a reaction on his fifth call.

'Yeah, who wants him?' The voice – male, Cockney – was not friendly.

So he'd found the right place at least. 'It's really his brother Dave I'm after. I'm a friend.'

'Didn't know the bleeder had any left,' muttered the voice and acknowledged the contact details Jamie gave him with a grunt. 'What's your connection with Dave then?'

'We met last year. When we were both, er . . .' Jamie's voice suddenly trailed off. 'Tell him it's about a job,' he added, suddenly aware of how dodgy that sounded.

'You've got a nerve,' the voice snarled and the phone was slammed down.

So now, as he stood on Ros Bradey's doorstep, he had no idea whether his message would be passed on or not.

The old farmhouse in front of him had recently been smartened up. The white paint on the door looked fresh and the brass knocker gleamed. Boots of varying sizes and functions were lined up neatly in the porch and the front garden behind him was obviously lovingly tended. From a window to his right came the sound of piano music, something stirring and classical, though not to his taste. Not that he knew what his taste was these days, after days and nights suffering the cacophony of the Garstone ghetto-blasters.

He was about to knock when the music faltered, stopped, then started again, replaying a complex phrase. Jamie realised he wasn't listening to a recording but to a person playing a real instrument. He was amazed. He couldn't claim he liked the torrent of notes that surrounded him but it was bloody impressive. He didn't dare knock on the door until it stopped.

Jamie had never met Ros Bradey before, since she'd arrived in the area after his imprisonment, but if she was being pursued by Toby Priest he had an idea what she would be like. For a start, he'd bet she'd be young enough to be Toby's daughter. In his mid-fifties, having seen off three wives, the Colonel's taste was for youth. The word around Ridgemoor was that there was always a vacancy for a stable lass if she was pretty enough – and prepared to accept some duties that lay outside the usual job description. Whatever the reason, there was always a high turnover of female help in the yard.

The woman who opened the door to Jamie, however, was no nubile stable lass. He couldn't guess her age. Petite and fine-boned, with wide-spaced brown eyes and a mass of treacle-coloured hair pulled off her face and fastened with a clasp. She wore no make-up and there were lines at the corners of her eyes and mouth. But her jaw was firm and the skin of her neck was as delicate as a schoolgirl's. She was a woman of some presence.

Even though she was a newcomer, Ros must have heard something about him but she gave no inkling as she offered a brisk handshake. She did not smile but scrutinised him dispassionately with a penetrating gaze.

'Let's see what you're made of then,' she said, pulling a padded winter jacket off a coathook and pointing back down the garden path.

Jamie didn't dare mention the music. As she shut the door behind them with some force he had the impression that she was closing it on a part of her life that he wasn't supposed to see. To refer to the piano-playing would be an invasion of her privacy.

She led him down a lane at the side of the house and through a five-barred gate. From here he could see a patchwork of fields arranged with practice fences and obstacles of various kinds. A couple of horses were being put through their paces. He noticed others being led towards a sprawl of old farm buildings, among them a large barn.

'That's my indoor school,' Ros volunteered as they got closer, 'but we'll be using the paddock.'

'How many horses do you keep?' he asked as they entered a yard of old wooden stalls.

'Not more than twenty, if I can help it. But occasionally a few more than that. Sometimes it's hard to say no.' These final words came out with a force that made Jamie wonder if she would have liked to say no to him. Had someone been twisting her arm? Toby, under pressure from Malcolm perhaps?

'We'll take Bramble,' she announced, calling to a girl who darted into the stall of a solid old bay. 'We keep him here as a schoolmaster. He leads any problem horses and gets people like you off the ground,' she explained. 'Have you ever been off the ground?' The insulting tone implied that Ros already knew the answer. Jamie could tell that she despised anyone who thought they could ride and yet had never done any jumping.

'Never.'

'Do you think you've got the nerve for it?'

This was question Jamie had been asking himself a lot recently, and the closer he got to finding out, the less certain he was of the answer.

'Of course.'

'Put Jamie on, please, Caroline.'

As the girl legged Jamie into the saddle, his immediate reaction was to pull up his stirrup irons.

'What do you think you're doing?'

Jamie looked at Ros with surprise. He'd never ridden any other way than short.

'Take your feet out of the irons, then cross the leathers over the front of the saddle. I want to see if you can ride or not. You'll never be any good at jumping unless you grip properly with your legs. And I don't want to see you hanging on to the horse's mouth either.'

Jamie did as he was told. Having his legs hanging loose on the horse's sides felt strange – like riding a bicycle without stabilisers for the first time. It altered his centre of balance and took a few moments to come to terms with.

'Right, just trot round and get used to him.'

As Jamie set off, out of the yard and into a nearby paddock, Ros called out one instruction after another. 'Shoulders back.' 'Grip tighter.' 'Let him have some rein.' It was incessant. After ten minutes of trotting around with no irons, Jamie was tired and irritable. Anyone listening to

Ros would have thought that he'd never ridden before. What he was being asked to do wasn't easy, but for a first time he felt he was making progress.

'OK, pull up and take a rest.'

The insides of Jamie's legs were burning. Even if he'd been riding regularly he doubted that he'd have coped with her demands.

Ros instructed Caroline to lay down a grid with a small jump. This was a line of poles on the ground for Bramble to step over, leading up to an obstacle. The poles were spaced at critical distances to ensure the horse kept to a rhythm and jumped off at exactly the right place.

Ros turned her attention back to Jamie.

'I want you to trot around the outside and then come down the line. Keep hold of some mane so that you don't pull him in the mouth, and lean forward as he takes off.' She took a couple of handkerchiefs from her pocket and placed them beneath the saddle and Jamie's knees. 'And don't let either of these slip out.'

Jamie walked away and set off around the paddock. He was so irritated at the way Ros was treating him that any thought of being nervous had completely vanished. He tried to concentrate on the task in hand.

Bramble had probably been through this a hundred times before but nevertheless, as Jamie turned him to face the line, he pricked his ears and broke into a canter. Jamie tried to pull him back but Bramble's mind was made up. The poles had been spaced for a trotting horse and, as a consequence, the moment the fast-moving Bramble was across the first one he had to adjust quickly to avoid standing on the next. That took him right on to the third pole and, from then on, it was like someone doing the hop skip and jump, with Jamie clinging on for dear life and both handkerchiefs gone.

Ros was less than impressed. 'I know you said you hadn't jumped before but I didn't realise you hadn't ridden either.'

In days gone by, Jamie would have given Ros a mouthful of abuse but Garstone had taught him to keep his rebellious feelings to himself. And, though he seethed inside, he knew he hadn't exactly covered himself in glory.

'Let me have another go,' he said.

Ros replaced the handkerchiefs without a word.

This time when Bramble went to canter Jamie was ready for him. The old horse trotted straight down the line and hopped over the jump with his ears pricked. Jamie looked down to see the two pieces of cloth still in place.

Ros showed no emotion. 'Do that once more and then you can do it without a saddle.'

Surprisingly, although it was more difficult without the saddle, Jamie could see what the exercise was meant to achieve. He could feel his legs moulding into Bramble's sides and the rhythm of the horse was easier to judge. The slight forward and backward movement as the animal took off and landed felt more natural.

'That will do you,' Ros said curtly as he asked if she wanted him to go again. 'I think the horse has had enough, even if you haven't.'

Jamie was thankful for the rest. He felt he'd done all right for his first attempt. Obviously his instructor was of a different opinion.

As had previously been arranged, Ros gave Jamie a ride to Ridgemoor after the lesson. From there Jamie would either hook up with Malcolm and get a ride back or call Pippa. Ros, it seemed, had a schooling session with one of Toby's jumpers.

The journey passed in silence, Ros driving fast, her face lined with concentration. To start with she took a back route and Jamie was unsure quite where they were. She joined the main road skirting the edge of the moor, heading upwards, and sudden dread gripped Jamie. He recognised the route as they crested the ridge and the road dived downhill, making a sharp curve to the right. In the months before the trial Jamie had made every effort to avoid this road – the scene of the accident that had killed Alan Kirkstall and stolen a year and a half of his own liberty.

As the car flashed past the drystone wall and the thin copse of trees overlooking the valley, Jamie caught a glimpse of red and white – a bunch of fading carnations tied to the new fence in front of the trees. Someone must be tending the spot, keeping it as a roadside memorial. Jamie's stomach turned over.

'Are you all right?'

He nodded, unable to speak, surprised that she had registered his unease. Hard act though she might be, Ros did not appear to miss much.

Toby himself came outside to greet them as the car pulled into the Ridgemoor courtyard. Jamie assumed it was because of his interest in

54

Ros but, after bestowing a polite kiss on her cheek, the trainer focused on his former jockey.

'Good to see you back, young man. We've missed you in this yard.'

'Thanks, Colonel,' said Jamie, a little embarrassed.

'Sorry to hear you're lost to the Flat,' Toby continued. He turned to Ros. 'Best apprentice I ever had. You'll have no trouble making a jump jockey out of him.'

'Not on the basis of what I've seen so far,' she said drily.

Toby laughed but Jamie didn't join in. He knew she wasn't joking.

'So where's this horse you want me to look at?' she asked Toby.

'I've put him in one of the back boxes. He's been in a filthy temper ever since he pitched up.'

The trainer turned and headed through the courtyard along a path that led behind the main row of stalls. Ros followed and Jamie hung back, aware that this was not his business.

'Jamie,' Toby shouted as he strode off. 'Come and make yourself useful.'

He set off after them. Apparently this was his business after all.

As they approached the rear stables a sound of crashing and banging, as of hooves battering a wall, filled the air.

'He's heard us coming,' said Toby. 'He's been trying to kick the place down for the past four days.'

They turned the corner into a cobbled yard, hemmed by black-and-white painted stables. Ten years ago, so Jamie had been told, this had been the hub of Ridgemoor's activities but Toby had expanded his premises since then, building more modern facilities to house his charges.

At first Jamie couldn't make out which box held the rebellious animal, as they all seemed to be empty. Then he caught a flash of movement behind the nearest door and the thump and shudder of a ferocious kick that set the wooden frame quivering. A big black head suddenly thrust itself into vision, the tendons on his neck taut and straining. At the sight of them the horse froze, glaring out of eyes as black as coal and rimmed with red.

'Oh Toby, he's magnificent,' said Ros with a passion that took Jamie by surprise. Maybe she wasn't quite such a cool customer after all.

'He's a handsome fellow, no question,' replied the trainer. 'I think that's the chief reason Malcolm bought him. The owners don't know much about horses apparently so it's best to have an animal that looks the part.'

'What's he called?'

'Beaufort Bonanza, as in Beaufort the travel company. Malcolm found him in Germany so the girls call him Adolf. Seems to suit his personality. Be careful, Ros, he'll take your arm off given half a chance.'

Ros had closed to within a few feet of the horse and was talking to him in a low, guttural whisper that Jamie couldn't make out. Adolf cocked his head quizzically. He appeared to be listening. Jamie caught a word or two and realised she was speaking to him in German. That was cunning of her – it was obviously the language he was used to.

The two men watched as Ros, still talking, reached up and patted his great neck. Adolf allowed the contact. Indeed, he appeared to enjoy it.

Without turning her head, Ros spoke to Toby. 'What's his problem?'

'He just won't settle. Every time he jumps a hurdle he takes off as if there's a lion chasing him. Someone must have beaten the poor fellow rotten at some stage.'

'He could do with some exercise to use up some of this destructive energy. Has he been ridden out?'

'Not today. He's got a cold back. When a lad got on him yesterday the horse fired him across the yard. Nearly broke his shoulder. He'll be off for a few days.'

For the first time in their short acquaintance, Ros smiled at Jamie. 'Lucky you're here then, isn't it?'

'You want me to ride him?' His voice came out strained and thin.

A finely plucked eyebrow rose quizzically. 'Why not? You wanted a bit more action as I recall.' She appeared to be enjoying his discomfort.

'OK,' he agreed. 'I'll go and fetch my helmet.'

When he returned a stable girl was tacking up Adolf in the yard. The horse seemed much calmer now he was out in the open.

Toby gave Jamie a leg up into the saddle and he felt the animal shift uneasily beneath him as it took his weight.

'What are you going to do with him?' said the trainer, turning to Ros.

'Are the poles with the rubber tyres still out in the paddock alongside the hay-barn?

'Yes.'

'Let's take him out there.' Ros looked up at Jamie. 'Just warm him up for ten minutes. Not that he looks as if he needs it. Do a few circles on either rein.'

The stable lass led the way and Jamie took a firm grip on the horse as he walked him into a field with a big black barn at one end. He'd rarely ventured down here when he'd worked at Ridgemoor. It was kept as a schooling yard for jumpers which, in those days, had been of little interest to him. Funny how times changed. He began the exercise Ros had prescribed, determined to follow her instructions to the letter – particularly after the Colonel's earlier endorsement of his skill. He couldn't let his former employer down.

Ros called out, 'I'm now going to show you how to stop a horse from running away at his fences in one easy lesson. Toby, would you give me a hand?'

With Jamie and Adolf at one end of the paddock, Ros stood with her back to the barn and paced out six good strides towards the centre. Then, with Toby's assistance, she set about building an obstacle out of poles and fence wings. When she had finished she stood back and admired her work. It wasn't big, standing at just a little over three feet, but it was solid.

'There, that should settle him,' she said, looking beyond the fence to the corrugated wall of the barn, just six strides off. 'If he takes on the barn you might end up short of a jockey but I guarantee you'll have a bloody good jumper on your hands.'

By now Jamie, watching from the other end of the paddock, had an idea of what she was up to. According to Toby, once Adolf jumped an obstacle he'd run off, defying his rider. By making the horse jump directly in front of the barn wall, Ros was cutting off his escape route and forcing him to remain under control. That was the theory anyway.

Ros turned and motioned to Jamie to bring the horse up to them. Adolf began to get jittery the moment he spotted the fence. Jamie patted his neck and spoke to him quietly, much as Ros had done. It didn't seem to have the same effect. He could feel the horse shiver with pent-up energy beneath him.

'Right, Jamie,' Ros said, 'just bring him straight in and over the fence. Don't try and slow him down and, when he lands, don't let him turn. Keep him facing the barn. Even he must realise he can't jump it, so call his bluff.'

Jamie noticed Toby exchange a glance with the stable girl and shake his head. He guessed that the Colonel had reservations about what Ros was asking him to do but had decided not to interfere. Since Toby was not slow in laying down the law, obviously he must trust her. Of course, *he* wasn't the one sitting on top of Adolf.

Two hours ago Jamie had never left the ground on a horse. Now he was being asked to jump an animal he doubted he could hold, a few yards in front of a solid wall. If it hadn't been for his pride he'd have told Ros what she could do. She wasn't being fair on him.

It crossed his mind that if anything went wrong he might get a cheap holiday from the horse's owner. The only trouble was that it would probably follow a spell in hospital!

He turned Adolf towards the fence. He'd hardly got him straight when the horse took off like a rocket. Jamie had no time to think about holding handkerchiefs in place but it was as if his knees were nailed to the animal's side.

Jamie had ridden long enough to know when a horse had spotted something it couldn't negotiate. But Adolf showed none of the signs as he took off over the fence and landed with his nose a few feet from the metal cladding of the barn wall.

There was a split second when Jamie thought Adolf was going to take off again then, just as quickly, the horse ducked out to his left. Jamie grabbed a piece of mane as he felt himself shooting out of the side-door. For an instant both of his legs were on the same side of the horse as his shoulder clattered into the wall. The force knocked him back into the saddle and he grabbed at the reins before the horse regained his stride and took off again.

'I told you not to let him turn.'

Jamie could hear Ros yelling at him as he struggled to get the horse back under control.

'Bring him back and do it again.'

Jamie could feel himself beginning to sweat under his helmet, a combination of effort and nerves. His shoulder was numb from the impact with the barn and muscles he'd not used for years were beginning to protest in his legs and back. But the blood was singing in his veins. Aches and pains could wait. This was the kind of thrill he used to live for.

He brought the horse in again, concentrating on keeping him on line. This time the manoeuvre went better. The horse still ducked away, but at a much slower pace. Twenty minutes later, with sweat pouring from every part of his body, Jamie had the animal completely under control, popping over the fence and pulling up on landing just a yard from the barn wall.

Ros then sent him over another jump, placed in the middle of the field. At once the horse began to pull, but nowhere near as badly as before. Ros called Jamie back to the fence facing the barn. Once more the horse reverted to his previous behaviour but Jamie was ready for him. He was determined to take him round until he had fully imposed his will on the animal.

At last, after another half an hour, the horse stayed settled no matter what was in front of him. Only then did Ros call them in. Jamie felt he'd learned more about riding in the past hour than he had in all his career. He was exhausted.

Jamie was surprised when Ros offered to drop him at Shelley Farm. At first he declined but there was no sign of Malcolm and it didn't seem fair to summon his sister when there was a lift on offer.

He almost fell asleep on the way back. He'd tried to keep fit in prison but there had been no way he could keep himself in shape for riding an animal like Adolf. He felt as if he'd gone a couple of rounds with Mike Tyson.

'Same time tomorrow then,' said Ros as she stopped the car in the drive. 'I'll meet you in the yard, no need to come to the house.'

Jamie nodded. He'd half expected her to suggest he found someone else to teach him and he wouldn't have cared. She looked at him as if he were a bad smell – maybe the Garstone stink still clung to him. However, if she was still game then he wasn't going to back off. He'd promised Pippa.

There was one matter, however.

'If you don't mind my asking, Ros – what do you charge?'

That bad-smell look again flickered across her elegant features.

'I mean,' he continued, 'what's this going to cost me?'

'A broken neck, I should think, until you learn how to handle awkward customers like Adolf.'

Jamie wasn't in the mood. 'I just want everything straight. Give me a bill at the end of the week, OK?'

'Jamie,' her voice was unexpectedly soft. 'There's no need. I owe Toby a favour or two and your lessons have been taken care of.'

Suddenly he didn't feel tired any more. He felt angry.

'What favours? Whatever goes on between you two's got nothing to do with me. You give me a bill and I'll pay it like anybody else.' He threw open the car door and jumped out. 'You think because I've just got out of prison I'm some kind of charity?'

'It's not that, Jamie.'

He paid no attention but spoke bitterly through the car window. 'You've got a nerve, Lady Bloody Bountiful. I don't care what kind of favours you give Toby or anyone else, with you and me it's proper business. All right?'

She looked at him calmly. 'If that's what you want. I charge thirty pounds a lesson plus VAT. I'll raise an invoice whenever you like.'

'Good.' For someone who'd been earning less than ten quid a week in the prison metal shop it seemed pretty pricy. But at least he now knew where he stood. And he had Malcolm's loan to tide him over. His fury vanished as quickly as it had arrived. 'Sorry, Ros, I didn't mean to get shirty.'

She nodded curtly and started the engine.

He trudged towards the house. Suddenly all his tiredness was back. After a bath he was going straight to bed.

Richard didn't want to make this phone call but he had no choice. Malcolm had been on at him, which was par for the course, then Toby had chipped in. For all Richard's recent success on the racecourse, he'd not yet learned how to say no to his father.

Toby had buttonholed him that morning on the gallops. 'Malcolm tells me you're keeping a friendly eye on Jamie now he's back.'

Richard reacted irritably. At least, out here alone with his father, he didn't have to keep up the pretence. 'But why *is* he back? In his position I'd find a job as far away as possible.'

Toby sighed. It was old ground. All three of them would have preferred Jamie to crawl into a hole in the ground so they could roll a boulder over the top. But Pippa had wanted her baby brother back under her wing and there was no way round that. Malcolm had termed their strategy 'damage limitation'. Richard knew it was just making the best of a very bad job.

Malcolm had been cosying up to Jamie, welcoming him into his home, bunging him cash and generally making Jamie feel like he was the best mate a man could have. The two-faced bastard was clever like that.

Now his father was asking him what *he* was going to do to keep Jamie sweet and unsuspecting.

The answer was this phone call. Richard hoped the grand gesture would get his co-conspirators off his back.

As Jamie slumped wearily in the kitchen, sipping a cup of tea, Pippa called him to the phone. It was Richard, summoning him to dinner that night and he wouldn't take no for an answer.

'You're coming, mate. No arguments.'

'Sorry, Rich, not tonight.'

'Look, you're out of prison now. You're allowed to have some fun. Anyhow, the table's booked and Vanessa's dying to get to know my best man.'

'What did you say?'

'Didn't I mention it? My wedding – next May. You're the best man.'

'Rich . . .' He floundered. Why would anyone want an ex-con for his best man? Especially – considering Richard and Malcolm had been his passengers at the time of his crash – an ex-con who'd nearly killed him. 'I don't know what to say,' he mumbled.

'Course you do. The word's yes. And just you be ready at eight.'

So he'd foregone his early night and togged himself up in his old clothes for dinner with Richard and his gorgeous fiancée of whom, he reminded himself, he was not supposed to have had carnal knowledge.

Richard was on his own when he picked Jamie up. Vanessa, he said, was meeting them at the Roman Arms. Jamie didn't smell a rat until they entered the crowded bar. He spotted Vanessa at once, perched on a high stool, all legs and blonde flamboyance. Next to her was another girl, a contrasting brunette, with legs maybe not so long and possibly more flesh on her bones, but out of the same stable nonetheless. The women turned as one as Richard and Jamie approached, their eyes gleaming.

'This is Georgie,' said Richard. 'She went to some boarding school with Vanessa where they had to wear green knickers.'

'Richard!' Vanessa sniffed in pretend disapproval.

'Actually, we didn't bother much with knickers,' said Georgie as she gave Jamie a firm handshake. 'Not in the sixth form anyway.' She gazed at him with a white-toothed smile and ill-concealed curiosity. Jamie remembered Vanessa saying at the races that she'd fix him up with one of her friends. Obviously she wasn't wasting any time.

Jamie was out of practice with small talk. Fortunately the others were less inhibited and he was able to take cover in some horse chat with Richard while he adjusted to being in the company of an unknown but available woman.

Up close he revised his first impression of Georgie. There wasn't that much resemblance to Vanessa. She looked older than her friend, with shadows under her eyes that make-up could not conceal. And she talked too quickly, her Home Counties vowels cutting through the bar-room Yorkshire chatter in a head-turning fashion. It occurred to Jamie that she was as nervous as he was.

The small restaurant upstairs was humming with enthusiastic diners and bustling service staff. Jamie found himself wedged onto an alcove banquette next to Georgie. He was instantly aware of her thigh, sheathed in a floral print skirt and flesh-toned tights, pressing into his.

'You two look cosy,' said Vanessa guilelessly from across the table. The witch.

Marie put down the phone and wandered into the front room where her father was watching *Who Wants to be a Millionaire?* At her approach he flicked the mute button on the remote control.

'Going out then, lass?'

She shook her head and slumped down next to him on the sofa.

'When I was your age you'd not catch me at home on a Friday night. Get out and have some fun.'

'It's OK, Dad. I don't feel like it.'

The television flicked up a caption beneath the worried face of a contestant.

'Thirty-two grand question. Money for old rope,' muttered Clem Kirkstall. 'You haven't fallen out with young Colin, have you?'

She'd been avoiding Colin for weeks but she didn't want to debate it with her father who was keen on him. Colin would take the trouble to sit with Clem and jaw about racing. He'd also been Alan's best friend. But that didn't mean she had to marry him, did it?

'It's not that,' she said, 'but there's no point in going out when I've got to get up at five in the morning.'

She'd said the same to Gail on the phone just now when she'd declined a trip to a club in Leeds. Once or twice she'd turned up for work after she'd been out all night and she'd barely made it through the shift. Her friends must think she was really boring. Getting old before her time.

'Go on, lad, it's ruddy obvious. February the fifteenth, 1971.' Clem was bawling at the television. 'Calls himself an economics lecturer, that one, and doesn't know the date of decimalisation.'

Marie laughed. She'd given up telling Dad to get himself on the programme. He knew all the answers. But if she thought he'd dropped the subject, she was mistaken.

'You don't have to go on a flaming great bender, you know. Get Colin to take you out for an hour or two.'

She could, of course, ring Colin. He'd change his plans and come running at the drop of a hat. But what girl wanted that? There was such a thing as being too devoted.

'Any road,' said her father, 'I've been asking around. They're looking for someone to help out in the surgery. Gooding told me when he popped in.'

Dr Gooding was an old friend of Clem's as well as his doctor. Time was when Clem would service the doctor's car – a reciprocal MOT arrangement, her father called it. It was a one-sided arrangement now.

'I'm not a doctor yet, Dad. At this rate I never will be.' Marie had always wanted to study medicine at university. A disappointing grade in Chemistry A-level had scuppered that prospect – which was why she was resitting.

Clem ignored her remark. 'Now they've got their new computer system running they want to sort out their records. Apparently they're in a right mess and they need someone to do a job short term. He says you're to call him in the morning.'

'Oh,' said Marie as she digested this information. Instinctively – like the business with Colin – she resented having her life organised for her.

'Mind you, if you want to carry on scrubbing toilets while the rest of the world is lying in bed then that's your business.'

The words 'Yes, it is' leapt into her mind but she didn't utter them. She wasn't that stupid. The prospect of jacking in the cleaning was too enticing.

'If you take my advice,' he added, 'you'll phone a friend.'

'I'll call in the morning,' she said and reached out a hand to grip his. 'Thanks, Dad.'

He turned up the sound on the TV.

The conversation moved inevitably to Jamie's time in prison. Georgie, it seemed, knew about his situation and was eager to find out more. Her curiosity increased with every glass of wine she put away.

It started with the appearance of the restaurant's menu cards. To Jamie the list of choices was bewildering. He'd once been told by an old con at Garstone that one of the problems of adjusting to the world after a stretch inside was accepting responsibility for everyday things. 'In here, you can't decide nothing for yourself. When you sleep, when you work, when you crap – it's all decided. You can't even open a door for yourself. It tell you, it's a ruddy great shock when you get outside.'

Jamie thought of these words as he read the list of dishes over and over. It was impossible to make a choice. He realised that the waiter was hovering with a notepad and the others were looking at him.

'Sorry,' he said. 'I'm a bit out of practice.'

Georgie leaned closer and a strand of raven hair brushed his cheek. 'The steak's the best thing here. And onion soup to start.'

'Er, OK.'

'He'll have the same as me,' she announced, taking the menu out of his hands and returning it to the waiter.

Jamie felt both grateful and foolish. It was hardly the way to impress a woman. He tried to explain and suddenly his time in prison was the primary topic of conversation, hard as he tried to head it off.

'Come on then, Jamie,' said Vanessa. 'What about sex behind bars?'

She was sitting directly opposite him, the fall of her hair screening her knowing look from Richard.

'Ooh yes, do tell,' cried Georgie. 'What goes on with all of you tough desperate men cooped up in one place with no women?'

For a split second Jamie was tempted to get up and leave. He'd found prison hard and degrading. Fear and loneliness had sapped his spirit from the first day to the last. He'd walked a tightrope of survival and all his energies had been harnessed to getting across in one piece. And throughout his time inside his sex drive had simply disappeared. When he'd thought of women, he'd yearned for warmth and comfort, of a body wrapped around his at night. Thought of carnal pleasure had not entered into it. He couldn't answer for his fellow prisoners but he guessed it was the same for many of them. A man's sensual imagination was the first casualty of a place like Garstone.

But this was not the occasion to pour cold water on his companions' ignorance. He'd been enough of a social flop already. And now he was a free man, the effect of Georgie's rounded hip rubbing suggestively against his was proof enough that the old urges were functioning again. More than that, they were raring to go.

'It's not what you think,' he said. 'Nobody ever accosted me in the showers. Mind you – I made damned sure I never dropped the soap.'

The joke had the desired effect. The pair opposite laughed and Georgie squealed with tipsy excitement. She leant all over him, her eyes dancing and one hand gripping his arm. Across the table, Jamie saw Vanessa observing this with quiet satisfaction.

Then, over Vanessa's shoulder, he noticed a middle-aged waitress approaching to clear the table of their first course. She too was looking at him but with a different kind of expression on her large pink face. Hatred, pure and simple. He'd seen a lot of it where he'd been.

The pink face was thrust into his own.

'Murderer!' she shouted, spraying him with spittle. 'They should never have let you out!'

With a sweep of her beefy forearm she upended everything on the table – dirty plates, glasses and bottles – onto Jamie and Georgie. Red wine and brown soup splattered everywhere.

'This bastard killed my nephew,' she shouted to the astonished spectators at adjoining tables. 'He's ruined my brother's life and he's free to go out with his fancy tart. There's no justice. He should rot in jail for what he's done!'

Jamie sat totally still as the place around him erupted. A posse of serving staff converged on the enraged waitress, who burst into tears as she allowed herself to be led away. Beside him Georgie, her clothes utterly drenched, screamed in outrage. Vanessa and Richard were on their feet as were many other diners. A man in a bow-tie – the manager, Jamie presumed – appeared, together with other senior restaurant staff. In the buzz of excited conversation, Jamie heard his name mentioned and then repeated. People were craning their necks to get a look at him.

65

There was even a smattering of applause from those who evidently approved of publicly humiliating drink-drive killers who escaped with piffling prison terms.

Vanessa had extricated Georgie from her seat now and was hugging her tight, trying to calm her hysterical friend.

'I am so sorry,' gabbled the manager as a waiter tried ineffectually to put their table to rights. 'This is quite unprecedented, I can assure you. Do you want me to call the police? I will if you want but I'm sure we can sort it out between ourselves. If you give us a few moments we'll have everything back to rights, I promise.'

Jamie stood up. 'No police, thanks. Come on, Richard, let's go.'

The manager fluttered around them on their bedraggled progress to the door. Georgie's sobs mingled with the whispered hum of conversation from the other tables. Every eye was upon them.

Outside they split up, Vanessa ushering Georgie straight into her car and driving off with an unhappy glance in Jamie and Richard's direction.

'Jesus Christ,' said Richard. 'You could sue.'

'No,' said Jamie. 'Just get me out of here please, Rich. As quick as you can.'

The two men drove home in silence, their thoughts loud in their heads.

Upstairs in her bedroom, her eyes glazing over as she stared, yet again, at the Periodic Table, Marie heard the familiar phut of a car bumbling up the lane and parking outside the house. She glanced at her watch. It was not yet ten – early for Auntie Joyce to be returning from her weekend stint at the Roman Arms.

A moment later the front door opened and was slammed shut with a bang that shook the house. Marie's fatigue vanished in an instant. Something was up.

By the time Marie got downstairs Auntie Joyce was sitting in the armchair in the lounge opposite Dad. She still wore her coat and her face was working with emotion. She appeared to be having difficulty getting her words out.

'Easy now, lass,' said Clem. 'Take your time.'

'That bastard came in the restaurant tonight. Laughing and boozing it up with a tarty piece hanging on his every word. I couldn't believe it. I was that upset.'

'Who came in, Joyce?' rumbled her dad.

'Him. Jamie Sullivan. I'd know that smug face anywhere. He didn't look so clever by the time I was done with him, I can tell you that.'

'What do you mean, Auntie?'

'I threw his dinner in his face and I told everyone just who he was – the murdering bastard who did for our Alan.'

'You never did.' Clem's mouth gaped in amazement.

'He should be rotting in jail, I said. For the rest of his miserable life.'

'My God, Joyce, you're a woman and a half.' Clem was grinning from ear to ear. 'So what did he do?'

'Nothing. Just sat there like he'd been caught with his pants down and his dinner all over him. I wish you could have seen him, Clem. Serve him bloody right to show his face.'

He began to laugh, a low wheezy shudder deep in his chest, and Joyce joined in, dabbing her florid face with a dainty white handkerchief that looked out of place in her large fist.

Marie was not so amused. Though the thought of Jamie Sullivan walking free tore at her, reminding her of the unfairness of their loss, to tip food over a person in public seemed so – childish. Just as the pair of them, her dad and her aunt, were childish in their glee. A great couple of babies, she thought, as her dad heaved himself to his feet and produced a bottle of liqueur brandy from a cupboard. The apricot brandy only came out at Christmas but this, she could see, would go down as a night of celebration. She didn't want to spoil things, but all the same she had to ask.

'What happened after that, Auntie? Did you get into trouble?'

Joyce fixed her with a steady eye, the glass poised halfway to her lips. 'Mr Duggan sacked me on the spot. Paid me for the night and told me to make myself scarce.'

'Oh, Auntie.' Joyce had worked Fridays and Saturdays at the Roman Arms for six years. And they'd all had happy evenings there in times gone by.

Joyce emptied her glass and held it out for a refill. 'What's that they say? Don't do the crime if you can't do the time. I don't care about the job. It were ruddy well worth it.'

Clem walked slowly but steadily up the slope to the seat overlooking the valley. It was a grand spot from which to watch the village below and people walking along the river, heading for the High Street shops. Some mornings he found the walk difficult but he was a stubborn beggar, always had been. Except when the weather was downright torrid he hadn't given up on his constitutional yet.

This morning he hardly thought about the comings and goings below or the weather or, even, his infirmities. His mind was on the events of last night and his sister's bombshell. Joyce was a heroine, showing Jamie Sullivan up in public with no thought for the consequences. He was right proud of her.

But in the cold light of day her bold gesture seemed merely that, an action of momentary substance. In the long run what had she got out of it? She'd given a murderer some public embarrassment and a dry-cleaning bill – which the Roman Arms would no doubt cover. He still applauded her but a gesture was all she'd made – and at the cost of her job.

If only it were possible to find another solution to the blight of Jamie Sullivan. Clem conjured up the jockey's face in his thoughts. Those wide eyes and innocent, little-boy-lost looks. How he'd like to batter those clean-cut features into a pulp. Clem had once felled an eighteen-stone drunk with a single blow of his big fist. Laid him out cold with one punch. He could still manage it, he had no doubt. Put Sullivan in front of him right now and he'd thump him into the next world with fists fuelled by righteous anger.

He'd do it, what's more, without fear of the consequences. What did it matter what happened to him? He was doomed anyway – his illness was slowly claiming him. It was wrong for Joyce to make sacrifices. It had to be him – while he had the strength left.

The wind whipped into his face, damp and cold. Time to get back. He rose slowly to his feet and at once was gripped by shortness of breath. He clung to the bench as the spasms shook his big frame.

Who was he kidding, dreaming of vengeance? In the state he was in, dreams were all he had left.

Chapter Four

14 January, 2002

Detective Inspector Jane Culpepper took one look at the cramped, jam-packed car park of the Deacon Parade nick and parked round the corner on a pay-and-display. She found the change for the maximum stay. She had no idea how long she'd be but she was taking no chances.

She wasn't looking forward to resuming her acquaintance with Superintendent Keith Wright. They'd got maudlin together at a leaving do two years ago when it turned out they were both reeling from divorce. Then he'd manoeuvred her into a cosy corner and she'd run off to be sick in the loo. They'd not seen each other since. With luck he'd forgotten all about it.

She was led up to his office straight away. 'He's waiting for you,' said the PC who showed her the way. That sounded ominous.

Time had not done the Superintendent any favours since they'd last met. He looked pasty and haggard, with even less hair. She hoped to God she'd weathered better than him.

'Good Christmas, Jane?' he asked. He didn't sound as if he particularly wanted to know. His eyes were still on the open file in front of him.

She took the seat he indicated on the other side of his desk.

'Very nice, thank you, sir,' she replied, which was stretching the truth a bit – nobody would call Christmas and Boxing Day at The Palm Tree Residential Home 'nice'. Though the staff were saints, in Jane's opinion, to see her mother there, in a wheelchair after her last stroke, was hard.

'I expect Robbie keeps you on your toes?'

All credit to Wright, even in these troubled times he had researched her son's name. Her curiosity was growing.

'You know teenagers, sir,' she replied, keeping up the facade.

The truth was she'd hardly seen her son during the past fortnight. She'd not thought it fair to inflict The Palm Tree on a fourteen-year-old at Christmas so he'd spent it with his father and stepmother. Then they'd whisked him off to Switzerland for the New Year on a skiing holiday – their present to him and very generous it was too. Deprived of his company it had meant she'd spent the entire holiday period feeling as if she were one step away from becoming a Palm Tree resident herself.

None of which was of interest to the Superintendent.

He looked at her with bloodshot eyes, finally giving her his full attention. 'You've heard about Leighton Jones?'

'Yes, sir.'

Of course she'd heard. Detective Chief Inspector Jones, the heaviest hitter in the Sketch Valley CID, had been sent home the day before, suspended on full pay pending an investigation by the Discipline and Complaints branch. Quite why Leighton was under investigation depended on who you listened to. But he'd made his name on the Drugs Squad and the whisper was that he'd become too closely associated with a couple of bad boys responsible for most of the drug trafficking in the area. But who could say at this stage? A chancer like Leighton walked a fine line – it would be easy to put a foot wrong.

'So you've probably already guessed why I've asked for you,' he continued.

That she didn't know, though she imagined it was to do with tidying up some mess of Leighton's. It couldn't be anything good, Wright was being too polite.

'DCI Jones was Senior Investigating Officer on a double murder. I'd like you to take over his role in the investigation.'

Jane's mouth dropped open and she shut it quickly. In the course of her career she'd been on several murder teams and, as Deputy SIO, had run an incident room. But she'd never acted as an SIO herself. This was a first. It made up for a few other things.

Wright registered her reaction. 'Don't get too excited. There's a school of thought that wants to scale this operation down. It's a couple of months old and a result looks doubtful. Two drug addicts in a burnt-out cottage.'

A distant bell rang in Jane's head. 'The Bonfire Night Murders?'

Wright nodded. 'You must have been reading the *East Lancs Journal*. I don't know why the nationals didn't pick it up. Murder, arson, torture – it's got everything. Except sex, of course.' He flashed her a quick, cautious smile. So he did remember. Pity.

'Torture?' she said, picking up on the one word that didn't sound familiar from what she'd read. 'I don't remember that.'

'It came to light later. Simon Bennett will fill you in. He is – was – Leighton's deputy.'

And now he was hers.

'Great.' Her enthusiasm was not faked.

Wright got to his feet and she followed suit. 'The logical thing to do was to put Simon in charge. He's a competent man. But . . .' he fixed her with a purposeful glare '. . . I want some fresh thinking on this. That's why I've brought you in – Acting Detective Chief Inspector.'

Her heart thumped with excitement. Acting DCI. This was a heaven-sent opportunity.

'Thank you, sir. I won't let you down, I promise.'

'Just give it your best shot, Jane. That's all any of us can do.'

It wasn't the most inspiring call to arms but it didn't dampen her spirits one bit.

It was a wet afternoon at Haydock Park, with storm clouds scurrying in from the Irish Sea, eager to dump their contents on the north-west of England. The rain, however, did little to dampen the enthusiasm of the racegoers in Box 13 of the Tommy Whittle stand. The guests of Beaufort Holidays – mostly favoured employees for this inaugural occasion – had enjoyed a substantial lunch and, armed with suitable lubrication, were looking forward to winning a few quid on the gee-gees. And the cherry on the cake, according to their generous host, would be the first sight of the company's own horse. Beaufort Bonanza, a handsome black gelding, was making his maiden appearance in the last race. Barney's excitement (and the brandy) had already turned his cheeks a hearty puce. Malcolm hoped his client would survive the afternoon. He knew one thing, if the old fart had a heart attack it wouldn't be him who administered the kiss of life. He'd leave that to Beverley who had seized the role of hostess with some aplomb.

71

'Sorry to see your wife's not here,' Malcolm had said to Barney over lunch. It was mischievous of him but the businessman had not turned a hair.

'Oh, she never comes to work dos,' he'd boomed. 'My job's to get out and earn a crust. Hers is to sit at home and scoff it. Isn't that right, Beverley?'

Malcolm couldn't help but admire the man. A doormat at home to push around and a woman half his age to parade in public.

As a concession to the occasion Beverley was wearing one of her less sober suits. The shade of pastel blue complemented her eyes which, today, were showcased by a pair of thin-rimmed oval spectacles. The jacket was nipped in at the waist, hinting at the curves beneath, and Malcolm noted several appreciative glances cast in her direction by the other men in the group. Barney patted her hip and squeezed her arm every chance he got. Now and again she shot Malcolm a conspiratorial glance. She was loving every second.

He'd tried to get out of attending this Beaufort bash once he'd discovered that there would be no chance of a get-together with Beverley later.

'I know one or two nice little hotels out that way,' he'd said the last time he'd paid a visit to her bedroom. 'We'll stop over.'

She'd lifted her head from his chest, her expression humourless. 'Not possible. I'm driving Barney back.'

'Well, when you've dropped him off. We'll go somewhere nearer home.'

'I don't know when I'll be finished.'

'You mean you'll bring him back here?'

She'd not replied to that but fastened her wide thin mouth on his to shut him up. Malcolm had a pretty shrewd idea Barney paid the rent on the cottage. Maybe it was done through the books of his company. Like the dress allowance that filled her wardrobe with designer clothes and her chest of drawers with expensive underwear. No wonder she was so devoted to the company cause.

The next day, on the phone, he'd tried to wriggle out of attending the meeting at all but she wasn't having it.

'May I remind you, Malcolm, that you have a very generous contract with Beaufort Holidays. Mr Beaufort will be most unhappy if you are not there to lend your support on the occasion of our first race.'

Malcolm could have told her to stuff it, of course. Women did not talk to him like this. On the other hand, while he still found her attractive, it amused him to submit.

'Yes, mistress,' he'd said, knowing the irony would pass her by.

So here he was, on this tedious company knees-up, surrounded by flushed and noisy office managers and tele-sales execs, all of whom were looking for a winner. And, as the acknowledged expert on horses, he was expected to supply it.

Malcolm fancied himself as a bit of a tipster – after all, he ought to be. But today was not one of his best.

'I don't think much to your fancies, Mr Bloodstock Agent,' said the loudest and largest of the company suits after Malcolm had recommended three duds in a row. 'Eh, Barney, I hope he's a better judge of horseflesh or your Bonanza will be a right duffer.'

Malcolm considered telling this fat clown where to shove it but that, of course, was not an option.

'Sorry about that,' he muttered as pleasantly as he could manage.

Beverley stepped in swiftly. 'What would you know about it, Roland? A clot like you couldn't tell a racehorse from a rocking horse without getting a second opinion.'

To Malcolm's surprise, Roland roared with laughter at this treatment. She leaned over and placed her hand on his pudgy knee. 'What you do is look for the horse with the biggest feet. You see how wet it is? If they've got big feet they're not so likely to get bogged down.'

This impressive argument kept everyone amused and, by some fluke, provided the name of the winner in the next two races. By the time Barney and his merry group of connections headed down to the parade ring for Beaufort Bonanza's race, expectations were running dangerously high. Malcolm hoped to God that Adolf would put on some kind of a show.

The last race on the card was significant not just for the first appearance of the Beaufort horse. It was the first race of Jamie's comeback and his first under National Hunt rules. He had not ridden competitively since the day of his accident and his win on Morwenstow. Haydock in the January mud on an unknown and unpredictable animal like Adolf was a far cry from Ascot in September. But a race was a race and this one represented a step back to the profession that had been his life.

'I've won here on the Flat,' he said to Ros as they stood in the parade ring, the wind whipping rain into their faces.

'I know,' she said. 'The Sprint Cup on Samantha Brown.'

Jamie was suspicious. 'Did Toby tell you?'

'As a matter of fact he did mention it, but I remember watching it on television. You came from ten lengths down in the last furlong. An astonishing piece of riding from an apprentice.'

He looked at her in amazement. Throughout their many sessions she'd given the impression that his past experience didn't count. To hear a word of praise from her unsmiling lips was as rare as winter warmth.

Now she was smiling, creasing the fine lines at the corners of her eyes. 'You were one of the best young riders I'd ever seen. I was pleased when you came to work with me.'

'You never said so.'

'Why should I? You were meant to learn. And you have.'

Jamie glowed with pleasure. The boost to his morale was timely. The race ahead was going to be a challenge.

Toby had not wanted to run Beaufort Bonanza so soon but the owners, so Malcolm said, were insistent. Like any other employee of Beaufort Holidays, Adolf had to earn his keep. And flying the company flag was more important than honing his skills in private.

'As far as Barney Beaufort's concerned,' Malcolm told them, 'he just wants an entry on the card. Then he can take a box at the meeting and swank to his corporate guests.'

So here they were at Haydock Park with Jamie preparing to step back into the racing arena on a temperamental novice. All the indications were that the ground wouldn't suit Adolf. The going had deteriorated in the steady downpour, making a notoriously sticky track even more testing. Jamie had secretly hoped that the meeting might be abandoned but no such luck. The going was officially described as heavy. Quite what Adolf would make of it he had no idea.

There was only one factor in their favour: the race was a bumper – a National Hunt contest run on the Flat. Neither horse nor jockey would have their newfound jumping skills put to the test. That was something.

A group of intrepid racegoers were squelching across the grass towards them, Malcolm at their head. Jamie recognised Barney Beaufort and the woman who'd accompanied him to Ridgemoor before Christmas to inspect the horse. Adolf's connections had arrived.

Barney greeted Ros with the words, 'I'm a bit disappointed your boss hasn't turned up.'

Jamie was amused to note a flicker of irritation cross her face. She counted nobody, not even Toby, as her 'boss'. She recovered quickly.

'Unfortunately he had a longstanding commitment to be at Southwell,' she said with a smile. 'He's most upset not to be here, I can assure you.'

'Well, I don't suppose he can be in two places at once,' said Beaufort grudgingly.

By now Adolf was making his way round the ring led by Trish, a Ridgemoor stable girl. Some of the Beaufort team greeted his arrival with a boozy cheer which earned glances of disapproval from more experienced groups of owners. As Adolf approached, pulling hard, Jamie saw, the Beaufort people surged forward and the horse reared away skittishly.

'Can I stroke him?' shouted one of the women.

'He looks right nervous,' said a man.

'May we have some room, please?' Ros's voice cut through the clamour. She quickly legged Jamie into the saddle. 'Get him out on the course quickly,' she muttered. 'Away from this lot.'

But Barney wanted to play out his two penn'orth for the watching throng. He had hold of Adolf's bridle and boomed, 'Now listen here, everyone. Red Rum had his last race on this course and I'm a proud man today to send out Beaufort Bonanza for his first.' He looked up at Jamie. 'Good luck, young fellow, the weight of history is upon your shoulders.'

He must have a screw loose, thought Jamie as he guided Adolf out of the ring.

As had been predicted by all apart from the enthusiastic Beaufort party, Adolf did not relish his first taste of competition. He stepped gingerly down to the start of the two-mile race, not enjoying the boggy turf. His race was the last on the card and the course had been pretty well churned up.

He mucked Jamie around at the start, bumping into the runners on either side and then, when the tape went up, he shot off down the course like a scalded cat.

'Calm down, you silly sod,' Jamie shouted uselessly, tugging as hard as he could on the reins to try and get some purchase on the horse's mouth. But Adolf's head was in the air, his jaw and neck locked solid, and there was no restraining the powerful beast. Even if there'd been a brick wall in front of him Adolf would have tried to charge through it.

They were way out ahead of the field, maybe some six lengths clear though Jamie couldn't risk looking back. The thought flashed through his head that this was the position he'd dreamed of being in the race – if only this were the last furlong and not the first.

Soon the heavy ground took its toll, the gluey surface draining the energy from Adolf. He began to struggle and, by the time they had completed the first mile, the other runners had overtaken them. Now they laboured in the rear, losing touch with every stride.

Jamie hunted over to the outside in search of better ground but that made little difference. He urged Adolf on with hands and knees, and then with kicks to the ribs and a crack on the shoulders from the whip. He might as well not have bothered. The horse was unhappy with the whole experience and had no intention of competing. After a mile and a half, with the rest of the field a distant vision ahead, Jamie pulled him up and then set off on the long hack for home, wondering what on earth to say to Barney Beaufort. Forget about Red Rum, the weight of history had done for the pair of them.

In the Beaufort Holidays camp, dismay was mixed with hilarity. When things go so disastrously wrong, what else can you do but smile?

'Never mind, Barney,' said the branch manager from Clitheroe. 'We all had a cracking day out.'

But Barney did mind, Malcolm could tell, as reproachful eyes were turned in his direction. He did his best to stick up for the horse, reaching into the well-used bag of racing phrases to explain the poor performance. But once he'd repeated that the ground was unsuitable, that the race had come too early for him and that the experience was part of a valuable learning curve, what else was there to say?

Barney nodded sagely. 'We live to fight another day,' he announced, neatly topping Malcolm's list of clichés.

'At least the horse has come back in one piece, Mr B,' said Beverley, tucking her arm companionably through Barney's and turning to whisper some words into his ear which even the alert Malcolm could not catch. The mournful expression on the businessman's face softened and he patted her hand. 'Time for one more drink, everybody,' he announced, 'and we'll hope for better luck next time.'

'Look at it this way, Barney,' cried Roland. 'He'll be a better price next time out.'

Malcolm wished he'd thought of that one. There was no denying the optimism of some punters.

He turned down a final drink. Time to beat a hasty retreat. After all, he'd done his duty. Beverley caught up with him as he made his way to the ground floor of the stand.

'Changed your mind, have you?' he said as her fingers sought his. 'We can still make a night of it.'

'I wish,' she said, tugging him to one side of the departing throng. 'I just slipped out for a moment to say goodbye.'

'Really?' Her arm had now crept beneath his coat to circle his waist and her face turned up to his, just inches away. 'Goodbye then,' he said and bent to kiss her. She darted her tongue into his mouth and pressed the length of her body into his.

It was a pretty stupid thing for the pair of them to do, to snog like teenagers in full view of the departing racegoers. Anyone could have seen them – even Barney. Malcolm was sure he could hear the travel agent's voice booming out not far away.

She broke away first, her face flushed. 'I've got to get back.'

'Dump Barney, for God's sake. Tell him you're sick or something.'

'I can't,' she said simply and walked off back the way she had come.

Malcolm watched her go, the well-cut suit emphasising the swing of her trim hips. He wasn't a man given to jealousy but the thought of her turning him down for the evening in preference to some florid, fifty-ish travel agent gave rise to a variety of emotions he didn't care to identify.

By the time he had reached his car he knew what was needed to assuage the feelings roused in him by Beverley's inflammatory antics. She was not the only woman at his disposal. He reached for his mobile phone.

Pippa caught the racing results on the radio as she waded through some admin in the office. Her secretary had left at Christmas and things were already getting into a mess. At the moment, however, she wasn't sure that she wanted to replace her. Losing Arabella Childs' horses in November, followed shortly afterwards by the predictable defection of

Lonsdale Heights, had hit her in the pocket. To be honest, the business could do with some new clients.

She'd had no runners that afternoon, which made the news of two successes for Toby at Southwell all the more galling. And a phone call from Jamie telling her of his horse's poor showing set the seal on her gloom. Things weren't going right at present.

She bundled the unanswered correspondence – bills, for the most part – back into her in-tray and locked up the office. As she crossed the yard to the empty house, weary and fed up, she decided she really must do something soon about the yard. So far all her grand talk about revamping her training methods had come to nothing. Jamie had promised to help her out but he'd been so wrapped up in retraining as a jump jockey that he'd not been much help. And his promise to call in an expert had amounted to a big fat zero.

Disgruntled, she stamped into the kitchen. She supposed she ought to get some supper sorted out. Before long her husband and brother would turn up and expect to be fed. How come neither of them ever pulled on an apron and turned out a hot meal at the end of the day?

To be fair, on working days she just defrosted meals from the deep freeze. Jamie was pretty good at spaghetti suppers while Malcolm insisted on doing the weekend grocery run. And, most of the time, she enjoyed putting the food on the table, regularly turning down their offers of help.

But tonight she would really welcome a hand. Someone to pour her a drink and tell her to put her feet up while they made some magic with the pots and pans. However, it looked like she was out of luck.

She was pulling frozen pizzas out of their packaging when the phone rang.

'Hello, darling.' Malcolm's voice was warm and sympathetic. 'How do you fancy a glamorous night out?'

She didn't, as it happened, but she loved being asked. And by the time they had finished talking her blues had vanished. On instructions, she ran herself a bath and prepared for a long soak. The prospect of an early night with her husband was all she needed to revive her spirits. In her opinion, the best place to eat pizza was in bed.

Jamie wondered where Malcolm had got to after the race as he was half expecting the offer of a lift home. On the other hand, he was quite happy to return in the horse box with Ros and Trish. Ros turned on the radio and tuned it to some orchestral music.

'Do you mind?' she asked. 'It helps me concentrate.'

'You're the driver,' said Trish but she rolled her eyes at Jamie. He could tell she'd rather have Radio One.

'It's nice,' he said. You hypocrite, he thought, who are you trying to impress?

'So what was it like?' Ros asked him.

He knew what she meant. He'd been worried about his return to the weighing room and how he'd get on when he was back in the old routine. Of course, the personnel were different now he was riding at a National Hunt meeting. He knew a few of the jump lads from the old days but most of the faces were unfamiliar to him. He'd been feeling apprehensive, as they would all know his recent history.

In the event, the warmth of his welcome had proved his fears groundless – even if his new companions had enjoyed a bit of fun at his expense.

'Got to give you credit for trying your hand at some proper racing,' said Tom Dougan, a red-headed rider from Limerick.

'It's a different game to the Flat, son,' said his pal, Josh Keane. 'I'd get myself some brown britches, if I were you.'

But they'd all wished him luck and he'd laughed at their jibes, even when they made jokes about prison and his car crash.

'Just one thing, Jamie,' Tom called out, 'never offer me a lift home.'

On reflection, that part of the afternoon had gone well. He'd missed the camaraderie of the weighing room.

'It was OK,' he said in response to Ros's question. 'Different, but OK.'

His knees gave way as he unbuckled his belt and he sat down abruptly on the changing-room bench. The hour in the sauna had left him weak as a kitten, but he'd had to shift a couple of pounds in a hurry to make the weight for his afternoon races. Mind you, it wasn't just the steaming but the boozing and the girls. Especially that last one, that Vanessa. She certainly knew how to drain a man dry.

He grinned to himself. Champagne and shagging were not recommended for the morning of a big race. The Colonel would tear him off a strip if he ever found out. But how would he? Little Miss Golden Thighs wasn't going to tell him. She was too keen to get a second helping.

'See you in the parade ring, lover,' she'd said as he'd finally dismissed her from his hotel bed.

'Make it the winners' enclosure,' he'd replied.

Anyway, even if the Colonel did find out, what could he do? The old man appreciated a pretty girl himself, he knew that for a fact. And the way Jamie was riding he reckoned there'd be no cause for complaint.

He stood up to kick off his trousers and felt his legs wobble again. He braced himself against the wall.

'All right, Jamie?' called his valet from across the room.

'No problem, Pat.' He put as much energy into his voice as he could muster. Old Pat had seen it all and didn't miss much. 'Got your money on my Diadem runner?'

'Haven't had a bet in twenty years.'

'Do yourself a favour. Mine can't be beat.'

The boast earned a barrage of comment from the riders changing around him – none of whom appeared to agree.

Then Jamie had a bright idea, one he couldn't resist. He stepped up onto the bench, leaving his trousers on the floor, and thrust his backside towards his audience.

'Get a load of my arse, lads. You lot are going to be looking at it all afternoon.'

A pair of socks and a chorus of jeers flew in his direction. A senior jockey in the opposite corner turned away, unamused. Well, sod him, thought Jamie. He's only pissed off because he knows it's true.

He made his way into the toilet and shut the door with a shaking hand. Maybe it hadn't been such a bright idea to clown around. But what was wrong with having a laugh? All the same, he felt like a limp lettuce and he had five rides ahead of him, all on good horses who carried with them a weight of expectation. Ascot was packed to the rafters on this fine autumn Sunday. It was a day on which nineteen-year-old rising stars made their reputation. He couldn't let anyone down – least of all himself.

It was just as well he had a couple of pills left. He took them now, swallowing them dry, and slumped on the toilet seat to conserve his energy until they kicked in. He'd be as right as rain in a few minutes. Then let battle commence. The rest of them would be watching his rear for sure.

*

Jane Culpepper had badly wanted to hate Clive's new wife, Susan – as any woman in her position would. Susan was younger than Jane by nearly ten years, was modishly skinny and had seduced Jane's husband during cosy office lunch-hours and weekend so-called golfing trips. What's more, Susan was a privately educated little rich girl, whose family owned a chain of chemists – the irony being that her presence in the clinic where Clive worked had not been brought about by economic necessity. Why on earth, Jane wondered when she had discovered the facts, work as a dental hygienist, poking around in people's smelly mouths, when you didn't have to work at all?

But once the dust had settled on Clive's decision to bale out of their marriage and she'd realised that Robbie wasn't fighting the new arrangement, she'd decided to make an effort with Susan. Thank God she had. Susan was eager to be friends, to act as a go-between and to be as much of a surrogate mother to Robbie as was permissible. Maybe it was the guilt of someone who knows they are privileged, but Susan was endlessly accommodating. As, for example, when Jane realised she'd not be out of Deacon Parade in time to pick Robbie up from Computer Club, as promised. She'd simply called Susan who happily agreed to give him supper at her house and make sure he did his homework.

'Do you want me to run him back later?' she'd asked. 'He could stay the night with us if you're busy.'

The woman was a treasure, Jane thought. And the icing on the cake, ignoble though it was to think it, was that Susan was plain. No chin and no chest and she hid her round sapphire-blue eyes beneath a way out-of-date fringe. What a petty little cow I am, thought Jane as she chucked her overflowing briefcase on to the sofa and made for the fridge. A large G&T was what she deserved after the rigours of the day.

She'd barely discovered that she was out of ice and the tonic was flat before her mobile rang. She'd already talked to Robbie and her mother so she was half inclined to ignore it. The number on the readout wasn't familiar.

'Boss?' The voice was deep and male. 'It's Simon Bennett.'

'Hi.' She'd spent most of the afternoon with him by her side, accompanying her to a variety of briefings concerning the Bonfire Night Murders. What did he want now?

'Fancy a spot of dinner?'

She looked at the fridge, full of pasta and sausages – Robbie stuff – and the bottle of flat tonic in her hand.

'You bet,' she said.

'I'm outside your place now, boss. You want to freshen up or anything? I can wait.'

Forget that, it was half past eight and she'd not eaten all day. She was famished. And even though Simon must have an agenda, here was her chance to get under the skin of her new job.

'I'm coming right now,' she said, slamming the fridge door shut.

'Just one thing.'

'Yes?'

'Shove the boss stuff for the evening, all right?'

Before today, Jane had heard two things about Simon Bennett – that he was joined at the hip to Leighton Jones, and that he went after women like a fox in a hen coop.

Sitting across the restaurant table from Simon, Jane could see that the second of these statements might well be true. He'd be pushing forty, a year or two older than her, but the signs of age on his face gave it a lived-in, crumpled look that took the edge off his still-boyish smile. Add to that thick dark hair, dancing green eyes and a voice of deep velvet and his reputation made sense. She wouldn't mind betting that Simon became more attractive the older he got. If only the same could be said for her.

The restaurant was small and Italian, pleasantly full of customers who seemed intent on their dinner. A stream of aromatic dishes was being ferried out of the kitchen by two middle-aged waiters who worked with such efficiency that they appeared to have three arms. One of them filled their glasses with a deep-hued Barolo while the other set a generous platter of mixed antipasti on the starched white tablecloth between them. '*Buon appetito*,' they murmured in one voice before gliding off to satisfy others' needs.

'I never knew this place existed,' she said, 'and I only live round the corner.'

Simon smiled a trifle smugly and raised his glass.

Jane ate and drank with gusto; this was an unexpected treat. There were salamis, smoked fish and olives, and vegetables in fragrant melt-in-the-mouth sauces that she didn't recognise.

'That's *caponata*,' Simon explained as she enthused over one mixture. 'Deep-fried aubergine in onions and celery. It's Sicilian.'

'Do you cook?'

'Occasionally.'

Of course he did. The vision of an intimate dinner, a man cooking for her, swam into her mind. It was high up on her list of favourite seduction techniques, not that she could remember when she'd last been a recipient.

The wine was heady, which probably accounted for what she said next. 'Is that your secret weapon with the girls? The Naked Chef act?'

The green eyes narrowed. 'What do you mean?'

'I heard you were a ladies' man.' She pushed on foolishly. 'You know, the Romeo of Deacon Parade. A swathe of broken hearts in your wake.'

His face was stony. 'I've heard things about you, too.'

'Really?' She tried to keep it light. 'Such as?'

He leaned closer. Flickering candlelight distorted his features. 'Such as you're the Super's bit on the side. That he's been slipping it to you since his wife walked out.'

She couldn't think what to say. She'd relaxed for a moment, lulled by the food and wine and by his easygoing manner, and suddenly the knife was between her ribs. Her impulse was to get to her feet and leave, maybe after throwing her wine in his face. But she fought it.

'There is nothing going on between Superintendent Wright and me,' she hissed.

'OK.' He leaned back, grinning amiably once more. She didn't trust his grin now. 'If you say so.'

'I do.' It didn't sound convincing even to her.

'Clear something up for me then. Explain how come you breeze into our incident room and take over. I was Deputy SIO. I've been on this job since day one. If anyone should step into Leighton's shoes it should be me.'

From his point of view she could see that her arrival must be galling. Tough on him. This kind of thing had happened to her in the past. It was about time the cookie crumbled in her favour.

'Simon, the point is that the investigation was going nowhere. I've come in as a fresh eye. Time's going by. If we're ever to solve this crime we need a new approach.'

He shook his head vigorously and drained his glass. 'We know who did it. We just don't have the firepower to bring them down. At least, not now Leighton's been shafted, we don't.'

'What do you mean, you know who did it?'

'It's one of Pete's drug pals.'

'So you don't know exactly.'

Simon helped himself to more wine. She tried to stop him topping up her glass but he went ahead anyway. What the hell, she didn't have to drink it.

'Look, you haven't had time yet to read the witness statements. And after all that gladhanding today you probably don't know whether you're coming or going. But – number one, Pete was a small-time heroin dealer. He made just about enough to fund his own habit. Two, on the night he was killed he had a visit from one of his regulars, Ian Barrable. Or Filthy Ian Barrable as we call him – you can imagine why.'

One of the waiters was hovering. Simon asked him to clear the table and hold the next course for a bit, if he didn't mind. The waiter didn't. Neither did Jane; she was full.

Simon continued, 'According to Barrable, Pete was in great spirits and wanted to shoot the breeze. Poor old Filthy was so strung out he just wanted to do his business and go but Pete kept him hanging on, saying that he was about to pull off a deal that would change his life. He said he'd soon be out of small-time dealing and Filthy would have to find another source of smack – Filthy remembers that, all right. Finally Pete sorted him out and Filthy left at about nine with what he came for. He surfaced two days later to find Pete was dead in the fire and, so he says, he knew at once it wasn't an accident. That was before we let on that the pair of them had been murdered.'

'So?' Jane wasn't sure where this was going.

'Barrable remembers Pete boasting about his new friends from Eastern Europe. Said he was going into business with them. And we've got witnesses who saw Pete on a train from York that evening. So, point three, there's a gang of Albanian gypsies living in York. Free housing, full benefits and they're into every scam going, including a drug connection via Turkey to the Middle East. It's a well-known route. These guys are new on the scene, keen to make a mark however they can and they don't play by the regular rules. Odds on they killed Pete and Amanda.'

'But why?'

'From what Pete told Filthy he'd at last got the cash together to fund a big score. He'd never made any bones about wanting to stop trading in wraps and tiddly amounts. Leighton reckoned – we all did – that he'd been in York to arrange to buy a quantity of heroin from the Albanians so he could move up the ladder and start supplying small-time dealers like himself. Kind of a career move. But his new pals worked him over till he told them where he kept his cash, then nicked it.'

Jane mused on this. She'd spent some time that afternoon going over the postmortems on the bodies. The reports clearly established, from the absence of smoke in their lungs, that Pete and Amanda had died before the fire had started. Though the partially burnt corpses had been removed from the house by the firefighters who had first arrived on the scene, the burn damage to the bodies was not extensive enough to obscure the evidence of what had happened to them. Both had been tied up and throttled. Pete's body also had bruising on the legs and body consistent with being kicked. Then there was the broken ankle and the charred flesh on his thigh.

Simon popped a last crust of bread into his mouth. He appeared to have recovered his good humour. 'I bet if someone shoved a hot poker down *your* trousers you'd soon tell them where you'd hidden your piggy bank.'

'Did any of the neighbours hear anything?'

He shook his head. 'No. But it was a noisy night with fireworks going off all over the place.'

'I was thinking of cries of pain. Edward the Second was killed in Berkeley Castle by a red-hot poker thrust into his anus. Reputedly his screams of agony were heard for miles.'

Simon's jaw dropped. 'No one heard anything like that. Good God, you've got a lurid imagination.'

'I'm a bit of a murder buff.' She grinned at him, happy to have scored a point or two. 'So you think Pete had a quantity of money in the house?'

'We know he did. He showed it to Filthy. A great brick of banknotes in a Tesco's carrier bag, apparently.'

'How much?'

'At least twenty grand, probably more. He didn't let Filthy count it, of course. Just flashed it at him to show off.'

'Was he really that stupid?'

Simon shrugged. 'He was a heroin addict. Native intelligence is not their strong point.'

'And the money and the bag were not discovered on the premises?'

'Funnily enough, they weren't. However, in the toilet upstairs, the lid of the cistern was lying on the floor and we found traces of dirt on the bog seat.'

'So you think that's where Pete hid the money and they tortured him until he revealed the hiding place?'

Simon nodded. 'Not the most original hidey-hole. Not worth getting a third-degree burn for, if you ask me. They'd have found it in five minutes anyway.'

He nodded at the waiter and suddenly plates and a large salad bowl appeared on the table. A dish of pasta was set between them.

Simon took over the serving duties and spooned ribbon-thin linguine studded with clam shells on to her plate. Their fragrance filled her nostrils. Maybe she wasn't as full as she had thought.

'So where do you think Pete got the money?'

'Dunno. Perhaps he won the pools. The important thing is we know it was in the house at nine, when Filthy left, and gone by midnight. So there's your motive. Robbery.'

'It doesn't seem worth killing two people for twenty thousand pounds.'

He laughed. 'I've known plenty killed for a whole lot less. And so have you, I bet.'

That was true. Her last murder investigation had been of a pensioner mugged for the contents of her handbag.

'But this is so callous. To kill the girl too.'

He sighed. 'Those Albanians don't muck around.'

'So what have you done about them?'

'Put them under surveillance, raided their lodgings and pulled some in for questioning. Funny how their command of English dries up in an interview room. We're working through interpreters who are probably related to the blokes we're interested in. There's a shifting population of adult males plus a whole caravan of women and kids. So far we've pinned nothing on them worse than pimping and possession of an offensive weapon. They favour serrated kitchen knives.'

'So, beyond Mr Barrable's statement, you have no evidence they have any connection to Pete and Amanda?'

'We know Pete was in York on the day he was killed.' He twisted linguine round his fork. 'But you're quite right – there's nothing on them we can use. Not yet anyway.'

Jane pushed her plate away. She'd been brought into the investigation to provide an objective view and she would do just that. Simon's scenario might well be accurate but she was determined to take nothing at face value. She'd go over all the statements and reports bit by bit until she came to her own conclusion. She thought of the bulging briefcase on the sofa in her flat.

'Are we finished?' she said, taking in the empty plates on the table. They'd done justice to the wine as well.

'One thing,' he said in his soft deep voice. 'I've got two ex-wives, a teenage daughter who treats me like a mobile cashpoint and a live-in partner who's just decided to live out. I go home, pick the bills off the mat and eat in front of the TV. If that's the life of a ladies' man, I hold my hand up.'

She didn't know what to say. It sounded depressingly familiar but she wasn't going to let on. She'd slipped up at the start of the evening by being too friendly; she wouldn't make the same mistake again.

'OK, Simon. I shan't make any more assumptions – provided you do the same for me.'

He smiled his pleasant smile – the non-sinister version. 'I never really thought there was anything between you and Keith Wright. You're far too classy for him.'

His eyes twinkled in the candlelight. It was definitely time to go home.

Matilda, Pippa's red setter, bounded ahead of Jamie down the dark path. Though Pippa's yard had long ceased to be a farm, some of the fields were leased out to the neighbour who farmed the adjoining property. He kept sheep there in the winter and, in the summer, turned the land into a campsite for summer visitors. So Jamie wasn't surprised to see a tent lit up by the flicker of a small fire on the other side of the hedgerow as he walked the dog. He wondered what kind of person chose to camp out in a muddy field in January. It certainly wasn't his idea of fun.

As he drew closer, the oncoming breeze bore the smell of smoke into his face – and something else that set his tastebuds tingling. Bacon. He'd not enjoyed his meagre supper earlier and there was something about the

smell of bacon cooked outdoors. It reminded him of camping trips as a kid, when his Uncle Bob would take charge of breakfast.

He stopped at the hedge and looked over. The small ridge tent had obviously seen better times but the campsite was neat and the fire burned in a shallow trench to protect it from the wind. A frying pan – presumably the source of the bacon aroma – sat on the ground next to the flames, as if it had just been removed from the heat. There was no one in sight, though the visitor could not be far off.

Jamie was about to call out a greeting. Maybe the happy camper would like directions to Shelley Farm should he run out of water or milk. But Jamie was forestalled by a scrabbling in the hedge ahead and the sight of a bounding four-legged shape charging towards the tent.

'Matilda!' he shouted, all too aware of what was about to happen. 'Don't you dare – heel!'

He was wasting his breath. Matilda was young, insubordinate and always hungry. In an instant she was by the fire, flipping the pan and its contents into the grass.

'Oy!' came a shout of outrage from inside the tent.

Jamie sprinted to the gate and vaulted over. In the dim light he could see a tall figure on his knees grappling with the dog, who was emitting a high-pitched squeal of protest. Something metallic flashed in the man's hand. A knife!

'Don't touch her!' Jamie screamed. He pelted towards them and threw himself at the stooping figure, grabbing the arm with the knife. The pair of them tumbled over with Jamie on top and there was an 'Oof!' of surprise from the man beneath him. Jamie pressed the other's face into the soggy grass and rammed his arm high and hard into his back. 'Let go of the knife,' he hissed, 'or I'll break the bone.'

The man beneath twisted to squint up at him, then began to shake, a strange gurgling noise coming from his throat. Jamie shifted his weight off the prone body though he still gripped the arm tight.

In the shadow Jamie could make out a shaved head beneath him, an earring winking in the lobe of one ear, and a mouthful of teeth bared in pain or – as he realised the gurgle was more like a chuckle – amusement.

He recognised the face at once though his brain was slow to put a name to it.

'And I had you down for a pacifist, Jamie mate,' said Dave Prescott. 'Glad you learned something in the nick.'

Chapter Five

Dave seemed less put out than Jamie by their tussle in the grass. He was still chortling to himself as he retrieved his frying pan and showed Jamie the 'knife' he'd been holding – a bent fork with a missing tine.

'I don't mind your dog scarfing my supper,' he explained, 'but I don't want her going off with my cutlery. I've had this fork a long time.'

'Sorry, Dave,' Jamie said for the umpteenth time. 'She didn't mean any harm.'

Matilda had made herself at home by the fire, her eyes following the movement of the frying pan in Dave's hand. He was giving it a quick wipe down and reaching for a plastic food-container. 'Think you can keep her under control while I cook some more?' he said.

Jamie put the dog on the lead and fastened her to a nearby fence post. Matilda looked at him in reproach but for once he ignored her.

'You got my message then?' It was a bit of a silly question but Jamie was still bemused by the events of the past ten minutes. 'Why didn't you call me?'

Dave looked up from spreading brown sauce on slices of white bread. 'I wasn't sure about it. It's not a good idea to hang around with the blokes you knew inside.'

Jamie couldn't agree more but it was strange to realise that someone might think that way about him.

'No offence, mate,' the thin man added, slapping bacon rashers between the bread. 'Want one?'

Of course he did, but it didn't seem fair to make further inroads into Dave's resources.

Dave saw him hesitate. 'Go on, take it.'

It was delicious. Matilda was whining in the background but that was too bad – she wasn't getting any of his.

'So, given that you've obviously decided to take a risk and look me up, what are you doing out here?'

Dave chewed thoughtfully. 'I knew you weren't in 'cos I kept an eye on your place. The bloke who let me camp here told me you were riding at Haydock.'

'But my sister's there. She'd have looked after you till I got back.'

Dave pulled a face, stretching his rubbery features out of shape. 'I dunno about that, Jamie.'

On reflection, looking at the glistening bald head of the spindly-limbed runner and the rope burn tattooed round his neck, maybe it wasn't such a bad thing he hadn't pitched up out of the blue and surprised Pippa.

'And before you say anything,' Dave continued, 'I prefer sleeping outdoors. I can't be doing with being banged up inside.'

Jamie wondered how Dave had managed to survive prison. Or was it being in prison that had made him like this?

'I know what you're thinking,' the runner said. 'I wouldn't describe myself as an actual loony. I'm more of a genuine eccentric.'

Jamie wasn't going to disagree.

Malcolm stretched lazily in the empty bed. He reckoned he deserved a bit of a lie-in after his exertions of the night before. Pippa had brought him a cup of tea when she'd got up for first lot but it had long since gone cold. He drank half of it in one gulp regardless. He'd drunk much worse. In his Army days, after forty-eight hours in the mountains without food or sleep, a cup of cold tea would have counted as nectar.

He swung his legs out of bed and trod on something small and hard. He smiled as he picked it up. It was the button he'd lost off his shirt when he'd been fooling around with Pippa last night. It was gratifying to think he could still make her lose her cool in the bedroom after two years of marriage.

He ought to knock his side interests on the head. Beverley had served her usefulness. He'd miss her babe-in-a-business-suit appeal but maybe it was time for him to be a good boy. It was only fair to the wife.

Plus, of course, he had his long-term prospects to think of. Pippa was in line for some decent money the day she and her brother sold the land they were sitting on. It would take a few years, maybe, but eventually the offers would be too good to refuse. Of course, if her frustration with the yard continued he might be able to persuade her to cash in her chips sooner rather than later. The way things were heading – like the crackpot idea of roping in some jailbird athlete – pay day was just around the corner. Maybe then, with the training bug out of her system, she'd get on with turning out a couple of sprogs and the pair of them could earn Brownie points with his father. That ought to prompt the old man to move aside at Ridgemoor and pass the yard on to the pair of them. He could spearhead the business and let Pippa handle the training side. Surely that was where their future lay.

On the other hand, he couldn't be expected just to think of the future. A man had to have his amusements to keep life interesting. And, with the long-term solid, an appetiser on the side like Bev certainly spiced up the main dish. That was his experience.

It was a nice problem to have.

He checked his mobile for messages. Surprise, surprise, there was one from Beverley, left half an hour ago.

'Malcolm, we need to schedule a debrief. I'm at home all morning and I expect to hear from you.'

He chuckled and pressed the Call button. Then he cut the connection. He had a better idea.

Ten minutes later he was driving out of the yard. He'd make that call in person.

'Pippa,' she looked up from rinsing mugs in the office sink, 'I want you to meet someone.'

She took in the tall bald man in a muddy tracksuit by Jamie's side.

'This is Dave Prescott.'

From what she'd heard, she wasn't predisposed to like this former jailbird and she had no confidence that he'd be able to help her out. However, she'd not wanted to dampen Jamie's enthusiasm and, being honest, she could do with some new ideas. But – from this bizarre-looking individual? She took in the tattoos and the earring and the enormous head perched on his skinny body. God help us.

Yet, as Dave extended his hand in greeting, she couldn't help responding to him. There was warmth in the size of his grin and the touch of his long bony fingers. His eyes held hers as he said, 'Really pleased to meet you, Ms Hutchison. Heard a lot about you.'

'I've heard about you, too.' Which was true. Jamie had found references to Dave's athletic career in a couple of old books. He really had been an international runner. The words 'oddball' and 'controversial' also accompanied reports on his races. Now she looked closely, the long nose and sunken eyes were recognisably the same as in the photos from the 1980s, though the hair – a shaggy mullet – was a thing of the past. A good thing too, in her opinion.

Pippa made them all tea and cleared a space on her desk to sit on – the paper pile was growing by the day – while Dave perched on the spare chair and Jamie leaned against the filing cabinet. The room seemed very small with the three of them huddled so close together.

'So,' said her gangly guest, 'what's this all about?'

Evidently Jamie hadn't told him. Maybe that was best. 'What do you know about training horses, Dave?'

He rolled his eyes. They were of a different hue, she noticed. One was more green than brown, the other more brown than green. It figured.

'Not a lot,' he admitted. 'That is, nothing at all. Sorry.'

'But you know about training athletes?'

'Sure.' He laughed, an engaging throaty cackle. 'It's about all I do know, as a matter of fact.'

She nodded, took a deep breath and said, 'Excellent. That's exactly what we want.'

He looked surprised. 'It is?'

'Absolutely,' she said with a confidence she did not feel. 'Just pretend my horses are people for the next couple of days and then tell us what you think.'

His cackle was more prolonged this time.

'Will you do it?' she said.

'We'll pay you for your time,' Jamie chipped in.

'Ok,' said Dave, setting down his empty mug. 'But why?'

Pippa explained about Black Knight, how the horse had improved out of recognition once he'd joined another trainer.

'Until then I thought I was as good as anyone. But I've rarely had horses leave to go to another trainer. Usually their owners take them hunting or send them to point-to-points. What I know about training I've learned from watching people round here at work and from reading up. It's not as if I've been all over the world working for different trainers. Now I'm wondering if I don't need some new ideas. Maybe I'm not very good after all.'

'In case you hadn't noticed,' Jamie said, 'my sister is suffering from a crisis of confidence. The truth is, she's brilliant with animals. She has a sixth sense when there's the slightest thing wrong with them. Anyhow, we'd like you to give us your opinion.'

Dave considered what he'd heard, then turned to Jamie.

'You must have ridden for lots of different trainers in the past. What do *you* think?'

'Actually, I did most of my riding for one gaffer back then. I'm sorry to say I wasn't very observant about his training methods. I was just keen to do well and I did what I was asked without thinking about it. In any case, training has probably changed a bit since then.'

Pippa stepped in. 'The bottom line is, Dave, we'd just like your input. If you tell me I'm not doing anything wrong I'll be thrilled to hear it.'

'And if you tell her she is, she won't take any notice,' Jamie butted in with a grin.

Pippa looked indignant. 'Come on. Let me show you round.'

As she led the pair of them out into the yard she noticed Dave trying to keep a straight face. He probably thought she was the oddball. Maybe he was right.

'I thought you wanted to discuss yesterday's race,' Malcolm murmured, staring at the rosebud-pink ceiling of Beverley's bedroom through the curtain of her blue-black hair. The ceiling toned nicely with the candy-striped wallpaper and cherry-blossom curtains. He could describe the décor of this room in detail. It was the only place in the cottage where he'd spent any time.

She rolled to one side of him and snuggled into the crook of his arm, her bare breasts nestling pleasantly into his ribs.

'Yeah, sure.' She sounded as if it were his idea.

'That's what you said on the phone. I presume you talked about it with Beaufort afterwards.'

'Barney was really disappointed.'

'I could see that. But I thought it didn't matter how the horse performed. Your company just wanted an entry on the card, remember?'

93

'That was my idea but Barney takes these things to heart. I mean, Adolf didn't just lose – he gave up. And the jockey didn't help either.'

Malcolm was taken aback. 'Jamie's a top rider.'

'Really?' She pulled away from him and sat up. 'Two years ago on the Flat maybe. The only publicity we got out of yesterday's race was about an ex-con making a comeback and losing. I tell you, Malcolm, it's not good enough.'

He stared at her in surprise, realising that their moment of intimacy had turned into a company broadside – and he was on the receiving end. Those pale blue eyes, for once unscreened, blazed with cold fire and her chin jutted aggressively. She was quick to spoil for a fight. He'd bet her subordinates at the office got it in the neck on a regular basis.

Beverley's full bosom positively quivered with her discontent. It was the first time he'd been given a dressing down by a stark-naked woman. There was no denying it was a bit of a turn-on.

'The first run means nothing,' he said calmly. 'Yesterday was good experience for Adolf. Next time he'll be used to race conditions. And we'll make sure the going isn't so heavy.'

The thin line of her mouth softened fractionally but she didn't look convinced. However, the belligerence had vanished from her voice when she spoke next.

'I'm just worried Barney will decide to pull the plug on the whole operation. It was all my idea. If he suddenly decides to get rid of the horse I'll be left with egg on my face.'

Malcolm didn't like the sound of that. He didn't want Beaufort trying to recoup his money on the horse – he'd get a nasty surprise if he did.

'It's far too early for all that, surely? Suppose I get Dad to give him a ring and talk up Adolf's potential? And you keep massaging his ego – or whatever it is of his you massage – *ow!*'

She had a pretty hefty backhander for a woman but she was laughing as she landed it. He scooped her into his arms and held her to his chest. That was better.

'It'll work out fine. Honestly, Bev.'

She lifted her face to his and he accepted the invitation. He knew how to take her mind off Adolf.

On reflection, he thought later, that was another reason why he couldn't pack her in at the moment, with her getting anxious about the horse. He'd just have to soldier on.

*

It was frustrating for Jane to come in so late on the November the Fifth investigation. On all her previous murder cases she'd been able to visit the crime scene within hours – on a couple of occasions within minutes – of the incident, usually with the body of the victim *in situ*. It made a hell of a difference to taste the sights and smells of the crime firsthand, shocking and repugnant as they usually were. Like most detectives, she'd always believed that the insights gained from standing on the spot were invaluable. It gave you a gut feel – and this time she had none. Though she'd visited the cottage, the trip told her little about what had taken place there on Bonfire Night. Possession of the fire-damaged premises had reverted to the owner at the end of the previous year and builders were hard at work. The word was that the owner, Pete's former landlord, was looking for a quick sale.

In any case, Jane realised that even if she had been on the case since day one, the on-the-spot insights she craved would have been denied her. Because of the fire and the actions of the fire brigade, the crime scene had been unavoidably corrupted from the start. Not even Leighton Jones had had the advantage of viewing the bodies in the position the killer – or killers – had left them.

Simon took her through the sequence of events.

'Filthy Barrable says he left the cottage when *ER* came on the box. Amanda wanted to watch it.'

'So he went?'

'Yes. He says he hates medical programmes – can't stand needles and blood. Bit rich coming from a junkie. Anyhow, that puts his departure at nine – we checked. The emergency operator took the call reporting the fire at ten fifty-two. It was a busy night, being November the fifth; all the same, the fire brigade arrived at two minutes past eleven. By then the front room was well away but the rest of the house wasn't too badly damaged. The brigade managed to prevent the thatched roof from going up, fortunately.'

There was no doubt the firefighters had done a remarkable job but their approach had been of the no-nonsense kind – out with the hoses, on with the breathing apparatus and in they'd bravely gone, smashing down the front door. According to neighbours it was likely that the occupants were at home as lights had been spotted earlier and their bone-shaker of a car was parked in the road outside. Within a couple of minutes the firefighters had discovered the bodies in the front room and hauled them out of the burning building. It was immediately obvious that the pair were past saving but only the subsequent examination revealed the true cause of their deaths.

The upshot of all that was the complete devastation of the crime scene. Little had been salvaged from the front room, where it was apparent the fire had started. Fire brigade investigators surmised that an accelerant had been used – probably liquid floor polish. The cottage owner said that he'd recently had the oak floor renovated and had left a supply of polish in the hope that his new tenants might care for it.

Partially protected in the coal scuttle, a fragment of cord had survived the blaze. Its thickness and weave was consistent with marks on Pete's wrists which suggested the victims had been bound before their deaths.

'Right,' said Jane, trying to fix the sequence of events in her mind. 'The killers arrived some time after Barrable left. Any sign of a forced entry? Or wasn't it possible to tell?'

'The back of the cottage was relatively undamaged. The windows and kitchen door were secure as far as we could see. And the firefighters had to knock the front door down to get in.'

'So Pete or Amanda must have let them in. Then they tied the pair of them up, kicked and assaulted them with the poker—'

'Just Pete. There were no injuries to Amanda's body.'

'OK, so they burned Pete to find the whereabouts of the money Barrable saw.'

'Which was hidden in the cistern upstairs. Looks like it, anyway.'

'Then they strangled Pete and Amanda. With their hands.'

Simon nodded. The pathologist's report had been clear. No ropes or scarves or makeshift garrottes had been used, just hands – probably gloved, there being no marks of fingernails.

Jane considered the method of execution. It was a hard way to end someone's life, to grip them by the throat and hang on until they were dead. It wasn't like pulling a trigger from yards away, or even plunging a knife into the heart. This was visceral, in-your-face slaughter. You'd have plenty of time to think about what you were doing as you pinned someone down and literally squeezed the life from their body. She'd never even wrung a chicken's neck, though she'd watch a grown man make a mess of it in a survival programme on TV. To strangle a person in cold blood would require some nerve.

'Do drug-dealers have a history of throttling one another?'

'I haven't come across it before,' Simon conceded.

'What about these Albanians of yours? Is this a regular Eastern European method?'

He shrugged. 'You've got me there. I've no idea.'

She pondered further. 'It's a sex-crime method, isn't it? It's what Christie did to all those women. Strangled them and had intercourse with the corpses.'

Simon pulled a face. 'Thanks, boss. This is bad enough without turning it into Rillington Place.'

She grinned. It was satisfying to ruffle his feathers. 'You get my point though. If this was a drug killing they'd have been shot or stabbed or had their heads caved in with a baseball bat. Now, if Amanda had been raped, it would make much more sense.'

'But she wasn't. There was no semen, no genital bruising, no sign of sexual interference at all.'

'I know.' She sighed.

'You women – you look for a sex motive everywhere.' This time he was grinning, pleased to get his own back.

'One thing about strangling,' she continued, thinking out loud, 'it's clean. Shoot or stab or batter someone and the odds are you'll get covered in blood. But cut off the air to the brain and you walk away without any sign of involvement. Maybe there's saliva on your hands or bits of fabric from the victim's clothes, but nothing obvious.'

'And our guys have had the best part of three months to clean up,' Simon added.

'You still like the drug-dealers, don't you?'

'Yes.'

'Even though you've got nothing to link them to Pete beyond his trip to York? And all of them,' she'd reviewed the extensive witness statements taken from a host of Eastern European suspects, 'have alibis for November the fifth.'

'They're lying for each other, boss. We'll nail them for something else and they'll start ratting on each other – then the truth will come out about this. You'll see.'

'Tell me again why you think they did it. I mean, Pete and Amanda were hardly much of a threat. Even if they could identify whoever robbed them, what could they do? We wouldn't have taken them seriously and they're not linked to any drug gangs, are they?'

'You must be joking.'

'Which is why you think it's the Albanian dealers.'

He nodded. 'Life's a whole lot cheaper in Eastern Europe than in East Lancs. There's also been two other junkie murders in the last six months. Leighton believed they were carried out by the boys from York.'

'Tell me.'

'Stabbings. Both victims were slow paying money. I bet there aren't too many slow payers on their books now.'

'But they weren't strangled like Pete and Amanda, were they?'

Simon sighed. He was obviously irritated by her reluctance to accept the obvious. And, she supposed, he had reason. She was reluctantly coming round to the drug rip-off theory. It wasn't exactly the fresh thinking the Superintendent had hoped for.

'Am I getting too old for horses, Doctor?' asked Ros as she lay on the bed in Lionel Gooding's consulting room. Yesterday, Spring Fever, a stubbornly earthbound gelding she'd been schooling as a favour for a friend, had got fed up with her and landed a surprise kick. She'd been trying to ignore the pain all morning but had finally decided to check it out.

Gooding's large hands moved along her swollen calf. He appeared not to have heard her question. Finally he spoke.

'I hope you're not fishing for compliments, Ms Bradey. You're a woman in her prime and as fit as a fiddle. I'm sure horses are in some measure responsible for your condition.'

'Except when they're kicking lumps off me.' She winced as he continued to probe.

He stepped back from the couch and stripped his gloves from his fingers.

'As far as I can tell there's nothing broken. Of course, I can send you for an X-ray if you would prefer a machine to issue a diagnosis.'

She shook her head. 'No, thank you, Doctor. I assume there's a chance you know what you're talking about.'

He peered at her gravely, as if deciding whether she was poking fun at him. It was a game they played whenever they ran into one another. Ros liked the doctor a lot.

'Assume nothing in this life, Ms Bradey,' he said as he took the seat behind his desk. 'Thirty-five years of general practice may well have eroded my judgement.' His fingers hovered hesitantly over the keyboard of his computer. 'I'll give you a prescription for anti-inflammatory tablets and some painkillers.'

'Don't bother, Doctor. I avoid medicine unless it's essential. If it's just bruising it'll get better in its own time.'

Gooding looked at her gratefully. 'Excellent. You've spared me entering into battle with this computer. It's a new system I haven't yet mastered.'

Ros slipped her foot gingerly into her shoe and stood. Time for someone else to benefit from the doctor's wisdom. But the doctor, for once, did not seem in a hurry.

'Ms Bradey, I hope you won't mind my asking, but does your horse-training establishment require many staff?'

'It's a schooling yard. I'm not a licensed trainer. But,' she added, aware that the distinction might be lost on the doctor, 'there are four staff apart from me.'

'And volunteer workers?'

'Oh yes, plenty of them. Horse-mad kids who'd probably pay *me* if I let them. It's how most of us start out.'

'Aha.' He beamed. 'So if I gave your name to a young lady I know who'd love to get back in the saddle, she wouldn't be turned away with a flea in her ear?'

'No, though she might have to take her place in the queue. There's a limit to the number of giggly schoolgirls I can put up with about the place.'

'I see.' His pale grey eyes probed hers. 'Marie's not exactly the giggly type and she left school last year. Her father is – well, let's just say she's had a difficult home life recently. She used to be a bit of a rider and I believe it would be to her benefit to take it up again.'

'So you recommend her?'

'Absolutely. She's helping us out here at the moment, just while we get our records sorted out. To be frank, she's got a much better grasp of the new computer than the rest of us.'

Ros was amused. If the rest of the practice staff were as technophobic as Dr Gooding that wouldn't be difficult.

'OK,' she said. 'Tell her I expect to see her tomorrow morning at six-thirty.'

Gooding nodded. 'Thank you, Ms Bradey. She'll be there.'

Ros had no doubt she would be. It was whether she turned up the following morning that was the real test. Mucking out horses in the early morning darkness usually sorted the wheat from the chaff.

As Jane drove across the Pennines she hoped the journey would be worth it. Apart from her trip to view Pete and Amanda's cottage, she'd spent the past few days in the incident room, talking to the investigation team and immersing herself in the case documentation. In the days and weeks following the murders, the detectives had been diligent. The HOLMES computer system had been fed with hundreds of witness statements, the product of house-to-house enquiries, close examination of phone records and background research into the lives of the two victims. Plus, of course, information gleaned from Leighton's network of drug informers across the county. Right now Jane couldn't see the wood from the trees. In fact, she doubted she'd recognise a tree if she bumped into it.

So when a call for Leighton had been received from Amanda's elder sister, Jane decided to drive to Harrogate and introduce herself as the new SIO. Maybe she could gather an insight into the personality of the dead girl by talking to a close family member.

Jane could hear the hullabaloo of toddlers at play as she stood outside the door of a house on a new development. All the surrounding dwellings had similar white doors with brass carriage lanterns on either side of the porch. People-carriers and four-wheel-drive vehicles were in the majority, all equipped with child seats. This was professional-family country. Amanda's sister, Elizabeth Jacobs, was married to a solicitor in Harrogate.

Elizabeth tried to usher her into a beige-carpeted front room but Jane said yes to a cup of coffee and followed her into the kitchen where three small children were nominally having their tea. The smallest, evidently still in nappies, was pouring juice from his beaker into a crisp packet while the other two were savaging a packet of Jaffa cakes and ignoring the puddle on the table.

Jane took charge of the kettle while their mother dived in to sort out the mess. Elizabeth was blonde, overweight and pretty. She issued directions firmly but kindly and the children did as they were told, which was impressive. Observing the mother's laughing face, Jane supposed that dealing with three children under five might limit the time available to grieve for the loss of a sister.

As Elizabeth cajoled the children into some kind of order, shooing them into a small playroom next door, Jane noticed her West Country accent. She'd read in the file that the family were from Cornwall. Elizabeth had gone to university in Leeds and horse-mad Amanda had followed her north, taking jobs first in Yorkshire yards then in Lancashire. Josephine, their younger sister, had resumed a round-the-world backpacking trip, having interrupted it for Amanda's funeral.

Once they had a few moments to themselves the light left Elizabeth's face. Now Jane had a chance to examine her more closely, she noticed shadows like bruises beneath her eyes. It was soon apparent that she shouldered a burden of guilt for her sister's death.

'Can you believe that when I first met Pete I thought what a lovely guy he was? Good-looking, generous – and the way he spoke, as if he was a BBC announcer. I encouraged Mandy to nail him down. "Don't let this one slip through your fingers," I said.' Elizabeth laughed bitterly. 'Turns out he was one of the biggest losers on the planet.'

Jane said nothing, just nodded sympathetically. It was evident that Pete, the public schoolboy gone bad, had been adept at making a good first impression. Apparently women were forever trying to wean him off his gambling and heroin habits. None had succeeded. The sensible got out or suffered the consequences. And Elizabeth's sister had suffered worst of all.

'She only died because of him. That's the most painful thing to bear. To think that she was just in the way when those drug-dealers came to kill him.'

'That's what you believe, is it?'

'Mr Jones said it was all to do with a drug deal. It was, wasn't it?'

'Quite possibly.'

'I'd like to know why you haven't arrested the animals who did it. Mr Jones said he was pretty sure he knew who was responsible.'

'Mr Jones isn't involved in the case any more. I'm now the Senior Investigating Officer.'

'Oh?' She glared at Jane. 'Does that mean it's all back to square one? You're never going to catch them, are you?'

Jane was stung. 'It doesn't mean that at all. I have every confidence that we will find the people responsible.'

'But?' Elizabeth prompted icily.

'But so far we have no direct evidence to link anyone with the murders. It's quite possible that Pete's drug activities were to blame. Nevertheless we have to re-examine every aspect of the investigation.'

'Is that why Mr Jones is off the case and you're here instead?'

Jane wondered what subject Elizabeth had studied at university. She was obviously no fool. 'Sometimes a change of personnel helps moves things along,' she said diplomatically.

The hostility had now disappeared from Elizabeth's face. She looked numb. Jane reflected that as a reassuring presence she probably came a poor second to her predecessor.

'My husband warned me it was all taking too long. He said you'd have made some arrests by now if you had a case.'

Fortunately, at that moment, a squeal of childish outrage from next door claimed Elizabeth's attention and she scurried off. By the time she returned, Jane was able to redirect the conversation.

'May I ask if you're aware of anyone who might have wanted to cause Amanda harm?'

Elizabeth was plainly taken by surprise. 'Like who?'

'A jealous ex-boyfriend maybe.'

She shook her head. 'Of course not.'

'Please think carefully, Mrs Jacobs. I don't mean any disrespect to your sister but I understand that before she moved in with Pete she had one or two admirers.'

That was putting it politely. According to Amanda's colleagues at the yard where she'd last worked, the stable girl had been as mad about boys as she was about horses.

Elizabeth's tone was defensive. 'Mandy was always popular with the lads – before Pete turned her into a recluse. She was ever so warm and bubbly. And really pretty.'

Jane thought of the photographs of the girl's partially burnt corpse. It was hard to reconcile the two images.

Obligingly, Elizabeth filled the silence. 'Out of the three of us, Mandy never had much luck with men. I met Cliff at my first job and we just clicked. Same thing with Jo. She's off travelling with a boy she's been going out with since she was fifteen. Mandy was always searching for the right guy.' She shot Jane a rueful smile. 'She used to enjoy the search though.'

'Did things end badly with any of these men?'

'Not that I can think of, but I wouldn't necessarily know. We didn't see as much of her after she moved. She used to bring her boyfriends round when she worked in Yorkshire. Ridgemoor's only thirty miles up the road.'

Jane nodded. She wasn't familiar with the horse-racing scene but Simon had given her a rundown on the various yards where Amanda had worked. It had struck her that the girl was as promiscuous in her employers as she was in her choice of men. There seemed to be plenty of both.

A further outburst from next door interrupted them. Jane gathered bathtime was approaching, which would effectively end their discussion. She wasn't sure that she'd managed to win Elizabeth over but, for now, she'd beat a retreat.

As she showed Jane to the door, Elizabeth said, 'I don't suppose you'd know what happened to all Mandy's photos?'

Jane shook her head. The cottage had been picked over in great detail in the days after the fire and everything that had survived had been released to the families of the deceased once they were adjudged to be of no further use to the investigation.

'Mr Jones let me have Mandy's personal things and there was a receipt for photo-developing in her bag. It made me wonder what happened to all her other photos. It would mean a lot to Jo and me to have them.'

'Where did she keep them?'

'In the sideboard. They were in an old biscuit tin, all loose.'

The sideboard had been in the front room downstairs, where the fire had started. Jane knew it was most unlikely they had survived the blaze.

'I'll check for you but I wouldn't get your hopes up.'

'No chance of that,' said Elizabeth as she closed the door on her visitor. 'I ran out of hope some while ago.'

Jamie struggled up the crumbling footpath, trying to keep pace with the lanky figure ahead. His vest was soaked with sweat from the effort of running uphill and his trainers were drenched from the brown puddles which lay in wait at every turn. It had been Dave's suggestion that he accompany him on a run across the moor. An hour ago it seemed like a good idea but he was seriously out of practice.

He crested the rise and found Dave jogging on the spot, his big bullet head capped by a woollen hat, like an egg cosy. He flashed Jamie a toothy grin. The sod was scarcely out of breath. 'You're just in time,' he said, pointing up at the western sky.

Through the leaden clouds a broad shaft of late-afternoon sun played over the moor like a spotlight, picking out the humps and folds of the hillside and the sparkle of the winter-swollen stream at their feet.

'Bloody marvellous,' enthused Dave. 'You've got a cracking spot here.'

Jamie nodded agreement. He was past speech. He dragged the keen air into his lungs in ragged gulps.

'A professional sportsman's got to keep in shape,' Dave observed. 'You were fitter in the nick.'

'Running's not really my sport,' Jamie managed. 'At least, not pelting uphill for miles with a maniac like you.'

Dave laughed over the stiff breeze now blowing drops of rain into their faces. 'Cross-country's the best, mate. Good for body and soul. Look at that.' He nodded towards the horizon where a rainbow was arching through the sky.

Jamie couldn't deny it was spectacular but the rain was getting heavier and the wind felt like ice on his skin. As they watched, the sunlight was swallowed by rolling grey clouds and the rainbow faded from view.

'I don't fancy your tent much tonight, Dave. Are you sure you won't settle for a bed indoors?'

Dave did not dignify that with a reply. He just shook his head and set off again, downhill this time, back the way they had come.

Jamie, much relieved, fell in beside him. 'You'll eat with us though, won't you? Give us a rundown on progress so far.'

'What progress would that be?'

Even jogging gently downhill it was an effort to keep up.

'You know, what you think about Pippa's horses.'

'I think that the horses are very pretty,' Dave sprang across a puddle that was fast turning into a lake, 'but not as pretty as your sister.'

Jamie splashed after him. 'And?'

'And nothing, mate. That's as far as I've got.'

Irritated by Jamie's questions or maybe by his lack of speed, Dave suddenly lengthened his stride and was away down the hill, safely out of earshot. Jamie plodded after him. There would be no catching the thin man this side of supper.

'Hey, Mum – I've got one for you.' Robbie's eyes gleamed from behind his wire-framed spectacles as he gazed eagerly at Jane from the doorway. She looked up from her paperwork piled on the table in the small sitting room. This was the third interruption in the past ten minutes. Elizabeth Jacobs wasn't the only one with demanding children.

'I thought you were doing your homework,' she said as sternly as she could. Here was her only child, fruit of a failed marriage, forced to bounce between two homes. The fight not to indulge him was carried out on a daily basis.

'Yeah, yeah,' he said dismissively. When his skin cleared up and he filled out he'd be a handsome lad, she thought. For the moment, however, he was a bit gawky. To be honest, more than a bit.

'Listen,' he went on. 'You're in a room with three switches. Outside in the corridor are three light bulbs. You can press any combination of switches but once you've left the room you can't go back again. How can you tell which switch controls which bulb?'

Jane groaned. This was typical of Robbie. He had an English essay to write but he'd do anything to postpone his proper work. It wasn't as if he didn't exercise his brain but he preferred to exercise it in a different direction. He loved intellectual puzzles, along with obscure science-fiction novels and computer games that never seemed to end.

Jane had vetoed a computer in his bedroom, concerned that he'd spend all night logged on to graphic porn-sites. Then she discovered that Clive had laid on internet access for Robbie at his place. She'd hit the roof until Susan had shown her on the screen a record of the sites Robbie visited. It turned out he spent most of his time online playing chess against opponents on the other side of the world. There was not an incautiously garbed female in sight. True to her mother's instinct, Jane had now begun to worry that her son wasn't interested in girls.

'So, what do you reckon, Mum?'

She knew she ought to be grateful. He was a bright boy, hardworking too. Even though some subjects bored him, he still knuckled down and did his best. And, as far as she was aware, he didn't smoke, didn't dabble with drugs or even overdose on unsuitable TV programmes. On the other hand, he avoided physical exercise wherever possible, preferred time spent in front of a computer to an hour in the park and had no female friends.

'Come on, Mum. Call yourself a detective?'

Jane couldn't begin to work out the puzzle he had set her. She was no good at them. Robbie was dismayed by her regular failures. How could she solve crimes if she had no talent for lateral thinking? Jane couldn't answer that one either.

'Shall I tell you the answer?'

She admitted defeat. 'I think you'll have to.'

His eyes gleamed with triumph. 'It's obvious. You turn on two of the switches and, after twenty seconds or so, turn one of them off again. Then you go into the corridor. One bulb will be alight – that's the switch you've left on. One bulb will be stone cold – that's the switch you haven't touched. And the third bulb won't be lit but it will be warm – that's the one you turned on and off. Easy.'

And so it was – now he'd explained it.

'Honestly, Mum,' he continued, eager to rub her nose in it, 'you're hopeless.' He said it with just the amount of affection in his tone to defuse the insult.

As he returned to his room, she dropped her eyes to the notes on the investigation. At the rate she was going, her son wasn't the only one getting away with murder.

Marie raked over the soiled wood shavings, savouring the once-familiar fug of the stables. In the much-missed days when she'd owned a horse, she'd never minded this chore – unlike Alan, who could be so lazy when he didn't feel like doing something. Once he'd sussed that she quite liked mucking out he'd left it all to her. 'Some people are born to shovel shit,' he used to say to her. 'Looks like you're one of them.' Her late-lamented brother could be a right pain sometimes.

She'd turned up at Ros Bradey's yard dead on time, at half past six, cycling the mile and a bit in the damp morning darkness. She hadn't minded the early start, she was used to it after her cleaning job. And this time she was off to do a job she loved – even if it was unpaid.

Ros had welcomed her politely, if briskly, and thrown her straight into the business of mucking out boxes. There'd been shouted introductions to a couple of other girls at the same chore and Caroline, obviously Ros's senior helper, had shown her round the small, twenty-horse yard.

Now Marie was on her third box, occupied by a nervous-looking chestnut gelding with a white nose who shied away from her when she entered the stall.

She talked to the horse as she raked through his soiled bedding. Alan had told her she was a nutter when she'd behaved like that with Misty, their old horse, but she'd not been able to get out of the habit. And now it was a Godsend to have someone to chat to. So she told the chestnut gelding about the good things in her life – swapping the office-cleaning for the doctor's surgery, getting down to some proper study for her resit and now, spending some time in a stables. By the time she'd run through that there was no time to get into the not-so-good things, like the fact that Dad and Auntie Joyce were driving her up the wall and she just knew Auntie was letting him smoke on the sly, and the recently discovered information that Colin was going out with a hairdresser with a pierced tummy – not that she cared, good luck to him, but she wished she hadn't heard it first from Gail.

'Tea?'

Ros was standing by the box door with a couple of mugs in her hand.

Marie looked up in surprise but Ros cut off the embarrassed apologies that sprang to her lips. 'You've done a good job on these boxes.'

Marie took her tea. 'Thanks. It's a while since I've mucked out.'

'And how's he been?' Ros indicated the chestnut who was watching them closely, as if aware he was under discussion.

'Great. He thinks I'm a bit funny 'cos I haven't stopped prattling but I don't think he minds really.'

With her free hand Marie reached out to scratch the big white muzzle. The horse allowed himself to be petted.

'Who told you to clean his stall?' Ros was looking at her keenly. 'I was going to deal with him myself.'

Marie was flustered. No one had told her, she'd just assumed it had to be done. 'Sorry,' she blurted.

Ros was smiling. 'Don't apologise. He gave me a nasty kick the other day and he's tried to bite a couple of other girls. But you two seem made for each other.'

'Oh.' Marie looked at the horse. He was licking her palm now, nuzzling into her like a great big softie.

Ros was appraising the pair of them. 'How much time have you got?'

'I'm supposed to be at the surgery by ten.'

'Then you've got plenty of time to ride him.'

'Oh yes, please!'

'Have you done any jumping?'

'I used to.' She'd been a medal-winning show-jumper at the age of twelve – but she wasn't going to boast.

'OK. I'm schooling him for a friend. I'll give you both a lesson, if you like.'

Marie certainly did like. She hadn't felt so excited for ages.

Malcolm sought Toby out on the Ridgemoor gallops during second lot. It was a good spot to bend his ear with no chance of being overheard. On the other hand, he had to battle for his father's attention as the trainer kept his eye on his horses being put through their paces.

'I need a bit of help with Adolf,' Malcolm began. 'The Beaufort people weren't too happy with the Haydock outing.'

'First time out, what did they expect?'

'That's what I said but Beverley Harris is getting her knickers in a twist. She's trying to score points with her boss.'

Toby took his time scanning his string of horses through fieldglasses as they galloped across the moor. 'What do you expect me to do about it?'

'Ring Barney Beaufort and reassure him. Tell him what a great prospect Adolf is.'

Toby grunted unhappily. 'So you want me to lie for you?'

'I want you to put the best gloss on the situation you can manage.'

'I don't like Beaufort or his horse.'

'But you do like the money, don't you, Dad? Thirty-odd grand for soft-soaping old Barney's not a bad day's work.'

His father lowered the glasses and glared at him nastily. Malcolm ignored the venom in his look. He'd made his point – money always talked with the old man.

'OK, I'll ring him if I must.'

'Thanks, Dad.'

It was hard work sometimes but his father always came through in the end.

Chapter Six

Filthy Barrable was not as poisonous a prospect in the flesh as Jane had been led to believe. Not from a distance anyway. His hair was neat and his broad face boyish and cheerful. The cheer faded as Jane reached the table in the corner of the motorway café where DC Lucy Jenkins had taken him for a free fry-up. Despite her eight years' service and black belt in judo, Lucy was as wide-eyed and dimpled as a school-leaver, which made her the ideal candidate to lure Filthy into the open. Jane could, of course, have simply yanked Filthy off the street for a formal interview but sometimes the heavy hand could be counter-productive.

'Aye up,' he said in a thick Yorkshire accent – as if he were an actor in a Hovis commercial, thought Jane as she took a seat next to him, cutting off the escape route to the door. Not that flight would do him much good – he'd need a ride out of the motorway service area.

Up close Jane realised Filthy had not been misnamed. A pungent aroma clung to him that could only be caused by serious neglect of personal hygiene. She had to force a smile as she introduced herself.

'So you're the one who's come on for Jonesie,' he said. 'I heard he'd put through his own goal.'

Lucy gave Jane a slight shake of the head. Whatever Barrable had heard about Leighton he'd not got it from her. The troubles of DCI Jones, the scourge of the Lancashire drugs scene, would have been seized on eagerly by dealers and customers alike. Filthy and his friends probably had a better idea of the beleaguered detective's prospects than his colleagues.

'I imagine you know what I'd like to discuss with you, Mr Barrable,' said Jane.

Filthy chased the last piece of fried bread round his plate and popped it into his mouth.

'I thought you might prefer these surroundings to an interview room at the station.'

He stared at her as he chewed. Then swallowed.

'Which,' she persisted, 'I could easily arrange.'

Finally he spoke. 'Got any burn?'

Jane was still translating the request in her mind when Lucy threw a packet of cigarettes on to the table. They were enveloped by Filthy's big grimy fingers in an instant. Jane watched him strip the cellophane from the packet and jam the white tube between his lips.

Were these the hands that had squeezed the life out of Pete and Amanda? Why not? By his own admission Barrable had been on the spot. He'd seen the money. He could have done it easily.

Filthy dragged smoke into his lungs and grinned at her. The packet had disappeared somewhere inside his stained denim jacket.

Jane knew he hadn't done it. His girlfriend had given him a lift to Pete's place and waited outside while Filthy went inside to score. After he'd done the deed the pair had driven back home to shoot up. Soon after, they'd joined in the Guy Fawkes party thrown by the students next door. He was solidly alibied from 9.30 pm until the early hours of the next morning. Even supposing he had committed the murders and torched the house, that meant the fire would have burned for another ninety minutes before the alarm was raised – most unlikely according to the fire experts she'd talked to.

In any case, Filthy had told them about the money which was presumed missing. Why would he do that if he'd stolen it? And why would he invent the money if it didn't exist? He might be a smelly individual but no one thought he was stupid. As far as this enquiry went he was of considerable importance. In any trial his testimony was going to be crucial.

So it was in a tone of scrupulous politeness that Jane asked if he would mind running through the events of the evening of last 5 November once again, for her personal benefit. 'I would really appreciate it,' she added softly.

He appeared to give the matter some thought. 'All right,' he said finally and began his tale.

It didn't vary in any significant detail from the account Simon had first given her, nor from his signed witness statement. He'd arrived, strung out, shortly after half-past eight. Pete, who was in a larky mood, had mucked him around. First he'd pretended he didn't have any drugs to sell, then he'd told Filthy he wasn't dealing in wraps and piffling amounts any more. Filthy had got fed up and made to leave, thinking of other sources he could try. Pete had then announced he was only joking and of course he could sort Filthy out. He'd gone on to boast that he was about to expand his operations. Filthy, having heard this before, said Oh yeah? and Pete had picked a plastic carrier-bag off the table and dumped it in Filthy's lap, saying Take a look at that, then. Inside was the money, three bricks of new-looking banknotes bundled together with rubber bands.

'Don't ask me how much there was,' said Barrable. 'There was red notes and there was brown and there was a lot. That's all I know.'

'Did you ask him how much?'

'Course I did but he went all coy. He said, "Enough to get me on the Orient Express." What he meant was, get him in with these East Europeans he was always on about. That's how he talked about them. The drugs come through Turkey, see.'

Filthy lit another cigarette from the butt of his first. 'I reckon he was about to tell me how much was in the bag when Mandy came in. She went ballistic when she saw me holding the money. She yanked it off me and screamed at Pete, had a real go at him. First I thought it was because he'd let me see it but it was because he'd told her he'd put it in a safe place and he hadn't.'

'Did you put this in your statement?' Jane couldn't remember this particular detail.

'Maybe not. I'll add it if you like. Anyhow, he calmed her down, said he'd stash it right away and she turned the telly on, well fed up. Pete gave me some stuff and I thought it was time I split, so I did.'

'He didn't say where he was going to put the money, did he?'

Barrable shook his head.

'Or where he'd got it from?'

'He just said he'd had a slice of luck.'

'Where do you think he might have got it?'

Filthy stubbed out his cigarette and leaned back in his seat. 'Haven't got a clue,' he said. 'Tell you what though, it's not my idea of luck.'

Jane nodded. She couldn't agree more.

*

'Got anything for me yet, Dave?'

Pippa was tired of asking this question. It was nearly a week since his arrival and so far Dave Prescott had made no pronouncement whatsoever. If it wasn't for Jamie, who so badly needed a friend, she'd have told him to get lost.

No, she wouldn't, she corrected herself, because she'd grown to rather like Dave on her own account. There was something comforting about his good-natured presence, despite his off-putting appearance. And though he'd not yet delivered the goods for which he'd been hired, he had his other uses. On his second day Pippa had caught him on the phone in the office and assumed he was making a call on his own behalf. It turned out that he'd been answering calls while the office was unattended and had compiled a neat list of messages for her to respond to.

After that, he'd put in a couple of hours every morning, manning the phone and sorting the paperwork. He was remarkably organised.

'What's so strange about it?' he responded when she'd said as much. 'I administered the East–West Cross-Country Run for six years. We had runners from all over the world and raised a mint for charity. Your little outfit here's a breeze compared to that.'

Pippa might have taken offence had he not accompanied this remark with a wink and answered the phone before she could open her mouth.

But this morning he'd taken a seat on the other side of the desk and produced a sheet of crumpled paper covered in the tidy handwriting she was becoming accustomed to. And in response to her regular enquiry, he'd nodded and tapped his notes.

'At first,' he began, 'I thought you were a bit of a fruitcake. Horses and humans run differently, as I'm sure you've observed. There's the matter of travelling on four legs rather than two. And horses can't talk either, so there's a communication problem right there. However, you seem an intelligent woman so I thought I'd give you the benefit of the doubt.'

'Thank you,' she said. It seemed appropriate.

'I've had a good look at what you get up to here. I'm thinking of it like the sort of training camp you get in East Africa where, say, the top Kenyan runners get together for months. I've been trying to put the differences between horses and humans out of my mind and concentrate on the similarities. So what you've got are a collection of elite athletes living side by side, training together every day, all with the aim of winning races.

'One thing strikes me straight off. Your horses have got it pretty easy. There's these teams of body slaves pampering them day and night, feeding and grooming and fussing around them. And when they're actually asked to put in a bit of effort, what do they actually do? Not much, as far as I can tell. You trot them up onto the gallops, get them to run around for an hour and then it's back home for tea and biscuits and another round of pampering. It's not exactly a heavy workload, is it? If these were athletes they'd be doing a hundred miles a week at least. I mean,' he continued, emphasising his point by prodding the desk top with a long bony finger, 'it can't be right that a four-legged animal weighing almost half a ton is doing less work than a ten-stone human being. Have you ever considered taking them out twice a day?'

Pippa sighed. He had a point. 'I know what you're saying, Dave, but it's the cost. The lads finish at lunchtime and they're off till four. If they stay all afternoon I'll have to pay them more and I'm on a tight enough budget as it is.'

The runner appeared to take her point, which was encouraging. Despite her natural scepticism she was hoping that he might be able to help.

'How about,' he said, 'instead of the lads spending their time doing evening stables, they ride out instead. I know at this time of year it's probably too dark but maybe they could start earlier. Whichever way you look at it, your horses have got to do more work.'

Pippa nodded in agreement. She knew that what Dave was saying made sense, but there was more to training horses than giving them physical tasks. In her experience there was a fine line between how much you could work a horse and how much you could get it to eat. If you overworked them they nearly always went off their food and once that happened you were in trouble.

Some trainers maintained that you needed to train horses to eat before you could train them to gallop. Once the animals were eating fourteen to eighteen pounds a day of solid food like oats and nuts you could train them hard, knowing that if their intake dropped a couple of pounds they'd still be getting a sufficient amount to survive on.

Pippa explained this to Dave. 'People tend to forget that thorough-breds have been bred and trained to race for centuries. They're highly strung animals, prone to fretting. You can't exactly say to them, "You've got a race coming up so you'll have to put in some extra work".'

Dave listened closely, nodding his large hairless head from time to time. 'Why don't you let me write out a training programme for a few of your more moderate animals. I'll aim to gradually increase their speed and endurance work. I bet I can talk four of your lads into helping and I'll get them all out twice a day.'

The prospect of trying something new appealed to Pippa. She also fancied that Dave was the kind of fellow who could persuade her lads to have a shot at something different. Provided she kept an eye on what he was up to, what did she have to lose?

'OK,' she said, 'let's give it a go.'

He held out his hand and she took it, her fingers disappearing into his firm warm grasp.

'Tell you what,' he added with a grin, 'if it's a complete fiasco, we can always blame Jamie.'

She knew she could work with someone who made her laugh.

The last time Jamie had visited Carlisle racecourse he'd arrived by helicopter. Having triumphed in two races at Ripon, he was just in time to boot home the winner in the last. He couldn't remember how he left the course but he'd ended up at a party in town and had a clear recollection of nursing a hangover in the back of a taxi the next morning all the way home to Yorkshire.

Today, accompanied by Dave, he'd arrived at a more sedate pace in the Ridgemoor horsebox, with Adolf and Feeding Frenzy, a six-year-old novice chaser, in the back. He was down to ride both of them. In his slow progression from Flat tearaway to professional jump jockey, this was a big day.

Apart from the race at Haydock, Jamie had so far restricted his riding to schooling with Ros and riding out on Pippa's and, sometimes, Toby's horses. Pippa had been urging him to ring Bertie Brooks to see if his former agent would find him some rides but Jamie had been putting it off. Among the many things his accident had smashed was his self-confidence. He wanted to be sure he had the skills to be a jump jockey before he offered himself for hire. Also, the thought nagged at him: if Bertie wanted to continue representing him, why hadn't he been in touch? He'd have heard by now that Jamie was out of prison. He suspected that these days, Bertie didn't want to know.

The offer to ride Feeding Frenzy had come from another trainer in the Ridgemoor area, Ferdy Gates. Ferdy ran a small operation often referred to as 'Gates' All-sorts', in that no one could predict what variety of performer would emerge from his dilapidated yard. He was as likely to pop up with a two-year-old sprinter as an old warhorse having a tilt at his umpteenth Grand National.

Jamie had once ridden a supposedly red-hot filly for him in a Guineas trial in which the horse had turned in a distinctly lukewarm performance, despite Jamie's best efforts. Ferdy had been cheerful enough about it and said he didn't blame Jamie but he'd never offered him another ride – until now. Jamie couldn't work out who'd put him up to it, though he suspected Malcolm. One of Mal's clients had a horse with Ferdy and, despite his brother-in-law's denials, Jamie had his suspicions. It was typical of Malcolm to avoid taking credit.

Malcolm was amongst the gang of connections assembled in the parade ring to see Beaufort Bonanza off on the second instalment of his racing life. Jamie recognised Barney Beaufort surrounded by a crew of beaming businessmen and hoped that this time they'd all be spared the death-or-glory speechifying. But this time Toby was present and Beaufort appeared happy to cede the top-dog role to the trainer, nodding his head in agreement as the Colonel briefed Jamie on the race ahead.

In reality, Jamie had already received his briefing from Ros an hour earlier when he and Dave had looked Adolf over in his box.

She'd delivered her advice in customarily no-nonsense fashion.

'Whatever you do,' she'd said, 'don't let him take a pull. He went off like a train last time and died. If you let him do it again, we'll all deserve to be out of a job.'

'He'll be all right,' Jamie said. 'He's a different horse to last time.'

'In my experience, young man, horses don't change that quickly. He may be good as gold at home but out here in a race, first time over hurdles, he might forget everything he's learnt. It's your job to make him remember – OK?'

'Don't worry. I'll keep him covered.'

'Good.' But she'd given him a long, hard stare before striding off.

Dave had been watching their exchange with interest and he rolled his eyes as she disappeared. He waited till she'd turned out of sight before he said slyly, 'She likes you.'

'What?'

The tall man chuckled. 'Attractive, too.'

'She's old enough to be my mother,' Jamie protested. But it was true, Ros was a classy-looking woman. It made her all the more intimidating.

Dave's words were in Jamie's head now as Ros appeared out of the crowd and, for a moment, took hold of Adolf's bridle. 'Remember what we discussed,' she murmured.

He nodded, aware of her dark brown eyes boring into his.

'Good luck then,' she said as he set off down to the start.

Carlisle is a small tight track with plenty of ups and downs. With a strong wind blowing in from the Irish Sea and some low winter sunshine playing peekaboo behind the scudding clouds there was plenty for horse and rider to contend with. Especially for a highly strung novice like Adolf on his first run over hurdles. At least, throughout the two miles one furlong of the race ahead, there were only six obstacles to contend with. In Jamie's opinion, that would be more than enough.

As they joined the group of hurdlers massing at the start, he could see the sense in Ros's words. Adolf did not feel like the same horse as the one he regularly rode out at Ridgemoor. That old jittery mood was back – 'buzzy' was the term Ros used – and he could feel the animal twitching with nerves beneath him, desperate to be off.

When the tape rose Adolf was out of his blocks like Linford Christie.

No, you don't, thought Jamie and jerked the reins back hard. It slowed the horse down but Jamie had to fight to keep him under control as the other runners caught them up. It was the start of a battle as Jamie strove to put the brakes on and Adolf tried to follow his instincts to bolt wildly into the blue.

Jamie held the upper hand as the first hurdle loomed. This was a moment of danger, Adolf's trouble being the urge to run out of control after a jump.

They soared over the obstacle and, as they hit the ground, he was pulling harder than ever, threatening to yank Jamie's arms out of their sockets. Cursing, he tugged hard at the horse's mouth, commanding him to slow down. Adolf faltered and other runners flew past, the first horse obviously leading his jockey the same kind of merry dance as Jamie's mount. He tucked in behind this leading group and at once Adolf began to settle. That was more like it. The key to the race, Jamie knew, was to keep his horse back in the pack, out of sight of a clear road ahead – keeping him covered, just like he'd promised.

The Beaufort Holidays group weren't party to the race tactics that Jamie was trying to impose on their runner. Nevertheless, they were mightily encouraged by events so far.

'He's in the lead!' shrieked one of the guests' wives. 'Oh no!' she moaned a second later as Beaufort Bonanza was overtaken by the pack.

'Thank God for that,' muttered Malcolm in Beverley's ear. She didn't reply but from the pressure of her leg on his he knew she'd heard. He'd managed to position himself behind her in the group massed on the Grandstand balcony. While everyone's attention was focused on the course, he insinuated his hand beneath her short jacket to gently circle the small of her back through her silk blouse. She wore yet another of her fetching suits, this one in pale apricot. He wondered what particular items of exotic lingerie might lie beneath.

There had been protracted debate ahead of Adolf's latest outing, with Barney demanding a new test of the horse's prowess as soon as possible and Toby wanting just the opposite. As far as the Colonel was concerned, Adolf's Haydock showing had clearly demonstrated that he needed a lot more work before being turned loose on the racecourse for a second time. Inevitably this difference of opinion had led to Malcolm and Beverley convening several urgent meetings to put their respective masters' points of view. As far as Malcolm was concerned the argument could have continued even longer, considering that it was conducted between the sheets in Beverley's pink boudoir.

In the end, naturally, Beaufort's view had prevailed – he was paying, after all – and Toby had found this modest novice hurdle race on one of the north's most appealing small courses. What's more, the Colonel had agreed to Malcolm's suggestion that he lend his own presence to the occasion, and he was currently elbow to elbow with Barney giving him his authoritative reading of the race.

Malcolm's hand slid round to the inflowing curve of Beverley's waist where it was stopped by the pressure of her fingers.

'Bonanza looks full of running,' said one of the party, as he tracked the horses through binoculars on the far side of the course.

Malcolm could pick out the scarlet-and-white Beaufort colours tucked in behind the leading group – most satisfactory. Everything, in fact, was turning out well this time, in contrast to Adolf's first outing.

He put his lips to Beverley's ear. 'If he wins I'm whisking you off tonight for a celebration. No arguments.'

He knew just where to whisk her to, as well. A small hotel overlooking Coniston Water where the beds were wide and soft and the service was discreet.

She squeezed his fingers in response. That had to mean yes, didn't it?

He turned his attention back to the race.

Jamie was beginning to feel confident – a long-forgotten feeling in a horse race. It had been a fight all the way round the circuit, with Adolf testing his strength and concentration with every yard they travelled. Not least of Jamie's problems was the difficulty of piloting a big, strapping animal who had a tendency to jump to the left, round a tight right-handed course. But he was managing it. All those hours in the paddock practising close control under Ros's keen eye were paying off.

So far Jamie had succeeded in keeping Adolf out of sight of open ground. Since the first hurdle Jamie had kept him tucked a couple of lengths behind the leading group, tracking a solid black horse called Jericho. He kept Adolf in line as they came out of the final bend and into the home straight. Adolf took the next two hurdles in his stride. Just one obstacle lay ahead. Once they'd cleared it, Jamie would shift the horse out into the open and give him his head. The way they were travelling, in a powerful rhythm across the ground, he was sure Adolf had the beating of the horses in front. The others had made all the running and he could see they were beginning to flag.

Familiar emotions came flooding back, giving him a rush he'd doubted he'd ever feel again. He was going to win this race!

And he would have done, he was sure, if Jericho, immediately ahead, hadn't completely mistimed his jump at the last and sprawled across the turf in a tangle of limbs.

Adolf cleared the hurdle and jinked instinctively to the left but there was no way he could avoid the faller. Jericho's trailing leg caught

Adolf's off-hind foot and then he was also plunging to the ground, slamming Jamie into the deck.

He lay there for a few seconds, stunned by the speed of events. He remembered this feeling too – of being suddenly ditched, robbed of victory at the last gasp. It was one memory he could do without.

A collective groan went up from the Beaufort party as their horse crashed to the turf. There were cries of disappointment, resigned shrugs from the cynical – a fall was only to be expected, after all – and general concern for horse and rider.

'He's on his feet, thank God,' said the man with the binoculars. 'The jockey's OK, too.'

'What rotten luck,' boomed Toby's voice, putting the official verdict on proceedings. 'But that's racing, folks.'

But these reactions were not of interest to Malcolm. The pressure on his hand vanished and Beverley stepped away from him with an impatient shrug.

The look she turned on him was one of fury. He was beginning to learn her moods. When things went wrong her first reaction was to look for someone to blame. The nearest person would do.

Coniston Water would obviously have to wait.

Jamie sat motionless in the changing room. He'd taken a battering down his left side from the fall but fortunately he'd been passed fit for his ride on Feeding Frenzy. It would have been a blow to miss that.

What hurt more than his bruises was the dressing-down he'd received from the Colonel.

'What the blazes did you think you were doing sitting behind Jericho? You had the width of the whole flipping course to run in.'

Jamie had been indignant but these days he knew better than to fly off the handle in response. 'I was keeping him covered, Colonel. Like we discussed.'

'Yes, but it was obvious that horse was going to fall. He'd run out of puff. We could all see him wobbling from up in the stand.'

It was true that he'd not really been concentrating on the condition of the horse ahead. He'd been entirely focused on Adolf and how they were going to win. Counting his chickens.

'I'm sorry, Colonel,' he said.

The trainer glowered at him. 'I gave Mr Beaufort and his friends a load of cobblers about it just being bad luck. One of the hazards of the game being brought down by a faller and so on, but in this instance I don't think it was. This one's down to you, Jamie, and I hope you learn a lesson from it.'

'Yes, sir,' he'd replied, feeling about sixteen – the age when he'd first ridden for Toby.

Ros watched the entire exchange without saying a word, her face inscrutable. Doubtless she'd give him the benefit of her twopennyworth later. He couldn't wait.

'You all right, mate?'

Jamie looked up to see Robin Price, the jockey who'd been on the winner of his race, crossing the room towards him.

'You took a bit of a bash, didn't you?' Robin said as he sat down on the bench opposite.

'It's only a bruise.' He was touched by the lad's concern. 'Congratulations, by the way.'

'Thanks.' Robin's face was split in two by the width of his grin. He looked like he didn't need to shave much. 'It's my first win.'

'Excellent.' Jamie found himself smiling broadly. The boy's pleasure was infectious. 'I hope you're going to celebrate in style.'

'You bet. Look what the owner gave me.' He held up a banknote – £50. 'With my win bonus I'll clear about two hundred and fifty pounds. We're going to have a brilliant night.'

A moment ago Jamie had been feeling like a kid; now he felt positively middle-aged.

'I'd invest this if I were you, lad,' said Desmond Hartley as he slipped the envelope into Jamie's hand. 'Ring me at the office if you'd like a few tips.'

'Thank you, sir. I might take you up on that.'

The envelope felt thick – three grand sort of thick – as he assessed it surreptitiously between his fingers. What with the percentage of the prize money from the Diadem Stakes, he might have cleared almost ten grand from that race alone. High-rolling owners like Hartley could be very generous.

'A classic piece of riding,' the owner said, Vanessa at his elbow, her eyes bathing Jamie with the light of admiration and newly fired lust.

Would Hartley have been so appreciative if he'd realised Jamie had already been the beneficiary of his daughter's own brand of generosity? 'Just don't leave it so late next time,' Hartley added. 'It's not good for my health. You must have nerves of steel.'

Jamie laughed and they all joined in. He had left his victory burst late, that was true, but he'd never had any doubt that he'd get there. Today was one of those days when everything was destined to go right.

He'd had two winners before he'd even lined up on Morwenstow, over seven furlongs and a mile. In both of those he'd come with a run in the last furlong and cruised past the leader in his own time, making it look easy – which it was. The Diadem was different. He'd been up against strong competition and Morwenstow had been nervy at the start, jumping out behind the field.

It was a short race, a six-furlong sprint for the line, a mere eighty seconds in the saddle. He had no time to nurse his mount along and get him in the mood. He had to impose his will and shake the horse out of his lethargy. He gave Morwenstow a smack across the shoulder and went to work. The horse did as he was told – he had no option.

There was a wall of horses ahead of him at the three-furlong mark. Halfway through the race and he was still last. But there was a fire in his mount now and he'd lit it. He plunged into the body of the pack. For a split second the horses closed in around him until it seemed he was touching riders on either side, the group of them pelting along like a many-legged beast. Then his rivals fell away and he saw open ground ahead.

At five furlongs he was two lengths down on the leading horses, four of them racing abreast. 'Come on,' he muttered, 'where's my gap?' And there it was – a sliver of daylight between the rail and the stand-side runner.

Jamie switched to the inside and gave Morwenstow the word. The pair of them knifed through the opening, seemingly creating space out of nothing. The rider outside them turned his head and Jamie glimpsed his mouth open in an O of surprise. He tried to close the door and shut them out but he was too late, Morwenstow held his station. For a few seconds the two horses raced shoulder to shoulder. The post shot towards them and Jamie squeezed the last ounce out of his horse.

The photo seemed to take ages but Jamie was calm. He had no doubt. Officially Morwenstow won by a short head but a nostril would have been a more accurate assessment.

'You deserve that, my boy,' said Hartley, pointing to Jamie's envelope. 'You've got a rare gift.'

Did he still have a gift? Jamie wondered as he trotted Feeding Frenzy up for a preliminary look at the first fence ahead of the fifth race, a two-mile novice chase over eleven fences. The rolling scenery and small crowd of racing enthusiasts, bundled up against the wintry breeze, were a far cry from the lush lawns of Ascot and the massed ranks of well-dressed southerners, high on champagne cocktails and Pimms. Once Jamie had been the darling of the rich, but could he perform before the country folk of Cumbria? In those days he'd been contemptuous of meetings like this, with their derisory prize money and rural clientele. Now he was just grateful to be allowed to take part.

'He's a grand sort,' Ferdy Gates had said of Feeding Frenzy on introducing the horse to Jamie, 'but he'll never set the world on fire.' Since then Jamie had ridden work on him and he had no reason to doubt Ferdy's assessment.

As the tapes went up and they set off, Jamie settled the horse at the rear of the nine runners. He was well aware that this was his second first of the day. He'd just ridden his first hurdle race and now he was having his maiden crack at a steeplechase. He prayed that this time he'd at least manage to finish the race.

Feeding Frenzy provided a different sort of ride to Adolf. For one thing, he did everything he was told without protest. And he jumped right-handed without having to be yanked in the correct direction after every obstacle. Even more important, he'd tackled jumps like these many times. The same could not be said for Jamie who'd only been over an open ditch twice, up on Ferdy's practice ground, and had never tackled a water jump at all. Yet here he was clearing the water in front of the stands with the shouts of zealous punters clearly audible over the drumming of hooves and the creaking and jingling of tack.

I could get a taste for this, he thought as they turned out into the open country. It was a relief to be on a compliant animal with nimble feet and he found himself gliding past a couple of back-markers, eager to take on the next fence.

Since his failure – as he saw it – on Adolf, he'd attempted to find out about the other horses in the race. Ferdy had marked his card, telling him which animals to be wary of. It wouldn't do to be brought down by another dodgy jumper.

The horse on his inside pecked at the open ditch and Feeding Frenzy cruised past. Jamie set his sights on the next two horses ahead, travelling side by side as they rounded the bend which led back to the home straight and the next open ditch. The horse nearest to him mucked it up and put his foot in, jerking the rider out of the saddle. Jamie congratulated himself on giving it a wide berth as Feeding Frenzy popped over the obstacle a length ahead of the next horse.

He was lying fourth, he calculated, with a couple of furlongs to go, and Feeding Frenzy was lobbing along nicely. The leaders were just five lengths ahead – plenty of time to reel them in.

He gave Feeding Frenzy a smack with the whip, time to get cracking. The horse took no notice but continued his steady progression towards the next fence.

Jamie hit him again. Come on, you dozy fellow, show me what you've got!

He tried everything he could to shake the horse up but there was no change in his pace. As they hit the uphill slope towards the finish, the leaders began to pull further away. It dawned on Jamie that his mount was already travelling as fast as he could. For all his sure-footedness, Feeding Frenzy was one-paced. As Ferdy had said, he was not going to set the world on fire.

At least he got his wish – he finished the race.

The horses had been loaded into the box and Jamie and Dave were about to take their places in the cab when Ros appeared.

'Jamie, can I have a word?'

Avoiding Dave's inquisitive glance, Jamie followed her across the yard. He had a fair idea what was coming. This was her bollocking to follow up the Colonel's criticism of his ride on Adolf. What's more, it was to be delivered in cold blood, hours after the event. How typical of Ros.

She turned to face him, her face unreadable. 'You probably don't realise what you've done today,' she began.

Oh Lord, what other balls-ups had he perpetrated? Whatever it was, he had no doubt she was about to tell him.

'When I agreed to help you I knew that you were a talented horseman. But you'd learned your skills on fast Flat horses. All you had to do was ride short and point them in the right direction. Your races barely lasted two minutes. Jumping's a different game. Jockeys have got to be stronger, smarter, able to change strategy in the course of a long race.'

All this was true enough, as he was finding out. He wished she'd get to the point.

'Frankly,' she said, 'you had it easy on the Flat and I didn't think you'd have the brains or the patience for jumping. Or the courage.'

Thanks a bunch, he thought, suppressing the urge to walk away. You didn't turn your back on your enemy – he'd learned that in Garstone.

'I just want you to know that I was wrong,' she said.

He stared at her. Had he heard correctly?

'Toby's entitled to give you his opinion of your race on Adolf but I don't agree with it. In my opinion, to put him in a position to win in your first hurdle race was brilliant. And the way you handled the steeplechase was a revelation. You've got no nerves at all, have you? You just want to win.'

She laid a hand on his arm. 'So, what I'm saying is, you should be very happy with what you've achieved this afternoon. I know I am. Well done.'

He took his seat in the horse box in a daze. Dave was smirking and he could see he was in for a journey full of sly remarks at his expense.

Not that he cared. Maybe Ros wasn't such a cold fish after all.

Simon Bennett was looking more crumpled than usual as he slumped at his desk, resting his head on one hand, a pen poised in the other. A pile of new CDs sat by his elbow.

'Is this a bad time?' Jane asked as he looked up.

He shook his head and she sat opposite him. She pointed at the CDs; Britney Spears was on top of the pile. 'Bit young for you, isn't she?'

He rolled his eyes. 'Very funny, boss. You tell me what to buy a stroppy little teenager who's got everything but thinks she's got nothing.'

She regretted her feeble joke. She realised now that he was preparing his daughter's birthday present. Since their dinner she'd shared the odd parental note with Simon. Tanya was turning fourteen and, so Jane gathered, adolescence was hitting her hard. Simon saw Tanya at weekends and on the occasions she walked out of her mother's house after a row or needed a lift home in the early hours from some forbidden club or party. In other words, he bore a fair amount of the brunt. Jane congratulated herself on producing a boy child. For all her anxieties about Robbie, he played by the rules.

He put down his pen and looked at her quizzically. Now she could get down to business.

'I've been talking to your friend Barrable. I believe him about the money. I just wish I knew how Pete had come by so much.'

'He could have got lucky on a horse.'

'I'm serious, Simon.'

'So am I. Pete gambled on horses – that's how he met Mandy. He'd chat up stable girls to get tips.'

Jane considered the matter for a moment. 'Has anyone tried to check that out? Did he have a regular bookie?'

'He used to have a phone account till he got blacklisted. We showed his photo round all the local bookmakers. They knew him all right.'

'And?'

'He was known as a small-beer punter. Whatever he won he'd end up paying right back, just like the rest of us. What's so funny?'

He'd caught her grinning.

'I don't think I've ever placed a bet in my life.'

He leaned back in his seat and smiled at her. His eyes gleamed and even beneath the washed-out strip-light of the office he looked impossibly handsome. 'What a goody-goody you are, Acting DCI Culpepper,' he said. 'I must take you in hand one day.'

Jane jumped to her feet. Time to bring this conversation to an end. 'Just give it some thought, will you? Where Pete got the money, I mean,' she added as he continued to smile at her lazily.

'Yes, boss.'

She was halfway to the door before she remembered. 'Do you know what happened to Amanda's photos?'

He looked surprised. 'No.'

'According to her sister, Amanda kept a collection of photographs in the sideboard downstairs. Ring any bells?'

He shook his head. 'They were probably destroyed in the fire.'

'I thought all the stuff in the sideboard survived.'

125

According to the scene-of-crime record the solid old sideboard had been badly damaged but its contents were recognisable – cutlery, plates and glasses, even packs of cards and old jigsaws.

'Yes, but I don't remember any photos.'

'Elizabeth says they were kept in a biscuit tin.'

'Aha.' Simon produced a cellophane envelope from the shelf behind him and shook some photos on to the desk. They showed the front room of the cottage after the fire had been extinguished. The fire debris was labelled though the main items of furniture were recognisable even in their burnt and blackened state – sideboard, table, chairs.

'There we are,' he said, pointing to a dark object at the back of the wide fireplace, behind the coal scuttle. Half of it was bent and twisted but the portion farthest from the hearth had retained its square shape. The remains of a biscuit tin.

'So it wasn't in the sideboard,' said Jane, digesting this information. 'They must have had the photos out and they got burnt when the place was torched.'

'There's mention of photo remnants in the fire-investigator's report.'

Jane nodded. So that was that. At least she could tell Elizabeth what had happened to the photos – that they'd not been put away and had perished in the flames.

She wondered when she'd be able to tell the poor woman some good news. She sincerely hoped it would be soon.

Chapter Seven

Marie looked up from her desk in the poky room at the back of the surgery. Most of the space was taken up by filing cabinets and the floor on either side of her desk was piled high with olive-green folders. The work of transferring patient details onto the new computer was a slow grind.

Lionel Gooding peered at her from the doorway. 'May I interrupt for a moment?'

It wasn't really a request. As the senior member of the medical practice he made the rules. Nevertheless he stepped into the room hesitantly and Marie was on her guard. As a rule – when he wanted her to sort out his computer messes, for example – he strode in and out as if he owned the place which, in a manner of speaking, he did.

'Is everything all right, Dr Gooding? I know I'm a bit behind with the records but they're all over the place. Well, some of them . . .'

He cut off her flow with a flap of his hands. 'Your work is excellent, Marie, and much appreciated by us all. I'd just like a word of a more personal nature. May I . . .?'

He indicated the spare chair and she swept a bundle of folders off the seat to make space. He'd closed the door behind him – it was ominous.

'I ran into Ros Bradey this morning.'

So that was it. Everything fell into place. He wanted to know why she'd stopped going to the stables.

'I suppose Ros is a bit disappointed in me.'

'I think she's as much puzzled as disappointed. As am I. You've been telling me how much you enjoy being around horses once more, and Ros is full of praise for your riding ability.'

She took a deep breath. 'I owe you an explanation.'

He stopped her. 'No, you don't, Marie. And you don't owe Ros Bradey one either – she says she's used to young girls changing their minds without letting anyone know what they are up to.'

She could just picture Ros saying the words.

'However,' Dr Gooding had got to his feet, 'she says there's someone else you should explain yourself to. A horse called Spring Fever who's wondering where you've got to.'

Ouch!

Malcolm didn't like being given the runaround. He'd spent the morning trying to get hold of Beverley but her phone was being answered by a gormless minion who could only tell him she was 'in a meeting'. The girl would not elaborate on how long this meeting was likely to last but when he got the same response at one-thirty he felt sure he was being deliberately snubbed.

It wasn't that he was particularly keen to discuss Adolf's latest cock-up straight away, but Beverley had barely spoken a civil word to him after the race. And when he'd tried to detain her at the end of the meeting – to float the Coniston Water idea in seductive detail – she'd simply brushed him off. 'Call me tomorrow. Barney's waiting,' she'd muttered as she strode off to the car park without a backward glance.

Frankly he was getting a little tired of her moody behaviour but it made her more interesting than the majority of women he'd been involved with. Most of the females in his life had fallen into the doormat category and, by the time he'd wiped his feet a few times, he'd been ready to move on. Pippa had been one of the exceptions and so, too, was Beverley. He had to admit she was intriguing. He'd been through her handbag once and come across some pills called Fluoxetine. Prozac by another brand-name – he'd checked it out. This secret piece of knowledge tickled him. So the super-smart executive was really a doped-up bag of nerves. She was certainly a challenge. And he wasn't prepared to give her up until he was sure he was on top.

At last he managed to get through to her assistant, a snippy type called Karen who had also, he was sure, been ducking his calls. Karen was Beverley's creature. Malcolm could reliably calculate his current standing in Beverley's affections by Karen's tone.

Right now she was all business. 'I'm afraid Ms Harris is still in conference with the chairman, Mr Priest. Is this a matter of urgency?'

'She asked me to call and arrange a meeting. Can you tell her I could manage drinks this evening?'

Karen's reply was encouraging. 'Let me just see if she can squeeze you in.'

Malcolm had no doubt the double-entendre was intentional. Things were looking up.

When Karen came back on the line, the wind had changed and her tone was distant. 'She says she can spare ten minutes in her office at five this afternoon. Or else it'll have to be next week.'

Malcolm agreed, trying to keep the fury out of his voice. Just wait till he got Beverley on her own.

Marie cycled up to Ros's yard after the surgery closed for lunch. There was no point in putting it off. The sun was out and she found herself pedalling faster as she caught sight of the indoor school across the sparkling green fields. She'd missed this short journey and didn't want her connection to end. But how in all conscience could she allow it to continue?

There was plenty of activity. She could see horses being led across to the barn and tackling jumps in the paddock. She looked for Ros amongst the figures in the field and couldn't spot her.

She rode round to the stables and parked her bike. The boxes seemed empty apart from one. A familiar white-nosed face regarded her with a luminous eye and a whicker in the throat.

'How are you?' she said happily as she reached up to pat Spring Fever's neck. 'Have you missed me?'

'What do you think?' said a voice from behind her.

To Marie's relief Ros was smiling. She was expecting a telling-off and maybe that would follow but, for the moment, it seemed Ros had other things on her mind.

'You've turned up just in time. I haven't got anyone to ride him.'

'Oh.' Marie was not prepared for that. She was dressed for an office not the stable.

Ros read her mind and was not to be thwarted. 'There's spare clothes in the tack room. Let's get you kitted out.'

Within five minutes Marie found herself on top of Spring Fever, gently warming him up round the paddock preparatory to tackling a series of jumps that Ros was arranging. As the pair of them soared over the first one, Marie felt happier than she'd been in days. Since she'd last sat on Spring Fever, in fact.

'It must be love,' said Ros afterwards as they rubbed Spring Fever down and settled him back in his box. 'He'll jump for you but he won't get off the ground for anyone else. Would you like to put him through his paces for his owner? Just to demonstrate that I've not been taking money under false pretences.'

'I'd love to, Ros, but . . .'

She ground to a halt. This was the point she knew must come – the point she was dreading. And she began to explain about her brother and the accident that had taken his life. And how, now she'd heard that Jamie Sullivan – the man responsible – also rode Ros's horses, she could no longer do so.

Ros took her into the scruffy room that served as an office-cum-kitchen and made them tea. When Caroline and a couple of other girls appeared at the door she shooed them away.

'Suppose,' she said at length, 'I could guarantee that you would not run into Jamie on these premises?'

Marie was surprised. Was Ros proposing to rearrange her schedule just for her? She didn't expect her to do that.

'Or,' Ros continued, 'is it the fact that I associate with him that causes you a problem?'

'Oh no! I don't feel like that. My dad and my aunt might, but I'm not like them. I don't think Jamie Sullivan's my enemy or anything. It's just – I hate the thought of bumping into him. You know, like him arriving and asking me to saddle up one of the horses for him. It wouldn't be right, would it? I can't come here if I think he might suddenly turn up.'

Ros put down her mug. 'He won't. There's other places we can work. And if he's going to be here I shall make sure you are not.'

Relief washed over her. Of course, she could have found other stables and ridden out elsewhere but it suited her here. She liked Ros and the other girls and the horses. And now she could carry on as before. Her face broke into a smile. 'That's brilliant.'

'So you'll come tomorrow?'

'Oh yes. Thanks ever so much, Ros. I can't believe you'll go to this trouble just for me.'

Ros dumped her mug in the sink and turned for the door. 'Don't kid yourself, Marie. I'm only thinking of my horses.'

All the same, Marie thought as she pedalled back down the lane, it felt as if she'd just been paid the most enormous compliment.

Beverley kept Malcolm waiting in reception, as he'd anticipated she would. By now he'd recovered his composure. He reminded himself that he and Beverley were playing a game that was mutually beneficial. Beverley had been sluttishly selfish in bed and he'd swear she was dying for more. And this – the official cold shoulder, the summons to the office – was her next move in the game, like intellectual foreplay. He'd go along with it. He was sure the consummation would be worth it.

He was put out, though, to find that Beverley was not intending to grant him exclusive access to her presence. When Karen finally ushered him into Beverley's office she took a seat on a straight-backed chair next to the desk and produced a notebook, obviously acting on instructions.

Beverley was at her most forbidding. She offered a cursory formal handshake and indicated the squashy sofa which Malcolm had squirmed around on during his first visit. This time she stayed firmly put behind her desk and launched into business without preamble. 'I've asked Karen to take minutes of our conversation, just for the record.'

'I didn't know there was a record,' he said.

'Surely you don't object to an official note of our discussion? It's more businesslike. Ultimately it's for the benefit of both parties.'

A few smart retorts sprang to Malcolm's mind but he kept quiet. His curiosity almost outweighed his suspicion.

'As you can imagine,' she continued, 'I have taken the opportunity to review with Mr Beaufort the progress of Beaufort Bonanza in the light of yesterday's disappointing performance.'

Malcolm couldn't contain himself. 'Now come on, you can't call it disappointing. That run was a great improvement on Haydock.'

'It could hardly have been worse.'

'We all know he got it wrong at Haydock, but yesterday he showed some real form.'

'He fell over, Malcolm, and failed to finish for the second time in a row. Now . . .' Karen was scribbling energetically on her pad, taking down every word. The sight was infuriating. '. . . Considering the amount of money the company has expended on the horse and the assurances we were given as to its potential, we feel we must take closer control over its management.'

'What are you on about?' Malcolm was close to losing his temper. 'I made no assurances about Adolf.'

'I can distinctly recall you saying that an outlay of eighty thousand pounds would provide a horse capable of competing in the Grand National within two years.'

'I didn't say that!'

Beverley gave him a wintry smile. 'Now you can see why we need an official record.'

Malcolm charged on. 'Anyway, what do you mean by closer control over his management? Are you and Barney proposing to come down to the stables and muck him out?'

She appeared to take his suggestion seriously – she wasn't much of a one for jokes. 'No, that's not what we had in mind. To be specific, we want to select the date and nature of all Beaufort Bonanza's future races without obstruction from the trainer. Naturally we will take his opinion into account but only insofar as it relates to the horse's physical condition.'

'My father won't like that,' said Malcolm.

Beverley ignored the remark. 'We also require complete control over the selection of a jockey. And I can tell you that from now on, Jamie Sullivan won't be riding.'

Malcolm opened his mouth to protest then thought the better of it. He was being stitched up in here. 'Anything else?' he said.

'Not at present.' Beverley glanced at her watch and stood up. 'I'm so sorry, Malcolm, I'm afraid I'm out of time.'

Karen stood up too, a smile lurking in the corner of her mean little mouth.

What a pair of bitches.

Jane was well aware from her frequent conversations with Superintendent Keith Wright that her honeymoon period was over. The Bonfire Night investigation was stuck and her 'fresh thinking' had not produced results – yet. As if Wright's evident impatience wasn't plain enough, the whittling down of her team made it clear she was no longer flavour of the month. She'd already lost two DCs to more urgent matters and there was talk of closing down the incident room. Double murder or not, there was a limit to how many resources a moribund investigation could tie up.

In some respects Jane didn't mind the depletion of her forces. There was no point in having an army if you marched it in the wrong direction. And, for all Leighton Jones's flair, she wasn't convinced that he'd deployed his troops correctly.

Where had Pete got that money from?

The question nagged at her. It was fundamental to most investigations that the truth was entangled in the money trail. Arson was a case in point – a crime that boomed in times of economic depression when failing businesses went up in smoke in the hope of salvation from an insurance cheque. And though in this case the reason for the arson seemed plain – to obscure the murders – the mystery of Pete's carrier-bag of cash wouldn't go away.

Leighton's team had investigated Pete pretty thoroughly. He came from an Anglo-Ulster brewing family living on past glories. He'd been educated at English boarding schools and dropped out of university halfway through a History degree. He drifted into teaching and, when full-time jobs became insupportable, private tutoring arrangements. For the past few years he'd been technically unemployed, though the investigation had unearthed a couple of local families whose children he had helped with their studies. From their statements it appeared he did a reasonable job, even if he wasn't always guaranteed to turn up. These families and a handful of disreputable friends had been the only mourners at his funeral.

Jane was curious about Pete's own family. His parents were dead but it appeared that he had a brother and numerous aunts, uncles and cousins. A note in the file of a phone conversation with the brother supplied the information that the family had washed their hands of Pete years ago – and he of them.

There was one remaining family connection, however – a monthly payment of a thousand pounds, transferred from Ireland into his bank account. This, the enquiry had discovered, was Pete's share of the family fortune, left in trust for him by his grandfather. It explained how he had managed to pay his rent and keep his costly habits afloat while doing little beyond giving the odd private lesson and small-time drug-dealing.

Jane wondered how much good all those thousand-pound handouts had really done him. 'Poor little trust-fund boy,' she murmured to herself.

But suppose, out of these regular payments and his dealing, he'd managed to get a good stake together, could he not have won the money in a bet? Despite what the local bookies had said, Pete did follow the horses and, through Amanda, could maybe get some inside tips. Perhaps they'd amassed this money through clever gambling? That's what Leighton had thought – when he'd thought about it at all.

Jane still wasn't convinced. Wouldn't Pete have boasted to Filthy about a big win, given that he'd boasted about the change in his fortunes? Isn't that what gamblers did? She was hardly familiar with their psychology, however. Perhaps she really should go racing with Simon.

She pushed the thought out of her mind and turned to Amanda's finances. Her records had been found in the upstairs back room of the cottage where they had escaped damage from the fire. Jane found herself looking at the conventional paper-trail of a young woman's financial life – credit-card bills, reams of bank statements and a building society passbook. All the accounts except for the latter were in the red but that had not always been the case. It was clear where the rot had started to set in – six months before her death. Hello, Pete, goodbye cash, Jane thought. It was entirely predictable.

Until that point, it seemed, Amanda had skimmed along, just about keeping her head above water. There'd been regular incomings from her employer and what looked like outgoings on the usual living expenses, with the occasional plastic retail splurge. But the end of her employment had signalled an irreversible decline in her finances. The building society passbook told the most interesting story. Until the previous summer it had been healthily balanced, containing over £7000. Since then regular withdrawals had reduced the holdings to less than a hundred pounds. The bundle of cash that Filthy Barrable had seen was sorely needed.

Jane flicked back through the pages of the passbook, which revealed the entire history of the account. Amanda had opened it with a deposit of fifty pounds seven years ago. After that, she'd added small amounts each month of ten or twenty pounds. Jane assumed the money was saved out of her earnings, in the time-honoured fashion of the thrifty, as Amanda tried to scrape together a lump sum. At that rate, however, Jane wondered how Amanda had managed to get it up to seven grand.

She found the answer in an entry for October 1999 when Amanda had deposited the sum of £10,000. Where had that come from?

Jane glanced at her watch. Was twenty to six a bad time to ring Elizabeth Jacobs? It might be suppertime or bathtime or bedtime – on reflection, any time was bad. With three young children to care for there would always be a reason why a mother's attention was engaged elsewhere. She punched in the number.

The phone was picked up on the fifth ring. 'Hello,' said a small voice. Child noises could be heard in the background and singing – Jane recognised the soundtrack of *The Jungle Book*.

'May I speak to your mummy, please?'

'Hello,' said the voice. 'Hello.'

Was there something wrong with the line?

Jane repeated her question. The voice repeated the answer: 'Hello, hello, hello.'

Just as she was on the point of ringing off, a woman shouted down the line, 'Is that you, Cliff? Hurry up and come home – they're driving me round the twist.'

There was an embarrassed pause when Jane introduced herself. This was obviously not a good time to talk.

'Do you mind if I pop round tomorrow morning?' she asked. 'At half ten, say?'

'I can't guarantee we'll have the chance to—' Elizabeth broke off and shouted something. There was a crash in the background and Jane heard a wail go up. Elizabeth spoke urgently, 'That'll be fine. I've got to go.'

Another receiver was picked up elsewhere in the house. 'Hello,' said a little voice. 'Hello, hello, hello . . .'

Jane put down the phone.

Malcolm took up his station in the White Rose across the street from Beaufort Holidays. He swallowed a large scotch to soothe his nerves then nursed a pint at a table by the window. From there he could see directly into the staff car park. It was less full than it had been twenty minutes ago when most of the office drones had fled the premises on the dot of six. Barney Beaufort's Bentley was still in gleaming evidence and, two spaces down, so was Beverley's Citroën. Malcolm's chief concern was that the pair would exit together. He had to get Beverley on her own.

The office door opened and a solid figure, astrakhan overcoat belted against the winter chill, strode towards the Bentley – unaccompanied, thank God. At last something was going right.

Malcolm knew how Beverley operated. He reckoned she'd be another five minutes, ten at the most. In her scheme of things the appearance of endeavour was as important as the thing itself. She'd make a point of remaining at her desk while the boss was in the building and exit swiftly once he was out of the picture.

He was not disappointed. Six minutes after the Bentley had rolled out of the car park, Beverley was standing beside the Citroën, keys in her hand.

'Not so fast, Ms Harris,' Malcolm said as he stepped between her and the vehicle.

She didn't appear surprised to see him. 'You still lurking around, Malcolm? What do you want now?'

'What do you think, Beverley? I want an explanation of that charade this afternoon. Who the hell do you think you are – Pol Pot in high heels?'

She looked at him neutrally, her expression giving nothing away.

'Get in the car,' she ordered and opened the door. He did as he was told.

With exaggerated care, unlike her usual driving style, she backed out of the car park and drove a hundred yards down the road, drawing to a halt in a dark side street.

She removed her spectacles and placed them on top of the dashboard, then turned to face him.

'Beverley,' he began, 'just what the hell are you playing at?'

But he got no further before she threw herself on him, pulling his head down to hers and kissing him with an open mouth.

He tried to hold her off. He was still angry. He needed explanations, a chance to express his frustrations. But she was rubbing and stroking him, her tongue in his mouth, her leg across his lap.

At last she relaxed her grip and laid her head on his shoulder, her arm hugging his chest.

'I've been wanting to do that all afternoon,' she murmured.

'What stopped you? Karen could have entered it in the minutes.'

She giggled. 'There's security cameras in the car park. That's why I had to bring you here.'

She was fondling him again, gently but with purpose.

'Beverley, you crazy witch, let's go back to your place.'

'I can't wait that long.'

'There's hotels here in town.'

'Mmm, yeah.'

'Come on then, let's go. I'll drive.'

She released him and sat upright. 'Whatever you say, Malcolm. You're the boss.'

Hardly.

It was just her bad luck, thought Pippa, that the first person she ran into in the parade ring at Southwell racecourse was the one she'd most hoped to avoid: Arabella Childs. It had been more than six months since Mrs Childs' horse Black Knight had been removed from her yard but the manner of the defection still hurt. She'd seen Black Knight's name on the list of entries and, for one moment, had considered finding another race for May Day Warrior, her own horse. But she'd dismissed the thought at once. She was running a professional business and could hardly allow her own feelings to interfere.

Mrs Childs was preparing to walk past without acknowledging her but Pippa wasn't having that. 'How are things, Arabella?' she asked.

The other woman barely broke stride. 'I can't stop, darling,' she said, 'I must discuss strategy with Toby.'

Pippa was left standing open-mouthed.

Dave watched the smartly dressed older woman scuttle off and muttered in Pippa's ear, 'Must be her strategy for the post-race cocktail party.'

She found herself grinning stupidly. 'Please, Dave, don't make me laugh. Here come my owners.'

The connections of May Day Warrior, the two founders of a software company and their female partners, were walking across the ring towards them. The men provided a contrast in sizes.

'Blimey,' said Dave. 'Little and Large.'

'Don't, Dave,' she implored, biting back laughter. She couldn't think why she was behaving so frivolously. It must have something to do with her lanky escort and – a sobering thought – the fact that Jamie was not with them. It wasn't his fault but the gloom that dogged her brother was infectious.

The May Day Warrior group were a cheery lot, out to make a night of it. It was obvious that their high spirits had already been fuelled by a few drinks. Nevertheless, Pippa was preparing herself to answer some searching questions on the horse's prospects. He'd come second last time out and she remembered saying (foolishly) that he'd be a cert to win his next race. She wasn't looking forward to being reminded of this remark but was saved in an unexpected fashion.

Little, the small round one, was still pumping Dave's hand following Pippa's introduction. 'I don't believe it!' he cried. 'You're *the* Dave Prescott! I saw you break the UK record for the five thousand metres at Crystal Palace.'

Dave grinned modestly. 'That was back in the Dark Ages, mate.'

'Yeah, when we last had world-class distance runners. I was at school and you were my hero. Hey, everybody!'

Pippa watched with surprise and increasing pleasure as the group turned their attention to Dave. She knew the two men were sports nuts and the women, thrilled by the occasion, mobbed Dave too. In the excitement, May Day Warrior and his rider were given a cheerful send-off and nobody quizzed her about his prospects.

'Thanks, Dave,' she said to her companion as they made their way to the stand. 'You've made their evening, whatever happens in the race.'

Jamie could have accompanied Pippa and Dave to Southwell but the prospect of a four-hour round trip in the car hadn't thrilled him. The fact was, the fall he'd had at Carlisle had shaken him up more than he cared to admit. Apart from the bruises, it had revived some aches and pains that dated back to his car crash.

He'd been dozing on the sofa, so when the phone rang it took him some while to lever his aching body upright and answer it.

'Are you all right, Jamie? You sound half dead.'

'I'm fine, Ros.' He wasn't going to admit to anyone, least of all her, that he was in pain. He'd just earned Brownie points for courage and didn't intend to lose them.

'Jamie . . .' She paused, for once sounding uncertain. 'Do you like music? Orchestral music, that is.'

'Yes,' he said without thinking. 'At least, I like it but I don't know much about it.'

You liar. You know nothing about it.

'I need an escort tomorrow night to accompany me to a concert. It's a private affair with some friends. Would you be interested?'

'Yes,' he said and instantly regretted it. He'd be stuck with a load of toffs, listening to music he didn't understand, while his aching body played a different kind of tune. 'Thanks, Ros, I'd love to.'

Now why on earth had he said that?

As the horses took their places on the far side of the course for the start of the race, Pippa's light-hearted mood evaporated. Through binoculars, she watched Black Knight being herded into his stall with a sour taste in her mouth. He had been one of her favourites and she knew she'd done a good job on him, nursing him through one niggle after another yet still producing him fit on race days. He'd won for her at Lingfield and been placed on three other occasions, which wasn't bad. If it hadn't been for Toby she was sure she'd be saddling him for this race. It wasn't fair.

Dave gave her an encouraging grin which she did her best to return. On the journey down she'd given him the background to the race.

'Basically, Dave, I used to train Black Knight alongside May Day Warrior and there was no doubt that the Warrior was the better horse. I'd never dream of entering them in the same race. But Black Knight's done well since Toby took him over. He won at Wolverhampton and the handicapper has raised him twelve pounds. So today's a big test. If Black Knight's really improved that much then I'll *know* I'm not that good at my job.'

Dave had listened without comment and then indicated the intricate timepiece on his wrist. 'You want me to put a stopwatch on them?' he'd asked, which was about the most useful suggestion he could make. Why hadn't she thought of that?'

The horses set off at a steady pace. With two miles ahead of them – one and a half circuits of the all-weather track – there was no need for anyone to go mad. Considering its class, there were some reasonable animals in the race but Pippa calculated that May Day Warrior was as good as any of them. The runners passed the stands and the winning post for the first time and headed out into the country, the Warrior lying fourth out of the eight runners, well placed on the rail, with Black Knight just behind him.

She wondered if Black Knight's jockey – her brother-in-law Richard – was deliberately tracking her horse. The pair of them seemed glued together all the way down the far side of the course. With ten furlongs gone some of the runners were flagging and the leading three began to come back to May Day Warrior. Rounding the top bend he cruised into the lead and entered the home straight five lengths clear.

As was her habit, Pippa found herself hopping up and down, her body a singing jangle of nerves as she willed her horse home. But though he'd left the rest of the field in his wake the Warrior had not yet beaten Black Knight. The two horses were level coming out of the bend with the long home straight in front of them.

Up on the gallops at home, Pippa knew that the Warrior would have burned off the other horse with ease. So it was with disbelief that she watched Richard put his foot down on Black Knight and ease smoothly to the front, taking the horse away from his erstwhile stable companion with each stride.

The victory margin was four lengths.

In bed at the Starlighter Hotel three miles down the road from Beaufort Holidays, Malcolm could tell that Beverley was becoming restless. She lay curled up in his arms, her back to him spoon-fashion, so he couldn't read her face as she murmured, 'I can't stay the night here, you know.'

'You women are all the same. You take what you want from a man, then leave him high and dry.'

'I'm serious, Malcolm. The staff know me in here – we use their meeting rooms for conferences sometimes. I can't be seen checking out with you in the morning.'

He took her point. He also ought to be a bit circumspect. Shacking up with a woman twenty minutes from the marital home wasn't the smartest way to behave. However, it was still a bit early – Pippa wouldn't be back from Southwell till late.

He kissed the nape of her neck, then nuzzled lower, teasing the top vertebra of her spine. She arched back against him – so she was still in the mood.

'I'm not letting you go just yet. Not after the grilling you gave me this afternoon.'

'I was only doing my job.'

'You're not saying you were serious?'

She turned on to her back and looked him in the face. 'I certainly was.'

'So Barney really wants to choose the races and give Jamie the boot?'

'Too right.'

Up close her milky blue eyes seemed bottomless.

'You have the most beautiful eyes.'

'Don't try and change the subject. You've got to do something about that horse, Malcolm. If it doesn't win soon Barney's going to want his money back.'

'Beverley, you know it doesn't work like that. I can't make the horse win.'

'Well, at least get it to finish – preferably in the first three. And you can get rid of that jockey with a criminal record. It's not good for the company image. Anyway, he's not much cop – even your father says so.'

Malcolm wasn't going to argue the point. He had more pressing matters on his mind.

'OK, Ms Harris. I agree on one condition.'

Her mouth pursed in suspicion. 'What's that?'

'You wear your glasses while I shag you rotten.'

Pippa didn't know how she would have survived the rest of the evening if it hadn't been for Dave. She wasn't the tearful sort but for a second, as he put a consoling arm around her shoulder, she felt like shedding a bucket-load.

Dave peered into her face, obviously gauging the extent of her distress. If, as others had done after a painful loss, he'd made sympathetic noises she'd have punched him. 'Never mind,' 'It's just one race', 'Better luck next time,' and all other well-meaning banalities made her puke. It implied that this defeat didn't matter and that there were more important things in life. Well, there weren't – not the way she felt right now.

'I don't understand. How could Black Knight run like that?'

He propelled her through the crowd. 'Let's save the postmortem till we've seen off Little and Large, OK?'

She nodded agreement and steeled herself for a conversation with the owners. Surely they'd be fed up too, having just seen their runner left for dead by a horse with an inferior ranking?

But if the owners felt that way they never said so, being jollied along by Dave once more as he congratulated them on coming second to a great performance by the winner.

'I got skinned by Seb Coe in a fifteen hundred metres once,' he confided. 'It was just like that. We were stride for stride into the home straight and then he turned on the after-burners. Beat me by about the same distance as Black Knight.'

Which neatly turned the conversation away from horse racing and on to athletics. Pippa scarcely had to say a word.

Later, nursing a glass of wine in the bar, she said, 'Is that true about Seb Coe?'

'Certainly is.'

'How did you feel when he beat you like that?'

'I was pig sick for about half an hour. Then I realised that he was better than I was.'

'But I'm sure Black Knight is *not* better than May Day Warrior.' She drained her glass. 'What were the times?'

He pulled an envelope from his pocket and showed her the figures he'd noted down. Black Knight: 3 minutes 50.2. May Day Warrior: 3 minutes 51.9.

'That's ridiculous,' she exclaimed. 'Black Knight's not four lengths better.'

'Maybe the other one had an off day.'

She shook her head. 'The Warrior's done pretty much what I'd expect. That's a good time for him around here. But Black Knight's improved again. Damn!' She slammed her hand on the table top, causing a few heads to turn.

Dave put a big hand on top of hers. 'Steady, girl, you'll get us chucked out.'

'It just makes me mad to see Toby take my horses and turn them round like that. I've got to do something.'

'That's why I'm here, isn't it?' He drained his orange juice with a flourish. 'Just you wait till I've finished with my lot. Suppose I improve them by two seconds too?'

She knew from the way he looked at her that he was only trying to cheer her up but it wasn't going to work. If Dave, who knew nothing about racing, could make her horses run faster then it would only demonstrate what she feared above all – that she was no damn good as a trainer.

She sighed. It was heartfelt. 'Would you like to drive my car, Dave?'

'No problem.' He pointed to her glass. He was getting good at reading her mind.

'Make it a large one,' she said.

Chapter Eight

Jane was kitted out for battle for her second visit to Elizabeth Jacobs' family compound. She was armed with a Disney video, a bumper pack of animal-shaped sweets and – her big guns – a selection of Danish pastries from a fancy cake shop. Based on observations from her first visit, when she'd seen Elizabeth popping leftovers into her mouth as she cleared the kids' tea, she had a hunch her plump hostess possessed a sweet tooth.

Though these precautionary offerings were accepted with gratitude and some surprise, they turned out to be unnecessary. This time help was at hand to keep the children at bay. In the kitchen, supervising a boiling kettle, was a middle-aged woman whom Elizabeth introduced as her mother-in-law. The lady was smartly dressed and icily polite. Jane wouldn't mind betting that she was not overjoyed at the circumstances of this social occasion. But then, who would be?

Elizabeth's mother-in-law served them coffee on a tray in the front room. She closed the door firmly behind her when she left, shutting out all possible interruption. What a relief.

'I've been trying to build up a picture of Amanda's life,' said Jane as Elizabeth pored over the plate of Danish pastries. 'I'm interested to see what she was like before she got involved with Pete.'

'She was a healthy, hardworking, funloving girl before she met that creep,' replied Elizabeth with venom and snapped her teeth into a gooey apricot slice.

'I can see that.' To show willing, Jane cut a corner off her Danish and nibbled at it. 'She was in full employment till a few months before her death, wasn't she?'

Elizabeth nodded, her jaw working.

'And I see from her building society records that she used to put aside a few pounds every month.'

Elizabeth's eating rhythm slowed and a furrow appeared on her smooth wide forehead. It was clear she wasn't sure where this was going.

Jane nibbled some more. 'Do you know if she ever came by more substantial amounts of money?'

'Stable girls don't earn substantial amounts. Mandy only did it because she loved horses.' Elizabeth had finished her pastry. She selected another, a currant whirl with icing. 'I think she earned tips though.'

'What for?'

'If one of the horses she looked after did well, the owners would tip her. Or if it was the best turned-out horse in a race she might get something.'

'How much money would that be?'

Elizabeth paused mid-bite. 'You're not working for the Inland Revenue on the side, are you?'

Jane shook her head. Perish the thought.

'She might get fifty pounds. A hundred maybe.'

'How about a few thousand?'

Elizabeth laughed, spraying crumbs. 'You're joking! My sister barely earned a thousand a month.'

Jane lifted her briefcase on to her lap and opened it. 'How would you account, then, for the ten thousand pounds she paid into her building society in October 1999?'

The laughter froze on Elizabeth's face. 'She never had that amount of money in her life.'

Jane passed her photocopied pages of the passbook and indicated the entry.

Elizabeth stared at it for a long time. At last she said, 'I didn't know about this.'

'Can you think of any way she could have come by such a sum? An inheritance, perhaps? Or a gift from someone in the family?'

Elizabeth shook her head vigorously. 'There's been nothing like that in our family. I'd have known about it.'

'Maybe she won it on a horse?'

'I doubt it. She used to give us tips but most of them were rotten. She thought every horse she worked with was going to win though they rarely did.'

'So she could have backed a winner?'

'Not on that scale. She'd never bet more than a tenner.' Elizabeth attacked her currant whirl again. 'God knows how she got that money. She never said a word to me about it. What do you want to know for anyway?'

That was a good question. Jane wasn't entirely sure herself. She decided to be honest.

'At present we're not making much progress with this enquiry and so I'm trying to explore all avenues that are available. We believe the motive for the murders was robbery. It seems, as I'm sure DCI Jones told you, that there was a substantial amount of cash in the cottage before the fire, at least twenty or thirty thousand pounds. Since the money is missing, it is reasonable to assume that whoever killed Amanda and Pete and set the fire, also took the cash.'

Elizabeth had polished off her second pastry by now and was wiping icing from her fingers. She put down the paper serviette. 'I thought it was a rival drug gang. I went through all this with Mr Jones – and with you last time. I suppose you're going to start going on about old boyfriends again. I can't say I'm very impressed, Inspector Culpepper. It's obvious who did it but you don't have enough evidence so you're barking up any old tree. And all this about Mandy's building society is a complete red herring.'

Jane regretted trying to take Elizabeth into her confidence. And bringing those pastries wasn't such a bright idea either. The poor woman, obviously upset, was starting on her third. It was like bringing a bottle when you visited an alcoholic – it didn't do them any favours.

She ploughed on, however. 'I understand your concern, Mrs Jacobs, and it may well be that you are right. My point is that a large sum of money was in their possession. I'd like to know how they got hold of it – even if only to complete our knowledge.'

'Not "they",' said Elizabeth vehemently. 'Pete had the money, he got it through dealing drugs. It was nothing to do with Mandy.'

Jane thought of Filthy Barrable's story – of how Amanda had shouted at Pete for not putting the money in a safe place. So she knew about the cash and was anxious for it to be hidden. Even if Pete had acquired it, she had a stake in its ownership.

'We can't be sure about that. It's one of the reasons why I'd like to account for the ten thousand pounds your sister came by a couple of

147

years ago. Maybe it's got nothing to do with the current circumstances but I'd like to be able to rule it out. Any light you can shed would be helpful.'

'Well, I can tell you one thing,' Elizabeth muttered begrudgingly. 'October 1999 is when she left Yorkshire. She stopped working at Ridgemoor and found a job in Lancashire.'

At last, some kind of response to her plea for information.

The door opened and Mrs Jacobs senior stepped in. 'More coffee?'

'Yes, please,' said Jane quickly. It had been hard work so far and she wasn't going anywhere in a hurry.

From the window of his small office at Ridgemoor Malcolm peered across the yard to the main building, an imposing old farmhouse where his father lived. These days it housed Toby's own luxurious suite of offices but it had once been the family home. After the departure of the third Mrs Priest Toby had spent a fortune remodelling the interior to suit his new lifestyle as businessman bachelor. God knows, Malcolm reflected, how he'd managed to afford it. But Toby, often thanks to his well-connected owners, had always been able to lay his hands on money.

Ros Bradey's car was still in the drive, which was a nuisance as Malcolm needed an urgent private word with his father. If the old man was romancing La Bradey – and who could blame him? – then he could be left twiddling his thumbs for a long while. On the other hand, he knew his father had a lunch meeting at Doncaster, in which case his tête-à-tête with Ros would not be prolonged. She'd been in there for the best part of an hour already.

Malcolm headed across the yard, impatient to get his chore over and done with.

He met Ros emerging from the front door. She didn't look as if she'd just disentangled herself from the arms of a lover. Her hair was piled on her head in an elaborate arrangement and she wore jodhpurs and brightly polished riding boots. And her manner was curt. She managed a tight smile as he held the door open for her. 'Good morning, Malcolm,' she said, adding, 'and good luck,' as she strode past.

What did she mean by that? he wondered as he admired her retreating rear view in an impersonal fashion. He'd often been intrigued by his father's women, and had a bit of luck with them on occasion. Right now, however, his hands were far too full even if he were so inclined.

'Hi, Dad,' he said as he entered the main office at the back of the house. It had been extended into the garden with a long glass window that gave onto a panoramic view of the Ridgemoor gallops and the hills beyond. First-time visitors were always impressed by the spectacular vista. Malcolm barely gave it a glance.

Toby was standing by his desk, hands in his pockets. He grunted a greeting.

So that was the reason for Ros's remark. His father was in a mood. For a second Malcolm considered postponing his conversation but dismissed the thought – he'd been waiting half the morning for this opportunity after all.

'Got a moment, Dad?'

Toby made a show of looking at his watch. 'I've got to be out of here in ten minutes. Talk to me while I get changed.'

Malcolm followed his father upstairs and into the room he used as a dressing-room. A suit and shirt had been laid out for him – the work of the live-in housekeeper, Janet. Malcolm stole a quick look into his father's bedroom and noted that Janet had been at work there too. The bed looked as if it had been made according to military regulations – further proof, if needed, that no hanky-panky had been taking place.

'I saw Ros as I came in,' Malcolm ventured. 'How's it going with her?'

His father gave him a sour look. 'Mind your own business.'

'Actually it is my business. That is, if you decide to marry her.'

Toby stopped in the act of unzipping his trousers. 'Who said anything about marriage?'

'I'm just thinking ahead. I know what you're like when you can't get them to drop their knickers. That's why you married the last one.'

Toby's marriage five years ago to wife number three had lasted not much more than a couple of years, enduring just as long as his interest in her willowy body. Subsequently the attempts of the lady in question – a widowed society hostess – to 'sophisticate' the horse trainer had foundered in predictable acrimony.

'You've got a bloody cheek,' Toby muttered, pulling on his clean shirt.

Malcolm felt better after this exchange. Sex was one of the few topics in which he felt the equal of his father. The pair of them shared the same acquisitive attitudes. Toby had bought Malcolm the services of a pretty tart for the night of his sixteenth birthday and had been amused, years later, to hear that Malcolm had lost his virginity two years before that memorable evening. The same birthday gift laid on for Malcolm's stepbrother Richard had traumatised him for weeks. Malcolm and Toby still liked to tease him about it.

Now was Malcolm's chance. 'About Adolf, Dad . . .'

Toby groaned. 'Not now, for God's sake. I spend more time discussing that animal than any other in my yard.'

'I know, but this is important.'

'Not to me it isn't. Don't ask me to spend another afternoon sucking up to that clown Beaufort. I've done my bit and you can deal with him yourself from now on.'

'I will, I promise. It's just that I've had a meeting with Beverley Harris about Carlisle and—'

Toby cut him off again. 'Beverley Harris is a bitch. Nice arse on her but complete poison.'

'If you say so, Dad.'

The trainer was fiddling with a cufflink but his eyes were on Malcolm, probing his face. 'You've not been playing away with her, have you?' he said shrewdly.

'We just have a business arrangement.'

'Rubbish – I can read you like a book. You're a fool, Malcolm. You've a damn fine woman of your own at home and it's about time you put her in the club, instead of mucking around with a ball-breaker like Beverley bloody Harris.'

'She's not going to break my balls, I promise. And don't worry, we'll be calling you Grandad soon. Pippa and I are working on it.'

Toby glared at him then resumed fumbling with his cufflink.

'Here, Dad, I'll do that.'

Toby allowed his son to take charge of his wrist. 'So, what do the Beaufort lot want now, then?'

'A new jockey and they pick the next race – subject to Adolf's fitness.'

The trainer shrugged. 'Is that all?' The sarcasm was heavy.

'He's got to win next time.'

'Tell me something new.'

'Seriously, Dad, he's got to finish in the frame at least.'

Toby put on his jacket and looked at himself in the full-length mirror that fronted the wardrobe. He looked distinguished. Respectable. Not the sort of man who'd dope horses.

'Can you do something?' Malcolm ventured. He didn't want to beg but his father was quite capable of making him do so.

'I'll think about it,' said Toby.

'Please, Dad. I'd be really grateful.'

'Huh.' Toby headed for the door. 'It's not *that* nice an arse, you know,' was his parting shot.

Jane smiled encouragingly at Elizabeth and sipped her fresh cup of coffee. 'Do you know why Amanda left her job at Ridgemoor?'

'She found a better one.'

'In what way?'

'You know, more responsibility, more money. We were sorry she went – we didn't see her so often. We also lost our best babysitter.'

'So she left of her own free will?'

'Of course. Well, as far as I know. Why is it important?'

'I was just wondering. If she were made redundant, for example, there could have been a lump sum of severance pay. Which might account for the ten thousand pounds.'

'Oh.' Elizabeth looked unimpressed. 'I don't think you've got much of an idea how things work in horse racing. I doubt if stable girls are ever made redundant. And if they are, they'd be lucky to get their bus fare and a bag of horse nuts.'

Jane had no doubt Elizabeth was right. The timing of Amanda's change of job and her windfall of £10,000 must be entirely coincidental. Reluctantly she changed the subject.

'I made enquiries about Amanda's photos, as you requested.'

'Yes?'

It was a shame to dash her hopes. 'I'm sorry, Mrs Jacobs, but we're positive they were destroyed in the fire. We can identify the remains of the tin they were kept in from the crime-scene photographs.'

'Oh.' Elizabeth opened her mouth to add something, then stopped. Jane could see she was making an effort to control her feelings. Eventually she said, 'That's a pity.' It was evidently more than that.

'But you do have photographs of your sister, don't you?'

Elizabeth nodded.

On impulse, Jane asked, 'May I see them?' It didn't seem right to get up and leave at this point.

Elizabeth left the room and returned with some green photo-developers' envelopes. 'I always mean to put them in albums,' she said, 'but I never get round to it.'

She began to pass Jane the snaps one by one, with a word of explanation on each. There were several different batches, taken on occasions during the past three or four years: in a playground with the kids, a Christmas meal, on the moors with a child in a backpack.

Jane recognised a couple of the shots – Elizabeth must have supplied them to help the investigation. But here were more of Amanda larking around with the children, pulling a squiffy face as she posed with a glass of wine, cradling a sleeping baby. It struck Jane that Amanda was more than pretty. Everyone in the pictures, from the children to adults such as Elizabeth's mother-in-law, looked at her with adoration. How they must have enjoyed her visits.

Elizabeth's commentary had dried up.

'You must miss her so much,' said Jane. It was a thoughtless remark but something personal needed to be said. It was hard to look at these happy family snapshots of a lost loved one and not empathise.

Elizabeth made no sound but began to weep openly. The tears ran silently down her face in a curtain and she made no effort to stem them. Jane took a bundle of paper tissues from the packet she carried in her briefcase and offered them to the distressed woman. Elizabeth ignored them and instead, grasped Jane's hand.

They sat like that for what seemed an age, Jane leaning forward awkwardly, her fingers held fast in the younger woman's painful grip, as her grief overflowed. At last the tears stopped, as suddenly as a tap being shut off, and Jane's hand was released.

'I'll be all right now,' said Elizabeth in a matter-of-fact tone, wiping her face. 'Sometimes it just has to come out. Though I try not to cry in front of the kids.' She blew her nose loudly.

'They still don't know she's dead. I bought them Christmas presents from Mandy and said she'd gone away for a while – like their Auntie Jo.'

'Do you get any help?'

'You mean counselling? Or grief-management?' There was contempt in her voice. 'No, thank you very much.'

'I was thinking more of Victim Support. Of talking to other people in the same situation. That might help.'

Elizabeth began to gather together the photographs now scattered across the table. 'We're having a memorial service for Mandy – will you come?'

'I'd like to very much.'

'I'll send you the details.' She was organising the photos into piles and putting them into the correct envelopes. 'I want to get as many of her old workmates as possible. So few people from Ridgemoor could get to the funeral. That bastard Toby Priest wouldn't give them the time off work.'

'Who's Toby Priest?'

Elizabeth picked up an envelope, one Jane had not looked through, and pulled out a photograph. 'That's him.'

Jane examined the shot. It showed a group of men, many of them stripped to the waist in the sunshine, waving at the camera. They looked sweaty and red-faced and one had his foot on a ball.

Elizabeth was pointing to an older man standing at the rear. He was square-jawed and his well-cut hair was streaked with grey. He posed with a whistle to his lips. Jane thought he looked familiar.

'Toby's the most successful horse trainer in the north,' added Elizabeth. 'Ridgemoor's his yard.'

That explained why Jane knew the face. He must crop up regularly in the news.

'What's this about?' she asked.

'The Ridgemoor lads played a lot of football. Toby sometimes used to referee.'

'And Amanda watched?'

'Mandy and some of the other girls used to go along.'

Jane reached for the other photos in the batch. It was interesting to get a glimpse into Amanda's working life. The three other photos in the envelope were identical.

'Are there any others of the yard?' she asked. 'These are all the same.'

'The rest were destroyed – that's what you just told me. These are the ones I got out of the developers with the ticket I found in her handbag.'

Jane remembered now. 'Why do you think she made copies of this particular photo?'

Elizabeth shrugged. 'All I can think of is that she wanted to give them to some of the lads.'

'But this must have been taken a while ago. She left Ridgemoor over two years before her death. Why do it after all that time?'

Elizabeth sighed. 'I like to think that she'd decided to get in touch with her old life again. You know, to ditch Pete and drugs and get back with her old friends. Do you think that's possible, Jane?'

It was the first time she'd used her Christian name. Jane was touched. She put her hand on Elizabeth's arm. 'Of course,' she said.

It was time to go. As Jane stood she picked up one of the football photos. 'May I borrow this?'

'Keep it,' said Elizabeth. 'I've got plenty.'

Many things about the evening ahead with Ros unnerved Jamie. The prospect of mingling with a cultured set of people and responding to music he didn't understand was part of it. In his days as a Flat jockey he'd mixed unselfconsciously with all types, particularly the wealthy horse-owning set. But he'd been a different person back then – young, brash and successful. Two and a half years down the track, Jamie's life was in bits and putting it back together was a struggle. He said as much to Dave.

The runner seemed surprised by Jamie's attitude. 'You're looking at it from the wrong perspective, mate. This is not some terrible ordeal you've got to survive – it's an opportunity to show people that you're alive and kicking.'

Jamie had not been convinced. 'They're all going to know I've been to jail for killing some poor kid. Half of them are going to hate me.'

'Maybe, but you've got to learn to live with that. Don't forget that most of them are probably damn lucky they're not standing in your shoes. I bet if anyone has a go at you they'll have a drink in their hand.'

Jamie smiled. Dave was probably right. He'd also put his finger on something Jamie was painfully aware of. Back in the old days, when he'd breezed through evenings like this, he'd been high on whatever he'd been able to lay his hands on. No wonder he'd not had a care in the world then – he'd been out of his mind. In prison he'd sworn to himself never to do drink and drugs again – and he'd stuck to it. He might nurse a glass of wine for show but that's all it was. The consequence was that he would have to face the evening ahead stone cold sober.

And he'd be in the company of Ros. That was his other cause of anxiety. Why had she invited him? Did she really like him, as Dave said? Till the other day he'd found her forbidding and cold. Those deep brown eyes observed him dispassionately, probing for every little fault in his riding. And that full pink mouth had simply nagged at him, barking orders, permanently turned down in displeasure. Physically attractive she might be, but he'd long come to the conclusion that the only thing she was passionate about was doing her job. Now he just didn't know.

Dave, naturally, had a go at him about his 'date'.

'It's not a date,' Jamie protested. 'She's got to go with someone and I'm just filling in.'

'You're squiring the lady to a romantic musical evening. Sounds like a date to me.'

But Jamie was grateful for Dave's interest in some respects.

'How are you getting to this concert?' he asked.

'Ros is going to drive.'

Dave shook his head. 'Not a good idea. I know you're banned but you've got to lay on the transport. Save her from the hassle. Then she can have a drop of vino if she wants – and reckon you're a considerate geezer for taking over the responsibility.'

Jamie wished he'd thought of that but was quick to take the advice. He'd tracked down a quality car service and hired their most luxurious vehicle for the evening. Then he'd taken great pleasure in overriding Ros's protests when he'd phoned to tell her he was arranging the transport.

'I don't mind driving,' she'd said. 'But if you insist . . .'

He'd insisted.

So now, as she emerged from the front door of her house, her face registered surprise as she saw the Mercedes saloon. The uniformed chauffeur had asked Jamie if he'd like him to wear his cap and Jamie had said yes.

Ros giggled. 'I'm very impressed,' she said, but the smile on her face was one of simple amusement. Had he done something wrong?

He was wearing a smartly pressed suit – Pippa had supervised the acquisition of a new wardrobe – and his tie matched the midnight-blue handkerchief that peeked from his top pocket.

'You look extremely smart,' Ros said. 'I feel positively under-dressed.'

Beneath her overcoat she wore a pale eau de nil sweater over a black pencil skirt. She had good legs – he'd never seen them before – and her hair hung loose for once, in a thick treacle-brown cloud. She looked great but she was not dressed for a gala evening.

The chauffeur held the door open for her and Ros settled herself appreciatively into the leather-upholstered seat. She was still grinning to herself.

'Where to, sir?' asked the chauffeur, turning in his seat.

'Clayton Valley Girls' School, please,' said Ros.

To his credit the driver registered no surprise. 'Certainly, madam,' he said and swung the car effortlessly out of the drive.

'It's a Year Ten concert,' she added for Jamie's benefit. 'My friend's daughter has a solo.' She put a hand on the sleeve of his silky new suit. 'I'm sorry, it's not exactly Glyndebourne.'

Jamie grinned, putting on as brave a face as he could manage.

He felt a complete prat.

Though not quite what he was expecting, Jamie's evening was far from a disaster. The school buildings lay between wooded slopes and acres of green meadow marked out for games. The Mercedes purred through the grounds to a conspicuous spot in the car park, where it drew a degree of attention from the girls in their blue-and-white school uniforms. The chauffeur – John, as had now been established – attracted even more, which he appeared to enjoy hugely.

Ros soon located her friends, a middle-aged couple with a distracted air. He gathered that Tom was some kind of doctor and Joanna he recognised as a show-jumper he'd seen on television. Thankfully they seemed to have no idea who he was.

'Quick, let's get a seat,' Joanna cried, the moment the introductions were made. 'I have to be near the front.'

'Madam's more nervous than Poppy,' muttered Tom as they followed his wife through the crowd of other mums and dads and mutinous-looking younger brothers.

They found places with a reasonable sightline to a stage on which the members of the school orchestra were arranging their music and unpacking their instruments. Jamie assumed that the large airy hall was used for school assemblies and a familiar dread gripped him as he sank onto the hard, straight-backed seat. His memories of such gatherings were shaped by boredom and, right now, he expected more of the same.

To his surprise, the evening passed swiftly as the orchestra lurched and sawed through a series of short pieces, each featuring a different soloist. Beside him, Ros provided a quick commentary on the music and the ability of the performers, which helped. Some of them, in Jamie's opinion, seemed remarkably good – but what did he know?

Poppy – Tom and Joanna's daughter – was on last. She was a sulky-looking dark-haired girl who, as she took her place at the piano, managed to give the impression she had done everyone a favour simply by turning up. She started hesitantly and there was a collective wince from her parents as she hit a wrong note.

'It's a rather ambitious piece,' Ros whispered in Jamie's ear.

He saw a flash of anger cross the girl's face, as if she were aware she wasn't doing herself justice. The sulky selfconsciousness vanished as she began to focus. Suddenly she was switched on, the notes rippling around the hall, the sound of the orchestra swelling behind her. Even Jamie could tell that this was music-making of a different order to what had gone before.

He watched the intensity on the girl's face as she played and recognised it. She was bringing all her doubt and dissatisfaction and adolescent anger to bear on the one special talent she possessed. He remembered doing just the same when he was her age, when he'd first begun race riding. As the music drove on, transporting everyone in the hall, Jamie knew he had to recapture some of the old passion. He'd turned into such a dreary stick since the accident – scared of life, playing it safe, afraid to trust in himself. God, if a fifteen-year-old schoolgirl could make music like this, then he could damn well win some horse races!

Poppy earned thunderous applause – even from the legion of younger brothers. She looked flushed and happy as she took her bow, trans-formed from the disgruntled child who had taken the stage. Her parents, too, were changed people. Tom's smile embraced the whole room and Joanna couldn't stop talking.

'I was convinced she was going to blow it. When she fluffed those notes at the beginning! My heart was in my mouth.'

They were swept along in the departing throng, back to the car park. 'What was that piece of music?' Jamie asked Ros.

'The first movement from Rachmaninov's second piano concerto. It's lovely, isn't it?'

'Yes.' Something was nagging at Jamie. A familiar phrase was repeating itself in his head. Suddenly he remembered where he'd heard the melody before. 'You can play it too, can't you?'

She stared at him. 'How do you know that?'

He grinned. 'I heard it standing at your front door, the first time I came to your yard.'

'Oh.' It was the first time he'd seen her unsure of herself. 'I wish I could play it like Poppy,' she said at last.

The young lady herself appeared at that moment, seemingly still punch drunk from her performance and the acclaim of those around. Jamie added his congratulations but her eyes did not meet his as she shook his hand; they were on John the chauffeur standing beside the Mercedes.

Jamie had a brainwave. Ros had explained that the five of them were going back to Tom and Joanna's house for a celebratory supper. Jamie ushered Poppy towards the Merc.

'Special transport for the star of the show,' he said.

John opened the rear door with a flourish.

'Oh gosh,' said Poppy, 'really?' and jumped inside without being asked twice.

'Well, that's made her night,' Tom said to Jamie. 'We'll see you back at our place,' and he steered his wife towards a mud-streaked Volvo further down the row.

Though Jamie enjoyed the rest of the evening, he couldn't work out why he had been asked along. Ros plainly knew the family well and hardly needed an escort, and it wasn't as if he was being paraded as a new boyfriend – not that he knew of, anyway. Only when Poppy, tired and squiffy after too much cake and a celebratory glass of champagne, had been persuaded to go to bed, did things become clearer.

'Have you told Jamie about Gates of Eden?' Joanna said to Ros as she emptied the wine bottle into her glass.

Ros shook her head. 'He's your horse. I'm leaving it to you.'

Jamie wondered if he'd heard correctly. 'What's this?' he said. 'I know Gates of Eden. I rode him for Toby.'

The last time had been the day he'd won the Diadem Stakes on Morwenstow. Gates of Eden had been his only ride that day where he'd not finished in the first three. He remembered the horse well – a big solid grey with a nice nature, but not quite quick enough for the company he'd been keeping that day at Ascot.

'You didn't own him back then, did you?' Jamie recalled an American woman in the ring beside Toby at Ascot. She'd almost lost her hat in the breeze as it whipped across the parade ground.

'No. I bought him from Mrs Truscott before she went back to the States.'

Mrs Truscott. He remembered her now. She'd told him he looked cute in his riding britches. She was nothing like Joanna.

'I was really after his stable companion who has the making of a show-jumper, but Mrs Truscott would only sell them as a pair. I thought I'd get rid of Gates of Eden but he'd strained a tendon and by the time I'd got him sound I couldn't bear to. He's a bit of an indulgence, really.'

'You said it,' added Tom.

Ros stepped in quickly. 'Joanna wants to try him over hurdles and she's asked me to school him. Given your past history, we wondered if you'd like to help.'

'You bet,' said Jamie, almost before the words were out of her mouth. Gates of Eden had been a real trier – maybe racing over obstacles would suit him. The feel of that broad-backed powerhouse beneath him stuck in his mind. 'I'd love to sit on him again anyway.'

Joanna beamed. 'We were hoping you were going to say that.'

'There's a problem with Gates of Eden,' said Ros as John drove them back to her house. 'I didn't want to raise it with Joanna. Come in for some coffee and I'll tell you. And I'm sure our chauffeur has had enough of us for the night. I can run you home later.'

As Jamie paid John off he looked at him closely, trying to read his expression. There was definitely a knowing twinkle in his eye as he wished Jamie good night. Since when had an invitation to have coffee come to mean something else?

Apart from that glimpse down the hall a few months ago, this was the first time Ros had allowed Jamie to see into her home. As she ushered him through into the kitchen at the back, he had the impression of antique furniture and walls full of pictures, a wood-framed settee with white lace headrests, vases of flowers and overflowing bookshelves. The kitchen was similarly cluttered with china on display and a fruit bowl on the square pine table.

Jamie watched Ros as she put on the kettle and ground coffee beans. She seemed to him such a mass of alluring contradictions. Though she worked with horses, no one could ever call her 'horsey'. And despite her country occupation, here in her home, surrounded by her books and paintings, she seemed more of a sophisticated city-dweller. This evening, the stableyard martinet had been replaced by a good-humoured and sympathetic companion. A glamorous one too.

Jamie was well aware he'd been hiding from his feelings. He'd made no attempt to make new friends since he'd left prison. He'd certainly not sought out any women. His sensual life was frozen in time, two and half years in the past. Back then he'd been a greedy, hell-raising kid, joy-riding through life without thought for the consequences. And when it had all gone smash he'd tried to distance himself as much as possible from his old self.

But that wasn't the answer either. The passions that had once inspired him were still there and, like Poppy and her piano-playing, he had to find a means of expressing them. He had to take risks again. To ride fast horses. To find a woman – one woman, not a succession of needy girls – and involve her in his life.

Ros, for instance?

She set his coffee in front of him and sat next to him at the table.

'What would your sister say to stabling Gates of Eden?' she asked.

He wrenched his thoughts back to the business at hand. He was puzzled by her question. 'Can't you keep him here?'

'Not if he's going to be entered for a race. I don't have a trainer's licence.'

Of course, the horse could only run from a registered yard.

'Isn't Ridgemoor a better bet? The Colonel's got a few jumpers already. Pippa only has Flat runners.'

'I talked to Toby about it this morning, but . . .' the full pink lips turned down '. . . we couldn't agree terms. I can speak to your sister directly though it might be better coming from you.'

Jamie thought about it. He liked the idea of bringing some business into Pippa's yard and he knew she had some empty boxes.

'What about schooling him? Pippa's not set up for that.'

'You're close to a schooling ground, aren't you?'

Jamie hadn't thought of that. Many people took their horses to the public facility just down the road.

'I'll talk to her tomorrow,' he said. 'Sounds like a good idea to me.'

She smiled. 'Excellent.' Then her expression changed, clouding over. 'Jamie,' she said. 'I hope you don't mind if . . .' Her words tailed off.

Her hand was on the table next to his.

Go for it, he thought. *Stop running away.*

He captured her fingers in his. Her hand was small and shapely. He turned the palm upwards and raised it to his lips.

She looked at him with wide mysterious eyes. He couldn't read her emotions but, made bold by her silence, he kissed the soft ball of flesh at the base of her thumb.

She made a sound, a sharp intake of breath, and her hand slipped around his neck, turning his head to look directly into her face. She was smiling again.

'Are you making a pass at me, Jamie?'

'Yes,' he said boldly.

She chuckled. Her fingers in his hair at the back of his neck began to stroke him. Like an indulgent owner strokes a pet dog. The chuckle grew into a full-blown laugh.

He jerked away from her. He'd misjudged her disastrously. He'd taken a risk and fallen flat on his face.

'Jamie, don't be angry,' she said. 'I'm flattered.'

'You're not. You think I'm a joke.'

'That's not true.'

'Then what's so funny?'

'Well, if you must know . . .' she hesitated. Was she dreaming up some good line to spin him? 'Put it down to middle-aged hysteria. It's not every day a woman of my age is propositioned twice.'

Twice?

She read the confusion in his face. 'I spent half the morning side-stepping Toby Priest. Whatever anyone cares to think, I have no desire to become emotionally entangled with a man like him.'

'Or me either.'

'Don't think I'm not tempted. You're young, gifted and gorgeous.'

'But?'

'Call me old fashioned but you need a girlfriend of your own generation.'

He didn't reply; he was still gnawing on his disappointment.

This time she took hold of his hand. 'I can't let myself fall for a man half my age. Do you understand?'

He rallied. 'Not really. Men go with young women all the time.'

'Quite.' The word was uttered with contempt. She pulled her hand back and stood up. 'Come on. I'm going to drive you home.'

Jamie didn't argue further. He followed her into the hall, still working a few things out.

'What happened with Toby – is that why you can't stable Gates of Eden at Ridgemoor?'

She pulled on her coat. 'He said he'd take the horse if I went away with him for the weekend. I turned him down but he's not good at taking no for an answer. Unlike you.'

She took his arm as they walked towards the car. He felt better about things now.

As they drove down the dark lanes she said, 'There's something I've got to tell you. It's what I was trying to tell you earlier.'

Before he'd got the wrong end of the stick.

'OK,' he said. After what had just gone on he didn't think anything she said would surprise him. But he was wrong.

She told him she had employed Marie Kirkstall.

Chapter Nine

Jamie didn't have to twist Pippa's arm to make room for Gates of Eden in her yard. The plain fact was that, after the recent defections from her string, she still had spare boxes. Given that Ros had undertaken to teach him in the nearby schooling yard, she seemed quite happy about the arrangement.

A day later the big grey arrived in a horse box from Ros's yard where he had been given the first part of his jumping education. He ambled cheerfully into his new stall and made straight for the feed bin.

'Cor, look at him scoff,' said Dave. 'He's carrying too much weight already. He's just a tub of lard with a tail.'

Jamie patted the animal's sleek flank and laughed. 'Three weeks ago you swore blind you knew nothing about horses, Dave. Now you're an expert.'

'But Dave's right,' said Pippa. 'He is a bit on the porky side.'

Jamie had noticed the way his sister had palled up with his former prisonmate. The four horses Pippa had given him to train didn't seem to have made any significant improvement under his new regime but it was still early days. Dave didn't promise to make them faster, but he seemed confident he could give them more stamina.

Whatever his uses as a so-called racing consultant – and the jury had scarcely begun deliberating – Dave had proved himself indispensable as a secretary, a driver and general morale-booster. May Day Warrior's defeat at Southwell had been a blow for Pippa but she'd not become down-hearted; instead she'd seemed even more determined to beat her jinx. Jamie put this down to Dave's cheerful presence.

He'd also noticed the effect Pippa had on Dave. After a night when incessant rain had lashed his small tent, she'd suggested that he get a roof over his head. She'd pointed out that he'd be no use to her if he got sick, and offered him a room in the house or use of the stable lads' digs. Dave had sloped off sheepishly and returned to say he'd moved into a caravan on an out-of-season campsite. Jamie had been persuading him to give up the tent for weeks, to no effect. One short conversation with Pippa, however, had produced results.

The arrival of Gates of Eden compensated Jamie for other matters that weren't so satisfactory – like having to own up to the real nature of his evening out with Ros.

'It's all your fault,' he reproached Dave as he related the story.

Dave enjoyed it hugely. 'I said get a taxi, mate, not a chauffeur-driven limo.'

But he could cope with the runner's good-natured ribbing. It was less easy to hide the disappointment that gripped him after a conversation with Malcolm shortly after Gates of Eden's arrival.

'I'm sorry, Jamie, but the owners want a different jockey to ride Adolf next time out.'

Jamie remembered Toby's attack on his riding at Carlisle.

'You mean the Colonel doesn't want me,' he said. 'He's still pissed at the way he got brought down.'

'Whatever, mate. I wouldn't get too upset about it – you've got other rides coming in, haven't you?'

That was true; his appearance at Carlisle had attracted attention, and other trainers in the area had asked him to ride work for them. As a result he had been booked for a race at Doncaster the next day, with the possibility of others to follow. He was looking forward to the rides but that didn't mean he was happy to surrender Adolf.

He said as much to Ros, wondering whether she was party to the decision to jock him off. Had she known about it the other evening? She was at pains to put his mind at rest.

'It's nothing to do with me, Jamie. Anyway, I'm out of the picture, too. Toby says he's going to look after Adolf himself.'

That made Jamie feel better. If Ros was also off the case then he couldn't be blamed entirely for the horse's failure.

She appeared to know what he was thinking.

'Jamie, the reason they are getting rid of us is that we've done our job. We've turned a temperamental no-hoper into an animal who can at least take part in a race.'

'I suppose so.'

'Of course, he'll probably bolt up next time out and other people will get all the credit but that's too bad. Promise me you won't brood over it.'

'OK,' he'd said as she squeezed his arm.

Things had changed between them since the other evening. She touched him often but not in a sexual way, prodding, urging and reassuring him with her hands – like a mother. He liked it.

The turning point, on reflection, had not been the failed seduction but the conversation that took place in her car after she'd explained about Marie. Jamie had told her about the car crash – as much of it as he could remember – and the way he was back then.

'When I think about it now, I was an accident just waiting to happen. And, to be purely selfish, I'm glad that it did. Being in hospital and in prison turned me round, so you could say I gained out of it. But that lad died in my place. I can understand why his family hate me.'

'Marie doesn't hate you, Jamie. But she doesn't want to run the risk of bumping into you. I promised I'd arrange it so she wouldn't.'

He'd nodded. 'Fair enough.'

'Just don't come up first thing in the morning – she goes to work at the doctor's surgery at ten. Anyway, I'll be seeing you at Pippa's. We'll keep working together.'

And that, luckily, was how it was turning out. Thanks to Ros, his riding had improved beyond recognition. After hours of riding without a saddle he now felt glued to any horses he rode. Ros had drummed it into him that the position of his head was the key to successful jump riding. 'Keep it still and keep it down' was her mantra. He must have jumped 200 fences while repeating those words to himself and now it was second nature. He no longer needed the reins to help him keep balanced while jumping over a fence: his legs and head position were taking care of that.

The other major benefit of learning to keep his head still was that it made judging the approach to a fence that much easier. The more he jumped, the better he got, and he was learning to adapt to each new horse he rode. As Ros said – frequently – there was no substitute for practice.

Dave parked Pippa's beat-up old Land Rover next to a sparkling scarlet Citroën two-seater in the courtyard at Ridgemoor. It was his first visit to Toby Priest's place and, from the scale of the grounds he'd just driven through and the new buildings that lined his route, he could see that this was a much larger operation than Pippa's. He felt like an impostor – or a spy in the enemy camp. In the normal course of events, there was no way an individual like himself would be let loose on these kind of premises.

He got out of the vehicle and looked around. His mission was to deliver Malcolm's mobile phone which had been discovered on the hall table at Shelley Farm after Malcolm had left that morning. Pippa had been tied up at work and so Dave had volunteered to drop it round.

Now he needed to locate Malcolm. Typically, though he'd seen plenty of staff as he drove up – out near the American barns and accompanying a string of horses out of the yard – the inner courtyard was deserted. Just as he was debating which way to go, a man in a white coat rounded the corner of the main house.

Blimey, he thought, they've even got their own scientists.

The man stopped when he spotted Dave heading towards him. There was suspicion in his eyes – Dave well knew he cut an unorthodox figure. The man relaxed when Dave mentioned Malcolm's name and explained his errand.

'You could leave the phone with me,' he said. 'Malcolm's in the bottom paddock with some visitor from Beaufort Holidays.'

But Dave's interest had been aroused by the Beaufort reference. He guessed they'd be working with Adolf and he fancied having a look himself. 'No offence, mate,' he said, 'but I think I ought to hand it over personally. Can't I just nip up there?'

The suggestion didn't go down well. 'We can't allow unauthorised personnel to roam where they please, you know. There's some extremely valuable thoroughbreds on these premises.'

Dave's grin broadened as he prepared to apply a touch of soft soap – always the best way of getting what he wanted, in his experience – when another white-coated figure appeared.

'Bloody hell!' the new arrival cried as he looked at the runner. 'It's Dave Prescott!' He held out his hand and said to the first man, 'I know this bloke – though he probably doesn't remember me.'

Dave looked at him closely. He was almost the same height as Dave, with bulging eyes and a receding hairline. It took a second or two to place him, to add hair to his head and chin, and glasses to the bridge of his nose. It must have been ten years since he'd last seen him.

His newfound friend supplied the name Dave was searching for. 'Walter Clark. We used to race against each other,' he added for his colleague's benefit.

Dave seized Walter's hand and pumped it enthusiastically. 'You old bastard,' he cried. 'What the hell are you doing here?'

'I'm a vet. We're part of the on-site medical team.'

Dave quickly told Walter of his errand. By now the first man was consulting his watch. Walter took the hint. 'You go ahead, Julian, I'll show Dave the way.'

For a moment it looked as though Julian was going to argue but, with an insincere, 'Nice to meet you,' aimed in Dave's direction and a meaningful tap of his watch-face intended for his colleague, he turned on his heel.

Walter pointed the way forward. 'Julian's all right really,' he said, 'just a bit of a goody-goody when it comes to the rules.'

'Not like you then, Walter.'

The vet gave Dave a sly grin. 'I'm a reformed character. Anyhow, you can talk. I read you got banged up.'

Dave grunted. There wasn't much to say.

They passed a row of old-fashioned horse boxes and Walter opened a gate which led onto a well-kept bridleway.

'I thought it was a bloody shame. We shouldn't be locking up our great athletes.'

Dave peered into the other's weathered face. He appeared to be sincere. 'Thanks, mate. But no one's above the law, that's what they kept telling me.'

They came to a clearing where the path divided. Walter pointed off to the left. 'I ought to get back and help Julian out. Meeting with the Colonel about some expensive beast's hip. Fifty yards that way and you'll come to a big paddock with a barn at one end. They're in there.'

They shook hands again. 'Do you still run?' Dave asked.

'Absolutely. Got to keep fit.'

'Give us your number then and we'll go out.'

'Really?' Walter seemed touched. 'I'll never keep up with you these days.' But he produced a small white business card from inside his coat and handed it over.

Dave mused over this unexpected encounter as he walked along the path. Walter had been a scruffy postgrad when he'd last seen him. His final sight of him had been his pony tail bouncing on the back of his neck as he overtook Dave in the last mile of the East–West run, bounding past him on what looked like spring-heeled legs to win the race by the length of a football pitch. Bloody demoralising it had been, too. That was the day when Dave had realised there were younger and better men ready to elbow him aside. Literally, as it turned out, because another three of them caught him before the finish that day.

Turning these memories over in his mind, he came to the barn Walter had told him to look out for and walked along the path to the paddock. He could hear the patter of hooves on turf and, as he turned the corner of the barn, he recognised Adolf with a lad on his back cantering away from him on the far side of the field.

Two people stood some twenty yards off by the last of a set of practice fences, watching the horse as he turned to take the jumps. They had their backs to Dave but he recognised Malcolm at once. By his side was a dark-haired woman, presumably his guest. She wore a short checked jacket and blue jeans designed, no doubt, by some high-fashion store. Quite apart from the stylish cut of the garment, Dave's attention was riveted by the hand exploring the straining contours of the curves they contained. The hand leisurely cupped one buttock then roved to the other, confident of its welcome. Malcolm was feeling up some female in broad daylight and, from the way she was leaning into him with her hip, the woman had no complaints.

Dave stepped back swiftly behind the wall of the barn, all thoughts of Walter and past cross-country feats completely wiped from his mind. The casual but carnal caress could only mean one thing – Pippa's husband was cheating on her.

He tried to persuade himself he had been mistaken. Perhaps that wasn't Malcolm – after all, he hadn't seen his face.

He could hear voices now. The riding sounds had been replaced by a three-way conversation. He peeped around the side of the barn and saw Adolf and his rider next to the man and woman he had been watching. They no longer had their hands on each other, which would be difficult since there was a horse standing between them, and so it was safe for him to emerge.

He strode across the turf towards them, a smile fixed on his face. The man turned towards him in surprise.

'You forgot your mobile, Malcolm,' Dave said by way of explaining his presence. 'Pippa thought you might need it.'

Not a flicker of concern crossed Malcolm's features as he thanked Dave. Surely he must feel a twinge of guilt at the mention of his wife's name? If he did he showed no outward sign as he turned to introduce his female companion.

Dave recognised her from the race meeting at Carlisle, where she'd been surrounded by a flock of men in suits. He'd pegged her as the bossy business type and he noted the calculation in her eyes as she gave him the once-over. Her gaze did not linger long. He was not her sort any more than she was his. Why on earth Malcolm was fooling about with her when he had Pippa at home, Dave couldn't imagine. And, frankly, he didn't want to know.

'Do you mind if we stop by my place?' said Jane as Simon Bennett pulled off the ring road and headed for the city centre. They'd spent a fruitless two hours in a police station sitting in on an interview with a Preston drug-dealer, a small-time operator like Pete. He'd hinted through his solicitor that he knew who was responsible for the Bonfire Night killings but it had been plain from the start that he was simply looking for a way out of his own predicament.

'That little toe-rag would have shopped his granny if he'd thought it would get him off,' muttered Simon, still musing on their wasted afternoon.

'I'd just like to look in on Robbie,' she continued. 'Make sure he's doing his homework.'

'And not polishing off your booze with the class sexpot?'

'He's not like that,' she said.

He snorted. 'They're all like that, given half a chance. I should know,' he added, 'I'm the father of the class sexpot.'

Was that why he was out of sorts? Had Tanya been upsetting him?

'Well, Robbie doesn't know any girls.' More's the pity, she thought, but kept it to herself.

Jane could hear the television even as she inserted the key in the front door and she could feel her mouth crimp at the corners. Simon had a sly grin on his face. God, what an old bag she must look.

Sure enough, her son had his feet up on the coffee-table, a bag of Doritos on his lap, and was watching some noisy sci-fi thing. He waved a hand at her, hardly taking his eyes from the screen.

'Robbie!' she shouted over the sound of an explosion. 'Turn that off,' and she grabbed the remote control before he could obey her instruction.

'What's up, Mum?' he said in an irritatingly unfussed manner. 'Oh, hi,' he added, catching sight of Simon.

Jane reined in her temper and introduced them. As Robbie got to his feet and shook hands, she realised she was over-reacting. He might be gauche but he was a well-mannered lad and he was entitled to relax after school – up to a point.

He knew what was on her mind. 'Just ten more minutes,' he said, pointing to the TV. 'I've got a heap of science and maths.'

'Why don't you start now then?' she said. 'The sooner you start the sooner you finish.'

The cliché was out almost by reflex. Robbie rolled his eyes and shambled towards the door, clutching the Doritos packet and trailing crumbs. She kept her mouth firmly shut.

'See you again, Robbie,' said Simon.

'Sure thing. Hey...' the boy stopped. A thought had occurred. 'Since you're both such hot-shot cops...'

'Robbie!' Jane's irritation was mounting. Since the age of five her son had been a past master of prevarication and she still didn't know how to deal with it.

'Just a quickie,' he said disarmingly. 'There's three prisoners, see, and they're called into the Governor's office.'

Jane groaned inwardly. Another of his impossible brain-teasers.

'The Governor shows them four snooker balls, three red and one black. He gives them one ball each but they can't see what they've got because their hands are tied behind their backs. OK?'

'OK,' said Simon.

'The Governor says that whoever is holding a red ball can walk out of his office a free man, but if a prisoner tries to walk out with a black ball, he'll serve an extra year on his sentence. And he tells them they're not allowed to talk to each other.'

Get on with it, thought Jane, but she kept it to herself.

'So, the prisoners stand around, wondering what to do. One of them can see the other two are holding red balls. Then he makes a decision and walks out of the office a free man. How did he know that he wasn't holding the black ball?'

Jane didn't have a clue. It must be something to do with the way her brain was wired up – she couldn't do cryptic crosswords either. Robbie, on the other hand, loved showing off his mental dexterity. He was looking at her now with a smirk of triumph on his face.

'Are you going to tell him, boss?' Simon turned towards her. 'Or shall I?'

'Go ahead, Simon. Put us all out of our misery.'

'It's obvious, Robbie. If our prisoner had been holding the black ball the other two would have seen it and walked out. Because they hesitated, he knew he also had a red ball. Correct?'

Robbie nodded. 'At last – a copper with some brains. Mum didn't get it though. How come she's your boss?'

Jane was speechless. How could he?

Simon just laughed. 'Because being a smart alec's only going to get you so far, Robbie. You need a bit of wisdom and I'd say your mother's wiser than you or me.'

'Oh.' Robbie didn't look entirely convinced but for once he didn't stay to argue the point. 'Catch you later,' he mumbled and ducked out of the door.

Simon caught her eye; he was grinning from ear to ear.

Dave was out of sorts all afternoon and found it hard to enter into the four-horse training programme that he had set up. He even shouted at Rosie, one of the stable girls who had volunteered to help out, when she didn't allow her horse time to ease off properly after a sharp piece of work. He saw her make a what's-up-with-him? face at Mick, one of the other lads.

When he stopped to think about it, Dave knew just what the matter was and it had nothing to do with the four game stable staff who cheerfully submitted to his bumbling instructions every afternoon. The discovery he had made about Malcolm, much as he desired it, would not be consigned to oblivion. The image of the big man's hand on that woman just wouldn't go away. And while, in the normal course of events, he'd have considered it cause for a laugh and something to be shared with his mates, this was different. This was not a joke. The knowledge that what he said could directly affect Pippa's happiness was burning him up.

There wasn't anyone he could tell. Jamie was his best friend up here but he could hardly let on his sister was being two-timed – or was it his duty, as a friend, to tell him exactly that?

Whatever, he was determined not to go blundering in. This wasn't his business. Besides, he might have got the wrong end of the stick – though that was hardly likely unless he'd completely misread Pippa. He supposed she could know all about Malcolm's habits. Maybe they had one of those marriages you read about – an 'open' marriage. If that were the case, he himself would be first in the queue to help Mrs Priest fulfil her end of the bargain. He didn't believe it for one minute. Open marriages were Sunday tabloid wish-fulfilment or, in his observation, bad marriages about to hit the rocks.

But only last week Pippa had told him that if she didn't turn the training around she might as well pack it in and have kids, like Malcolm wanted. That didn't sound like a man unhappy with his wife. Unless, of course, the thought suddenly burst upon him, her refusal was why her husband was playing touchy-feely with Beverley Harris.

'What now, Dave?' Jill, Pippa's travelling head lad who tagged along when she wasn't racing, was at his elbow.

'Um . . .' He hadn't been paying much attention. 'What do you think?'

'I think Stickleback's had enough because that cut on his off-hind still looks sore. But don't you want the others to let rip?'

She was poking fun because he always got them to finish off with a head-to-head gallop, yelling, 'Go on, let 'em rip!'

'Yeah, I suppose I do. You tell 'em.'

She did as he asked and then, as they watched the three horses streak across the turf away from them, she asked, 'Are you all right, Dave?'

But she didn't get an answer. His thoughts were elsewhere.

Jamie was no stranger to stage fright. As an apprentice, faced with his first professional rides, he'd been consumed by nerves – barely sleeping the night before, vomiting in the toilet before the race, standing tongue-tied in the parade ring. Fortunately, the symptoms had vanished the moment he rode down to the start. Then he'd been ice-cool, able to make split-second choices by instinct, reacting quicker than most riders. In the crazy rush of a horse race it seemed he had more time than others.

At first he'd reasoned that the distress he suffered beforehand was counterbalanced by his efficiency in the saddle. It seemed a fair trade-off. Then he hit a rough patch – twenty rides without even being placed, and on some good horses too. And when his mount decided not to run, or got knocked off line in the crush, or simply ran out of steam with the post in sight, Jamie had still gone through an agony before climbing on board. It no longer seemed fair.

Round about this time, he took his first drink 'to steady his nerves'. It had worked like a charm, calming his racing blood and banishing the butterflies in his stomach. He started winning again, too, and he decided it couldn't be a coincidence. If he could ride well without sleep and half dizzy from being sick, surely he could perform even better after the calming effect of a little drink? It seemed like a licence to indulge – and he had.

In retrospect, Jamie could see that back then he'd been like a ticking bomb. His wild behaviour had guaranteed that it wasn't a question of *if* but *when* the bomb would go off. And it had. He'd be living with the consequences for the rest of his life.

So now, in the weighing-room at Doncaster, he fought the urge to step into the toilet and throw up. Instead he took a deep, controlled breath and accepted discomfort as his lot. It was the price he paid for getting back into the saddle fuelled with nothing but his ability.

He knew the reason his nerves were running riot. Ahead was his biggest test yet as a jump rider and he was facing it on his own.

Jamie had travelled to Doncaster to ride a hurdler for Ferdy Gates. He'd cadged a lift in the horse box with Ferdy's stable staff. He could have asked Dave to drive him in the Land Rover or Ros might have been free. But they had business of their own to attend to and it was time he stood on his own two feet.

The two-mile race had passed uneventfully with his mount putting in a safe-and-steady performance – they'd finished sixth out of a field of thirteen. There had not been anything Jamie could have done to improve matters, since his horse had never been in touch with the leaders.

'I'd try him over a longer distance next time,' Jamie said to Ferdy afterwards. 'I'd like to ride him again if I could.'

After that minor excitement Jamie had changed and sat twiddling his thumbs in the weighing room, waiting for his ride back at the end of the afternoon. Suddenly a large woman with a weatherbeaten face had appeared and asked for a word. Irene Bolt had got his name from Ferdy.

'I've a spare ride going,' she said. 'Jockey hasn't turned up – I won't use that little sod again. You interested?'

So now Jamie was facing the prospect of riding High Sierra, a seven-year-old novice chaser, in a two-and-a-half mile handicap.

'I can't say he's the most popular fellow in my yard,' Irene had said. 'He's raw but he's got potential.'

'I'd watch out, if I were you,' called another jockey as Jamie returned to change back into his riding clothes. A couple of the other lads also told him to be careful. Irene Bolt reputedly had a stable full of lousy jumpers with little or no steering. It seemed Jamie was the only jockey in the country who didn't know what you were up against when you rode one of her dodgy animals.

It was too late to do anything about it now. Jamie strode into the ring with a reasonable amount of trepidation. There had not been time to look up the form – there had barely been time to change into the right colours – and he was keen to see what he'd let himself in for.

High Sierra was a mean-looking bruiser of a horse. He gazed at Jamie with a disdainful eye, his tail twitching. Jamie noticed he was sweating heavily.

'Watch out for him biting the other runners,' Irene said cheerily as she gave him a leg-up. 'It's jolly embarrassing when he does that.'

'Bad-tempered, is he?' Jamie asked.

'He can be. The lads call him Psycho Sierra. He's quite a character.'

That was one way of putting it, thought Jamie. No wonder his jockey hadn't turned up.

The horse pulled hard on the way to the start and Jamie took a firm hold, keeping the animal's head twisted over the running rail to prevent it bolting. The irony of the trainer's surname might have raised a smile had he not been hanging on for dear life.

High Sierra sullenly obeyed but Jamie could sense that rebellion wasn't far off. They joined the fourteen other runners milling round before the start. Mindful of the trainer's remarks about biting, Jamie dragged his head away from the grey horse on his left. High Sierra appeared to obey instructions then suddenly jerked backwards. An oath split the air from the grey's jockey.

'Watch that sod. He tried to kick mine!' the rider shouted at Jamie.

Bloody hell! What had he got himself into? Jamie pulled his horse away, out of the line, to prevent any further interference. At that moment the tapes went up, stranding them at the start as the rest of the field raced away.

It amounted to the worst possible start – literally. Jamie urged his troublesome mount after the others with murder in his heart – which probably made two of them, he thought.

It was almost a relief to play tail-end Charlie round the sharp end of the pear-shaped course. The tight corner didn't suit the big lumbering Sierra and Jamie took it with care and at no great speed. At present his aim was simply to get the animal down the back straight and over the fences in a smooth rhythm. If they got to the start of the long sweeping curve for home in one piece, then he could think about the contest itself.

This jump racing was a far different method of riding to what he had been used to. As Ros had pointed out, riding for the best part of five minutes over obstacles required a different mental technique to a minute-long wham-bam sprint on the Flat.

Now he'd got the horse thinking about running and jumping, instead of beating up his fellow competitors, the animal was moving smoothly. Or maybe Psycho Sierra simply wanted to catch up with the other horses so he could take his bad temper out on them.

Whatever the reason, the horse was employing his massive strength in a steady gallop. By the end of the outward straight – the big end of the pear – they had caught up and passed half the field. When Sierra decided to apply himself, he could certainly shift.

The horse sailed over the open ditch on the shallow curve of the bottom end and pinged the first fence leading into the home straight. He was eating up the other runners as fast as he was devouring the ground. Suddenly, Jamie found himself assessing his position in the race. There were five horses ahead of them and four fences to go. They took the next couple with powerful leaps, leaving two more of their rivals in their wake.

The three leading horses were a few lengths ahead, racing almost abreast. Jamie kept his mount wide on the stand side, praying he could keep up this remarkable display for another couple of furlongs. If they could just nose out one other runner they'd be in the places and that would be something.

But the three ahead weren't giving up and Sierra made little impression. Jamie gave the horse a smack with his stick as they approached the second to last and felt him respond. He saw the nearest horse clout the top of the fence just before Sierra took off. The other horse faltered and they were past him in a blur of wind and mud. Third – fantastic!

They were level with the second horse going into the last fence. Jamie looked to his left and saw his rider giving everything he'd got. It didn't seem to be doing much good; the animal was operating on auto-pilot.

Sierra was also tiring, Jamie could sense it. They only scraped over the last fence. For a moment, as his horse stumbled, he thought they were about to fall but he yanked Sierra's nose up just before it kissed the turf and the animal stayed on his feet. That was their chance gone, though. They finished six lengths behind the winner in second place.

Irene was delighted. 'I say, how marvellous!' she crowed. 'I knew he had the ability but it's not easy to get the best out of him. You two got on like a house on fire.'

Jamie made a noncommittal noise and grinned; he didn't want to spoil the party atmosphere.

'You're a marriage made in heaven!' the big woman continued. 'You will ride him next time, won't you?'

Five minutes earlier, Jamie's first instinct would have been to say no, loudly and forcefully. But a ride was a ride – was he in any position to be choosy at this stage of his new career? And, to be fair, once he'd got going the horse had done nothing wrong. If he was to get to the top of this jumping game, Jamie knew he'd have to ride all sorts of animals, not just the good ones.

'I'll look forward to it,' he said.

'Bloody well done on Psycho, mate,' said Ferdy's travelling head lad, Padraig, as the horse box turned onto the A1. 'I'd have had a couple of quid on him if I'd known.'

'Known what?'

'That you were going to ride him. I found out too late.'

'Really?' Jamie was chuffed. If knowledgeable lads like Padraig were beginning to rate him, then he must be doing something right.

The journey back passed quickly. After just under an hour and a half they turned into the Ridgemoor Valley, past the familiar landmark of the Lord Nelson public house. A shadow fell over Jamie's good spirits as its Victorian bulk loomed. He'd been down this road before.

Jamie gunned the car into the pub car park and reversed it at speed into a spot by a battered Mondeo. It had been a hard but exhilarating hammer north from Ascot and the thought of a long drink had been tantalising him since he'd got off the motorway at Leeds.

He flashed his new Rolex and turned to his passengers. 'Two hours fifty-six,' he announced proudly. 'Told you I could do it in under three.'

'You drive like a maniac,' murmured Richard from the back seat.

Jamie noted that he looked a bit green around the gills. Rich could be a wimp sometimes. 'A thirsty maniac,' he said. 'You guys owe me a beer.'

'I thought you were buying, maestro.' Malcolm opened the passenger door. 'You're the day's big winner.'

That was true enough. First past the post three times at Ascot, including a cracking performance in a quality race like the Diadem. A nice present stuffed in his back pocket from a top owner. And that didn't include the morning in bed with the owner's daughter. It was his day all right. And the way he was going there'd be many more like it.

Jamie ordered a pint of lager and the same for Malcolm. Rich asked for a slimline tonic. Jesus.

'Sure you don't want a proper drink? Go on, man, live dangerously.'

Rich didn't laugh. He was being a bit of a misery this evening. Well, screw him.

'You know your problem, Rich? You're afraid to get stuck in. You had a gap in that last race and you hesitated, so you missed your chance.'

Rich's face crumpled, like a kid who'd dropped his ice cream, so Jamie knew he'd hit a nerve.

'It's the same with women. You hang back and some other bugger's off the mark ahead of you.' Jamie turned to Malcolm. 'Some other bugger like me.' They both laughed.

'Seriously, mate,' Jamie continued, 'you've got to stick up for yourself more. I reckon the best thing you could do' – he'd been meaning to get

this off his chest for a while and now seemed a good time – 'is jack in working for your old man.'

'What's that got to do with it?'

'It's not very impressive working for your daddy, is it? I mean, people will always wonder why you got the gig. I think you should go and sling your leg over some other trainer's horses. You know, just to prove you can. What do you say, Mal?'

Jamie could tell that Malcolm was enjoying watching his brother squirm.

'Jamie might have a point, Richard,' he said. 'I bet Dad would be impressed if you made your way at another yard.'

Richard glared at him. 'You can talk. You don't wipe your arse without his approval.'

'I spent six years on my own in the Army, mate.'

'And came running straight home when you ballsed up.'

Jamie was amused. Talk about light the blue touch paper and retire.

'Now then, lads, you're spoiling my night.' He pulled a £50 note from the bundle in his pocket and caught the barman's eye. 'I'm switching to vodka – what about you?'

Richard declined, of course, but Malcolm opted for Scotch. Jamie cast his eye around for other likely recipients of his generosity. He had a good feeling about tonight.

There were some Ridgemoor stable staff in the far corner, lads and lasses who worked all hours for not much. When his drinks arrived Jamie handed the barman the banknote. 'Stick this behind the bar, would you, Charlie? Anything that lot over there wants is on me. And yourself, of course.'

Charlie grinned. 'I'll take a half, thanks.'

Jamie added a splash of Coke to his vodka – Diet Coke, of course, as he had to keep an eye on his weight. 'Let me know when the cash runs out. There's plenty more.'

'Been a good day, has it?'

'You could say – and it's just getting going.'

Richard had taken himself off to talk to some of the lads and Malcolm had been joined by one of the Ridgemoor stable girls, a blonde bubbly sort. Jamie moved in swiftly, aware it was his brotherly duty to keep an eye on his sister's boyfriend. Not that it was any of his business what either of them got up to.

The rest of the Ridgemoor group joined them and congratulations rained down on Jamie, inspired by his Ascot exploits and the free drinks. He was the man of the moment and it felt damn good.

The vodka hit him after a quarter of an hour. He got up to go to the Gents and sat straight back down again. It was if he'd been sandbagged behind the knees. Well, he had been living on the edge all day. By rights he ought to be spark out somewhere, recharging his batteries. Stuff that, though, he was having too good a time.

The trouble was, he had no more of his magic pills and what he needed right now was a pick-me-up. Booze was all very well but there was nothing like a chemical stimulant to keep a man's motor running. He looked around for assistance. This crowd wasn't cool enough or rich enough to be carrying what he needed. Their idea of a wild night out was getting blatted on Alco-pops.

He looked around the bar and recognised a couple of girls at a table on the far side of the room. His luck was in – of course. He took it carefully crossing the room – he could do without an attack of the wobbles. His target was a woman in a scooped-out pink top with appliquéd sequins and a leather skirt. He knew she was pretending not to see him.

'Hi, Cassie,' he said.

She looked up in feigned surprise. Her companion, Helen, followed her glance and said, 'You can get lost for a start.'

Jamie ignored the spotty bitch. Quite why Helen had it in for him he wasn't sure – it wasn't her he'd dumped, after all.

'Can I have a word, Cassie?'

'No, you bloody can't,' said Helen. 'You've done enough damage.'

But Cassie took no notice and got to her feet, as he'd known she would. He put his arm around her waist and led her away from the table.

'Have you got anything on you?'

She stared at him without comprehension.

'Pills? Coke? Anything but hash.'

He felt her stiffen. Oh God, surely the silly cow hadn't thought he was still interested in her?

'Sorry, Cassie, that came out wrong. It's just that I'm in a rush tonight. I was going to call you.'

'Were you?' Her mouth softened. 'Were you really?'

They'd spent a boozed-up weekend in bed three weeks back. Just long enough for Jamie to enjoy all that she had to offer and leave well satisfied. The trouble was, her appetite had only just been whetted – or so he gathered from the phone messages and notes that had followed him since.

'Look, I'm tied up tonight but what about tomorrow? We could do dinner out or pizza in, you choose.'

She was wavering, he could see. 'I'd like that,' she said at last.

'Great. I'll call tomorrow morning.' Fat chance. 'But I'm dead on my feet, Cassie. I just need something to keep me going.'

He knew she usually carried some stuff – their weekend stimulants had not all been served in a glass.

'I've got a little coke,' she admitted.

'Great! I'll buy it off you.'

'No, you bloody well won't. What do you think I am?' She pulled away from him and stalked through the door that led to the toilets.

He followed and caught up with her in the passage. She rummaged in her bag and extracted something.

'Promise you'll call me.'

'I promise. Tomorrow night's a date.'

She leaned against him and slipped the small cellophane packet into his shirt pocket.

He had to kiss her, it was only fair. She tasted of cigarettes and Bacardi and smelt of something sweet and heavy, her familiar perfume. It was OK and so was the kiss. But he'd moved on since then, he thought as he pushed open the door of the Gents and made for the cubicle. Perhaps he'd call Vanessa tomorrow instead.

The bog in the Lord Nelson wouldn't win prizes but at least the cistern had a flat top. Jamie wiped the porcelain clean with his shirt sleeve and carefully tipped the white powder onto the gleaming surface. He chop-chop-chopped the powder with his Visa card, then scraped it into two thin lines – one for each nostril. Excellent.

He pulled out one of Hartley's fifties and rolled the red banknote into a tight tube. He was going up in the world all right. The last time he'd sniffed some coke he'd used a bent straw.

He walked back into the bar with a spring in his step and set a course for the Ridgemoor table, steering well clear of Cassie and her stupid friend.

A hand tugged at his elbow. Richard.

'Have you seen Malcolm?'

'No.'

'I can't find him.'

Jamie shrugged. 'So?'

'If I flush him out can we get going?'

So that's what it was. Richard wanted to go home. Jamie was tempted to tell him to cadge a lift off someone else. On second thoughts, it might be a good idea to get out of Cassie's sight. He could nip down to the Rose after he'd dropped the Priest boys off. The new barmaid was a looker.

'OK, Rich. Give me ten minutes.'

His place had been saved at the table and a couple of fresh drinks were lined up. He splashed Coke into the two vodka glasses and downed the first in one.

'Thanks, lads,' he said though, come to think of it, it was probably his money that had paid for them. Which reminded him. He looked round at the Ridgemoor gang. Malcolm had reappeared. He was at the back with that blonde.

'I've got a toast,' Jamie shouted and all heads turned in his direction. 'Horses can't run and jockeys can't ride without lads and lasses like you. I've had a bloody good day today but it's all down to you lot. Cheers!' He raised his glass then drained it.

The group responded enthusiastically and voices called out their appreciation.

'Fantastic performance today, Jamie.'

'Great riding, mate.'

Jamie got to his feet, fumbling in his pocket. 'Hang on,' he said, pulling Hartley's wad from his pocket and tossing four £50 notes on the table. 'I'm off but bung this on the tab. You all deserve to get pissed!'

Their gratitude was heartfelt – God, it was easy to be popular if you bought your round and told people what they wanted to hear. Not that he didn't mean it.

He broke away from the noisy, back-slapping group and pushed Malcolm in the direction of the door. Richard followed.

As they stepped out into the twilight he murmured to the big man, 'Don't think I didn't notice you slipping off with that lass.'

Malcolm's reply was lost as the fresh air hit Jamie, sending his thoughts into a whirl and turning his legs to jelly. He grabbed the other man's arm to save himself from pitching headfirst onto the gravel.

'You all right, Jamie?' came the anxious voice of Richard.

He steadied himself and took a deep breath. 'I'm fine,' he said carefully, the words coming from a distance. 'Never felt better in my whole life.'

And that was all Jamie could remember of the night that changed his life.

Chapter Ten

It was ironic, Jane thought, that she should be clearing out her desk at Deacon Parade when Elizabeth Jacobs came on the line to give her directions to Amanda's memorial service that afternoon. She promised to be there and put the phone down without saying anything about the latest development in the case. She didn't think Elizabeth would be overjoyed to hear that it was being abandoned.

Of course, that wasn't the technical term for it and Superintendent Keith Wright would have considered such a reference as heresy. But how else did you explain the closing down of the incident room and the reallocation of personnel to other cases? She herself was still nominally in charge but she'd have to put the Bonfire Night Murders back in the queue behind other 'more pressing' matters. The file was still open, as Wright had put it, but she knew that he and almost everyone else had marked it shut for the moment. They all thought the East European drug-dealers had killed Pete and Amanda and that they might be able to pin it on them at some indeterminate point in the future. But murder, robbery, fraud and a host of other serious offences were being committed right now and police resources were finite.

In theory, Jane was all in favour of taking fresh aim in the fight against crime. And in this case she too was convinced the Albanians were responsible – well, almost. Maybe she still entertained doubts because it was her first time as SIO on a murder and she didn't want to leave it in this inconclusive state. But she'd come in late, when the case had already turned into a pig's ear. No one could blame her for its failure. Not even that slimy sod, Keith Wright.

'Not your fault, Jane,' he'd said at the end of their interview. 'Buy you a drink later as consolation?'

She'd ducked that one as best she could. She didn't want to find herself backed up in the corner of some loathsome pub swapping divorce war stories again. If she was going down that road there were others she'd prefer to travel with.

'So long, boss,' said Simon, the fellow-traveller she was thinking of.

'For God's sake cut out that boss stuff,' she protested. 'I can't stand it.'

'Sorry.' He grinned – how did he keep his teeth so white? 'Let's get together soon, eh?'

What did he have in mind? Her imagination went into overdrive – she couldn't help it. 'Er . . .' she said, caught offguard. Not very impressive.

His face fell. 'Just to keep in touch about this business, I meant. We shouldn't just forget about it.'

'OK,' she said. 'Call me.'

She watched his broad shoulders disappear through the door. Whether he called her or not, she had no intention of forgetting about the Bonfire Night Murders.

Joyce Kirkstall couldn't say she enjoyed her part-time job at the Post Office and general stores. Her function was manning the grocery till at the front of the shop, while at the back, behind a glass window, Mr and Mrs Jennings carried out the important tasks, such as doling out pensions and weighing parcels. It didn't pay much and old Jennings was a pain in the backside. He was a former British Rail station manager with a neurotic addiction to punctuality and an obsession with 'the rules', most of which he made up himself.

There were compensations, however, to working in the busiest shop in the High Street. Nearly everybody, at one time or another, dropped into the Post Office and many had nothing better to do than hang around and gossip. Joyce was happy to pass the time in a spot of conversation, though she had to be careful with Jennings in attendance. Mrs Jennings, however, couldn't be bossed around. And she did like a good chinwag.

Since taking the job Joyce had been able to add to her knowledge of many locals she'd known little about. It was impossible not to overhear what was said. It wasn't a large shop and, from her station at the till, she could hear every word spoken at the Post Office counter. Though she'd never counted herself as that nosy, it amused her to earwig on the local comings and goings, even when she didn't know exactly who they were talking about.

A favourite subject under discussion was 'that Ros Bradey' and, within a fortnight, she'd noted the woman herself – a Lady Muck type, Joyce had thought at first, with her expensive-casual clothes and low, well-modulated voice. She was irritatingly elegant and slim and she'd obviously not spent her working life skivvying for others as Joyce had. But she looked Joyce in the eye when she paid for her goods and said her pleases and thank yous as if she meant them. Then Joyce heard that she was one of the horsey lot running a business teaching animals to jump. So she must have done a fair amount of hard work in her time – horses being more labour intensive than small children even.

So when Marie started getting up early to work 'at Ros's', Joyce's attention was well and truly attuned to whatever was said about Ros Bradey.

Old Freddy Ferguson was getting in a muddle counting out the change for his pipe tobacco when Joyce heard the words 'you'll never guess the latest about Ros Bradey' from the Post Office counter.

Joyce impatiently plucked the correct coins from Freddy's open purse and banged up the sale. She looked across the shop and recognised Mrs Hargreaves thumbing an Air Mail sticker on to a large and shapeless packet – handmade baby clothes bound for her new granddaughter in Australia doubtless; the new arrival had been a hot topic for months.

'She's got herself a toy boy,' Mrs Hargreaves continued. 'He must be half her age.'

'I wouldn't mind a toy boy,' mused Mrs Jennings, earning a reproving glance from her husband. 'Course, chance would be a fine thing.'

'You haven't heard who it is yet,' said the new grandmother. 'It's that jockey who went to prison.'

There was an intake of breath. 'What – Jamie Sullivan? Never!'

'It's true. He took her out the other night all done up like a dog's dinner. He hired a chauffeur-driven car and ended up at Ros Bradey's place for the night. I know that for a fact.'

There came a loud coughing noise from Mr Jennings and Joyce caught sight of him making furious hand signals to Mrs Hargreaves.

'Australia, did you say?' cut in Mrs Jennings to cover the confusion as Mrs Hargreaves swivelled her head to stare in Joyce's direction. Her antipathy to Jamie Sullivan was well known – no doubt the Post Office clientele had jawed for weeks about her assault on him at the Roman Arms back in November.

A hearty conversation about grandchildren was struck up but the damage had been done. Joyce busied herself straightening the array of crisps, her unthinking fingers muddling the flavours. So Marie was working for the mistress of the man who'd killed her own brother.

She could scarcely believe it.

Clem Kirkstall stared at the pen on the carpet by his foot. How in blue blazes did it get there? He cursed softly to himself.

He was alone in the house, so there was no use calling for Joyce or Marie to come and pick it up for him. He'd have to manage himself or do without. And he didn't want to do without. The morning crossword was at hand on the table by his chair.

He considered his plan of action – his condition required him to do that, he found, or you could end up in some nasty spots. If he'd just bent forward to reach for the pen, as any normal person would – as he would have done himself just a few months ago – then his chest would be resting on his knees and the breath driven from his body. He didn't have enough breath to spare to risk that.

No, the thing to do was to slip to his knees first and reach for the pen on all fours. He could pick it up and put it back on the table, then climb back up into the chair, pulling himself up by his arms. That would put pressure on his chest, of course, but if he took it slowly he should be all right.

First he used the inhaler. He hadn't wanted one when Gooding had first made the suggestion. He'd said it would make him look like an asthmatic or something, and the doctor had given him a hard unfriendly stare. 'Just what is it you think you are, exactly?' he'd said and Clem had kept his mouth shut after that. He used the inhalers now, all the time, in fact, as he fought off the constant shortness of breath.

He tried to relax as he slid his right foot back round the side of the chair and lowered his knee towards the floor. But his stockinged foot seemed jammed in the thick pile of the carpet and it was an effort to even slide forward in the big old chair. With his thighs splayed and teetering on the edge of the seat, it wasn't that easy to relax. But he forced himself. He took a breath, a short gulp of air that seemed to stick in his throat. He could feel himself beginning to sweat.

He shoved his body forward and suddenly he was on the move, his knees jerking forward and landing with a window-pane-rattling thump onto the floor. Hell and tarnation. All because he wanted a ruddy pen.

Sinking onto his haunches he gauged the distance to the object of his discomfort. It was four feet away but it looked like forty. He shuffled towards it on his bottom. Like a big baby, he thought.

Oh Alan, thank God you can't see your big tough daddy now.

Marie had been about to leave the surgery for the day when her phone rang – a rare occurrence. It was Caroline from Ros's yard.

'You couldn't come up and help us with Spring Fever, could you? You're about the only one who gets on with him.'

'What's the matter with him?'

'He's being a right pain in the arse. He gets halfway across the yard then just stands up on his back legs.'

Marie was puzzled. 'Where's Ros?' Ros could handle Spring Fever. She'd bet Ros could handle anything.

'She's gone to the sales in Ireland and won't be back for a few days. Could you come – please?'

It wasn't in Marie to play hard to get where a horse was concerned. She'd cycled up to the yard straight away. She found the place in a bit of a tizz with Caroline, inclined in the past to be a little on the snippy side, pitifully grateful to see her.

'Ros said to do some Flat work with him in the paddock,' she said, 'but we can't even get him that far. He keeps rearing up or else he stands still and won't budge. We can't get him to do a thing.' Marie guessed she was worried what Ros might say.

Excited – and just a little fearful – Marie quickly changed into riding clothes. She'd seen Spring Fever's bad-tempered side before. Even though she adored the horse, he had a foul temper when he got into a state.

He was in a state now all right, standing four square in his stable.

'We left him here when you agreed to come,' said Caroline. 'He might have calmed down a bit by now.'

Marie thought so too as she stroked his white muzzle and gazed into his big wet eye.

Caroline led him out and gave her a boost into the saddle. Marie let her leathers down a few holes so as to get the maximum contact on his flanks with her legs. If he reared up she wanted to be as secure as possible.

Marie began to walk the horse slowly round the yard, patting his neck and talking to him all the time. She remembered that he'd been difficult before when it came to going out. He was fine within the confines of the stableyard, but each time she went to head him in the direction of the paddock his body tensed and his nose lifted in the air, as if he was preparing to rear up on his back legs.

Every time he did this, Marie pulled him left-handed and completed another circuit.

'He's taking the piss,' said Caroline, who had been standing at the exit to make certain Marie didn't come to any harm.

Marie knew that Caroline was right. Spring Fever was taking the mickey. As she felt him begin to duck out the next time, she brought her whip down on his shoulder with a force that surprised even herself. But the cord covering had barely made contact with Spring Fever's skin before he was upright and Marie was hanging helplessly around his neck.

'Jump off him!' screamed Caroline.

Spring Fever was vertical and looked ready to fall over backwards onto the gravel driveway.

Marie was too frightened to move. She just gripped the horse's mane tight and kept her weight as far forward as she could, hoping to keep him balanced. The few seconds she hung there seemed to last for ever, but eventually the big chestnut horse dropped back onto his front feet, his hoofs crunching into the gravel.

'Right, get off him,' cried Caroline, 'and put him back before he kills you.'

Dave dropped Jamie at the gate of Ros's yard, as Jamie had requested.

'Sure you don't want me to wait?' he said.

Jamie shook his head. He knew Dave had a busy afternoon, running his training session at Shelley Farm then meeting up with some guy he used to race against.

'I can walk back. Get a bit of exercise,' he added for Dave's benefit. He'd not been running for weeks and Dave was always on at him about it.

Jamie shut the gate behind him and headed down the familiar path. Ros was away for a couple of days but she'd left a race video for him to pick up from the office.

As he approached he heard the sound of a woman's voice raised in distress.

'Get off him now, please. He's going right back in his box.'

That sounded like Caroline, Ros's head lass.

'But we can't let him beat us!'

Jamie didn't recognise that voice but he could now see its owner, a girl on top of the horse who'd given Ros a kicking. She was obviously trying to get the animal out of the yard but he wasn't having any. His feet were planted on the ground as if they'd taken root.

Suddenly the horse reared up on its back legs. The girl clung on gamely. 'No!' she shouted. 'Get down!'

Jamie could see that the girl was determined not to let the horse get away with it. He called to Caroline over the gate, 'Can I make a suggestion before someone gets hurt?'

She whirled round, surprised to see him and, from the look of her, pleased too. 'Do anything you like. I'm terrified he'll topple backwards on top of her.'

Jamie could understand that. The lass was brave but, in his opinion, suicidal. She'd be squashed flat if an animal that size landed on her.

Jamie called to the girl on the horse to let him stand still for a moment. He then ran to the hay barn and returned a minute later with a couple of lengths of orange-coloured baling string.

'Pick up his front foot, would you?' he instructed Caroline. 'I don't want him kicking me and he can't do that on three legs'

Caroline did as she was told.

People used to say that Jamie's Uncle Bob had a touch of the gypsy in him. Jamie's mum would bridle at the suggestion, but her brother was dark and handsome with a gleam in his black eyes – as was Pippa. Whatever the truth of it, Bob knew a few useful Romany dodges when it came to horses and he'd delighted in passing them on to his niece and nephew. On occasions they could be handy – like now.

'What are you doing?' shouted the girl, a note of anxiety in her voice.

'I'm going to stop him rearing.'

Jamie captured the horse's tail and trussed it with one end of the baling string. Then he passed the string between the animal's back legs, pulling the tail through with it, and secured it around the leather girth. Now the tail no longer flowed out behind Spring Fever but rested up against his belly.

He stood up with a smile on his face. 'There we are. He won't be able to stand on his back legs now.'

'What have you done?' asked the girl.

'Tied his tail down tight. He can't rear up because he won't be able to balance. Horses can't stand upright unless they can use their dock to balance. Try him now.'

The girl prodded the horse into action and Jamie and Caroline watched as she walked him away. It was evident Spring Fever wanted to rear but just wasn't able to.

'Make him go in and out of the yard a few times until you are happy with him,' Jamie said, 'then take the string off and see if it's made any difference.'

This time when the horse stopped, his rider walloped him and he moved forward reluctantly.

'Thanks, Jamie,' said Caroline. 'If anything happened while Ros is away she'd kill me.'

'That's a nasty habit. People get paralysed by horses toppling backwards on them.'

'Where did you learn that trick with the string?'

'It's an old gypsy dodge.' Jamie felt pretty pleased with himself. 'Who's the girl?' he asked.

'Marie Kirkstall from the village.'

Jamie no longer felt so chuffed.

'Stubborn lass,' Caroline continued. 'Wouldn't get off him when I told her. Canny rider though.'

'Look, I've just got to pick something up from the office.' The girl didn't seem to have recognised him. If he went now he might be able to get away with it.

'Hang on a bit, Jamie. I'm sure she'd like to say thanks. There's smashing blonde hair under that helmet, you know.'

But Jamie was off, heading back to the gate. He raised his hand in a general farewell as he went but he didn't look at the rider on the horse.

What was Marie Kirkstall doing here at this time of day?

*

At first Jamie couldn't find the video tape in the small cluttered shed that passed for an office. Then the phone rang and he felt duty bound to answer it. By the time he'd taken a message and spotted a Jiffy bag marked 'Jamie' leaning on the bookshelf, he could hear the sound of horse's hooves from the yard outside.

It would be Marie, returning Spring Fever to his stall. She'd take his kit off and settle him down. If he waited a few minutes he could slip away unnoticed while she was with the horse in his box.

He heard Caroline's voice. 'I'll take him if you like.'

Jamie froze. Where was Marie going? Caroline must have told her his name by now. Maybe the experience had so spooked her that she was leaving straight away. He'd better stay right where he was and give her time to get clear. He didn't want to run into her in the small courtyard outside or in the narrow lane where there would be no escape. The tiny office was even worse.

She appeared in the doorway. 'Jamie Sullivan.' A statement, not a question. She hesitated, maybe wondering whether he knew who she was.

He cut in quickly. 'I didn't expect you'd be here. I'm sorry.'

She was close enough to touch, her back to the light and her face in shadow. He could make out her expression, however. The pale oval was sombre, with deepset unreadable eyes and a downturned slash of a mouth.

'Thank you for your help with Spring Fever.' She spoke formally. It was the kind of duty-bound sentiment you made because you had to.

'That's OK,' he said. 'Is he all right now?' The question was out before he could think. Maybe he wasn't supposed to talk to her.

'Oh yes. He behaved beautifully after that.' Her face relaxed a fraction. 'I think I was being a bit stupid. Caroline told me off for not putting him back in his box.'

'You've got guts,' he said. 'Most girls would be screaming their heads off if a horse tried that trick on them.'

'And boys wouldn't?' The slash of her mouth had changed shape, softened. Her neat, firm chin jutted impudently.

'Sure, boys would too.' Jamie was not prepared for this situation. Least of all the fact that she was so lovely to look at.

He plunged into the pause in their strange conversation. 'Look, Ros said you wouldn't be around at this time. I'm really sorry – I'll make sure in future.

She nodded and turned. 'Don't bother on my account,' she mumbled as she left. At least, that's what he thought she said.

He waited in the office till he was absolutely sure she had gone.

Amanda's memorial service was held at a small church in the Dales. Elizabeth told Jane she'd chosen it because the vicar was well disposed to the racing community. Also it was positioned not far from the yards in Yorkshire where her sister had worked.

The narrow pews were packed, mostly with youngsters whose natural exuberance was masked by the solemnity of the occasion. Jane gathered that these were stable staff, released from their chores on a non-racing afternoon.

The service was affecting. Amanda's favourite pop music was played. Elizabeth's eldest, four-year-old Grace, and a couple of nursery-school classmates sang a hesitant 'I'm a Little Teapot' as, apparently, they had once done for their Auntie Manda. A stable colleague delivered an amusing account of Mandy's first day in the yard when she'd paraded the wrong horse for an owner, who hadn't noticed the mistake. Then two high-mounted TV screens showed a video prepared by Amanda's youngest sister, Jo, on her travels in Australia. She stood on a cliff, high above a beach where surf pounded in a flickering white line, and cast seeds into the wind. Finally, Elizabeth delivered a halting but passionate address and the vicar led the congregation in prayer. Jane could have done without Elton John's Princess Diana tribute which accompanied their exit into the grey spring afternoon, but she put away her cynicism as she noticed tears on many cheeks.

It had been her intention to slip away quickly but Elizabeth caught her up.

'Won't you come back to the house, Jane? We've laid on some drinks.'

'I can't.' It was true – she had a case conference lined up about a suspected infanticide and she had to get back.

'In that case, I'm going to tell you now before I change my mind.'

'Tell me what?'

Elizabeth looked around but, for the moment, they were alone in the crowd. 'I've been thinking over what you said about Mandy's boy-friends, but I swear they were all harmless. It's just – well, this one was different.'

Jane held back her impatience. She'd waited long enough for this information. A few more seconds wouldn't matter.

'He was her boss and about thirty years older than she was. She'd never got involved with anyone like that before. I think it really screwed her up. And the bastard didn't even have the grace to show up today. His sons made the effort but he didn't.'

'I'm sorry, Elizabeth, I don't know who you are talking about.'

'Toby Priest. The guy who owns Ridgemoor.'

The older man in the football photo. The one playing referee, Jane remembered.

'Did it end badly?' she asked.

Elizabeth shrugged. 'I never got all the grisly details, if that's what you mean. It was all very sudden. One moment she was there in a new job and all was hunky-dory, next thing she's leaving to work in Lancashire, bloody miles away. I'm sure it was because of Toby. You want to know who gave her that money? I bet he did. He was still married at the time, so he just paid her off like some tart.'

'Or . . .' Jane hesitated. Her sympathy for Elizabeth ran deep and she didn't want to upset her unnecessarily. On the other hand, there was no way round it.

'Or what?' the other woman said.

'Could she have been pregnant? And the money was more than just a pay-off.'

'My sister would never have had an abortion, if that's what you're suggesting.' Elizabeth held Jane's gaze without wavering. 'She was passionately pro-life. Unlike me, ironically.'

Jane was trained not to take things at face value but she believed her nevertheless. She took Elizabeth's hand and squeezed it. There were other people gathering round now. 'Thank you,' she said. 'It was a lovely service.'

She walked quickly back to her car, musing on Amanda and Toby Priest. It might not be much to go on but it was more than she'd had before.

*

Dave considered his naked body in the mirror – mirrors, plural, in which, through the steam and condensation from his recent shower, he could view multiple images of his skinny self, reflecting and counter-reflecting into infinity. The blue-and-white mosaic of floor tiles seduced the eye and the extensive array of bathroom fittings gleamed with understated Italian style – or so Dave assumed. He made that glib assumption on the basis that Adriana, Walter Clark's wife, was from Rome and it was she who had been responsible for assembling their home with such loving care. Such care evidently extended to the bathroom of the 'guest suite' where Dave was towelling himself dry after an energetic run over the moors with his old adversary.

Dave lived the simple life, not entirely out of necessity, but that didn't mean he wasn't interested in more complex lifestyles. Walter possessed a five-bedroom mansion surrounded by three acres of landscaped garden, a Toyota Lexus and a seven-seater Galaxy in the drive and a flat-screen television the size of a small cinema in his games room in the basement. He also had two coal-eyed children whose smiling faces peered from a gallery of photos, chronicling their triumphs at prep school sports days. And there was also the afore-mentioned wife, a curvaceous black-ringleted stunner who could have been ordered from a mail-order catalogue of Italian brides – at a price.

Not being the covetous type, Dave thoroughly enjoyed the way Walter displayed his trophy home and family. It helped, of course, that he had never coveted the kind of things that Walter possessed.

When he'd first known Walter he'd been a long-haired student living out of baked bean cans. The reason he had so much hair, some reckoned, was because he couldn't afford a razor. Certainly no woman who was even half-decent-looking cast him a glance of interest away from the athletics track.

Now, as Dave faced Walter across the dinner table, he realised the truth about the hairy student. He'd grown it to cover up his modest appearance. But, weak chin notwithstanding, he had landed the sumptuous Adriana and spawned a brace of children who had inherited their mother's looks and their father's athletic ability. Dave was delighted for him.

'Congratulations, mate,' he said as he pushed back his plate. 'You've done really well for yourself.'

Walter gave him a self-conscious grin. It struck Dave that his old friend was desperate for his approval. He was happy to give it.

So far the conversation, with Adriana in attendance, had focused on Dave, with Walter egging him on to talk about his glory days as an athlete. Dave had played along, tossing as many bouquets in Walter's direction as he could. Not that Walter had seemed keen to catch them.

'Your old man left me for dead last time we competed in earnest,' Dave said to Adriana. 'Caught me at the end of a ten-mile cross-country race like he was on roller skates. He should have kept up serious athletics. He could have been an international.'

Her soot-flecked eyes had widened and the corners of her blush-pink lips relaxed just a touch. She patted her husband's hand as she stood. 'I knew it, darling, you could have been famous,' she said and swished off – to the kitchen, or so Dave presumed.

Having admired the elegance of her retreat, Dave said, 'Kids would be queuing up to be vets if they could see how you live.'

'Well . . .' Walter looked sheepish. 'Not all vets are as lucky as me.'

'How so?'

'I'm a specialist in racehorses. There's a lot of money connected to top-class thoroughbreds.'

'You mean you get good tips?'

Walter laughed. 'I don't bet. It wouldn't look too good if I started gambling on races which included runners I'd been treating.'

Dave thought further. 'You say you're a specialist. You mean, like the average vet is a sort of GP and you specialists are the Harley Street consultants?'

'In a way.'

Adriana came back into the room bearing a colourful platter of sliced fresh fruit which she set down on the table with a flourish. As she moved to the pale-wood sideboard to collect serving dishes she momentarily obscured the view through the picture window of the long green lawn sloping down to Walter's trout stream. If Dave shifted his head he could just catch a glimpse of the conservatory at the side of the house. Further round there was a rockery and a fountain and in the wood on the other side of the football pitch a tree-house for the kids. And so it went on – the Clarks didn't want for much.

This business of being a specialist horse vet, Dave mused to himself, seemed like a licence to print money.

*

Clem wasn't a selfish man but, with his illness closing in on him like a slowly tightening vice, it was hard sometimes to think outside his world of stolen breaths and shrinking mobility. Nevertheless he was attuned to the shifting moods of the women in his life. Something had shaken them up, he was sure of that, and it bothered him.

Last night he'd played cards with Marie, gin rummy, like they often did. It wasn't the greatest game but what card games were any good with just two players? And Joyce wouldn't join in, she never had done.

He'd played cards often with the kids when they were young. Alan had loved gambling games, which were the best sort, of course. Clem remembered the three of them playing poker and wagering with marbles. Edie, his wife, had been upset. 'You're giving them all your bad habits,' she'd said when he'd tried to laugh it off. 'You won't think it's so funny when your son's wasting his life in some casino.'

Shows how much you knew, Edie. Our poor lad never even got the chance to play the slot machine in a pub.

So they'd played rummy instead of poker and recently Marie had been keen to revive the habit.

'Haven't you got something more exciting to do with your life, young lady?' he'd grunted but they'd played all the same and he loved her for it. Only sometimes, especially this winter when most of her friends had gone off to college, he'd wondered if he wasn't the one doing her the favour.

Last night her mind had not been on the game. Deep thoughts had been rolling round her pretty head and she'd kept them locked in there despite his probing.

Joyce had been distracted, too, brushing aside Clem's questions when he asked her what was up. Something was. She'd plonked his breakfast in front of him as if she didn't care if it ended up in his lap. And when he'd asked her to fetch him the TV remote control which had wandered from its place on his table, she'd said, 'What now?' – as if he'd been nagging her all morning.

It was not like her. He wondered if he'd done anything to upset her. Anything beyond being an invalid, that is. He was a burden, he knew that, and one that was getting heavier.

Today's televised race meeting was at Wetherby, a proper Yorkshire-man's jumping course and one of his favourites. Clem subscribed to the view that if an animal could win at Wetherby he could win anywhere. He banished thoughts of domestic discontent and opened the racing paper.

But even there he found no refuge from his troubles. A horse he'd had his eye on for a while, Senegal Sunshine trained by Marcus Pine from across the valley, was being ridden by one Jamie Sullivan.

Marcus Pine was angling to be known as one of racing's eccentrics. He spoke like a toff and favoured coloured waistcoats, muttonchop sideburns and, on occasions, a monocle. He wasn't yet thirty, however, which rather spoiled the illusion from Jamie's point of view. However, since the TV cameras often singled him out at the racecourse, doubtless the charade was serving its purpose.

Fortunately there was no mucking around when it came to briefing his jockey.

'Sunny likes a run round here,' Marcus said to Jamie as Senegal Sunshine was led round the parade ring. 'He jumps left-handed so this course is just up his street. And he should act on this ground – he's happy with a bit of cut in the turf.'

Jamie nodded; he had already looked up the horse's form. He'd run at Wetherby nine times, including his debut in a bumper. 'How should I ride him?'

Marcus tugged thoughtfully on his sidewhiskers. 'You handle it as you see fit but I'd be inclined to track the bay, Butterfingers – he's a grand sort who stays on. Finish ahead of him and you'll have done well.'

Jamie reconsidered his opinion of the trainer. He might be turned out like a clown but the number of trainers who could tell you anything about anyone else's horses could be counted on the fingers of one hand.

The instructions simplified things, especially when Butterfingers tucked in behind the leader who set off at a less-than-threatening pace around two and a half miles of the chase course. Jamie kept the bay in view and concentrated on giving his mount a clear sight of the fences whilst keeping tight to the running rail.

As an apprentice on the Flat he'd been taught that even if you weren't on the best horse in the race, you should at least give him the best chance of winning. That meant going the shortest way and anticipating any problems ahead.

He'd learnt that your whip should always be on the open side, or in the hand closest to the wing of a fence. When you rode with your leg against the paint there was always a chance that a horse might try and run out through the wooden uprights. A good rider could sense what was about to happen and, if your whip was in the correct hand, you could give the horse a crack down the shoulder and save yourself. Jamie prided himself on being comfortable with his whip in either hand, but it amazed him how many of his competitors weren't.

Sunny was a nice horse to ride, with a broad back and a seat as comfortable as a familiar armchair. Fences, ditches and water jumps came all the same to him and he sailed over them with ease. Jamie felt he could have sipped a cup of tea at the same time and not spilt a drop.

Completing the first circuit, Butterfingers had had enough of the leader's sedate progress and slipped past him at an improved clip. Jamie was alert to the move and nudged Sunny on, not letting the bay horse steal a march on them. At the turn for home, Butterfingers' rider darted a quick look over his shoulder to gauge Jamie's proximity and began to pile on the pressure.

Jamie urged Sunny into another gear. The horse was still jumping with effortless style and seemed to have plenty left in the tank.

Together they closed the gap on Butterfingers as the last obstacle arrived. Jamie kicked Sunny into the fence and the pair landed neck and neck. Next to him, Jamie could hear his rival whipping the bay on.

With no fences remaining, this was now a Flat race uphill to the winning post. Jamie realised that he'd been in this situation many times before. He felt his old confidence flow through him. The horse beneath him was tiring but still game – he just had to help the animal dig deep into his last reserves of strength. Keep his rhythm.

The post was arriving fast now and the bay had his neck in front. Jamie stayed cool. Time seemed to have slowed for him, just as it used to do. Riding high on Sunny's shoulders, his hands in close contact with the horse's mouth, he applied the accelerator and Sunny slipped past Butterfingers on the line.

It was his first winner over jumps and it felt just like the old days.

Clem witnessed Jamie's victory with ashes in his mouth. He could have predicted the outcome – in fact, he had. 'Senegal Sunshine will win,' he'd said to his bookie on the phone. But he'd not been able to put his money down – not with Sullivan on the horse's back.

Instead he'd kept his powder dry and watched the race with ghoulish fascination, hoping fervently that the winning jockey would fall off and break his neck.

Jamie spent an exhilarating five minutes in the unsaddling enclosure after the race. It seemed he knew more people on the course than he'd realised. Among the crowd was Desmond Hartley, Vanessa's father.

'I'd recognise that smash-and-grab style of yours anywhere,' the owner said. 'If you'd left it any later you'd have been in the next race. Good to see you back, old boy.'

So Jamie lined up for his second race – a two-mile novice hurdle – on a high. He banished the euphoria of his victory, and the deluge of congratulations that had followed, from his thoughts. He didn't deserve it. The young lad he'd killed would never enjoy moments of success like this, so why should he?

He tried to push the guilt to the back of his mind but it was there all the same, like a cloud over the sun.

Many people, it seemed, shared Desmond Hartley's pleasure at seeing him back winning races. What's more, in a snatched phone call with Pippa, he'd learnt that Bertie Brooks, his former agent, had left a message for Jamie to give him a call. With Bertie representing him he could soon be very busy indeed. It was an enticing prospect.

He shut it out and focused on his mount, Brindisi, a well-made five-year-old trained by Ferdy Gates. The trainer had only recently taken charge of him and Jamie had the impression the horse was a bit of an unknown quantity. If he possessed any special attributes it would be up to Jamie to unearth them during the next four minutes.

Brindisi shot off brightly and Jamie had to pull him back into the pack. The only advice Ferdy had offered was to keep the horse from hitting the front in the early stages. On the way down he'd felt relaxed, just taking a nice hold of his bit, but as the tapes flew up he'd suddenly come to life and Jamie had to take a firm grip.

The horse jumped well and, until halfway round, seemed keen on the task in hand. Then he began to lag. Jamie tried to shake him up a bit. But Brindisi's enthusiasm had faded. It seemed he'd come to the conclusion that this running and jumping lark was too much like hard work.

On reflection – and Jamie had plenty of time for that as a result of what happened next – maybe he tried too hard with the horse in an effort to throw off his lethargy.

As they approached the last hurdle on the far side, he went after the horse with his stick. Brindisi took off two full strides from the obstacle, his front legs paddling desperately as he tried to clear it. He failed. The next moment Jamie was flying through the air and landing with a thump on the springy turf. As he rolled over, a hammer descended on his head.

Clem hadn't been enjoying his afternoon. Racing, particularly National Hunt racing, was the one thing that took his mind off his disability and made the time pass quicker. In the scheme of things his bets were not important – a few pounds here and there – but like any punter he enjoyed his winners and cursed his losers. This afternoon there had been plenty of cursing.

But the big blot on the landscape of his pleasure was Jamie Sullivan's victory. This was the first time he'd seen the jockey ride since his release from prison. Obviously it would not be the last. Despite his antipathy towards the man, Clem could recognise a skilful rider when he saw one and Sullivan, there was no denying, had a future in National Hunt. The thought of many more afternoons in this chair, gasping for breath as Jamie Sullivan rode winners, was profoundly depressing. Hadn't the man robbed him of enough?

He considered his prospects, as he had done many times before. He was hard-headed about his illness. It could not be cured or alleviated. Ahead lay only a further diminishing of his life and, in the end, a painful death. He didn't intend to let it get that far. At some point, he had long ago decided, he would take matters into his own hands. But he'd hoped that would be at a time in the future when Marie had fled the family nest. In an ideal world she'd be with a good man, considering a family of her own. That would be the point to relieve everyone, including himself, of the burden of his existence.

The next race, a novice hurdle, had begun while these unhappy matters churned around in his head. He was miserably aware that Jamie Sullivan was riding once more though not, thankfully, on his own fancy, Palace Party, a 10–1 chance who was running strongly in the leading group.

Slowly the race began to exert its familiar magic. Clem's worries were pushed to one side as the excitement of the moment began to grip. Palace Party was lying second as the commentator announced a faller out of shot. Clem cursed as the producer switched to a riderless horse then back again to the leading runners.

Approaching the last, Palace Party strode clear. The horse flew the final hurdle and galloped to the line to win by five clear lengths.

'You beauty!' growled Clem, savouring the small moment of satisfaction in the gloom of his afternoon.

Then, as the camera switched away from the winner's smiling connections back onto the course, Clem began to realise that something more momentous had taken place. The picture showed a knot of paramedics surrounding a man-shaped bundle lying on the track. An ambulance was in attendance and the voiceover spoke in concerned tones. The race began to run again onscreen, cutting to the point where a runner clipped a hurdle and unseated his rider. Clem clearly saw the jockey rolling over the turf ahead of the last runners in the race. His body spun towards the galloping animals. They passed within a whisker and then, at the last, a trailing hoof smacked the jockey squarely on the back of the head.

'Yes!' roared Clem in triumph.

He'd wanted Jamie Sullivan to break his neck – and it looked as if he just had.

Chapter Eleven

The doctors insisted that Jamie spend forty-eight hours in hospital under observation. After the injuries he had suffered in the car crash, which included severe trauma to the skull, no one was prepared to take any chances. The consensus of opinion was that he had been lucky. All he appeared to have suffered was bruising and a nasty headache.

Jamie didn't mind the restriction – he was used to being confined in one room, as he reminded his many visitors. One of the first was Vanessa. She told him she'd been at the course with her father and seen the incident. She'd followed the ambulance to hospital and kept Pippa up to date on his progress until she could get there herself. Then Vanessa had fielded all enquiries, including press interest, and run errands for Pippa throughout the night. She'd been a heroine.

'You've been on my conscience,' she explained to Jamie when he'd said as much. 'I promised I'd find you a girlfriend and I've done nothing since that ghastly night with poor Georgie. Anyhow,' she continued, 'organising my wedding is turning out to be such a hassle, I just leapt at something else to do. Sorting out one crocked jockey is easy-peasy compared to dealing with my mother and a seating plan for two hundred.'

Back at Shelley Farm, Jamie found himself the recipient of get-well wishes from many quarters. One of the oddest came from Irene Bolt. 'You're a bloody fool, young man,' she bawled down the phone at him. 'I've got High Sierra down for Catterick next Tuesday. I suppose you'll have to miss out now. Unless, of course, there's a chance the doc might give you the all clear?'

With a show of regret Jamie had dashed her hopes. What Palace Party had started, there was a good chance Psycho Sierra would finish off.

An elaborate flower display had been received from the office of Bertie Brooks. The message *I'll call when I get back from Dubai* was scrawled on a card embossed in gold leaf with the letters BBG. It took a moment for Jamie to work out that this stood for the Bertie Brooks Group. Since when had Bertie become a group? Five years ago, he'd been just another bandy-legged jockey scratching around for second-division rides. And the elegant handwriting that flowed across the card was not his, unless he'd been back to school recently. Jamie had to laugh.

The message which most captured his attention was less eye-catching, just a postcard of the Dales stuffed into an envelope. It read: *I was sorry to hear of your accident and hope you make a good recovery. Thank you for helping me with Spring Fever. Yours sincerely, Marie Kirkstall.*

Now, why on earth had she done that?

Dave directed Walter down the rutted path, the Lexus cruising through the puddles, spraying water into the hedgerows. Finally the caravan, its weatherbeaten sides flaking paint and the wheel arches stained with rust, came into sight.

Dave could see that his friend was appalled.

'You don't really live in that, do you?'

'It's not so bad. Come in and I'll make you a cuppa.'

Nevertheless, as he poured boiling water over tea bags in the tiny galley, he noticed Walter staring round uncomfortably. The moth-eaten curtains and cheap plastic fittings were not, Dave knew, to be compared with the Italian chic chez Clark.

They'd spent the morning in an amiable five-mile jog with a couple of Walter's running mates, followed by a session in the pub which Walter had cut short at Dave's request. The meeting had been instigated by the vet, who was plainly enjoying their past association. Dave would have thought that his prison conviction and public fall from grace might have taken the gloss off his reputation. But that was not the case where Walter was concerned. Dave had been paraded like a trophy of the glorious past.

Walter's eyes were flicking back and forth, taking in every detail of their shabby surroundings. They came to rest on Dave. He opened his mouth to speak, then thought the better of it. Dave watched with amusement, wondering how long it would take.

'Can I ask you a question?'

Dave nodded. Here it comes, he thought.

'Are you happy living like this?' Walter pushed a bony index finger along a grime-ridden crack in the Formica of the table top. 'I mean, you're one of the best athletes this country has ever produced. You've held national records at every distance from the three thousand metres to the marathon. You've represented your country at the Olympic Games.'

Dave said nothing; best to let him get it off his chest.

'People with half your experience are all over the radio and TV. They write columns in newspapers and give after-dinner speeches at five grand a pop. You could do the same. At least get together with some journalist and write your autobiography – you've got a great story to tell.'

'Why would I want to do that, Walter?'

The other man's eyes bulged incredulously as he shouted, 'To make some money, of course! Surely you don't want to live in shitheaps like this for the rest of your life?'

Dave said nothing in the silence that followed. Walter looked anxious, worried maybe that he had offended his hero. He pressed for an answer; however, his voice was low this time.

'Come on, mate – you can do better than this. I can help.'

Dave sipped his tea. The truth was, life was simpler without possessions and expectations and all the baggage that went with having a 'career'. Before he'd been banged up he'd had plenty of things – a flat, money in the bank, a girlfriend. All of that had gone down the tubes when he'd been convicted. He'd sold up and spent the money on lawyers. The girl had kissed him goodbye on the day he went to court with his overnight bag and he'd not seen her face since. Apart, that is, from the photographs in the paper illustrating her lurid account of their life together.

'Thanks, Walter, but I'm quite happy as I am. I'm not bothered whether I've got a couple of cars and a Jacuzzi.'

The vet exhaled noisily, trying no doubt to curtail his exasperation. It was plain that the number of cars a person owned bothered *him* a lot.

'But surely you don't object to money on principle?'

Dave was tempted to say yes, he did, just to enjoy Walter's reaction but he didn't want to upset him. He guessed there was at least one topic on Walter's agenda that wasn't a subject for jest.

'Well, I don't mind a few quid in my pocket, if that's what you're suggesting.'

Walter looked relieved. 'Thank God for that.' He leant forward, elbows on the table and said, 'Look, I'm going to give you a little steer. Do yourself a favour and make a note of it.'

Dave was intrigued. 'Oh yes?'

'I shouldn't be telling you this but there's a horse running at Newbury tomorrow.'

'You told me you didn't gamble.'

'I don't.' Walter was indignant. 'I just want to help you out, that's all.'

'Is this a horse you've been treating?'

'I'm not answering any questions, Dave. Let's just say I know of the animal and it's got a good chance. I'll lend you the stake money if you're short. Pay me back if you win.'

'And if I don't?'

Walter shrugged. The possibility appeared not to have entered his head. Dave was curious.

'OK, I'll buy. What's the horse's name?'

'A novice hurdler in the fourth race. Beaufort Bonanza.'

Now Dave was seriously intrigued.

Malcolm drove to Newbury with confidence that this time Adolf would pull off a victory and justify the hoopla that surrounded his every appearance on the track. And when that happy event took place, Malcolm expected to be the recipient of Beverley's gratitude.

He was sorely in need of Beverley's hands-on appreciation. He'd not seen much of her since he'd persuaded his father to go along with Beaufort Holidays' plans for the horse. She'd visited Ridgemoor once to run her eye over a new jockey – they'd agreed on the yard's top apprentice who'd been schooling the horse intensively – and gone along with Toby's suggestion that Adolf have a stab at a longer distance. Barney had been all in favour of an outing at Newbury on the basis that it spread the Beaufort Holidays word in the southern half of the country.

But it had been some while since Malcolm had enjoyed a cosy evening tucked up with Beverley in her pink boudoir. The closest they'd been recently was during that trip to the yard when he'd steered her into the woods after watching Adolf run through his paces. It hadn't been entirely satisfactory. Though there was something to be said for reliving your teenage thrills, these days he preferred a large double bed behind a locked door. And that's what he'd be angling for with Ms Harris once Adolf brought home the bacon today.

Jamie was in two minds about watching Adolf's latest race. He'd been jocked off enough horses in the past not to feel too sore about it but this situation was a bit different. He'd spent so much time with Adolf in recent months that, cussed animal that he was, Adolf did seem like 'his' horse. On the other hand, even if Jamie had originally been booked for the ride, he'd have had to cry off. His jockey's licence had been marked with red ink at Wetherby, and until the last entry was initialled in blue by a Jockey Club doctor he wouldn't be allowed to ride anywhere in the world. Anyhow, at present, he didn't feel fit enough to sit on a garden swing.

To Jamie's surprise, Dave sat down to watch the race with him, cutting short his afternoon training session with Pippa's horses.

'Your sister was right. If horses are happy, you can do what you like with them,' he said as he sprawled on the sofa. 'It's taken me three weeks to discover that that big grey one loves being in front. He's a different horse when he's leading. He works better, eats better. It's amazing.'

Jamie smiled. He was glad of the company and pleased that his friend should be having some success, no matter how small. One of the animals his sister had passed to Dave had gone lame and would be off work for at least six weeks. That left him with only three, to which had been added the grey jump horse, Gates of Eden. As Pippa had pointed out, each time a racehorse goes lame on you, it chips away at your confidence. Then you ease up on the workload of the rest of the string and only a winner will put you back on track.

Unfortunately Dave hadn't yet got one of his animals on the course – though Gates of Eden was entered in a hurdle at Carlisle. Jamie hoped he'd be fit enough to ride him and he was encouraged to hear of his progress, though he couldn't remember whether he was a front-runner or not. In fact he couldn't remember much of anything at present. He seemed to spend most of the time by himself, drifting woozily in and out of consciousness under the influence of painkillers.

'Don't let me go to sleep,' he said to Dave. 'I can hardly keep my eyes open these days.'

207

'There's no chance you'll get any kip with me around. I'm a bit
noisy when I've got money on a race.'
That woke Jamie up. 'You're having a bet?'
'Sure. That's the point of watching horses on the box, isn't it?'
'And?'
'And what?'
'Who's your money on then?'
'Adolf, of course.'
Jamie was flabbergasted. This was only Adolf's third race and he'd
yet to finish. What's more, he was attempting half a mile further than
he'd run before.
Dave was grinning at him, waiting for Jamie's objections.
'You obviously think he's going to improve now I'm not on him.'
'If you want to put it like that. I've got a good price, too.'
To Jamie's way of thinking, that was about the only aspect of the
wager that made sense. Much as he was attached to Adolf, the horse
was no champion in the making. He'd need to improve from his last run
just to get a place.

Having paid his respects over a glass of champagne, Malcolm gave the
Beaufort hospitality box a wide berth for much of the afternoon. He
bought drinks for a couple of trainers he'd worked with in the past and
chatted up an investment banker who was thinking of wasting his
money on some fancy horseflesh – not that Malcolm sold the prospect
to him in those terms. But as the time of Adolf's race approached,
Malcolm could not put off his return. A knot of discomfort had formed
in his chest – an increasingly familiar sensation when a certain person
came to mind. He didn't understand how a woman like Beverley could
have sunk her hooks so deep, but she had. And the prospect of seeing
her cosy up to Barney while the big-mouthed businessman paraded her
in public filled Malcolm with fury and an emotion that he'd never felt
before. For the first time in his life he was jealous.
His only consolation was that, on this occasion, there was every
chance that Beaufort Bonanza would put on a good show. Steps had
been taken. Like certain top cyclists, endurance athletes and, undoubtedly, some other racehorses, Adolf was about to benefit from the effects
of a drug that increased the supply of oxygen to his muscles. Some said
EPO didn't work and that it put the horses in danger. So far, to

Malcolm's knowledge, his father had achieved only good results. Fingers crossed, the success would continue.

The mood in the Beaufort box was less raucous than usual, possibly because these southern guests were less impressed by the generous liquid hospitality and more aware that the horse flying the company flag was facing failure for the third time in a row. Malcolm could see the tension in Barney's face and Beverley, while chatting animatedly to those around her, looked straight through Malcolm when he tried to catch her eye.

Guy Greaves, a well-tailored individual to whom Malcolm had been introduced earlier, appeared at his elbow. 'So, Mr Priest, what are our chances of finally seeing a return on the company investment?'

Malcolm recalled that Greaves sat on the Beaufort board. He looked like a sharp customer.

'Every chance, I'd say.' Malcolm sounded more bullish than he felt. 'He's had a couple of handy trial runs and now I expect to see the best of him.'

'What makes you think he can last an extra half mile?'

That was a good question – one that Malcolm was prepared for, however. 'My father's observation of him in training, really. He's not the fastest but he's built to last. We think he'll benefit from a longer trip.'

'Really?' It was obvious from his tone that Greaves was sceptical. 'I see the bookmakers don't share your optimism.'

Adolf was priced around 16–1 in the ring.

'All the more reason to get your money on, Guy.' Malcolm produced his own betting slip from his pocket. 'I've got a Beaufort Holidays Luxury Leisure Break riding on this.'

He had his eye on Beverley's shining dark hair as he spoke – he knew exactly who he intended to accompany him if he won.

Jamie looked at the list of runners in the paper. 'I see young Carlo's got the ride on Adolf. He's half Italian, you know.'

As it happened Dave did know. Carlo was the lad he'd seen riding Adolf on the day he took Malcolm's phone over to Ridgemoor. But Dave had no intention of letting on about that. He was still trying to pretend he'd not seen Pippa's husband all over that Beaufort woman.

'I hope he's tough enough,' Jamie mused. 'Adolf pulls like a train.'

Dave was well aware that Malcolm was one of the Beaufort party at Newbury for the race. She'd be there too, that Beverley. It made Dave's blood boil – Pippa didn't deserve such treatment. He'd almost put his foot in it with her just that morning.

'Aren't you going to Newbury with Malcolm?' he'd asked.

'Don't be daft,' she'd said. 'I've got too much to do here.'

'I just thought – he's away a lot, isn't he? Don't you fancy going along sometimes?'

She'd given him a funny look. 'We've both got our own businesses to run, Dave. I can't go tagging after him even if I had the time. He'd think I didn't trust him.'

Well, quite. Dave had shut up after that. It was none of his business after all. Not really.

'Look, Adolf's gone all buzzy again. Carlo's going to have to hang on tight.'

Jamie's remark brought Dave's attention back to the screen. The horses were lining up for the start of the race, two miles five furlongs round a wide, left-handed oval over eleven hurdles. Dave picked out the scarlet and white of Adolf's colours and the shape of the big horse as he jostled impatiently amongst the other runners.

The tape went up and Adolf got a flying start, bolting straight into the lead.

'Go on, you beauty!' yelled Dave.

'Calm down, mate. You don't want him belting off like that – he'll shoot his bolt before he's gone a mile.'

'I always like to see my money in front.'

Jamie laughed. 'There speaks the great race tactician. Is that how you used to run yourself?'

While Dave was searching for a smart retort, another horse came out of the pack and, clearly out of control, stormed past Adolf, closely followed by another.

'That's better,' said Jamie. 'Carlo can hide him behind those two maniacs and settle him down.'

Dave supposed Jamie was right. 'Come on, Adolf,' he roared, just for the fun of it.

*

In the Beaufort box Malcolm was feeling considerably better now the jockey had Adolf under control and tracking the leaders. He'd gone along with Beverley's demand to dump Jamie because it was easy to comply with but there was no denying that his brother-in-law was a forceful rider. Inexperienced though Jamie was over jumps, Malcolm would have been happier if he were still in charge. But Carlo seemed to have weathered the storm. All he had to do was keep the horse tucked in behind the leading two and let the horse's natural ability – in this case his enhanced natural ability – take effect.

The horses were rounding the far bend out in the country, with the best part of a mile still to run. Adolf was travelling well, taking the hurdles in his stride and keeping out of trouble.

'Are you still confident?' murmured Guy Greaves's voice by his side.

Malcolm didn't take his eye off the runners as he tracked them through his field glasses.

'Very,' he replied – and he was.

'Oh yes, my son,' yelled Dave, bouncing in his chair. 'It's in the bag.'

Adolf had taken up the running from three furlongs out with No Sanctuary, the favourite, also making ground a few lengths behind.

'Don't count your chickens. No Sanctuary's a good horse.'

But Jamie's words of caution were wasted on Dave. Even the sight of the more fancied horse steaming up on the outside could not dampen his confidence.

The pair were neck and neck at the beginning of the long home straight, with three hurdles remaining. Adolf pecked at the first and lost ground.

Dave groaned.

Apparently unfazed, Adolf came back at No Sanctuary only to slip back at the next hurdle.

'The other horse is a better jumper,' said Jamie, 'but Adolf looks stronger. It's as if he doesn't even notice the hurdles. He just gallops straight through them.'

Adolf was a length up going to the last, took it out by the roots and powered five lengths clear before he had crossed the line, with No Sanctuary flagging in the rear.

'That was amazing,' said Jamie. 'He's never run that distance in his life.'

Dave was on his feet, punching the air. And it wasn't just the thrill of backing the winner that fuelled his excitement. He now had a fair idea why Pippa's horses kept losing to Toby Priest.

Barney Beaufort milked the moment for all it was worth, which came as no surprise to anyone, least of all Malcolm. The company's own photographer was on hand to take shots of Barney with an exhausted Adolf, accepting the piddling winner's cheque from the race sponsor and posing with assorted guests and dignitaries. Malcolm had no doubt that the next edition of the Beaufort Holidays newsletter – to which he appeared to be a subscriber – would require some extra pages.

Back in the hospitality suite the jollity continued with, inevitably, a degree of ceremony attached. Barney evidently considered it a prime duty of the chairman and CEO to dignify every public occasion with a speech. Malcolm reckoned you'd have to shoot the old windbag to keep him quiet – a notion that had its attractions.

Nevertheless, he charged his glass as instructed and listened to Barney's meandering account of the events which had led to this historic moment. His own name was bandied about and he took a modest bow, as requested, when he was identified as the connoisseur of horseflesh who had brought Bonanza to the company's attention.

From then on, the spotlight shifted to the real heroine of Barney's tale, the young executive blessed not only with a bonny face but a brilliant mind, Beverley Harris. She it was who had championed Bonanza's cause in the face of company scepticism, had stuck up for the horse when he'd under-achieved on his first outings and who had brought about the changes in racing strategy which had led to this victory.

Malcolm nearly choked on his Scotch. All Beverley knew about horses was which end produced manure. He looked up and found himself staring into Guy Greaves's pale shrewd face, now brimming with amusement.

'Laying it on a bit thick, isn't he?' murmured Guy. 'Of course, there's a reason for that.'

'And what would that be?' Malcolm wasn't in the mood to listen to gossip about Barney and his Marketing Director – he was only too aware of their relationship. At least, he thought he was.

'Dear Beverley's been such a tower of strength since Barney's wife walked out.'

'What? She's left him?'

'Last year. Val found someone younger in advertising. Better-looking and just as rich. Barney was very cut up. Couldn't look at any other women.'

Malcolm was considering Greaves in a new light. The man was a bitchy little gossip.

'It took simply ages for Beverley to get romance on the agenda but she cracked it in the end. The smart money says she'll be the new Mrs B once the divorce comes through.'

'When did she crack it exactly?'

Greaves pulled a face. 'Well, I couldn't give you a precise timetable.'

'Go on, have a try.'

The businessman thought for a moment. 'If you ask me, the time she really began to fill in for Val was when the business of buying a horse came up.'

Malcolm thought as much. He'd always known she was tricky – that was part of her appeal – but he didn't like being the one who was tricked.

Applause was echoing round the room as Barney's tribute came to an end. Beverley beamed in appreciation. Malcolm knew it was impossible from this distance, but as her gaze swept over him he fancied he saw triumph in those milky blue eyes.

He'd never been beaten by a woman before and he didn't like it one bit.

Marie stayed late at the surgery which wasn't entirely sensible since (a) she wasn't paid for overtime (b) once she'd finished the clerical backlog she'd be out of a job altogether and (c) her Chemistry A-level resit was looming and she was behind on her revision. But the prospect of returning home was so gloomy.

There had been an atmosphere in the house for a few days, ever since she'd come in to find her dad and Aunt Joyce cock-a-hoop in front of the television.

'Look at this, lass,' her dad had shouted, more excited than she'd seen him for months. Then he'd replayed her a section of a horse race which he'd recorded. This wasn't that unusual. He often recorded races and played back his winning moments for her appreciation. But this was different.

She'd watched in alarm as a jockey had been unseated and then, as he spun across the turf, the camera had clearly picked out the moment when a horse's hoof had smacked into him, sending his head rocking on his shoulders. Why on earth did he want her to see this?

'You know who that is, don't you, sweetheart?'

'No, Dad.' But she'd known, really, even before her father told her.

'It's that little bastard Jamie Sullivan. Almost kicked his head clean off his shoulders, didn't he?'

'Is he all right?' she'd asked, fear twisting her stomach.

Her father had laughed long and loud. 'What do you think? They've carted him off to hospital. Next stop the funeral parlour, with a bit of luck.'

She'd wanted to smack the smug grin off his big red face. 'Sometimes, Dad,' she'd said, 'you really disgust me.' And she'd stormed off to her room.

The next day, sick of hearing her father and Aunt Joyce glorying over Jamie's accident, she'd scribbled a hasty postcard to the jockey, wishing him a swift recovery. It was a small gesture to offset the unChristian feelings of the rest of her family. She knew why they felt the way they did but it wasn't right.

Now she felt guilty. Dad and Auntie Joyce would be furious if they knew what she'd done. She'd betrayed them. Jamie Sullivan was, after all, the man who had killed her brother – he ought to suffer. So what if he'd served his prison sentence? He should suffer and suffer and suffer until he was dead like Alan. That's how Dad and Joyce felt and wasn't it her duty to support them?

Not exactly. They weren't due her uncritical backing, not if it meant going against her personal beliefs. And she did not believe in the hate and malice that fuelled their every thought of Jamie. As far as she was concerned, she could not be expected to like a man who had, through his negligence and contempt for the law, been the instrument of her brother's death. But he too had paid a price for his actions and, if he had any decent feelings, would carry on paying for the rest of his days.

The truth was that all of them – Dad, Aunt Joyce and Jamie Sullivan, too – had to get on with their lives. They must live as best they could, not letting the bad things of the past poison the future. It was now two and a half years since Alan's death. Where was the sense in picking at old wounds? Surely it was time to heal.

All of which was very noble, but her father didn't have much of a future before him and she'd betrayed him by writing to the man who'd robbed him of his son. As for Aunt Joyce, the way she looked at her these days and quizzed her on her whereabouts – it was as if she knew. Knew that she'd met Jamie at Ros's yard, had talked to him and sent him a get-well letter.

She picked another file from the pile on the floor and opened it. She wasn't going home just yet.

Jamie was walking but his feet didn't seem to touch the ground. He concentrated on keeping upright. Someone was by his side holding him. That was good. He couldn't fall with that strong grip on his arm, pushing him forward. It had been a long time since somebody had held him like this. Probably since he was a kid, being dragged along by his mum. But he wasn't a kid any more, was he? If he could ask the question, then he couldn't be, surely?

'Come on, Jamie, old son. The car's just over here.'

Who was that? The mummy-person, it had to be. The strong one, dragging him along.

'What's going on, Malcolm?'

That was someone else. A woman. He could see her now. Worth looking at, too. Pretty little blonde. Bit plump maybe but highly shaggable. He knew her, didn't he? What was her name?

'Is he all right?'

'Yeah, just a bit pissed. We'll get him home, Mandy, don't worry.'

Mandy, that was it, the one Malcolm had been cosying up to. Perhaps he should offer her a lift.

'Jesus, Malcolm, you're not going to let him drive, are you?'

Of course he was going to drive. It was his car. Nobody drove his car.

'Don't be stupid, mate, you can hardly stand.'

So what? You sat down to drive.

'Very funny, Jamie. Rich, look in his pocket for the keys, will you?'

If Richard laid a hand on him, he'd smack him in the mouth.

'Go back inside, Mandy. We'll deal with him.'

Yes, go back inside. He'd drop these two silly sods off and come back for her later.

215

'Are you sure you'll be all right?'

'We'll be fine, won't we, Rich?'

She was gone and they were walking again. Where were they going? Oh yes, to the car. He was going to drive now. Fantastic – no need to worry about moving his legs. Wheee!

Just as well this was a dream. You could do what the hell you liked in dreams.

'Malcolm!' Beverley looked amazed to see him standing on her doorstep at seven-thirty in the morning. 'What on earth are you doing here?'

'Let me in and I'll tell you.'

For a moment he thought she wasn't going to. She wore a blue-patterned, thigh-high dressing gown over not much and her legs were bare.

'I'll make you breakfast while you get dressed,' he said, to make it clear his intention wasn't just to turn up and park himself in her bed. Not that he didn't have hopes but it was best to let Bev think she called the shots.

'OK,' she said grudgingly and stood aside to let him in. He couldn't resist sliding his arms around her for a good morning kiss but she turned her cheek then slipped out of his grasp.

'Just coffee for me,' she said, pointing to the kitchen. 'I've got to be out of here by half past.'

While the kettle was boiling, he hunted for some coffee beans and unearthed some eggs. He ought to eat something to counter the flutter of excitement in his stomach. From above he could hear the creak of floorboards as Beverley moved around her bedroom. He could picture her standing naked in front of her dressing-table, selecting her underwear, buttoning her blouse.

He'd only spent the whole night with her once in this house, at the beginning of their fling, and he'd lain in bed the next morning savouring the sight of her dressing for work. He'd often thought that the sight of a woman getting dressed was as much of a turn-on as the process in reverse. On that memorable occasion he'd been so turned-on by the time she zipped up her skirt that he'd virtually torn it off her and she'd had to dress herself again half an hour later. How would she react this time, he wondered, if he went upstairs and repeated the treatment?

He was sorely tempted to find out. But then he thought of her recent snubs, the unreturned phone calls, the conversation he'd had with Guy Greaves at Newbury and concentrated on grinding the coffee beans.

Finally her heels clacked on the stone-flagged kitchen floor and she took the mug of coffee he held out to her. She wore one of her most severe suits, pinstripe charcoal, her shirt was pinned at the throat with an old-fashioned cameo brooch and the coils of her hair were pulled off her face, accentuating the dark frames of her spectacles. The message could not have been clearer if she'd worn a sign saying *Don't touch.*

He indicated the pan of scrambled eggs and a rack of toast. 'Sure you're not hungry?'

She shook her head. 'I suppose you're wondering why I haven't been in touch since the Newbury meeting,' she said. 'Before you start, there's letter on its way to you.'

'A letter? What's wrong with the phone?'

'We wanted to formally express our appreciation following Beaufort Bonanza's success the other day.'

He buttered a piece of toast. 'Sounds like you're giving me notice.'

'No.' She sat opposite him. 'But I will if we can't put our relationship on a more professional footing.'

'Oh really?' He felt his pulse beginning to quicken. 'So what does a professional like you charge for a bunk-up then?'

Her eyes blinked as she absorbed his remark. 'That's not funny, Malcolm,' she said softly.

He chewed his food without tasting it.

'What I mean is,' she continued, 'you and I can't continue to see each other except on business. It's been great fun but I think it's run its course.'

'Bollocks.' He pushed his plate away and watched it halt dangerously close to the edge of the table. He wished it had smashed to pieces on the stone, scattering gobs of egg and china fragments over her shiny black square-toed shoes. 'What you mean is, you've got what you want out of me and now you'd like me to sod off.'

She sighed. 'I'm sorry, but one person always has to be the first to pull out of a relationship that's not working.'

'Come off it, Beverley, I know what you've been up to. You've been using me to get at old man Beaufort. He was cut up when his wife left him and you couldn't get him interested. So you started putting yourself about with me so he could see what he was missing. Now he's hooked and you don't need me any more.'

Behind her spectacles her pale eyes narrowed. He imagined he'd surprised her and she was wondering whether to contest the point.

She switched tack. 'Malcolm, what possible future could you and I have? You're not going to leave your wife for me, are you? As far as you're concerned I'm just a bit on the side.'

'And old Beaufort's the love of your life, is he?'

Beverley got abruptly to her feet. 'Barney's not old, Malcolm. He's in his mid-fifties and as much of a man as you are. What's more, he's a good man and he needs me in all sorts of ways. You only want to get me into bed.'

Malcolm couldn't argue with that.

She dumped her mug in the sink and stood with her back towards him, her head bowed. 'You'd better leave me alone from now on.'

'Or?'

She turned to face him. 'Or I'll take steps to ensure that you do.'

Was she threatening him? She had balls, he'd give her that.

She looked at her watch. 'Time to go. I don't want to be late.'

He decided to leave quietly – this time.

'How are you feeling?'

'Better for being out here.'

Jamie and Vanessa were leaning on a gate overlooking the section of moor that Pippa used for her gallops. Dave's group of horses were racing across the turf in the near distance, tracked by an old Land Rover.

'I recognise that horse.' Vanessa pointed to the big grey animal in the lead.

'Gates of Eden. He's our only jumper – used to run on the Flat.'

'You rode him at Ascot, didn't you? I remember.'

Jamie nodded, wishing it was him out there on Gates of Eden right now. Ros and Pippa had thought including the grey in Dave's sessions might help build up his stamina. It had certainly helped remove some of the extra weight the animal had been carrying.

But much as Jamie wished to get back on board, he'd be a fool to mount a horse at the moment. He still had a stiff neck and wobbly legs. To be honest, however, his problems were as much mental as physical.

Though Jamie had been spending most of his days lying in bed, semi-comatose, he never seemed to get any proper sleep. It seemed he could shut his body down, but not his mind – and the result was that he felt permanently exhausted. And there was nothing to do. He couldn't concentrate on books or television. If he showed his face in the yard Pippa chivvied him away and Dave was too busy just to keep him company. It had been a relief when Vanessa turned up to check on his progress and suggested going for a walk.

'When's he going to race?' Vanessa was still assessing Gates of Eden.

'He's entered at Carlisle in about ten days. I was worried he wouldn't be ready. Now I'm not sure I'll make it.'

Vanessa tucked her arm through his. 'Cheer up, you old misery guts. You'll be fine by then.'

'Yeah.' It was true, he was being a bit down in the mouth. Time to change the subject. 'Can I ask your advice?'

He didn't wait for her reply but plunged on to tell her about Marie Kirkstall – Ros asking him to avoid the yard, finding Marie in difficulties on a horse and the card she'd sent wishing him well.

'After the crash, I was in hospital for a while. It took a long time for me to realise exactly what I'd done, because I had no memory of the accident. When I finally understood that I'd killed someone I wanted to write to the family. To acknowledge my guilt, I suppose. But I couldn't do the simplest things. I could barely write my own name. I wasn't capable of writing the letter and I didn't want to get someone else to do it for me – it wouldn't have been right.'

He stopped for a moment, gathering his thoughts. She squeezed his arm in encouragement.

'As time went by it got harder to think exactly what I'd say – it seemed more and more like a self-serving exercise. Like I was looking for forgiveness for an act that couldn't be forgiven. So I never did write to them. Then there was a lot of nasty stuff in the papers about the family's grief and how much they hated me for what I'd done. And, of course, I knew I was going to go to prison. So I just sort of shut down. In self-preservation, I suppose.

'But now I've met Marie and though she said she didn't want to see me she came looking for me at Ros's place and she's sent me a get-well card. Why would she do that? And what should I do?'

Vanessa considered the matter. 'Sounds like you want to send her that letter you couldn't write before.'

It was true, he did.

'Do you think I could? I don't want to upset her but I think it would help me.'

It would be like an offender coming face to face with his victim. It would be painful but it would be worth it.

'Do it then, Jamie. She's given you the opportunity.'

'Thanks,' he said. She'd confirmed his opinion. He'd write to Marie and ask Ros to give her the letter. He wouldn't ask for forgiveness, just for the opportunity to express his sorrow. The fact that he hadn't written to Alan Kirkstall's family had been preying on his mind. Maybe when he'd done it, he could go forward properly with his life.

They strolled back down the hill. There was a spring in Jamie's step.

'Maybe writing to Marie will sort my head out,' he said. 'I've been having the strangest dreams about the accident.'

'I thought you couldn't remember it.'

'I can't, but you know what dreams are like. You get all your worries and neuroses all muddled up in some weird scenario that seems absolutely real. Last night I dreamt I was leaving the pub on the night of the crash, absolutely legless, and that poor girl Mandy turned up.'

'The girl who was killed?'

'Yes. In my dream she started having a go at Malcolm for letting me get in the car pissed and I told Richard I'd thump him if he took my car keys off me.'

'Is that what actually happened?'

'God, no. I can't remember what happened. But this stuff has been flying round my head ever since I got kicked last week. Maybe if I write to Marie it will put an end to it. Do you think?'

She suddenly threw her arms round him and hugged him tight, giggling as she did so.

'What's so funny?' he asked when she'd let him go.

'You.'

'Sorry, I don't get it.'

Her face straightened and she looked him squarely in the eye. 'OK. What does Marie Kirkstall look like?'

He was puzzled. 'What's that got to do with it?'

'Is she pretty?'

He thought about it. 'She's a damn sight better-looking than pretty.'

The irritating woman was still laughing by the time they got back down to the yard.

Chapter Twelve

'I really didn't like that man,' said Jane as Simon drove down the country lane that led away from Toby Priest's yard. 'There's something slimy about him.'

'He's a pillar of the racing establishment.'

'He was trying to look down my blouse.'

Her colleague chuckled, a rich fruity sound that filled the car. 'Well, you are looking quite fetching today, boss.'

'Oh, shut up,' Jane snapped. She wasn't his boss any more but she couldn't deny she was looking her best. She wore her new navy suit and a pastel blue shirt which was only comfortable if she left the top two buttons undone. She'd made an effort with her hair and even applied a touch of eye make-up. It was pathetic really, titivating herself for a man who'd never shown the least romantic interest in her. But so what? She might as well boost her own morale.

She'd not seen Simon for a good ten days, not since they'd been instructed to back-burner the Bonfire case, and the drive to Yorkshire on a fine spring morning had been a treat – even if the point of it was to spend some time in the company of a puffed-up piece of work like Toby Priest.

To her surprise Simon turned off the road and parked in front of a pub with a thatched roof and a garden bathed in midday sunshine.

He turned towards her. 'Time for a quick sandwich?'

She shouldn't really. She had a pile of stuff she ought to be getting on with back in Preston. On the other hand, they'd been on the go since half eight and their surprised interviewee hadn't even offered them a glass of water.

'Good idea,' she said.

As yet there were few lunchtime customers but the barman was putting the finishing touches to a seductive-looking menu chalked on a blackboard over the fireplace.

'This is my treat,' she said firmly. It was too good to resist.

Ten minutes later they were tucking into a substantial lunch in the garden. The food was hearty – home-made steak pie and roast vegetables – and she'd bought Simon a pint on the basis that she would take over the driving. A fresh breeze rippled over the nearby duck pond, sharpening the appetite.

'So,' she said when the issue couldn't be put off any longer, 'what did you think of Toby Priest?'

They'd arrived at Ridgemoor at ten and had been left kicking their heels for some time in the house while the trainer had been summoned from the yard. He'd eventually turned up, wearing a face like thunder, obviously irritated at the interruption to his morning affairs. He'd been immediately mollified by Jane's hint of cleavage – or so it seemed to her – but had reverted to annoyance when the purpose of their business became apparent.

'Amanda Parkin? The poor girl who was murdered? I don't see how I can help you.'

'We understand that she used to work for you.'

'Only for a few weeks.'

'Almost six months, actually, Mr Priest. We'd be interested to hear why she left.'

'How do you expect me to remember that? I've got over forty staff at this stable. They come and go like day-trippers sometimes, I can't keep up with them. You'd be better off talking to my head lad.'

'Surely you remember Amanda, Mr Priest? We understand you had a close relationship with her for a while.'

That had surprised him and he'd looked at them suspiciously for a moment, obviously wondering just how much they knew. Jane thought he might deny the relationship, but he didn't.

'There's no law against a man falling for a pretty girl, is there? I was in the middle of a divorce at the time and she was kind enough to cheer me up.'

Jane kept quiet, hoping that Priest might volunteer more information. It worked, up to a point.

'I was very sad when I heard what had happened to Mandy. Very sad

222

indeed. Drugs are a terrible thing, as I'm sure you two officers know better than me. If she'd stayed here at Ridgemoor I like to think we could have given her the kind of pastoral care that would have saved her from such a fate. Everyone, no matter how junior, counts at this yard and we look out for each other.'

You hypocrite, Jane thought. A couple of minutes ago the trainer had said he wasn't responsible for his rapid turnover of staff, now he claimed he was head of a big happy family.

'Did you try to persuade Amanda to stay?'

'Yes, I did but she'd made up her mind. To be honest, I couldn't blame her. Once we'd had our fun why would she want to carry on working for me?'

'Would you say the relationship came to an amicable end?'

'Absolutely. No hard feelings on either side. I accepted that she really needed to settle down with a man her own age.'

'So she went with your blessing?'

'That's right.' He sounded hesitant, as if he didn't know where this was going.

'Did she leave with anything else? Like a sum of money?'

'Why would I give her money?'

'I wondered if, as an employee, she was entitled to a redundancy payment.'

He guffawed loudly. 'I've never made a stable groom redundant in my life. I'd have a hard time claiming I didn't need staff to muck out the horses. What on earth are you on about?'

Jane thought it was time to come clean. So she told him about the £10,000 payment into Amanda's building society account.

'We just wondered, given your professional and personal association with Amanda, whether you might know how she came by it.'

For a moment he looked confused. Then he amazed her. 'I do know, as a matter of fact. I gave it to her.'

Jane was flabbergasted. In the silence that followed, Simon spoke for the first time.

'But you just told us you didn't. "Why would I give her money?" I believe you said.'

'I'm sorry, I forgot.'

'You forgot you gave Amanda ten thousand pounds?' Jane found her voice but she couldn't keep the incredulity out of it.

'It slipped my mind.' Priest had some nerve – he barely looked embarrassed.

'Are you in the habit,' said Jane in as neutral a tone as she could manage, 'of giving your old girlfriends such substantial sums of money?'

The trainer smiled; his confidence had evidently returned. 'I hope most of my former lady friends would consider me a generous man.' He turned to Simon. 'I regret that my ex-wives might not put me in that category, however.'

Simon remained poker-faced. 'So the ten thousand pounds was just a gift?'

'That's right. I was very fond of Amanda. If you want to analyse our relationship I suppose it had a touch of father and daughter about it. Like any good father I wanted to send her off into the world with some money in her purse.

'Anyway,' he added, shifting his defence, 'in my business ten thousand pounds is not that significant a sum. I've got horses in my yard that were worth millions as untried yearlings. It cost one of my owners ninety thousand pounds just to make a late entry for the Derby. And if one of my stable jockeys rides a couple of classic winners he could probably retire on his share of the stud fees. I'm sorry to say this probably puts your police pension in the shade but it also places my little gift to Amanda in perspective, wouldn't you say?'

'Karen, hi – it's Malcolm.'

'Miss Harris is still in a meeting, Mr Priest.'

'Come off it, sweetheart, she just doesn't want to speak to me.'

'If there's an urgent message I can get it to her when they break for lunch. Otherwise, I'm sure she'll be dealing with her calls later. I'll make sure yours are on top of the pile.'

'You're an angel, Karen.'

'Thank you, Mr Priest, but I'd prefer not to be called sweetheart or angel. May I also suggest that there's no need for you to call again?'

'But then I wouldn't have a chance to talk to you, Karen honey. Oh – whoops. I bet I'm not supposed to call you honey either.'

'Have you been drinking, Mr Priest?'

'That's a very personal question, Karen honey. Why don't you and I get together to discuss it? We could do it over a drink. What do you say? If I can't have the organ-grinder, maybe I could have the monkey.'

'I'm going to put the phone down now, Mr Priest, and I would strongly advise you not to ring any more.'

'And I'd strongly advise you to take the poker out of your arse.'

But Malcolm was talking to the dial tone – which was probably just as well.

The wind was picking up, sending ripples racing across the surface of the pond, and scudding clouds were interrupting the sunshine. But, internally fortified by her substantial lunch, Jane was not conscious of the changing weather. She was waiting for Simon's reply to her question.

'What do I think of Toby Priest?' He polished off his pint and set the glass down with a bang. 'Personally, I think he's a nasty piece of work. Massive ego. A bully. As two-faced as they come. If he wasn't a successful horse-trainer he'd probably make a top politician, a captain of industry or,' his green eyes flashed wickedly, 'a Chief Constable.'

Jane couldn't disagree. 'Which makes it all the more puzzling why he admitted giving Amanda that money. He denied it at first then changed his tune. Why?'

'Beats me. Let's go inside and have a coffee. You're not dressed for spring in Yorkshire.'

It was true, she wasn't. Gratefully, she allowed herself to be steered indoors.

'Are you thinking what I'm thinking?' she said as they took their coffee to a far corner.

'Unlikely,' he said. 'I'm thinking how much that pastel blue suits you.'

'For God's sake, Simon, keep your mind on the job.'

'Sorry, boss, must be the beer.' His teeth were white in the gloom of their corner as he grinned at her. She mustn't allow herself to be distracted.

'Look,' she said, 'it's obvious he was telling the truth in the first place when he said he hadn't given her the money. And when he laughed at the idea of making redundancy payments to stable staff – that rang true, all right. The horses might cost a lot but you can bet the stable girls earn a pittance. Ten grand would have been a fortune to Amanda.'

Simon nodded patiently. She knew that look; he was waiting for her to make her point. And so she would – in her own time.

'So his first reaction was the truthful one but, when he thought about it, he changed his story and admitted he'd given her the money. Then he had the nerve to come out with a load of sentimental tripe about being a father to her.'

'You can get locked up for being that kind of father,' muttered Simon.

Jane ignored him. 'So the question is, why did he admit to doing something he didn't do?'

'I'm sure you're going to tell me.'

'I certainly am. He did it to protect someone. He knows who really gave her the money but he doesn't want us to find out. So he said he did it instead. Who's he covering up for? That's what we need to find out.'

'Correction, Jane, that's what *you* need to find out.'

'You disagree then?'

'No, I don't. I agree he lied just as you say and there's probably some hooky horse-racing reason why Amanda had ten grand from him. Like, maybe, he was giving her money to lay bets on sure things. You can imagine him trying to impress her. Men will say anything if they think it will get a girl into bed. Anyhow, she banked the money instead and took off with a younger bloke. Whatever it is, I bet you it's got nothing to do with who killed her. That's down to some out-of-order drug-dealer who fancied pinching Pete's wedge and she just happened to be in the way, poor kid.'

Oh.

'I'm sorry, Jane,' he said. 'That's just the way I see it.'

He was probably right. Whatever, she didn't have the time or resources to take it any further.

'Another coffee?' he asked.

She nodded and he headed for the bar. She watched him go. Had he really complimented her on the colour of her shirt? Was that the kind of thing *he* said when he wanted to get a girl into bed?

But he wasn't interested in her. Was he?

Pippa was out in the paddock with Dave. They were watching one of the lads, Micky, school Gates of Eden over some small fences when her mobile phone rang. She broke off to take the call.

She didn't recognise the voice – a female with a flat Yorkshire accent – but the name was familiar. She knew that Beverley Harris worked for one of Malcolm's clients. Why was she calling her?

'I don't know how you've come through on this number,' she said. 'Malcolm's at his office.'

'Actually, it's you I want to talk to, Pippa.'

Pippa? They'd never spoken before.

The voice dropped, taking on a confidential tone. 'I thought we needed a chat. Woman to woman, if you know what I mean.'

Pippa certainly didn't. The voice pressed on slyly.

'It's about your Malcolm. He's a bit of a ladies' man, isn't he? We've had to spend a deal of time together on this horse-racing business and I'm afraid he's inclined to overstep the mark.'

'I don't follow you, Miss Harris.'

'Look, Pippa, I'm a grown woman and I know how to handle a man with Desert's Disease.'

'What?'

'Desert's Disease – wandering palms. Surely you've heard the expression? Well, anyway, you get my drift. Malcolm is inclined to put his paws all over a girl. I meet all sorts of men in the course of business and most of them are like little boys. Show them a sweetie and they think they can pop it straight in their gobs. It's like that with your Malcolm. Let him glimpse an inch above your knee and next thing he'll have his hand up your skirt.'

Pippa was racking her brains. Surely this was a practical joke? This conversation could not be real.

'Excuse me, who did you say you were again?'

The woman's voice changed, grew harder. 'You know very well, so don't pretend you don't know what I'm on about. Your husband's been trying it on with me for weeks and now he's started pestering my staff. Can't you keep him under control? It's flaming obvious he's not getting what he needs at home and I reckon it's down to you to sort him out.'

Pippa was shaking. She wanted to end the call but she couldn't. There was something compelling about this awful voice and the poison it was pouring into her ear.

The woman reverted to her earlier note of assumed friendship. 'I'm not blaming you, Pippa. After all, it's not as if you need to wear a bag over your head. I've seen your picture. You could be a real babe if you made more of an effort. Buy yourself some tarty knickers – never fails, if you ask me – and make sure your feller gets his oats at home. You do understand what I'm saying, don't you? And there's one other thing. You can tell him I know about his friend in Germany – Mr Hans-Jurgen Bach.'

While Pippa was on the phone Dave had sounded Micky out about Gates of Eden. He was aware that if Jamie wasn't up to riding at Carlisle, the lad might have to take the race.

All the time he kept an eye on Pippa. It was obvious the call was causing her distress as she walked, head down, listening intently, to the corner of the field and out through the gate. When she didn't reappear after five minutes he went after her.

He found Pippa in the lane, standing by a hedgerow of fresh-leaved hawthorns. At first he thought she was still on the phone but she was holding the mobile down by her waist, staring at the little instrument.

'Pippa?' She didn't turn towards him. 'Do you want to keep going with Gates? Only, I need a bit of help.'

She looked up, clearly surprised to find him by her side. She seemed different somehow. Her eyes were dull and her mouth was twisted, like a child fighting back tears. He knew at once that something was badly wrong.

He put his hands on her shoulders. 'What's the matter? Has something happened?'

She swallowed. It seemed she didn't trust herself to speak. In their short acquaintance he'd seen her upset but not like this. His imagination raced wildly.

'Has there been an accident?'

'No.' The word was just a whisper, scarcely audible.

'Who was on the phone? Was it Malcolm?'

The moment he said the name he made the connection. Light flared in her eyes and her jaw set firm in pain and anger. So she must know what he knew, about Malcolm and that Beverley Harris.

She was struggling to speak but he stopped her.

'It's all right, Pippa,' he murmured, though it was anything but. Then he folded her into his arms and she clung to him like a drowning woman.

*

228

So far it had not been his day, Malcolm reflected as he spooned coffee powder into a mug. He probably shouldn't have hit the office Scotch at eleven-thirty in the morning but the frustration of being fobbed off by Beverley had got to him. Making sarky remarks to Karen wouldn't do him any good. Quite the contrary. The skinny bitch would speak to Beverley the first chance she got and there was no chance she'd pull her punches.

He had a list of other calls he ought to make – trainers he should talk to, owners he'd promised to report back to and potential clients he ought to schmooze. But he couldn't concentrate on anything else but Beaufort Holidays right now. His last conversation with Beverley played and replayed in his mind. There were issues that still had to be debated. Like Beverley's feelings for Barney. She'd never said she was in love with him, had she? She'd just said he needed her and that was a different matter. And no matter how virile Barney might be now, what about in fifteen years' time? Beverley would be barely forty – in her prime – and Barney would be over seventy. Leaving aside his personal feelings, it was his duty to point this out to her forcibly.

There was also the matter of business – they hadn't discussed Adolf the other morning and it was imperative they did so. In the euphoria of the Newbury win Malcolm had been instructed to fix up another race for him as soon as possible. Toby had now entered Adolf for a run out at Carlisle at his new distance of two and a half miles. Malcolm couldn't imagine that there would be any objections but he wanted company approval on the record.

The door burst open and a familiar presence strode into the room. Even though he was a fully grown man, the sight of Toby fired up with fury still turned Malcolm's stomach to water and took him back to the days when he was just a terrified little boy, helpless in the face of his father's rage.

Toby stood over him, leaning on the desk with both hands, his face inches from Malcolm's. His eyes blazed. He was angrier than Malcolm had seen him for a long time. Something serious was up.

It was a moment before Toby spoke. When he did so his voice was cold and distant. Malcolm well knew the self-restraint his father was imposing on himself.

'I've just had a visit from the police.'

Malcolm's first thought was of Adolf, and of the other horses. A doping scandal would put his father out of business – no wonder he was upset.

But what Toby said next took him off-balance. The surprise was like a kick in the guts.

'They asked me about Amanda Parkin.'

'Poor kid.' He had to say something and that was the kind of thing they all said about Mandy. A wasted life. Drugs are terrible. Poor kid.

'That's not what you said about her when she had your nuts in her hand, as I recall.'

Malcolm said nothing. Mandy had always been a sore point between them. It was one thing inheriting the odd girlfriend from your father, not such a good idea for them both to be poking her at the same time.

'Don't you want to know what they asked me? How she came by ten thousand pounds in October 1999.'

'How did they know about that?'

'She paid it into her building society.'

The silly cow. You give a girl a bundle of cash on a matter of utmost secrecy and she stashes it somewhere where it sticks out like a sore thumb.

'Why on earth are they interested in her building society?'

'God knows.' Toby slumped into the chair on the other side of Malcolm's desk. His anger appeared to have dissipated. Now he just looked weary. 'I rang Jack Kenny' – Kenny was a retired Yorkshire detective who advised on yard security '– and he had a word with some Lancashire Superintendent called Wright. They're convinced she was the victim of a drug double-cross and the whole business was down to that useless boyfriend of hers.'

Well, that was a relief.

'Anyway,' Toby continued, 'I told the police *I* gave Mandy the money.'

'Why on earth did you do that?'

'Because the police aren't stupid. They must know something otherwise they wouldn't turn up here, would they? If Mandy was daft enough to put the money in the building society, she might have written something in the pass book about where she got it.'

That sent a shiver down his spine. Jesus!

'But they didn't . . .' his voice trailed off.

'Come to interview you?' His father finished the sentence for him. 'Count your lucky stars, my son. At any rate, I reckon I've still got a broader back than you.

'If you ever get to be a father you might understand.'

'Thanks, Dad. I really mean it.'

Toby sighed heavily. Malcolm knew his father had been fonder of Mandy than he'd ever let on. 'I just hope to God they catch the bastards who killed her.'

Amen to that. The sooner they pinned the murders on a couple of dodgy drug-dealers the better.

After Toby had left, Malcolm made himself another coffee. His hands were shaking as he poured hot water from the kettle. Nerves – maybe he was getting past it.

There was only one good thing about his father's intervention – he'd not thought about Beverley Harris for a good half hour.

Then Pippa came on the line.

Jamie was having problems. It was all very well deciding he was going to write to Marie, but quite another to actually do it. The passage of time since the accident had not made the letter any easier to write.

He sat in his bedroom, hunched over the writing pad – this wasn't a task he wanted to be seen doing. But the doing was hard. Every attempt at expressing himself seemed to come out wrong, making him seem insincere and clumsy and just out to get himself off the hook. He stared out of the window.

He noticed Malcolm's car pull into the yard and saw Mal get out. He seemed in a rush. The downstairs door banged. Soon afterwards, as Jamie struggled with his impossible task, he heard voices from the room below.

It had been the one drawback to taking the room in the attic, that he should be directly above Pippa and Malcolm's bedroom. He'd been acutely aware that he was in danger of trespassing on their privacy, though they'd always reassured him on that point. He'd soon become used to noises from downstairs – the murmur of voices, the muffled drone of the radio, the sound of running water from their adjoining bathroom. But it was the sound of husband and wife making love that he was wary of. It made him feel like an intruder, poking his nose into

231

his sister's affairs. Even worse, it emphasised his loneliness, reminding him of the emptiness in his own life.

Strangely – thankfully – it was not a sound he heard very often.

What he was hearing now was intimacy of a different order – the sound of raised voices. The predominant note was sounded by Pippa. He'd had enough teenage rows with his sister to recognise that tone – outraged, furious, insistent. But it had been a long while, if ever, that he'd heard her sound so upset. And in the hurt and anger there was the unfamiliar note of bitterness.

This was a test of living in others' pockets – any couple were entitled to have rows and it was none of his business. Nonetheless it was impossible to ignore. There was certainly no hope of writing his letter now.

Jamie couldn't hear what was being said, for which he was grateful, but occasional phrases burst clearly upon his ears.

'Do you take me for a fool?'

'I thought you loved me.'

'It's a question of trust!'

Try as he might, these anguished words from his sister's lips lodged themselves in his head and there wasn't much chance that they'd go away.

What on earth had been going on?

He only knew he mustn't ask.

Malcolm drove back to his office on auto-pilot, his mind like a nest of snakes, alive with venomous thoughts. His day was continuing to slide downhill.

His mission to appease Pippa could hardly be counted a success. He was not entirely clear how much Beverley had revealed of their affair but Pippa appeared to have only a partial view of events. It seemed he had been painted as an all-round lech, prone to indiscriminately groping any females in his vicinity.

'Don't be ridiculous, Pippa,' he'd protested. 'The woman's a fantasist – she's making it up!'

Unfortunately the prosecution had not been impressed by this line of defence, being only too aware of his previous convictions. He'd nearly been caught once or twice in their boyfriend/girlfriend days but his protestations of innocence had been accepted at the time. A year into their marriage he'd not been so lucky when Pippa had walked in on him in the tack room with one of her own stable girls. That had been downright stupid of him and he'd had to grovel very hard to keep the marriage in one piece. The incident had taught him lots of lessons, the most important being: never dirty your own doorstep.

So now he only played away and he made all the right noises when he was around Pippa – though, to be honest, he had let things slip on the home front during this Bev business. He was paying for that now. A few more nights tucked up with Pippa recently and he might have been able to argue more convincingly that Beverley Harris was simply a malicious troublemaker.

The upshot of the confrontation was that Malcolm had uttered an outraged denial and sworn complete devotion to their marriage. Pippa, only slightly mollified, had ordered him out of her sight while she considered her options – one of which, she made it plain, was to talk to a solicitor.

Malcolm wasn't entirely unhappy to be left to his own devices. Given time, he was confident that he could get back on the right side of Pippa. After all, she had no real proof. Not yet, at least, and he aimed to prevent things going that far. Now was the ideal opportunity to deal with Beverley.

At the computer Malcolm ran off a fax proclaiming his delight that, as per instructions issued at Newbury, Beaufort Bonanza would be running in a two-and-a-half-mile hurdle race at the forthcoming Carlisle meeting. He sent it to Beverley with a copy to Barney Beaufort himself. It was a small matter but best to get it sorted right away.

As he worked he allowed his thoughts to shift to the other issues that were nagging at him. The worry that had flared up like toothache when his father confronted him and which Pippa's tirade had also touched off. There wasn't much he could do about the officers who had visited Toby, except hope his father's smokescreen would protect him. It was quite another matter to be threatened by Beverley.

How had she found out about Hans-Jurgen? Had she managed to get a look at the horse's passport on one of her trips to Ridgemoor? The address of a German vet, maybe even a phone number, would be on the document. She could have tracked the dealer down that way. Not that it mattered how she had come across the German who had sold him Adolf. More important was whether she had discovered Malcolm had bought the horse for £8000 and passed the animal on to Beaufort for ten times that amount.

She obviously wasn't as dumb about horses as she made out.

An ugly picture took shape in his mind. Of Beverly cuddling up to Barney in her pink bedroom. Of her whispering sweet nothings in his ear. Sweet nothings which included Malcolm's name and a scam to relieve Beaufort Holidays of something over £70,000.

What would Barney do about that? He'd hardly take it on the chin. He'd put Malcolm's sales documentation under the microscope for a start. His next step would doubtless be to call the police.

Malcolm didn't like this development at all. This was one triumph Beverley could not be allowed to enjoy.

Parked by the side of the old village school, Malcolm waited for nearly forty minutes before Beverley's Citroën swept past and made the turn down to the river. There had been plenty of time for him to mull over his plan for the evening ahead. Plenty of time, too, for him to wonder if Beverley wasn't coming straight home from work. But he'd dismissed the thought. He knew she'd come – she had to. And if she didn't turn up tonight there was always tomorrow.

He set off after her on foot, a bit self-conscious about carrying champagne and an elaborate display of flowers. They were certainly eye-catching, but hopefully his face wouldn't attract attention. In the event, he was lucky – there wasn't a soul in sight as he reached the river. Beverley's car was parked on the road outside her front gate. The next vehicle was twenty yards along. Good. If she'd had visitors he'd have had to turn tail.

He crunched up the garden path to her front door. This was the tricky bit. One of them, anyway. He held the flowers in front of him, up against the frosted glass of the door and, as it opened, announced, 'Special delivery.'

She was still in her work clothes, though over her shoulder he could see her jacket hanging on the newel post at the bottom of the stairs. Her eyes glared at him suspiciously above the foliage.

'No, Malcolm,' she said.

'Peace offering,' he replied, injecting as much warmth into his smile as he could.

'You're not coming in,' she stated flatly.

'Fine. I understand. I just wanted to bring you these.'

She glanced at the sumptuous display of roses and carnations. 'Very pretty. I'll give them to Karen, shall I?'

'I'm sorry I was a bit off with her. I hope she wasn't too upset.'

Beverley's misty blue eyes narrowed. 'What are you after?'

'Nothing, honestly. I promise to get out of your life completely. Well, I have to, don't I, after you put the poison in with Pippa.'

She permitted herself a self-satisfied grin. 'You don't want to mess with me, Malcolm.'

'Right.'

The grin vanished as she took the flowers from him. 'On your bike then.'

He turned to go. Then stopped. 'There's one thing.'

'Yes?' Her eyes brimmed with suspicion.

'About Adolf.'

'What about him? Think I might be planning a trip to Bavaria?'

'No. I was wondering if you were thinking of moving him to another trainer.'

'So that's what's behind this. You're worried you and your old man might be out of pocket.'

'It's just that, if you were, there's something you ought to know. Like how Adolf won at Newbury. It wasn't exactly under his own steam.'

He could see the thoughts connecting in her head as the implication sank in. The prospect of Beaufort Holidays being involved in a doping scandal would be setting the alarm bells ringing. After all, it had been her idea to get involved with racing. Barney would be less than impressed. 'Are you saying what I think you are, Malcolm?'

He shook his head. 'Not out here, Bev.'

She sighed and took a pace backwards. 'Oh, all right then. Come in and tell me.'

Success!

He closed the door behind him and eyed her swivelling hips as she led the way down the hall.

Dave whistled to himself as he stirred sausages in a frying pan on the hob of his tiny stove. The other ring hosted a kettle just coming to the boil and in the oven a baked potato sat on a plate in a pool of baked beans. The caravan door was open to the evening breeze. It was the simple things, Dave thought to himself.

Thus preoccupied he didn't hear his visitor approach. He'd just turned to reach for the eggs, when he caught sight of Pippa standing in the doorway, framed against the evening sky, her face a tragic mask. His heart tripped in his chest. She was too beautiful to be real.

'Pippa,' he cried, aware of the false jollity in his voice. After her mini-collapse earlier in the afternoon she'd pulled herself together pretty quickly, called off the training session and disappeared into the house. Dave had been trying hard not to think about the way she'd clung on to him. Maybe he'd got it wrong and it hadn't been anything to do with Malcolm. Maybe.

'Cuppa tea?' he said brightly. 'Or how about a sausage and baked beans? I'm thinking of opening a caff.'

The last was a stupid remark which he instantly regretted. Very cool, Dave. But she was saying nothing – it was unnerving.

Finally she spoke. 'Have you got anything to drink?'

Oh dear. Depressed woman asks for alcohol – it was always a bad sign in Dave's book. He found a bottle of cheap brandy he kept with his medicine kit and poured her a small measure. 'That's all you're getting till you've eaten,' he told her and sat her on a chair outside.

She stared dully at him as he deftly divided the food on to two plates and, using a stool as a table, served it up. He squatted on the caravan step.

'You can't beat eating outdoors,' he said. 'Best get a move on before it goes cold.'

He was gratified to see that she did as she was told, reluctantly at first, then with enthusiasm. She cleared her plate and mopped up the eggy leftovers with a crust of bread.

They shared an apple and a bar of fruit and nut for pudding. Then he allowed her another tot of brandy which she nursed as if it were ten-year-old cognac. They watched the dusk quickly thicken into night.

'Dave,' she said at last, 'why did they put you in prison?'

Up to this point he'd have been happy to talk to her about anything under the sun. But naturally she'd picked out the one topic that he really wished to avoid. What could he tell her? Only the truth.

'Because I was in possession of a quantity of illegal steroids.'

'They sent you to prison for that?'

236

'And a loaded handgun.'

She stared at him, those boundless black eyes searching his face. 'Why?' she said simply.

'They were in a bag in my possession.'

His bag which he'd lent to his brother. Chris hadn't told him he was using it to store dodgy gear or that the police had turned over his club. When he'd pitched up at Dave's place at three in the morning he'd just asked Dave to keep an eye on it for a couple of days. He'd not told him what was inside but Dave knew better than to ask. 'No one's going to come hassling *you*,' that's what Chris had said. But he'd been wrong.

'Was the gun yours? And the drugs?'

'No, they weren't. But I was guilty, Pippa. Guilty of being stupid anyway.' That wasn't how the prosecution had put it, he'd been pilloried as a golden-boy-gone-bad, a once-fine athlete who'd betrayed his talent by going into business with drug cheats. And he'd not put up a defence because that would have placed his brother in the dock instead. He'd refused to do that to Chris, a father of three with a business to run.

'You don't want to talk about this, do you?' she said.

'You're entitled to ask. I was called a malign and evil influence and a corrupter of young minds. You ought to know who you're working with.'

She lapsed into silence which, in the circumstances, was a relief.

Finally she said, 'Personally, I've only one complaint about you, Dave Prescott. You're a mean man with your booze.'

It could have been worse.

Then he took her home.

'So?' Beverley said, staring at him across the kitchen table. 'What's this all about?'

Malcolm raised the bottle of champagne he'd been clutching. 'How about a drink?'

She shrugged. 'I've got one.' She picked up a glass from the counter. Ice clinked. A vodka-and-tonic, Malcolm assumed, her usual after-work tipple. 'Tell me about the horse.'

'If you remember, my instructions were that Adolf had to win at all costs in his next race.'

'Actually, Malcolm, we simply requested closer control of his management.'

'You gave a pretty good impression of someone who wanted a winner. Don't tell me you'd rather he'd finished halfway down the field.'

Malcolm had fished two glasses from a cupboard and extracted the cork from the bottle. He poured the champagne and pushed one glass across the table towards her.

'So you doped him,' she said. She shook her head. 'You're a real operator, you know that?'

'Takes one to know one.' He raised his glass. 'Salut.'

Her glass was empty. She reached for the champagne. 'Up yours,' she said. 'I'm not sure I want to hear this.'

'I'm only telling you because our relationship is undergoing a change.'

She laughed. 'It's bloody well coming to an end, you mean.'

'Exactly. I accept that. But if you want to move Adolf from Ridgemoor, you should realise he might not be back in the winners' enclosure for a while. If ever.'

She sipped her drink and thought for a moment. 'I haven't raised the matter of finding a new trainer. There's no reason why Barney should want to move him.'

'Excellent. So we can carry on as before.'

'Not exactly, Malcolm. Don't you try and weasel round me. We've had a lot of fun but it can't go on.'

'I agree. I'll keep myself to myself, I promise.'

'Good.'

'Though I can't promise to keep my thoughts to myself. You're a bit special, you know, Bev.'

'Watch it or you're out of here.' She drained her glass. 'Go on then, I suppose you'd better tell me about Adolf.'

'Have you heard of EPO?'

'It's what distance athletes take, isn't it? Adds something to the blood.'

'That's the stuff. It enhances the oxygen-carrying capacity and gives the runner extra stamina. It works on horses too.'

'Is that why you put him in for a longer race?'

'Clever old you.'

She kicked him under the table. 'Don't patronise me.'

He rubbed his shin. 'Ouch.'

She laughed, a little tipsily, he thought. He refilled her glass.

'I'm on to you,' she said. 'You're trying to get me drunk.'

'Why would I want to do that?'

'Because.' She smiled at him knowingly. 'You want to get me upstairs for a last ride around the park.'

'Honestly, Bev, that's not true.'

'Don't lie to me.' She kicked him again but with stockinged feet this time. 'You're just a randy bastard. You'd climb on anything in a skirt.'

'Anything in a business suit and spectacles, maybe. You've spoiled me for other women, Bev.'

'Bastard.' Her foot kicked out again and remained where it landed, on his leg just below the knee. 'I bet your Pippa gave you a right good going-over after our little chat.'

'You could say that.'

'You've got some nerve showing up here begging for a last shag then.'

'Is that what I'm doing?'

'That's exactly what you're doing.'

Her foot had wormed higher up his leg. He caught it in his hand and ran his thumb over the ball of flesh at the base of her big toe, then up into the arch. He knew she liked that.

'Suppose you're right,' he said, 'what are my chances?'

'I'm not in the mood. I've just got in from work. I'm tired and dirty and not nearly pissed enough to climb back into bed with you.'

'I see.' He carried on massaging her foot. 'Suppose I ran you a bath and poured you another glass of champagne?'

'You'd be wasting your time.'

'I can't think of a better way of wasting it.'

A quarter of an hour later, Malcolm was ready. This was the trickiest bit of all. He ascended the stairs slowly. In his hand was the bottle of champagne, barely a glassful left in it. He'd wiped the bottle clean of his fingerprints and now carried it, like a waiter, wrapped in a tea towel. In his pocket was the key to the bathroom – just in case Beverley had been inclined to lock him out. However, there had been no objection from her when she took possession of the room – she'd probably not noticed its absence.

He knocked on the door and opened it in one movement. There was no squeal of protest.

'I wondered how long it would be before you turned up.'

The bath took up most of the small room. The water magnified the riot of her sumptuous pink flesh as she reclined full length. She made no attempt to cover herself.

He raised the bottle. 'I thought you might like a refill.'

She gazed at him myopically, her face altered without her spectacles. Her bedroom face, as he thought of it.

'You just want to have a gawp,' she said, but she held out her glass all the same, her breasts swelling briefly above the waterline.

He emptied the bottle into her glass and set it down on the floor by the bath. He stood over her, looking down at her body.

She drank then set the glass down carefully on the bathroom ledge. 'Like what you see?' she asked.

'Oh yes,' he said truthfully. 'Very much.'

It was simple to kill her. A damn sight easier than getting rid of Pete and Mandy. He began to soap her feet, caressing her gently as he had done in the kitchen.

'That's nice,' she murmured, allowing herself to sink slowly up to her neck in the warm water.

Suddenly he seized Beverley's ankles and yanked them upwards hard, plunging her head under the surface.

He'd heard about this method years ago, from a veteran Sergeant in the Army. The Sarge had said if it was done right, the mouth and nostrils filled so quickly with water that the victim blacked out instantly. Since the man was drunk at the time, the other guys had dismissed it as a joke – especially when he'd referred to his technique as 'the ultimate wife-deterrent'. But Malcolm had not forgotten. Later, he'd made enquiries about the Sergeant and was impressed to discover that the man's wife had indeed drowned in the bath.

It was all over for Beverley in seconds, the surprise such that she had no time to grab the sides of the bath. So his old Army pal had not been lying. 'The beauty of it,' he'd said, slurring his words as he reached for his pint pot, 'is that there's no struggle, no mess and not a mark on her. It's the shock, see. They black out just like that.' As Malcolm could now testify, the Sarge had not been lying.

He held Bev by the ankles, head under the surface, for as long as it took to make sure she was dead. Then he lowered her feet back into the water and left the room.

There was a certain amount of cleaning up to be done before he left – some surfaces had to be wiped, his champagne glass needed to be washed and put away and, nice touch this, he thought, the flower display had to be removed from the hall table. He carried it back to the car and set off for home.

It would take more than a fancy bunch of flowers to smooth Pippa's ruffled feathers, but it was a start.

Chapter Thirteen

Marie was in a hurry. She'd spent too long brushing Spring Fever. This was her preferred time of the day – returning from exercise and putting the horses back into clean stalls with lots of straw banked up around the sides and a full hay-net. It was a wrench to leave the stables every morning and make her way, with a detour home to change, to the dingy back room in the surgery.

She was about to mount her bike when she heard Ros call her. Didn't she realise how late it was?

Marie propped her bike against the wall and turned towards the other woman. Ros looked out of sorts, as if she had something difficult to say and didn't know how to go about it. Marie instantly forgot that she was running late. She had a funny feeling she knew what was coming.

'Caroline told me you ran into Jamie Sullivan here last week.'

Marie nodded. She'd half expected Ros to raise the matter before but had been grateful that she'd not done so. She wondered why she was mentioning it now.

'I'm sorry,' Ros continued. 'I did promise I'd make sure both of you weren't here at the same time.'

'It's OK. I'm glad I met him – he was very helpful. Just as long as my dad never finds out.'

Ros looked relieved. 'So it didn't upset you?'

She shook her head. 'I don't hate him like my dad and my aunt do.'

'I gather you wrote to him after his fall.'

She flushed. 'He told you that?'

Ros looked awkward. 'He was very touched that you should take the trouble. He's written you a reply.'

'He has?' A spark of excitement flared momentarily inside her, followed by a pinprick of guilt. How could she be moved by hearing from her brother's killer? What a sick individual she must be. 'I haven't received anything,' she said.

Ros pulled an envelope from the pocket of her jacket and offered it to Marie.

She didn't have to take it. Now was her chance to honour her father's feelings and turn her back on Jamie Sullivan for ever.

'Thanks, Ros,' she said as she accepted the letter.

Joyce accompanied Clem up the hill to his bench, as she did most mornings before she went off to work. Sometimes it was slow going as he stopped frequently to catch his breath. But she'd learnt not to hover too anxiously and to let him take his time. He didn't like being fussed, as he called it – he could get there under his own steam.

He could, too. Sometimes she was amazed how resilient he was. A month or so back, when it was frosty underfoot, she'd slipped over and he'd hauled her back to her feet. She'd been shocked at the strength that remained in those big arms, picking her twelve stone off the floor as if she were a toddler.

'By God, Clem,' she'd said. 'You're a powerful man for all your coughing and wheezing.'

He'd grinned at her. 'Aye, well I used to jack up trucks for a living,' and they'd both laughed.

But there was no laughter this morning. He was out of sorts and she knew he wouldn't tell her why, she'd have to ask. Joyce had never been married but she guessed that lots of couples ended up like her and Clem, attuned to each other's mood swings and resentful of them at the same time.

'You all right then?' she said as they finally reached the bench.

'Aye,' he wheezed. 'You can get going now.'

'Not until I know what's up with you.'

'Nothing's up with me, woman. Now get yourself off.'

She glared at him. It was a familiar process. There was something the matter and she was obliged to force it out of him. It occurred to her that if they were a married couple she wouldn't have to put up with it. She could up sticks and walk away. She could hardly do that to her ailing brother.

Finally, he muttered, 'The little bastard's on the mend.'

She didn't have to ask who that was. There was only one little bastard in their lives. Sullivan. May God rot his soul.

'He's going to be fit to race at Carlisle. I heard it on the radio.'

Joyce sighed. Her hatred of the jockey was no less intense than her brother's but it didn't loom so large on her horizon. What with the everyday hassle of work, domestic chores and caring for the invalid, there wasn't much time left over to brood on the continued existence of Jamie Sullivan. The opposite was true of her brother.

'Do yourself a favour, Clem. Try and forget about him, eh? He's not worth it.'

His face softened and he laid a heavy paw on her arm. 'I'm sorry, Joycie. You put up with a lot from me, don't you?'

'Aye, I do.' She grinned. All her resentment vanished in a flash. Even if Tom Jones was waiting for her at the bottom of the hill in a chauffeur-driven limo she'd never leave her brother. 'That's the truest thing you've said all morning.'

'Listen,' he leaned closer, his breath hot on her cheek. 'I need a favour from you.'

'Yes?'

'I don't reckon I've all that much time left—'

'Rubbish, Clem. Don't say that.'

'Let me finish. I've not a lot of time left to do what I have to do. Now, you've got something of mine. You took it from me.'

She shook her head and tried to step away but he held her fast.

'Don't deny it,' he continued urgently. 'You know what I'm talking about. I never said anything about it before because I reckoned you knew best. But it's different now, Joyce. I need it back.'

'I can't do that. I got rid of it.'

He stared at her in outrage. 'I don't believe you.'

'Please yourself but I threw it in the river years ago.' She pulled her arm from his grasp.

'That was mine, woman! You had no right.'

'Too bad,' she said and stomped off down the road.

Had he gone mad? The last thing she'd return to her unhappy, homicidal brother was a gun.

Marie stopped on her way home to read Jamie's letter. It was handwritten in blue Biro on a single sheet of unlined white paper.

Dear Marie Kirkstall,
Thank you for your kind wishes after my recent fall. I'm recovering well and expect to be riding again soon.

This is a difficult letter for me to write and I apologise if I express myself badly. I should have written it at the time of the car accident but I wasn't fit enough. Then as time went on it became harder and harder to do and I'm ashamed to say I bottled out.

I can't imagine how much pain I have caused you and your family. Not a day goes by when I don't think of the harm I have done you. Believe me when I say that if I could swap my life for your brother's then I would.

I had no idea I would run into you at Ros Bradey's yard. I would never have gone there if I'd known. Can I say, though, that I thought you a very gutsy rider.

This must be the ninth or tenth time I've tried to write this letter and I still don't think I've got it right. I hope it doesn't sound like I'm asking for forgiveness because I'm not. I'd just like you to know that I accept responsibility for the terrible thing I did and I'm trying to live my life better because of it.
Sincerely,
Jamie Sullivan

Marie read the letter over several times then she remounted the bike and pedalled back to the yard. She was going to be late for the surgery but she didn't care.

Ros looked startled as Marie reappeared and walked towards her across the paddock. She broke off from attending to one of the girls. 'Are you all right?' she said. 'I thought you went ages ago.'

Marie spoke urgently. If she didn't ask now she might never have the courage again. 'Ros, will you do me a favour? Will you ask Jamie if he'll meet me?'

Ros pursed her lips, then put her arm around Marie's shoulder. 'Do you really think that's wise?'

'No, I don't,' Marie blurted out. 'But I don't care. Will you help me fix it? Please?'

Malcolm had spent an exhilarating morning on the golf course with the owners of a pizza-delivery operation who were thinking of spending some money on a horse. They were cheerful, if unsophisticated, company. Early in their discussion Charlie, the senior partner, had said, 'Don't you worry whether we've got the cash – there's plenty of dough in the pizza business.' It wasn't the only time he said it.

Not that Malcolm gave two hoots. He was feeling good today. He'd slept like a baby – in the spare room, but so what? – and he felt he'd dealt decisively with yesterday's challenges.

When he'd arrived home at around nine the previous evening, Pippa had already gone to bed and locked the door. Jamie had been watching the television with one eye open but he'd opened the other when Malcolm and the flower arrangement came through the door. Malcolm had explained that the flowers were a peace-offering for Pippa – was Jamie aware they'd had an argument? Jamie evidently was. Malcolm had not gone into details, just implied it was a domestic misunderstanding and Jamie had asked no questions. Most tactful of him.

Then Malcolm had raided the fridge – funny how keen his appetite had been – scribbled a card to go with the flowers and turned in. He'd slept in late to give Pippa time to get out of the house and headed for the golf course making sure not to bump into her. There was a good chance she'd be more reasonable tonight.

The fast-food guys were good enough to stand him a decent lunch in the clubhouse, where pizza was definitely not on the menu, and he set off for Ridgemoor at around half past two. As he drew into the yard his mobile rang. He recognised the caller's number – Beaufort Holidays. How interesting.

'Karen, sweetheart,' he said cheerily. 'How delightful to hear from you.'

'I'm sorry to bother you, Mr Priest, but has Miss Harris been in touch with you today?' There was a gratifying note of anxiety in her reedy little voice.

'Has the great Beverley been in touch with me? I can't believe you're seriously asking this question.'

'She's not been into work and she's left no messages and we can't get her on any of her numbers.'

'I see.' He pretended to give the matter thought. 'Well, Karen, my angel, as you know from the way the pair of you have been avoiding my calls, I am possibly the last man in Yorkshire she's likely to have talked to over the past twenty-four hours.'

'Oh dear.' She moaned in disappointment. 'We're really worried. She's never done this before.'

'Don't you believe it. Knowing Miss Harris as I do, I expect she's locked in meaningful negotiations with a hunky new client in a hotel bedroom somewhere. You know how time flies when you're having fun. Or maybe you don't know much about that kind of fun, Karen sweetheart.'

'You're despicable!' she cried. He could imagine her pale spinsterish face tightening with distaste.

'And you've still got a poker up your arse,' he murmured as she slammed the phone down.

Marie was nervous, more nervous than she could remember. She hadn't expected Ros to move so quickly.

She'd been asked back to the yard to collect a present from Spring Fever's owner – at least, that's what Ros had said. However, when she arrived and walked into Ros's office, Jamie was sitting there.

Jamie looked as tense as she felt. He offered his hand and she took it. It was odd to be formally shaking hands in these circumstances but it seemed right. He had clear hazel eyes and long lashes, like a girl. But his shoulders and arms were muscle-packed. She liked the way he looked – she couldn't help it.

'You were lucky that horse didn't kill you the other day,' he said, rushing his words as if he were embarrassed.

Marie sensed his awkwardness at being close to her. In a strange way it gave her a confidence she wouldn't normally have possessed.

'I could say the same to you after your fall at Wetherby,' she replied boldly.

They both laughed.

'I read your letter,' she said, looking him straight in the eye.

'I hope it didn't upset you.'

'No. I thought it was brave of you to be so honest. I wish you'd written earlier, like you said.'

'Sorry.' He looked away. 'I mean, sorry for everything. For what it's worth.'

It was worth a lot but she needed more.

Malcolm couldn't concentrate on his paperwork. He was in the middle of a game of Freecell on his laptop when he got a call from his father.

'Come up to the house for a drink.' It wasn't exactly a request.

Toby already had a glass in his hand when Malcolm arrived. He poured Malcolm a generous splash of Scotch and stared moodily out of the big window at the steel-grey sky above the moor.

Malcolm filled the glass to the brim with soda; now was not the time to dull his wits. 'What's up?'

Toby turned to him. 'It's about Beverley Harris.'

'You don't have to worry, Dad, it's all over with her. After we spoke I packed her in. You were quite right.'

His father's face didn't change. 'Sit down.'

Malcolm did as he was told and waited for his father to spill the beans. He needed to get his reaction just right.

'I've just had a call from Barney Beaufort's office. Beverley's had an accident. She's dead, son.'

'No!' cried Malcolm, jumping to his feet. 'I don't believe it!' Liquid slopped over the side of his glass and dripped down his fingers to the floor. He pretended he hadn't noticed, staring at his father in wide-eyed alarm. Not too bad, he thought.

'When she didn't show at work, Beaufort went round there. Seems he had a key. He found her dead in the bath.'

'Jesus.'

'They think she'd been there since last night.'

'Oh my God.' Malcolm allowed himself to subside back into the chair.

'I'm very sorry, Malcolm. This'll be a bit of a shock to you.'

'Do they know how she died?'

Toby shrugged. 'There'll be some sort of inquest, I suppose. People pass out in the bath sometimes, don't they? Do you know if she was on any sort of medication?'

Malcolm laughed bitterly. 'All sorts, Dad, including the kind you get in an off-licence. I'm afraid Bev was a bit of a lush.'

'Well, there you are then. This might sound callous, lad, but you're better off without a woman like that.'

Exactly.

Marie and Jamie walked to the wood up the hill from Ros's yard. They talked about horses – an undemanding topic. She mentioned her show-jumping experience and he told her of his hopes for Gates of Eden at Carlisle.

They sat on a bench overlooking the valley and the conversation dried up. She knew he was taking his cue from her. She was the one who had instigated this meeting, so it was up to her.

Into the awkward silence she said, 'Will you tell me about the accident?'

He looked surprised. 'Do you really want to go through all that again? I mean, you must know all about it.'

'Not from your side, I don't.'

He took his time telling her, describing his day at the races and the drive back north with another jockey and his brother. 'I was dead chuffed with my new car. It was a red Mercedes 220 and I'd only had it four weeks. Actually, it was about ten years old but it was new to me and it was quick. I drove it like I rode horses – like a maniac. I was absolutely fearless. I never thought anything bad could happen to me. I'm sorry, Marie.'

She was irritated. 'Don't keep saying that. Just get on with what happened.'

He told her about stopping at a pub and meeting the stable staff from Ridgemoor. He'd had several drinks and also snorted cocaine in the toilet. Then he'd left with his passengers, Richard and Malcolm Priest, to drive home. He fell silent.

'Go on,' she said.

'I can't.'

'Jamie, this is the part that matters. Please tell me.'

'But I can't remember. I took a blow on the head in the crash and have no memory of it or what happened just before. A doctor told me it's called retrograde amnesia.'

'How convenient.' She supposed she shouldn't have said it but she didn't care.

'Don't think I don't know that. I've tried hard to remember and I really wish I could. It's like my mind playing tricks on me, trying to protect me but it only makes it worse.'

They sat in silence for a moment. She'd wanted to hear from his own lips how he had killed her brother, so she could honestly test her own feelings. Listening to a sincere confession she'd know whether, deep down, she could forgive him. But she'd been robbed of that. The disappointment was overwhelming.

Jamie spoke again. 'Believe me, Marie, I don't want to avoid my responsibility. If I could remember anything else I'd tell you. For my own sake I wish I had a clear memory of the crash so I could face up to it and put it behind me. But the whole business just goes on. Since I had that fall the other day I've been having nightmares. I get flashes of the night of the crash mixed in with weird images dredged up from somewhere in my head. I'm scared I'll never be able to get over it.'

She didn't know what to say. She was sorry for him and she found him powerfully attractive but that wasn't enough to allow her to forgive him. She had to go away and think.

'I'm cold,' she said. 'Let's go back.'

They walked down the hill in silence.

Malcolm found Pippa in the office on her own. Good.

She glanced up briefly as he entered and then looked down again at the papers on her desk. 'Go away, Malcolm,' she said in a small cold voice.

'We have to talk.'

'I have nothing to say to you.'

'OK. Listen then.' He sat down. 'You obviously haven't heard about Beverley Harris.'

That got her attention all right. Her eyes blazed at the mention of the name.

He pressed on. 'She's dead. She drowned in her bath, apparently. Beaufort Holidays rang Dad about an hour ago.'

She stared at him as she took in the news. 'An accident?'

'I imagine it's a bit early to tell. Look, it's not a nice thing for me to say in the circumstances but, considering what's been going on between you and me – you should know she had problems with pills and drink.'

'What are you saying? That she was drunk and drowned in the bath?'

'What I'm saying, Pippa, is that she was a depressed alcoholic with a mean temper. She got on to you out of pure malice because I wouldn't sleep with her.'

'Why didn't you say this before?'

'Would you have listened if I had? I told you she was a fantasist but you didn't want to hear my side of it. But now this has happened, it makes it painfully clear.'

'Do you think she killed herself?'

251

'I don't know what to think. It's a possibility, I suppose.'
'Oh God. Malcolm, I'm sorry.'
He took her hand in his. 'Me, too.'

Marie had changed her mind about Jamie half a dozen times before she reached home. He seemed so sincere when he spoke about his remorse and he'd said all the right things about being responsible for what he'd done. Yet, when it came down to it, he couldn't face up to telling her what had happened. He said he'd lost his memory but surely that was a cop-out – a convenient psychological block that prevented him from really owning up to his past.

The strange thing was, *he* obviously felt that way about it, too. It was as if he was stuck in limbo, unable to go forward till he'd truly confronted what he'd done. And she felt sorry for him because of it. That had to be the wrong way round.

With these thoughts churning round in her head, she went into the front room to say hello to her father. He was asleep in his chair in front of the television, where a police drama plodded across the screen. She considered waking him but thought the better of it.

There were no welcoming supper smells coming from the kitchen, which was unusual. To her surprise she found her Aunt Joyce sitting at the table in the dark, a half-full ashtray at her elbow.

'Are you all right, Auntie?' It was a silly question. She could see from the jut of her big square jaw that she was far from all right.

'I've been waiting for you to show your face,' Joyce said in an ominous tone. 'Sit down.'

Marie took a bottle of milk from the fridge and poured herself a glass. She was hungry, tired and not in the mood for a row, though she could see that she was in for one. She did not often clash with her aunt but they'd had their share of screaming matches in the past. She took a seat as instructed. What was this all about?

Joyce took an envelope from her apron pocket and laid it on the table between them. Marie recognised it at once – Jamie's letter.

'You've got some explaining to do,' her aunt said.

A few seconds earlier Marie would have said she was too weary to be angry but fury gripped her in a flash.

'Where did you get that?' she hissed.

'From your bedside table.' Joyce's words were measured.

'You've been in my private things!'

The older woman was unabashed. 'That's right. I don't make a habit of it, if that's what you're thinking. But I've had my suspicions about you since you started riding with Ros Bradey. I heard about her and her toy boy, Sullivan. Turns out I was right to be suspicious, wasn't I?'

Toy boy? What kind of ridiculous gossip had she been listening to?

Joyce jabbed a large pink finger at the envelope. 'What does this mean, Marie? I hope you've not been going behind our backs.'

'I met him by accident, that's all. I didn't want to have anything to do with him.'

'But you've written to him, haven't you? It says so in here. What do you think your father would say?'

So she hadn't told him yet – that was something.

'He'd go mad, I know. But I can't let what happened destroy my life like it's ruining his. Jamie's not some ogre. He didn't do it deliberately. We've all got to make peace. I don't know how but we must.'

Joyce's face darkened. 'You don't know what you're talking about. You lost your own brother to a selfish drunken hooligan. You can never make peace with scum like that.'

They stared at each other across the table, divided by the letter and all it stood for.

Marie snatched it up. 'You've got some nerve poking around with my stuff. You're not my mother. If I want to talk to Jamie then I will and you can't stop me. I've got my own life to lead.'

As Marie stalked out of the room it occurred to her that nothing much had changed. She'd ended up losing her rag and running away just like she had in her darkest teenage years. Only this time she hadn't slammed the door, much as she had wanted to, in case she woke her father.

She didn't know what she'd do if Joyce told Dad.

Dave tagged along with Jamie on his evening walk with Matilda. He'd have preferred a brisk run over the moor but Jamie had claimed he wasn't yet up to it.

'If you're not fit enough to go for a little jog,' Dave said, 'how come you're riding next week?'

'That's different. I'm not using my own legs.'

Dave conceded the point. Strolling with the dog, chucking her the occasional stick and waiting for her to emerge from the enticing undergrowth, gave them a chance to chew over the hot news – Beverley Harris's death.

'Funny way to die, isn't it?' Dave said. 'I can imagine falling in the shower and smashing your head open. But not just sitting in the bath.'

'She was drunk, apparently. Or maybe the booze reacted with the pills she was taking. That's what Malcolm says.'

And he would know, Dave thought. 'How's he taking it?'

Jamie shrugged. 'You can never tell with Malcolm, can you? He's always pretty cheerful. Except when Pippa's on his case.'

Pippa and Malcolm's argument had been the talk of the yard that morning, though no one had known the cause of it. Dave had kept his mouth shut, just as he had about Pippa's visit to his caravan the night before. He had rather hoped she might turn up again tonight but Jamie had appeared instead, with Matilda cavorting at his heels.

'Thank God, they've made it up,' said Jamie.

'What was it all about?' It was naughty of him but Dave couldn't help asking the question. He was dying to tell Jamie what he'd seen going on between Malcolm and Beverley – all he needed was an indication that Jamie already knew. But he was to be disappointed.

'I haven't a clue. Ignorance is bliss, if you ask me. I just keep my head down.'

Fair enough but it was frustrating. How come Jamie didn't see Malcolm for the two-faced sod that he really was? At times like this Dave had to remind himself that Jamie was a lot younger than he was.

'All I know,' Jamie continued, 'is that they are busy making it up tonight. So I'm not in any hurry to get home, if you follow.'

Dave followed all right but he wasn't happy about it. It sounded like Malcolm had got himself off the hook.

Joyce remained where she was in the kitchen, smoking the last of her cigarettes. What with Clem's condition she'd tried hard to cut down and she never smoked indoors. Tonight she didn't care.

She knew she couldn't stop Marie from seeing Jamie Sullivan if she wanted to. She was a young woman with a mind of her own – even if it was misguided.

That jibe about not being Marie's mother had hurt. It was an old wound, made a long time ago, but it was ripped open heartlessly every time they had a confrontation. She knew Marie had only said it in the heat of the moment but that didn't lessen the pain.

But there were other, greater pains that worried her. Jamie Sullivan was not just the hooligan who had carelessly knocked their lives off-track, he was a continuing menace. She missed her old job at the Roman Arms and he'd robbed her of that. Now he was a threat to Marie.

The girl wouldn't see it like that, of course, but Joyce knew more about men than she did. Suppose Marie fell in love with him – where would they be then? It would finish Clem off.

The one thing certain to draw Marie to Sullivan was for her to be banned from seeing him. Joyce was well aware that forbidden fruit tasted sweeter than any other kind. And she, stupidly, had just taken the first step in pointing Marie in that direction. She wished now she'd thought the matter through before confronting her niece.

She lit her last cigarette. There was one course of action left open to her but it terrified her. Her conversation with Clem that morning had shaken her up until it had been driven out of her mind by her discovery in Marie's bedroom. But the two problems were tied together and maybe the solution was too. Of course, the personal consequences were frightening but she wasn't sure that she cared about that.

She'd lied to Clem that morning – she'd not thrown his gun into the river. When she'd confiscated it during his terrible depression after Alan's death, she'd meant to get rid of it. But that was easier said than done. She'd imagined dropping it in the sea or throwing it down a pothole. Then she'd pictured it being found and traced to her and Clem. Just the thought of it gave her the willies. It had been easier by far to leave it where it was, hidden on the top of her wardrobe, and to forget all about it.

But she'd remembered it now.

Marie's mobile finally burst into life an hour after she'd left the message. It must be Jamie returning her call. She checked outside her room to make sure she wasn't going to be overheard – she had to be careful.

'Marie?' He sounded puzzled, as well he might be. They had parted politely enough but she knew they'd both felt the meeting had been a failure.

'Hi,' she said, suddenly hesitant. When she'd fled from her aunt she'd known just what she was going to say but suddenly her mind was a blank. She plunged in. 'Look, I've been thinking about what you told me. I don't think I was very nice to you this afternoon. After all, it's not your fault you can't remember what happened in the accident.'

'I don't expect you to be nice to me, Marie.'

'Well, I'm sorry anyway.'

He chuckled. 'Saying sorry is forbidden. Remember?'

'OK.'

There was a silence. He was obviously wary of her.

'Can we try again, Jamie? Could you bear to go through it once more?'

'If you think it would help.' He didn't sound sure.

'I do,' she said confidently. 'I definitely do.' And sod you, Auntie Joyce. It's my life.

Clem smelled the cigarette smoke as he lumbered painfully upstairs. God, how he'd love one but he knew better than to ask.

He guessed his conversation with Joyce that morning must be responsible for her black humour. Well, that was too bad. Women were moody, it came with the territory. If Alan were alive they'd have had a laugh about it. But he was doomed to spending the rest of his days in the company of women.

Marie was the same as Joyce. When she'd come in to see him earlier, as he was snoozing in front of the box, she'd been in a right funny state. Hugging and kissing him, saying, 'You know how much I love you, don't you, Dad?' When a father gets that kind of treatment he knows what the score is.

'How much do you want, love?' he'd asked and she'd burst into tears.

Then she'd said he must remember that when she went off to live on her own she'd be fine and not to worry about her and she'd always, always love him, even if she didn't see him every day.

He'd told her to cheer up and said that even though he'd miss her when she went away to university he'd be damned proud of her.

Honestly, what was that all about?

He'd reached his room by now and he flipped on the light, standing in the doorway to catch his breath. He noticed something on the bed but it took a few moments for him to realise what it was. And when he did so, a grin spread slowly over his face.

So Joyce had not got rid of his gun after all.

The weapon was still in the old shoe box that the man from Leeds had given him all those years ago. His name was Terry – or so he said – and the gun was in payment for a no-questions-asked turnaround on a pair of dodgy vehicles.

Clem wondered now why he had wanted it. Who had he been trying to impress? Himself, probably – a thirty-year-old self with no family ties and a romantic idea of the future. He'd been finding the legitimate motor trade a trifle boring and had been considering a walk on its wilder side.

Thank God that had never happened. He'd probably have spent the intervening years locked up. Instead he'd met a woman – sexy, irresistible and moody, of course – and married her instead.

He shuffled to the bed as fast as he could, eager to be reunited with this reminder of his past.

He removed the lid of the box. Everything was just as he remembered it: the yellow cloth wrapped round the gun, the dull glint of metal, the box of ammunition. The weapon was sleek and menacing, heavy in the hand. It would be old-fashioned now, out-matched and over-shadowed by the fancy automatic weapons that criminals used these days. But Clem had no doubt it would still work. 'Thank you, Joyce,' he muttered silently in honour of his ever-loyal sister.

Chapter Fourteen

Jane peered closely at the varieties of salami in the Polish deli. Despite her best intentions, she didn't often get the chance to shop in Preston Market. In the end she plumped for three different kinds which, she was assured, were all absolutely delicious. Judging by the moist flecks of fat and odour of garlic she had no doubt they would be. Robbie was in for a treat.

By the time she reached the café on the upper floor she was loaded down with bags. It had been impossible to pass the stalls of fruit and veg, cheese and fish and other foodstuffs without adding to her haul. Elizabeth Jacobs raised an eyebrow as she hove into view.

'So you are human,' Elizabeth said as Jane sat opposite her. 'I thought you were some robot who only ate and drank out of sufferance.'

'It's not all for me. I have a teenage son. It's like living with a boa constrictor – he devours things whole.'

Elizabeth laughed. She looked more relaxed than on any of their previous meetings. She'd left her brood at home with her mother-in-law, which probably accounted for it.

'There's nothing new on the case, I'm afraid,' Jane said, aiming to get the bad news out of the way. 'I'm very sorry, Elizabeth. I did say as much on the phone.'

Elizabeth was visiting Preston to buy material for a bridesmaid's dress at the market. She had been insistent that they meet. Jane had not felt able to say no.

'Did you learn anything from Toby Priest?'

'Not really.' Jane had no intention of mentioning the details of their conversation.

Elizabeth stared at her over the rim of her teacup. 'Are you still interested in knowing about Mandy's love-life?'

'Sure.' Jane had rather let her interest slide but, as Elizabeth was here and at last prepared to volunteer information, 'I'm listening.'

Elizabeth put down her cup. 'I should have told you this when I mentioned Mandy's affair with Toby, but I was livid with him for not coming to the memorial service. Also, I suppose, I wanted to protect Mandy's reputation.'

'I don't make judgements, Elizabeth.'

'Well, anyway, since I've told you about Toby I ought to complete the picture. When Mandy was working at Ridgemoor she was also seeing Toby's son, Malcolm.'

'At the same time, you mean?'

'Yes. That summer and autumn she was involved with both of them.'

'Did they know about each other?'

'No. She thought it was a great laugh, playing one off against the other.'

'She told you at the time?'

'Oh yes. Mandy was quite shameless about it. She was having a great time. Then of course it all went wrong.'

There was a surprise. In Jane's experience it was hard enough keeping one relationship going, let alone two at the same time.

'There was a nasty car crash and a local boy was killed. The driver was one of the jockeys from the yard and he ended up going to jail.'

That rang a bell with Jane. 'Is he the man who got out recently and went back to riding?'

'Jamie Sullivan. He's now Malcolm's brother-in-law.' Elizabeth leant forward in her seat. 'The crash changed everything. Malcolm was a passenger in the car, and though he wasn't badly hurt, Mandy was worried about him. She decided she really cared for him and broke it off with Toby who, of course, went up the wall when he discovered she'd been seeing Malcolm.'

Jane was just about keeping up. 'When was all this taking place?'

'The crash was in September 1999. Mandy left a couple of weeks later – when she found out Malcolm was intending to marry Jamie Sullivan's sister. Does this help at all?'

She had to be joking! But Jane did not want to sound ungrateful. 'It's all good background.'

'I'm glad I got it off my chest, anyway, even if it's not much use.'

'Hopeless,' Jane muttered to herself as she made for the escalator, trailing her bags. As ever, she was running late. It only occurred to her as she reached her car that Elizabeth had at least filled in one of the gaps in her knowledge. She'd been puzzling over who Toby Priest had been covering up for in the matter of the money. Now it seemed obvious. Surely it was the other man who'd been having an affair with Mandy and who was engaged to a third party. His son, Malcolm.

She wondered if Simon would appreciate hearing the news.

Dave could never see the point in going for a run and finishing off the evening in a pub, flooding the system with alcohol. But he supposed it was better a middle-aged man like Walter Clark indulged in both pastimes than in just one. It was obvious which he'd choose for preference.

Walter was on his third pint, and Dave on his second orange juice, when he judged it right to raise a tricky subject.

'Thanks for the tip on Beaufort Bonanza,' he said.

Walter smiled expansively. 'I hope you made a few bob.'

'I certainly did. About fifteen quid.'

'Christ, is that all? What did you put on – a pound?'

'Each way.'

Walter groaned loudly. 'For crying out loud, mate, I told you I'd stake you. Fifty quid would have been more like it.'

'I never bet more than a pound.'

Walter rolled his eyes. 'Look, Dave, I'll give you another chance.' He pulled his wallet from his pocket and counted out five £20 notes. 'He's running again at Carlisle in a few days. Put this on the nose – you know what that means, don't you? A hundred pounds to win. The odds won't be so good after last time but you'll do all right, I guarantee.'

Dave fingered the notes. 'How can you be so sure he'll win?'

'It's not a cast-iron certainty, of course.' Walter took a long pull on his pint and set it down carefully. 'Let's just say he might have an advantage over his competitors.'

'You mean the kind of advantage you used to have over me ten years ago?'

The smile faltered on Walter's face. 'Eh?'

'Come off it, Walter. I guessed at the time that you were running on more than adrenaline. There was no other way to account for the improvement in your times.'

Walter's mouth flapped like a landed fish. 'Dave, I am shocked that you should say that.'

'No need to be. I'm not exactly whiter than white myself.' Though I've never cheated to win a race – but he kept that sentiment to himself. This wasn't about recrimination. He needed Walter's cooperation. 'I've done time for drug abuse, remember?'

Walter was still spluttering protests and Dave allowed him to let off steam for a moment.

'Look, Walter, I'm not interested in what you get up to or how you pay your bills – though I imagine you've got plenty of those. But I am concerned about Beaufort Bonanza running at Carlisle.'

That focused the vet's attention. 'What do you mean?' he said.

'My boss has got an entry in the same race and I don't want her up against a horse that's on rocket fuel, or whatever you give them.'

Walter said nothing, just went back to his pint.

Dave continued, 'For the avoidance of doubt, as my solicitor used to say, I don't mind if our horse is beaten fair and square by yours. That's OK by me.'

Walter's eyebrows rose in surprise. 'Just supposing that things are as you imagine, how on earth will you know?'

'I won't. But I'm going to trust you, Walter. For old time's sake and all that.'

The vet turned the matter over in his mind. 'You're assuming that this is in my control?'

'It had better be. You ought to realise that I'm not quite so naïve as you think. I know one or two journalists who've got a bit of clout. If I see Adolf flying in the last half-mile like he did at Newbury then I shall be renewing my acquaintance sharpish.'

'You've got no proof.'

Dave laughed. 'What's proof got to do with it? A juicy rumour usually does the trick. And I don't suppose Toby Priest would appreciate the *Racing Beacon* turning up at Ridgemoor to check it out.'

Walter stared sullenly at him. 'Can I have my hundred pounds back?'

Dave was still holding the notes in his hand. He peeled off the top one and passed the rest across the table. 'I'll just get you another drink, Walter. It looks like you need it.'

After she'd finished her early-morning chores at Ros's yard, Marie usually got a chance to ride out. The morning after she'd called him, Jamie turned up and gave her a few riding tips as she took Spring Fever over the practice jumps. That had been fun.

She'd had to dash to work so they'd not had time to talk, but that was OK by her. It made sense to get to know one another a bit better.

This morning she'd kept an eye open for him but he'd not showed up until she was on the point of leaving.

'I'll walk with you for a bit,' he said and took charge of her bicycle, wheeling it along the lane to the gate.

'I've been thinking about what you told me,' she said. 'I can't speak for my family, but as far as I'm concerned we all ought to put Alan's death behind us. We've got to live in the future, after all.'

'That's good to hear. Thanks, Marie.'

'I also think you've got to ease up on yourself. It seems to me it wasn't all your fault.'

He stopped. 'What do you mean?'

'If you were that drunk when you left the pub, why didn't your friends stop you driving?'

He thought about it for a moment. 'I don't know.'

'Couldn't one of them have driven?'

'Richard didn't have a licence. I don't think he even knew how to drive in those days.'

'What about the other one?'

'Malcolm? He wanted to but I wouldn't let him. I said I was all right.'

Marie wasn't convinced, but what was the point of grilling Jamie about it? Hadn't she just said they ought to put it behind them?

They were now at the junction with the main road. Time for her to get on her bike.

Walter was slow in dragging himself out of bed and forcing a bowl of branflakes into his hung-over system. He'd hit the brandy bottle when he'd returned last night from the pub. But despite anaesthetising himself to the point where he couldn't manage to squeeze the toothpaste tube, the bony features of Dave Prescott had grinned at him throughout his dreams. And now he was running late, which was a big mistake as it gave Adriana a chance to buttonhole him on her return from the school run.

'I am *so* bored,' she cried as she strode into the kitchen and threw her car keys onto the silver Alessi coffee tray with a clang that rattled Walter's skull. 'When are you going to take me away from this tedious place? You promised me, Walter.'

Had he? Disenchantment with domesticity was her latest bug-bear. She'd been happy enough when they'd been doing up the house, spending money on architects and builders and interior decorators. Then he'd turned her loose on the garden and she'd spent a fortune out there too, landscaping and remodelling and replanting. Now it was all perfect, she was itching to start again somewhere else.

The problem was, she had no friends. The svelte, stylish Italian didn't exactly fit in with the local housewives. And she didn't much care for horses, which was a drawback, all things considered. In fact, according to the latest bulletin she hated the wretched creatures almost as much as she loathed Yorkshire and its beastly cold wet climate.

'I want to go home,' she announced, dragging a straight-backed kitchen chair across the stone floor with a noise like fingernails on a blackboard. She dropped onto the seat, crossing her long legs in sprayed-on denim jeans and jiggling a foot just in Walter's eye-line. Those trainers cost over £120, thought Walter irrelevantly.

'Take me back to Roma,' Adriana demanded with a pout of her oyster-pink lips.

'No,' he said shortly. 'It's too damned hot.' He wasn't in the mood for soft-pedalling. They'd had this argument before. He knew what was coming next.

'Let's go to the south, then,' she said. 'You can get another job where they have all those nice race courses like Ascot.'

Adriana knew about Ascot. She liked to bitch about the women's clothes on Ladies Day at the Royal meeting.

'No,' he said, getting to his feet. 'Listen to me, darling. We're doing all right here at the moment. The kids are in good schools and money goes a lot further up here than it does down south. Look, I'm late, I've got to rush.'

He beat it out of there before she could carry on whining. As it happened, he wouldn't mind a move. The right job at the right yard could work out well for all of them. But first he needed the right connections. It was a long-term proposition. In the meantime he had to deal with a short-term problem.

It had been stupid of him to start giving Dave Prescott racing tips. It just showed what happened when you tried to do a mate a favour. Then you found out he wasn't a real mate at all.

Whatever happened, Dave must not be allowed to carry out his threat of blowing the whistle on him to the press. Even if nothing could be proved, he'd be scuppered and the present job – let alone future ones – would evaporate quicker than a journalist could type EPO. At present there was no definitive test for the drug, whatever the papers might say. But at the back of his mind was the thought that one day there would be. And if there were too many rumours about its use the Jockey Club might start storing blood samples for future testing. Then the game really would be up.

He'd had his orders from Toby about Beaufort Bonanza. The horse had to put in another big performance at Carlisle. The owners – Beaufort Holidays – were in mourning for the death of the director who'd championed the acquisition of the horse and the occasion was to be dedicated to her memory. In other words, Adolf had to win.

But . . . any number of things could go wrong with horses. So far EPO had proved a very successful means of enhancing performance, but there had to be a failure sometime. It sounded as if the time had come.

Walter drove to Ridgemoor in a happier frame of mind. He'd simply omit to administer the drug and, when challenged, claim it hadn't had any effect. By the law of averages there had to be a cock-up soon – and this was going to be it.

One of Jane's regrets about the Bonfire Night Murders being shifted to the bottom of the intray was that she no longer saw much of Simon. She knew he was up to his eyes in an assortment of cases and he always popped into her office on his infrequent visits from Deacon Parade. However, the call she'd been expecting to repeat their evening out had not arrived and she couldn't keep engineering cosy drives to Yorkshire. The ball was now in his court and, she had to face it, he did not seem inclined to kick it in her direction.

Nevertheless, she entertained hopes, as a single woman with healthy appetites still does whenever an attractive man of partnership potential shows up on her radar. And the last person she wanted Simon to see her with was Superintendent Keith Wright.

Jane's office door was flung open just as the Super was launching into a waffly preamble about manpower restrictions. Jane saw Simon's face fall at Wright's presence.

'Good afternoon, sir,' he said, adding; 'I'll catch you another time, Jane,' as he retreated.

Wright scarcely registered the interruption but Jane cursed under her breath. Apart from anything else, she wanted to tell Simon what she'd learned from Elizabeth about Malcolm Priest. Instead she was doomed to be bored by Keith Wright while he doubtless worked round to asking her out (again).

To her astonishment she heard him mention a familiar name. 'I thought you'd be interested to hear the latest on the Priest family over in Yorkshire.'

That got her attention all right.

Keith grinned at her smugly. 'You didn't think I knew about your visit to Toby Priest, did you? Not much gets by me, Jane. He had a moan to an old pal of mine who advises him on security at his yard.'

'It was a long-shot, sir, but I'll follow up anything to get a handle on that double-murder.'

'Quite right too,' he said pompously. 'Bit of a waste of time, though, I expect.'

'Yes.' She didn't want to go into details. 'What's your news on him?'

He smiled at her in a self-satisfied fashion. She wondered how she was going to wiggle out of the inevitable invitation that would follow whatever information he was about to favour her with. 'As a matter of fact, my dear, it's not about Toby. It's one of his sons – not the jockey, the other one.'

'Malcolm?' There was surprise in her voice and eagerness too. It wouldn't have escaped him.

'That's right. I understand there's an anonymous female ringing Harrogate CID alleging that he's just killed someone.'

What?

Wright had all of her attention now and he was obviously enjoying it. 'A woman called Beverley Harris was found dead in her bath a couple of days ago. She worked for a holiday company with whom Malcolm Priest has a business association.'

'So he's a murder suspect?'

'Not exactly. It looks like an accidental death. Harrogate would like to interview the anonymous caller though. They're trying to track her down.'

'Who's in charge of this, sir? I'd like a word.'

'I'm sure I can discover that little detail for you, Jane. Why don't we get together out of the office – tomorrow evening, say? It'll give me time to make a few calls.'

Damn. She knew the oily sod would have something up his sleeve.

'Do you mind awfully, sir, if you just give me a buzz?'

His moist little mouth turned down at the edges. 'Don't want to be seen with me in public, is that it?'

'No, of course not. It's just that –' the idea came out of the blue '– I'm seeing someone and he might get the wrong end of the stick.'

'Oh.' He was not happy to hear that. Good. And the beauty of it was that she was permanently off the hook.

'I'm sorry, Keith.' She smiled. Best to let them down easy, that's what her mother had always said.

'Oh well, in that case, I shall retire gracefully.' He got to his feet. At the door he turned to face her. 'I'd like to meet this lucky fellow of yours. Perhaps the three of us could get together.'

Jesus. Now she'd have to make excuses for herself and someone who didn't even exist. What the hell was she supposed to say now?

'You already know him, sir. It's Simon Bennett.'

Even as she spoke the words she knew she shouldn't have said that.

Clem made his mind up when he saw the declarations in the paper for the following day. He told Joyce in a tone of voice that brooked no argument and, to his surprise, he got none.

'I'm going to Carlisle Races tomorrow,' he said, 'and don't try to stop me.'

Once he'd been a regular racegoer, sneaking off to midweek meetings when he could and delegating things at the garage. He'd been a couple of times in the year after Alan's death but his failing health had put a stop to that.

'How are you going to get there?' she asked.

'Taxi, train – don't you worry about me.'

'Of course I worry about you, you daft fool,' she replied with her familiar belligerence. 'I'm not having you puffing and wheezing around railway stations. If you insist on going I'll drive you.'

That's what he'd been hoping for, of course, but he'd not dared to ask.

'But what about the Post Office? Can you get the day off?'

'I'm taking it, whether old Jennings likes it or not.'

'Joyce, you're one in a million.'

'Don't give me that rubbish,' she muttered as she whisked away his breakfast tray.

But she was a grand lass. No question.

Jane wondered at which point in the day she could start nagging Keith Wright for the name of the Yorkshire officer dealing with the anonymous phone calls. Maybe she should have held out the promise of a date until she'd got what she wanted? But mind and body rebelled at the thought. Anyhow it was too late now, as she'd said to Simon when she'd phoned him last night.

'I've got a confession to make,' was how she'd opened the conversation and, 'I wish I'd never said it but it's too late now,' was how she'd ended. She doubted he'd heard, however, as he appeared to be having a choking fit.

'Are you all right?' she'd shouted into the phone, which had attracted Robbie from his room, any excuse not to be doing his English. She'd waved him back angrily.

The breathy, gulping noises on the other end of the line arranged themselves into a more familiar pattern and she realised, with relief and fury, that he was laughing. It took a while for him to control himself.

'I'm sorry,' she said finally, 'but would you mind playing along for a bit, just to get him off my back? Unless . . .' and a horrible thought struck her '. . . you're involved with someone at the moment. In which case, I couldn't ask you. That would be wrong. I'll just, well, I'll think of something else.'

He chuckled a bit more – a lazy, deep brown, patronising chuckle this time. She knew she was going to suffer for her stupidity.

'Don't worry, Jane,' he said finally. 'As it happens, I am theoretically unattached at present and I'm flattered to be your – what is it I am exactly? – your sleeping partner?'

'Thank you, Simon. With luck Wright won't mention it at all but I had to tell you.'

'OK, but if he does I'm going to need a bit of background. Like what movie we saw last night or what we're planning to do at the weekend.'

'For God's sake, Simon.'

'I'm serious – we've got to get our stories straight. I'm going to need a full breakdown of all those little details known only to those with whom we share our most intimate moments.'

'Oh sod off.'

'This was your idea, darling.'

She'd slammed the phone down and looked up to find Robbie grinning at her from the doorway.

'Have you got a thing going with him, Mum?'

A thing? Just what had she started?

Now the phone on her desk rang and she snatched it up, hoping it was the Superintendent with the information she wanted. It was Simon.

'I've just passed Wright in the corridor and he was all over me about you. He didn't look happy. This had better not stuff up my career.'

'Simon, I'm sorry. I'll go and talk to him today and straighten it out.'

'There's no need to do that. Just tell me one thing so I know next time he asks me – what exactly do you wear in bed?'

She hated him.

Marie's mind was only half on the job as she worked through the slowly dwindling pile of files. She'd played and replayed in her head her conversations with Jamie and her argument with her aunt. Out of it all one comment kept returning to bother her. What had Joyce meant by calling Jamie Ros's 'toy boy'? It shamed her that such an obvious piece of unfounded gossip should dominate her thoughts. But it did and it wouldn't go away. And she didn't know how to go about laying it to rest. She certainly wasn't going to raise the matter with Jamie or Ros or – least of all – her aunt.

An uneasy truce was in place at home. Marie was being polite but distant towards her aunt and Joyce was being distant without bothering with the politeness. So far, fingers crossed, she didn't appear to have said anything to her father. That was something to be thankful for.

She opened the next folder and was unprepared for the physical shock that seized her. She read the patient's name over and over, repeating it in her mind, just to make sure she wasn't somehow fooling herself. But the file really was headed: *Sullivan, James Robert*. Jamie's medical notes.

When Dr Gooding had employed her he'd stressed the importance of maintaining patient confidentiality. It had counted in her favour that he'd known her all his life and, so he'd said, trusted her as if she were his own daughter. She had signed a document binding her to secrecy and so far she had stuck to it faithfully. Nothing she had learned from the files had been passed to anyone else and she had put aside the medical histories of those few people she knew personally for someone else to deal with.

Jamie's folder was different. She couldn't resist reading it.

Compared to most files it was thin. Jamie had been a pretty healthy child. There was a history of sinus problems, which had vanished in puberty, and a few knocks, including a broken wrist, which Marie guessed had been the result of falling off horses. In 1999, however, came the car crash and a sheaf of reports from specialists on his injuries. She noticed references to his amnesia, which gave her a twinge of guilt as she recalled her reaction to his claim that he couldn't remember the accident.

But the piece of paper that interested her most, that riveted her attention as she read it through, was from the Accident & Emergency Department at High Moor Hospital. These were the notes compiled on Jamie's admission immediately following the crash. He had a suspected punctured lung, crushed ribs, a fractured arm and head trauma. One symbol was repeated throughout the list, the letter 'L' in a circle, meaning 'left'. Jamie's injuries were predominantly down the left-hand side of his body.

But how could that be, if Jamie was sitting in the driver's seat on the right-hand side of the car?

Jane arrived home late. Robbie was having supper at his dad's so there was no pressure to rush back and put food on the table. She dumped her bulging briefcase on the floor and once more dialled Harrogate CID. She'd finally got the name she wanted out of Keith Wright – DC Colin Stewart. But Stewart had not been answering his phone earlier and had obviously left for the day. She resolved to ring again in the morning even though she wasn't on duty.

She was taking the next day off to keep Robbie company – his school being shut for an inset day. Like every other parent, Jane couldn't understand why teacher training wasn't undertaken in the holidays – the schools were shut for long enough, for God's sake – but Robbie wasn't complaining. The deal was that he came back and worked hard tonight, and tomorrow they'd find something to do together, even if it was only going bowling or a cinema trip.

Unfortunately she had a load of stuff to get through first, of which tracking down DC Stewart was just one task. She explained as much to Robbie when he returned.

'What've you got to do?' he asked.

She sometimes told him about her cases, though she kept the details general and shielded him from anything disturbing. Maybe she shouldn't breathe a word but she believed that children of Robbie's age ought to be educated on the realities of the world around them. Criminals were no respecters of the innocent, she could attest to that first-hand. There had to be some advantages to being the child of a police officer and if she could give Robbie an insight into society's underbelly without injuring him, then she would.

She gave him a rundown of her tasks, which involved getting up to speed on a domestic assault and a departmental budget report. And there was still the matter of the Bonfire Night Murders. The latest information from the dead girl's sister had piqued her curiosity. Her intention was to research Jamie Sullivan's court case, and with luck Malcolm Priest's involvement, on the internet.

'I'll do that for you,' said Robbie.

'You've got your own work to do.'

'I've done it – well, nearly. Please, Mum, I'm much better on the net than you.'

There was no denying that but it didn't seem right to involve him so directly.

Her mobile rang and a familiar deep voice sounded in her ear.

'Just thought I'd better check in to see what I'm having for supper.'

'Get lost, Simon.'

'Why don't I say you made me your legendary *coq au vin* because you're a fabulous French cook? Please don't tell me you're not, it would shatter my illusions.'

She shouldn't have done but she began to laugh.

'OK, I'll say we had a Chinese takeaway. All right?'

She was still laughing as she put the phone down. Robbie was giving her a funny look.

'You *are* having a thing with him, aren't you?'

'No, I'm not.'

'It's all right by me, if that's what you're worried about.'

'Just clear off and do your homework, will you?'

He ambled towards the door. 'I'll have a trawl on the net for you when I've finished, shall I?'

'No.'

'OK.' He shrugged lazily. 'You know you could do worse than Simon, Mum.'

Infuriating child.

Malcolm was on his way out when a girl bicycled into the yard. He didn't recognise her at first but he gave her a thorough once-over as she explained that she'd come to see Jamie. She was a bit young but a cracker all the same. She could come and muck out *his* stables any day of the week.

He took her up to the house and yelled for Jamie. The girl seemed nervous, as if she'd bolt at any moment, so Malcolm ushered her into the hall. From above came the sound of feet on the stairs.

'Marie,' Jamie said, obviously taken aback by her presence. 'What are you doing here?'

Malcolm was intrigued. In the light of the hallway the girl seemed familiar. For two pins he'd have stuck around just to see how his brother-in-law handled this surprise package. The old Jamie would have whisked her upstairs in short order to see his etchings, but post-prison Jamie was seriously out of practice on the lady-killing front.

However, Malcolm was running late and, in any case, now was not the time to show the slightest interest in any member of the opposite sex, especially under his own roof. Whiter than white was how he must be – for the moment, at any rate.

He put his foot down as he drove to the Fox and Hen, which was equidistant between his home and Ridgemoor and thus a convenient spot for a meeting with his brother. He'd kept Richard waiting twenty minutes already but the get-together wasn't his idea. Richard had sounded panicky on the phone and refused to say what was up. That was typical of his little brother. When it came down to it, he was simply an old woman.

Richard was at a table by himself in the saloon bar, his eyes on the door as Malcolm strolled in. Jesus, he looked all of a twitch.

Malcolm took his time fetching himself a drink and exchanging pleasantries with the barmaid. Eventually he dropped into the chair opposite his brother.

'So,' he said, 'what's eating you then?' There didn't seem much point in beating around the bush.

Richard leant forward and muttered, though there was no one nearby and Elvis was booming away on the pub sound system, 'His memory's coming back.'

Malcolm wasn't going to make it easy for him. 'Who are we talking about exactly?'

'Jamie. He can remember the accident.'

Malcolm sipped his drink. They stocked a reasonable malt at the Fox, probably because the landlord came from Skye. 'If you ask me, my brother-in-law's never been the same since that car crash.'

Richard grabbed his arm. 'I'm serious, Mal. When he took a whack on the head the other week it got his memory going again. He can remember staggering around the car park and us getting the car keys off him.'

'How do you know this?'

'Vanessa told me. She was at Wetherby with her dad when he had the fall so she's been keeping an eye on him. He told her he's been having these weird dreams about the car crash.'

'He's been having dreams?'

'That's what he's told her but it's probably only a matter of time before he realises.'

'Rich, they *are* dreams.'

'He even remembers about Mandy being there.'

Uh-oh.

'Doesn't change a thing. Fact – he pleaded guilty and served time. Another fact – he took a bang on the head which so scrambled up his brains he got a personality transplant. However, if I were you, I wouldn't encourage my sexy little wife-to-be to spend time alone with Jamie discussing bedtime fantasies.'

273

Richard reacted angrily. 'That's not funny, Malcolm. Not everyone thinks through his dick like you and Dad.'

'I seem to remember that Jamie never used to think at all when it came to girls like Vanessa. They've run into each other before, you know.'

Richard plainly didn't. 'What are you on about?'

'I'm on about Jamie and your fiancée screwing their brains out a couple of years back. When he had that ride for old man Hartley in the Diadem.'

'I don't believe you.'

'Pippa told me. Swore me to secrecy, of course, which is why I'm only mentioning it now for your own good. Vanessa was a bit smitten, apparently. Used to write him letters from Australia.'

Richard was looking sick, nervously sipping from his glass even though it only contained a wedge of drowned lemon. 'She never said she knew him.'

'Well, she wouldn't, would she? Not if she had something to hide. According to Pippa,' he added, just to twist the knife, 'she was the last woman he had before he went inside. And there's probably been no one since, as far as I can tell.' Unless, of course, he was back in the saddle with little Marie.

Richard looked shattered, in an even worse state than when Malcolm walked in. Serves him right for winding me up about Jamie, Malcolm thought savagely. He got up from the table. He'd better get back to Pippa, since he was still on his best behaviour.

'Don't give Vanessa too hard a time, Rich,' he said before he went. 'Once you walk her down the aisle I'm sure she'll be as good as gold.'

He was still chuckling as he got into his car when his good humour was punctured by a sudden thought. *Marie*. He knew who she was now. Marie Kirkstall, the little sister of the boy on the horse. Was Jamie discussing his 'dreams' with her too?

Malcolm didn't like it. A talk with his brother-in-law was long overdue. He needed to find out exactly what was going on in his head. Then, if necessary, he could deal with him – just like he'd dealt with the others.

He hardly noticed the road as he drove home, he was thinking so hard.

Memory was a funny thing all right.

*

Marie found herself babbling, trying to explain to Jamie that she needed a word with him, and because she knew he wouldn't be at Ros's the next morning she'd cycled up here now and she was sorry but it wouldn't wait. She knew she was sounding foolish but nerves kept her talking.

A dog appeared out of nowhere and saved the situation. A big soppy red setter bounded down the hall and flung itself into her arms as if she were its dearest friend and, at that moment, she was.

'Get down, Matilda,' shouted Jamie and dragged the animal off her.

'I don't mind,' said Marie. 'I think she's absolutely lovely.'

The pair of them fussed over a squirming Matilda who was licking fingers and faces in an ecstasy of delight.

A dark-haired woman appeared in a doorway to what was probably the sitting room. 'What's going on?'

Jamie introduced his sister though there was no need. Marie knew who she was, just as Pippa had known her. They'd sat close to each other in the public gallery of Leeds Crown Court on the day of Jamie's sentencing trial. Marie had felt sorry for her and she'd guessed the feeling was mutual. They'd never spoken till now.

'You obviously like dogs.'

'Oh yes. We used to have a red setter.' And they'd had to find the dog another home after Dad's breathing problems got bad – but she didn't want to talk about that.

'Why don't you both take her for a walk? She's always game for an outing.'

That was clever of Jamie's sister and Marie was grateful to her. It got over the awkwardness of her unexpected arrival and would give her a chance to talk to Jamie in private.

'What's so urgent then?' said Jamie as they walked up the path that led to the foot of the moor. Though the sun had long since set the light lingered longer up here.

'I've got some questions about the accident.'

'I'm sorry but I still don't remember any more.'

'You remember your injuries though, don't you? Like – which arm did you break?'

'My left.'

'And what about your ribs – which side was hurt?'

'The left. I was pretty smashed up all down that side of my body.'

Matilda bounded up out of the dusk, just to make sure they were following, then scampered off again.

'How come you want to know about my injuries?' he asked.

'I saw your medical notes today at the surgery. Honestly, I didn't go looking for them. They turned up by chance.'

'So why are you asking me then?'

'I need to check – you don't mind, do you?'

There was a pause. She couldn't read his expression. 'You can ask me whatever you want, Marie.'

'OK, then. Your car, was it a regular right-hand-drive model?'

'Sure. Are you going to tell me what this is all about?'

It was about time she came clean.

'I'm very puzzled, Jamie. I know about the accident. I read the reports and the police explained it to us. Your car came up behind my brother on Misty, knocked them both off the road, crashed through the stone wall on the bend and finished up in some trees. I saw photos of it afterwards. It was a burnt-out wreck but you could see that the left side was all crumpled and bashed in. Two people got out of it with hardly a scratch but they carted you off to hospital in bits.'

They could hear Matilda woofing in the distance, probably after a rabbit or some other creature she'd never catch.

'What's your point, Marie?'

'My point is that the car was damaged on the left-hand side and so were you. The passenger side.'

He stopped in his tracks.

'Jamie, are you sure you were driving?'

Jamie slept badly that night. He often did before a race but this wasn't race nerves. Marie's visit had put him in a spin. He couldn't understand why she was trying to get him off the hook. He'd never tried to make excuses for what he'd done, so why should she?

He'd explained that in car crashes the weirdest things happened. He'd read about it. The forces were so immense, the twists and turns of an out-of-control vehicle so unpredictable that no logical conclusions could be drawn about his injuries. For all he knew, the car could have been travelling upside down.

But she'd remained sceptical and now so was he. Just imagine if he hadn't been driving, after all . . .

The hedgerow flashed by on his nearside, the leaves and grass stems in the verge ghostly in the headlights. Jesus, this was quick.

There was laughter and shouting in the confined space, his own whoops mingled with the others.

'Fantastic!' yelled a voice at his side. 'She goes like a bomb.'

'Slow down, you bloody idiot,' cried another from behind.

Out of the window a big familiar shape. A horse and rider. A dappled grey coat and a riding boot so close it almost kicked in the glass.

And a thump and a rumble beneath the wheels and the higgledy-piggledy stones of a moorland wall closing in.

An explosion of light in his head.

Then darkness.

Chapter Fifteen

Jane spread her notes about the Bonfire Night Murders across the kitchen table. There was a new addition to the file – a sheaf of A4 that she'd discovered that morning on the floor outside her room. Robbie really was the most disobedient boy. She'd told him not to look up the Sullivan drink-drive case on the internet but he'd gone ahead anyway.

It was hard to be angry with him, however. He'd saved her a task and she had something to read while she waited for the hands of the clock to creep round to nine – the time when she could put in her first call to Harrogate CID. She was determined to talk to Colin Stewart as soon as possible.

She ate a banana and some grapes as she read. Robbie had pulled off local newspaper reports which, to begin with, focused on the lad who had been killed and the grief of his family. It was sad and sober reading. Imagine what it would be like to lose Robbie. She put the thought out of her head – she couldn't get emotionally involved in this. It was hard though not to feel that this drunken dare-devil jockey had got off lightly. If it had been her son, she'd have wanted him incarcerated for life. At least he'd had the sense to plead guilty and spare the family the ordeal of a full-length trial. The court appearance was for sentencing only and had lasted just one day.

Nine o'clock had come and gone by the time she picked up the phone. It was answered after one ring – thank God for that.

Jane was prepared for a fight for information, since the officers of North Yorkshire weren't always entirely cooperative with their Lancashire counterparts. The reputation of some of the old-school detectives was that women like Jane were only welcome in the CID room if they wore stockings and took charge of the kettle.

DC Stewart, however, was obviously not of the old school. What's more, he sounded almost as young as Robbie.

'Sorry I didn't get back to you yesterday, ma'am, but I was a bit tied up.'

Ma'am? She suddenly felt about sixty. She explained her interest in the death of Beverley Harris and he ran through the facts for her without further preamble.

The woman's body had been discovered late in the afternoon by her employer, Barney Beaufort, who had called the police. The uniformed officers who had first attended had summoned CID and so Stewart had attended the crime scene – if that was what it was. The death had been reported to the coroner who hadn't yet registered it as enquiries were still in progress.

'She was lying on her back in the bath,' Stewart told her, 'and she'd obviously been in the water some while. It's a bit difficult to pinpoint the time of death because the heat of the bathwater would have affected the body temperature. But the likelihood is that she'd been in the bath since the night before. The lights were on in the bathroom and in the rest of the house.

'There was an empty champagne bottle by the side of the bath and the pathologist says there was plenty of alcohol in her system, plus some anti-depressant drug. He says there were no bruises on the body or other signs of violence. No evidence of sexual activity. The bathroom was well ordered – the floor was dry, a bathmat was laid out and there was a clean towel hanging on the radiator. She had a cupboard stuffed with medicines, all sorts of over-the-counter painkillers and some prescription drugs called Fluoxetine.'

'Is that the anti-depressant?'

'Yes. Her doctor said she'd been on them for about a year. She was a bit of a high-flyer at work but the job stressed her out. The doc said she'd never been suicidal though.'

'So what do you think?'

The detective paused, probably to gather his thoughts. 'My first impression – given that there was no sign of a third-party presence, no forced entry or anything like that – was that she got drunk on champagne which reacted with her medication. The bath was too hot and she fainted and drowned. I checked it out with people who supervise hot spas. They have to be careful that people don't collapse when the water temperature gets too high. It would be a funny way to deliberately kill yourself. She could have taken some of her pills if she wanted to do that. There was no note and no indication from her colleagues that she was that way inclined. Apart from the anti-depressants, of course.'

'You think it was an accident?'

Another pause. 'I said that was my *first* impression. Then we got a phone call from a woman who said she couldn't prove it but she knew Beverley had been murdered and we ought to talk to Malcolm Priest. This got passed on to me but I hadn't got round to checking it out before she came on again. This time she gave her name – Karen Robinson. She worked as Beverley's assistant at Beaufort Holidays. I've now got a statement from her and she didn't hold back. Gave me all sorts of stuff about Beverley's love-life. Seems she was sleeping with Barney Beaufort himself, which explains why he had a key to Beverley's cottage. But she'd also been knocking off this Malcolm Priest. He's a bloodstock agent who'd acquired a horse for the company.'

'I know who Malcolm is. He's the one I'm interested in.'

'Oh yes?' Stewart sounded interested himself. 'I'm going to pay him a visit shortly. According to Karen, he's a cross between Fred West and Ted Bundy.'

Jane chuckled. Colin Stewart was obviously a student of serious crime. A man after her own heart. 'What did she say?'

'Plenty, but it's all based on her personal animosity to this Malcolm. He's rubbed her up the wrong way and no mistake. It seems he was smitten with Beverley and when she gave him the boot he wouldn't take no for an answer. He was on the phone to the office all day and Karen was left to field the calls. I got the impression he took it out on her and now she's getting her own back. I'll talk to him, but frankly, there's no evidence that she was murdered.'

Maybe not, Jane thought, but something else had just occurred to her.

'Colin, you just mentioned Ted Bundy. Before you talk to Malcolm Priest, can I give you another name?'

'Of course.'

'George Joseph Smith. Go and look him up.'

'May I ask why, ma'am?'

She wished he'd stop doing that.

'Certainly,' she replied. 'He's also known as the Brides in the Bath murderer.'

Gates of Eden was running in the second race on the card so Pippa insisted on an early start. She'd not run the horse before and she was keen to make sure he was well settled in unfamiliar surroundings. From reading his record, he'd never experienced the undulating delights of Carlisle as a Flat runner and now here he was in his first race as a hurdler. She wanted to make sure he was as comfortable as possible.

But as the Land Rover growled across country, her real concern was her travelling companions. As ever, Malcolm was making his own way, with a stop at his office en route, and she was travelling with Jamie and Dave.

Jamie grinned at her reassuringly every time she turned to glance at him in the rear seat but she knew he was only putting on a cheerful face for her benefit. That fall at Wetherby had knocked the stuffing out of him and she was worried he was coming back too soon. She'd tried to get him to postpone his return but he'd been insistent.

'I'm fine, Pippa. The headaches have cleared up and I've got a clean bill of health. I'm really looking forward to getting back on Gates.'

That might well be true, she thought, but she could tell there were other things on his mind. That visit from Marie Kirkstall, for instance – what was that all about? She'd tried to ask him after the girl had gone last night but he'd not wanted to talk about it.

'I met her up at Ros's,' was all he said.

'But what did she want? Why would she come up here to see you?'

He'd given her an anguished look. 'I can't tell you now, Pippa. I need to think.' And he'd gone straight off to bed.

Dave was also giving her cause for concern. He drove silently, concentrating on the road ahead. Usually he made a lot of noise, entertaining her with a stream of stories and irreverent comments. It was unlike him to be silent and out of sorts. But then, what did she know about him really? They'd worked together for just a few weeks. He was entitled to have an off-day like anyone else. Except, now she thought about it, this was more like an off-week. He'd not been himself for a while. Maybe he was worried about the race. This was the first time a horse he'd worked with had come under orders.

'Cheer up, Dave. It won't be your fault if Gates of Eden nose-dives at the first.'

'Thanks,' he said.

She'd meant it as a joke but he'd taken it seriously. What was the matter with him? She sneaked a look over her shoulder. Jamie was staring blankly out of the window, deep in thought.

What was the matter with the pair of them?

'Who's the Brides in the Bath murderer, Mum?'

Jane hung up the phone. How typical of Robbie to turn up just at the wrong moment. He lounged in the kitchen doorway, dressed in a sweatshirt and baggy pants, looking as if he'd just dragged himself out of bed. It suddenly struck her that he seemed older, his shape filling up the doorway, his voice deeper as he repeated his question.

'A man called George Smith,' she replied. 'He married women and killed them to inherit their money and their life insurance.'

'And he killed them in the bath?'

'He pulled them up by their ankles so their heads were suddenly plunged underwater. People die very quickly like that and it leaves no sign of injury. It was only when his third wife died in the same way that he got caught.'

Robbie was shaking some sugary cereal into a bowl. 'Wicked,' he said. 'Have you got a case like that?'

'No, Robbie.' But North Yorkshire CID might have.

Why had she mentioned the Brides in the Bath Murders to Colin Stewart? She didn't seriously think Malcolm Priest was another George Smith, did she? No, but given her suspicions, she had to mention it.

So what exactly were her suspicions? Only the fact that Malcolm Priest was connected – tenuously – to two separate incidents of unexplained death. Was that enough to act on?

Robbie plonked himself down beside her, shovelling her papers aside and spilling them across the table.

'Careful,' she said.

'What's this?' Robbie was holding the photograph Elizabeth had given her of the lads at Ridgemoor larking around after a football match.

'It's the staff at the yard where Jamie Sullivan worked.'

He peered at it closely. 'It's got a date on it. Twenty-first of September 1999.'

She tried to place the information in context. 'It must have been taken a couple of weeks after Sullivan's car crash.'

'So you read that stuff I printed off for you.'

'I told you to leave it to me, Robbie. What time did you get to bed?'

He ignored the question and pointed to the photograph. 'Who are this lot then?'

'That one's Toby Priest.' Jane tapped the familiar image of the horse trainer. Even in the photo he gave her the creeps. 'I don't know the others.'

Robbie looked at it closely. 'That's Malcolm.' He pointed out a tall square-shouldered man without a shirt.

'How do you know that?'

'His photo's in that internet stuff. Here.' He leafed through the sheaf of papers and quickly found the page he wanted.

Jane saw at once that he was right. The same man in a suit and tie was identified arriving at court with the accused jockey. Now she looked closer she could see the family resemblance to his father.

Robbie had taken off his spectacles and was squinting at the photograph from a distance of about two inches. It was one of his tricks – his myopia enabled him to see with great clarity from close up.

'Have you noticed this?' he said at last, pointing to a mark on Malcolm's shoulder.

She looked at it for a moment. 'It looks like a bruise.'

He shot her an exasperated glance. 'Of course it's a bruise,' he said, jumping from his seat and rushing out of the room. A moment later he was back with a magnifying glass in his hand. 'Here, take a look.'

It undoubtedly was a bruise, a mulberry stain of extravagant hue that spread over Malcolm's collar bone and across one side of his chest.

Robbie had replaced his spectacles and was grinning at her with the infuriating look which invariably accompanied one of his ridiculous brainteasers. 'So what conclusion do you draw from that, Mum?'

'I don't draw any conclusion at all,' she said. 'Apart from the obvious one that he probably got it in the car crash.'

'And?'

'And nothing. If you've got some bright idea, Robbie, just spit it out.'

'Well, don't you reckon he got it from a seatbelt? It cuts right across his shoulder and diagonally across his chest – just where a seatbelt goes.'

That was true, it did. She looked through the magnifying glass again and thought she could make out a line where the edge of a strap had bitten into the flesh of the pectoral.

'Very good, Robbie. I'd say you're probably right.'

'In which case, why is the mark on the right side of his chest?'

She stared at him blankly.

He rolled his eyes, infuriated at her stupidity. 'Come on, Mum, you've read the reports. If Malcolm had been sitting in the front passenger seat as he claimed, the seatbelt bruise would be on his other shoulder.'

At last she got it. Malcolm was driving the car. Not Jamie. And, on the day she was murdered, Amanda had ordered four copies of the photo which proved it.

In the back seat of the Land Rover Jamie was lulled by the rhythm of the powerful engine. After Marie's unexpected visit he'd not had a good night's sleep. And he needed all the rest he could get if he was to do himself justice on Gates of Eden.

Flames flickered in the darkness. There was a stench of smoke and petrol in his nostrils and a roaring in his ears. He could feel the heat, the fire was getting closer. He knew he had to get away but he couldn't move.

'Jamie! Jamie!' Hands tugged and pulled at his limbs. 'Can you hear me?'

He wanted to respond, scream, 'Help me!' as loudly as he could, but his voice wouldn't work. Nothing was working.

'We've got to get him out.'

'It's OK. I've got him.'

'Quick, Malcolm.'

Then he was outside in the fresh air, being tumbled across the grass.

'Jamie!' Richard shouting in his ear. Hysterical. Fingers were prodding him, groping at his wrists. Clumsy. You won't find a pulse like that, Rich.

'Is he OK?' Malcolm.

'No!' More pummelling and poking. *'Jesus Christ, Mal, he's dead!'*
'Are you sure?'
'Yes. He's not breathing.'
'Oh God.'
But I'm not dead. Honestly.

The ringing of Jane's mobile interrupted a debate with Robbie on the chances of Jamie Sullivan losing his memory of the car crash. On reading the reports of the accident and trial, Jane had been of the opinion that the jockey's amnesia was a convenient excuse for not facing up to the consequences of his actions. Now, if Robbie's conclusion was correct, it looked more convenient for Malcolm.

She was surprised to discover the call was from Colin Stewart.

'I thought you'd like to know that I can't get hold of Malcolm Priest at the moment. He's off to a race meeting in Carlisle and I don't think my guvnor would approve of me going after him.'

'I can understand that, Colin.'

'I'll try and catch him when he gets back though. I really fancy him after what you said about George Smith. I looked it all up.' He sounded quite excited. 'The pathologist says it's possible Beverley could have been killed like that.'

'It could be difficult to prove,' she said in an attempt to calm him down. Her initial suggestion hadn't been entirely serious.

But the young detective wasn't listening.

'We've had a Ripper in Yorkshire. Just think, we could have a Brides in the Bath killer too.'

Lying on his back, looking up at the stars. In the distance, the sound of sirens. Up close, two voices.
'I don't understand, Rich. I just didn't see that horse.'
'What happened to the lad who was riding?'
'He's up on the road.'
'Is he OK?'
'He's dead too.'
'Oh, Jesus.'
'Listen to me, Rich. Before the police get here – Jamie was driving, right?'
'What do you mean?'

'Just say that Jamie was driving. It won't matter to him, will it? He's dead.'

But I'm not. I'm not!

'Mal – he moved. He's alive!'

'That doesn't change anything. It's his car. He was driving. It's two against one – right?'

Jane called Simon but was told he wasn't on duty. She found his home number. To her relief he didn't start on the cod boyfriend act. In fact his tone was grim.

'Is this a bad time?' she asked.

'Not exactly. I'm just having a constructive discussion with my daughter about how we are going to pass the day. I'm not in favour of spending it watching MTV.'

So Simon was in the same boat as she was. Tanya's school was obviously closed like Robbie's.

'Why don't you both come over here?' she said. 'It's about time Robbie met a female of his own age. And I've got something to tell you.'

'Not about Keith Wright, I hope.'

'It's the Bonfire Night Murders.'

'Right you are then, boss.'

As he put his foot down on the motorway, Malcolm was regretting being quite so hard on Richard the night before. At times his brother irritated him so much that he forgot the importance of keeping him on-side. Certainly venturing into Vanessa territory was dangerous. He'd have to smooth it over, say he'd misheard Pippa and it was some other blonde strumpet who used to be stuck on Jamie. And if he didn't swallow that there were other ways of making Richard toe the line. After all, if he went down he'd make sure little brother did too.

What to do about Jamie was a tougher problem to resolve. Just what did his brother-in-law remember of that night? His loss of memory had been very opportune so far and it would be handy to prolong it. It was a pity that Jamie's recent bang on the head appeared to have cleared the mists. Perhaps a harder thump would ensure they descended for good.

It might come to that.

*

Robbie had been aghast at the thought of some unknown girl invading his home space and had disappeared into his room for half an hour. But when the bell rang he beat Jane to the door. He'd changed into a fresh set of sweatshirt and loose pants and Jane noted the gel in his hair. Her stomach contracted with nerves – she hoped this idea wouldn't backfire.

Her anxieties increased when she clapped eyes on Tanya. The girl was taller than she was, with almond-shaped eyes and the kind of complexion that defied the existence of adolescent skin problems. She wore a denim skirt appliqued with glitter that finished halfway down her slender golden thighs and a skimpy yellow top which hinted at fast-growing curves. This was a girl of fourteen?

'Pleased to meet you,' Jane said.

Tanya flashed a perfunctory smile. 'Hi.' The almond eyes did not meet Jane's; they were focused to her left. On Robbie.

'You wanna Coke or something?' he mumbled in his new bass voice.

'Cool,' she replied and followed him into the kitchen.

Jane was left alone with Simon in the hall. She realised he was as on edge as she was. From the kitchen came Robbie's indistinct rumble, followed by a peal of high-pitched laughter.

'So far so good,' Simon murmured. 'Why don't you tell me what's on your mind?'

'Cool,' said Jane and led him into the sitting room. She'd hardly got started with her suppositions about Malcolm Priest, when Robbie stuck his head round the door.

'Hey, Mum, can me and Tanya get a video?'

She looked at Simon who shrugged – it was OK by him. She handed over a £10 note.

'Actually we might get a couple. And a pizza.'

Simon produced another tenner.

'Thanks, Si,' the boy said and vanished.

Jane bit her lip and avoided Simon's eye until she heard the front door slam. Then the pair of them began to laugh.

When they'd recovered, she said, 'We're just going to get in the way here, you know. Would you be happy to leave them on their own?'

'What have you got in mind?'

'A trip to the races to have a word with Malcolm Priest. I don't see why we shouldn't have a crack at him before Harrogate CID.'

*

On arrival at the racecourse Malcolm made straight for the Beaufort hospitality box to see how the land lay. He'd been a trifle cavalier in his treatment of Karen but he imagined she wasn't senior enough to appear at this kind of gathering. He was relieved to see that he was right.

Though there was a sombre atmosphere in the room in contrast to previous occasions, Malcolm observed that food and drink – particularly drink – were plentiful. He accepted a whisky and was drowning it in water – a clear head was called for this afternoon, all things considered – when Barney Beaufort appeared by his side.

'Malcolm,' said the travel agent in the tone of an actor about to launch into a speech, 'I appreciate your attendance on this sad occasion.' He wrung Malcolm's hand with both of his.

Malcolm hadn't clapped eyes on Barney since Newbury and there was an appreciable change in his demeanour since then. He wore a black tie and a tragic air. His once-ruddy face was pale and smudged with dark hollows.

'I considered cancelling,' Barney continued, 'but Beverley wouldn't have wanted me to do that. I drew the line at champagne though – it wouldn't have been right.'

Malcolm nodded in agreement. Champagne would have been in very poor taste indeed.

Barney sighed deeply. 'Beverly was a brilliant woman. Dedicated to the Bonanza initiative.'

Malcolm didn't know what to say to that. He wasn't sure which script the old ham was reading from.

Barney leaned closer. 'I found her body, you know. A terrible shock. But even in death she was beautiful, just as she was in life.'

Barney seemed to be enjoying his role of newly bereaved employer. Malcolm said nothing. He could hardly add that, in his opinion, Bev looked bloody terrible lying dead in the bath.

He was rescued by a well-groomed woman in a bright flower-print summer dress who took Barney by the arm. 'Do you mind awfully if I steal him away?' she said to Malcolm. 'There's an old friend of mine over there who he simply must meet,' and she led him off without a word of protest.

'Who's that woman?' he asked Guy Greaves who'd come up for a refill.

'Val Beaufort.'

289

Malcolm was at a loss. 'But you told me she'd left him.'

'She came running back in his hour of need. A good woman in a crisis, is Val.'

'What about the younger, richer advertising man?'

'I don't think he was quite as rich as he made out. But I only pick up the odd whisper. I know nothing for certain, unlike you.'

'Me?' Malcolm was startled. Was the Beaufort rumour mill linking him with Beverley? It would only take a whisper or two from that flat-chested piece of poison, Karen.

'You were right about Bonanza last time,' said Greaves. 'I want to know if he's going to do it again.'

Malcolm was relieved. This was a topic which he could discuss with some certainty. 'I'd stick your money on quick, Guy. Before the price gets any shorter.'

Simon put his foot down on the motorway. It was ninety miles to Carlisle and he'd promised Jane he'd make it in close to an hour. He'd made it clear he thought the whole expedition was a bit of a joke, but he'd hardly stopped grinning from the moment she'd suggested it.

'This is a damn sight more fun than trailing round the shops with Tanya,' he said, 'and nowhere near as expensive.'

Nevertheless he listened closely as Jane first told him about the death of Beverley Harris, and then about the Jamie Sullivan case.

'So, basically, we're haring up to Carlisle to confront this poor sod based on your knowledge of a Golden Oldie serial-killer and one of young Robbie's way-out theories.'

'It's not that way out.' She was immediately on the defensive. 'If you examine the photograph closely it really does look like a bruise on Malcolm's shoulder. And it's on the wrong side if he was a front-seat passenger, as he claims.'

She could see he was not impressed.

'Never mind, Jane. I like a day at the races. I can show you how to place a bet.'

She realised she hadn't told him about Elizabeth's latest revelation – that Toby and Malcolm were having an affair with Amanda at the same time. That made him think a bit.

'So your theory is what, exactly?' he said at last.

Good question.

'Suppose Malcolm and his brother allowed everyone to think that Jamie was responsible for the accident. Then suppose Amanda found out that Malcolm was the driver.'

'How?'

'I don't know. She was sleeping with him – maybe she was suspicious of that bruise, too, and that's why she ordered four copies of the photograph.'

'You've lost me, Jane.'

'I'm saying –' and suddenly it appeared in her mind as an inevitable sequence of events '– I'm saying that she was blackmailing him. He paid her off in the first place and she hopped off to Lancashire with ten grand in her building society. Then she fell for the ghastly Pete and two years later found herself out of work with a habit to feed. Pete would have jumped at the possibility of going back to Malcolm and milking him for more money. So the pair of them threatened him with exposure, using that photo as leverage, and he paid them the money that Pete showed to Filthy Barrable. Then, after Barrable had left, Malcolm turned up at the cottage, killed the pair of them and took his money back.'

There was silence in the car apart from the drone of the engine.

'What do you think then?' she said at last.

Simon shook his head. 'How long did it take you to dream that up?'

'No time at all. It just occurred to me.' She was pleased with herself. It felt right.

'God, you're a stubborn woman, Jane. The lengths you'll go to avoid the obvious. Which is that some evil little drug-dealer did the murders.'

Jane didn't bother to argue. Robbie would be proud of her theory. What was more, Simon didn't have a suspect and she did. She was looking forward to asking Malcolm Priest what he was doing on the night of 5 November.

'Oh no,' he groaned suddenly.

'What's up?' But the question was redundant. She could see the traffic clogging up the lanes ahead and the dreaded red-and-white signs. Roadworks for ten miles.

'Let's hope he's there for the rest of the afternoon,' Simon muttered as he slowed the car to a crawl. 'It might take us that long to get there.'

*

291

For once Joyce parked in the disabled car park with a clear conscience. In the years she'd been driving Clem's car, with the disabled sticker on the windscreen, she'd often been challenged when taking advantage of it. But this time she was fully justified.

They'd not spoken much on the journey. She'd asked him once or twice if he was all right but he'd told her to shut up and stop pestering him so she'd concentrated on the road ahead.

Now, as they prepared to get out, she turned to him. His face was grim.

'Are you sure you're up to this, Clem?'

'No, I'm not,' he said, pushing his door open. 'But we've not come all this ruddy way for nothing.'

She kept her thoughts to herself as she helped him on with his big old waterproof coat. It was heavier on the right-hand side and she noticed the way his hand nervously patted the bulge in his pocket.

'Why don't you give it to me?' she said.

'What?'

'The thing in your pocket. Let me shoot the little bastard.'

He looked at her, a swirl of emotion in his pale grey eyes. 'I can't, Joyce. They'd lock you away. It doesn't matter what happens to me.'

She began to protest but he stopped her. 'I've got to do it,' he said. 'He was my son and it's my job.'

She nodded her head. She'd tried.

'Which way?' she asked. This was her first time ever at a racecourse.

He pointed across Durdar Road to the entrance. 'Come on, lass,' he said with a sudden smile, 'just you follow me.'

It was quite like the old days.

Jamie put everything out of his head for the race. He was a professional and the dramas of his personal life had to be banished from the saddle. After all, this race, humble as it was in the great scheme of things, was more important than the Gold Cup to some people. The owner, Joanna Price, for one. He'd met her again in the saddling box and she could hardly contain her excitement. And Pippa, who'd gamely taken on the responsibility of saddling a jump horse and who was still gloomy about her prospects as a trainer. Then there was Dave, a complete novice in the world of racing, who'd been allowed to have a crack at getting this horse fit.

But Jamie preferred not to think about the human beings involved. His focus, for the moment, was on the horse beneath him as they mingled with the other runners before the start. Gates of Eden had made the same career move as himself, from Flat to jumps, from big money to small beer, from pacy performer to long-distance plodder. It's welcome to the real world for both of us, he thought.

Gates of Eden didn't seem perturbed by his change in status. His ears were pricked and he was alert. He probably recognised the situation he was in. Though it had been a couple of years since he'd last raced, Jamie knew that horses, like elephants, forgot very little.

He lined up beside Carlo on Adolf.

'Sorry, Jamie, he's mine now,' cried the Ridgemoor lad. 'I ain't swopping.'

'And you're welcome to him,' said Jamie, though he did feel some regrets. For one thing, he doubted if he'd be this close to his former mount at the finish if Adolf showed his Newbury form.

He wasn't sure how to ride this race and Pippa hadn't been much help. 'I'm leaving it to you,' she'd said. 'You know him as well as anybody' – which had pretty much summed up Ros's feelings when he'd canvassed her opinion earlier.

Dave was the only one who'd said anything useful. 'He loves being at the front. He doesn't like anything to go past him when he's ahead of the others.'

Adolf, by contrast, couldn't be allowed to hit the front too soon. Jamie knew Carlo would try to hide him in the pack before unleashing him over the last half-mile.

Jamie decided to keep Gates of Eden up with the leading runners but to hang back from pole position for as long as possible. He was well aware what a strength-sapping ordeal the undulating Carlisle track could be, especially when slogging uphill. Let some other horse do the front-running donkey work, if possible.

Fortunately, a local favourite called Climbing Party was happy to take on the pace-setting duties and sped to the front of the field of fourteen. Gates of Eden followed on keenly and would have headed them all if Jamie had let him.

'No, you don't,' he muttered to the big grey head beneath him, 'you've got a long way to go.'

It was an undeniable thrill to be riding this horse in a real race once more. The rhythm and athleticism were there just like before, but this time Jamie knew the horse would not be left behind for speed. The question was how he would handle the jumps and the distance. Two and a half miles was a long way on a testing track in soft ground.

The field was strung out as they completed a full circuit of the tight right-handed course. Gates of Eden was handily placed in second, leaping the hurdles smoothly and eating up the ground with his powerful stride. Even if the horse blew up now, the outing would have been well worth it.

But the grey showed no signs of flagging yet, unlike Climbing Party who had led from the start and was now beginning to pay the price. Jamie noticed him jinking at the last hurdle before they rounded the bend into the home straight.

Now was the time to give Gates of Eden his head. 'Let's see if you've got anything left,' Jamie muttered as he kicked on. To his delight the grey lengthened his stride and overtook the leader as he sailed over the first hurdle in the straight.

Dave's done a hell of a job, thought Jamie. Gates of Eden was galloping with complete freedom now he was in front, seemingly in his element. Surely he wasn't going to win? But when he glanced to his left, away from the rail, he realised that they had a fight on their hands. Adolf was on his shoulder and Carlo was working him for all he was worth.

The two horses jumped the next hurdle neck-and-neck and charged towards the last.

As they took the final obstacle Jamie realised that Gates of Eden was the stronger horse. He was not going to let Adolf past. Suddenly the black horse's challenge was over. He could hear Carlo behind him urging Adolf on but his race was finished.

Gates of Eden won by six lengths.

Clem knew how he was going to shoot Jamie Sullivan. He had an image in his mind, one he'd carried for forty years, of how it should be done. Even though Sullivan might be surrounded by other people it should be possible to get up close and fire straight into his chest. Just the way Jack Ruby had killed Lee Harvey Oswald in the crowded basement of Dallas police headquarters all those years ago.

But the spectators around the winner's enclosure were closely packed and not keen to yield to pressure from behind. Eventually Clem found himself wedged between two burly punters in anoraks on the perimeter of the ring. A few yards ahead the winner was led to his station and welcomed with polite claps and some enthusiastic pats from his connections. The jockey slid from the horse's back and was embraced by a woman Clem recognised as Sullivan's sister.

For a moment he toyed with the idea of pulling out the gun and shooting from where he was. Surely he couldn't miss from ten feet?

His hand was in his pocket, holding the weapon, but he kept it there. He'd only ever fired it once, years ago, up on the moors. He remembered the deafening roar and the kick of the recoil – and the fact that he couldn't hit a soft drink can from a similar distance to that which separated him from his target now. His only hope was to get right in close. One shot in the centre of the chest, that would do it.

Clem waited a few moments while the jockey talked to the beaming owner and a photograph was taken. Then the crowd began to disperse. The pressure on either side of him eased and he could move his arm more freely. The jockey, holding his saddle, was walking towards him. Suddenly he was a yard away, no more. This was Clem's opportunity.

But his hand wouldn't move. The weapon was caught in the folds of his coat. And his breath was short in his chest, paralysing his whole body.

Sullivan had passed him now, walking briskly back towards the weighing room.

Clem's chance to avenge his son had gone.

Jamie had just finished changing when he got word that some bald fellow was looking for him. He found Dave outside the weighing room standing next to an enormous rucksack from which protruded rolled-up camping paraphernalia.

'Congratulations,' Jamie cried, seizing the big man's hand. 'Your first winner with four legs.'

Dave shook his head. 'Not much to do with me. It's down to you and the horse.'

'Call it teamwork, then. What are you doing with all this gear? You off to climb Everest?'

It was a joke, naturally, but Dave didn't smile.

'I'm going back down south. I've just come to say cheerio and give you these.'

Jamie took the keys he was offering. They belonged to Pippa's Land Rover. He wondered if he'd heard correctly.

'It's a bit sudden, isn't it? When are you coming back?'

'Well . . . I can't say really. I'll keep in touch. It's been great, mate. Good to end on a winning note.'

The penny was slowly dropping. Dave was going for good. Jamie was thrown.

'Hang on, what does Pippa say about this?'

Dave looked away. 'I was hoping you might tell her for me. Say I'm really grateful for everything.'

'Tell her yourself. You can't just walk out like this.'

But Dave was already hoisting his pack onto his shoulders.

'She's going to be upset, Dave. What shall I say?'

Dave held out his hand. Jamie took it with reluctance.

'I've had a fantastic time. Been a real education.'

'Where are you going now?'

'Cab into town, train to London.'

'Don't go like this, Dave. Stay and talk to Pippa. Let us give you a proper send-off.'

But the tall man was already walking away.

Malcolm was seething. He couldn't get Walter on his mobile so he called his father instead.

'He ran out of steam. The race was his and he just stopped running.'

'I know,' said Toby.

'But that's not meant to happen.'

'That's horses for you.'

'Oh come off it, Dad. You know what I'm on about. He didn't perform like last time and somebody's arse needs a good kicking.'

'I've just kicked it, Malcolm. He says there's no guarantees.'

'But I thought that's what we were paying for – a guaranteed winner. I'm going to do some kicking as well as you.'

'No, you're not. He's allowed one failure. We'll make up for it next time.'

'We'd better. Or I'll slaughter the chinless little turd.'

He would too. Anyone who stepped out of line with Malcolm Priest took his life in his hands.

'Pippa, Dave's left. He gave me these,' Jamie held out the Land Rover keys, 'and asked me to tell you he's gone back to London. For good,' he added.

'He can't do that.'

'Of course he can.'

'No, he can't. Not now. Not till he's talked to me.' Her face had turned white.

'He can do what he wants. We don't have a contract with him or anything. We can't keep him against his will.'

'Oh sod it.' She stamped her foot, just like she used to do when their mother wouldn't let her stay out late. 'Did he say why?'

'No, he didn't.'

'I don't suppose you ruddy well thought to ask him. Where is he now?'

'He said he was catching a cab into town.'

She snatched the keys out of Jamie's hand. 'I'll find him. I'll give him a lift to the station if that's what he wants but not before I find out what's going on in his stupid thick head.'

And she vanished without saying goodbye.

Pippa halted the Land Rover at the taxi rank and sprang out. Dave was on his own. Not many punters forsook the course halfway through the afternoon's card.

'Get in!' she shouted at him.

'Hello, Pippa,' he mumbled unhappily.

'Get in and I'll take you to the station.'

'It's OK, I'll wait.'

'No, it's ruddy well *not* OK!' She had him by the arm and was dragging him towards the vehicle. 'Get in!' she ordered.

He did as he was told.

Finally, after forty minutes of stop-start, then crawling bumper to bumber along a coned-off single carriageway, Jane and Simon emerged from the maze of roadworks. Ahead lay a seductive vista of empty three-lane highway. Like every other frustrated motorist, Simon stamped his foot to the floor and burned rubber.

'What was that all about?' he complained. 'I didn't see one workman or one machine in operation.'

'You're doing a hundred, Simon.'

'Going to give me a ticket, are you?' He eased his foot off the accelerator all the same.

'Calm down,' Jane said. 'We'll be there in time for the fourth race.'

Malcolm Priest had better not leave early.

Bag in hand, Jamie left the changing-room. Gates of Eden had been his only ride of the day and he was rueing the fact. Till he'd walked into the weighing-room he'd not realised how much he had missed the place during his lay-off. His jump-racing colleagues had welcomed him back like a longlost friend, even though he'd only been one of their fraternity for a few weeks. And he'd just ridden a cracking winner so at least some part of his life was falling into place.

The way he felt right now, he'd even take on one of Irene Bolt's dodgy animals. But there were no spare rides today and now he wasn't even sure how he was going to get home. If Pippa didn't reappear, he supposed he could always ride back with the horse. He decided to head in that direction and maybe leave his stuff in the horse box.

'Hey, Jamie!' It was his brother-in-law, making his way through the crowd towards him with a broad smile on his face. 'You rode a stormer. Brilliant stuff.'

'Thanks.' The big man's generous praise, earned at the expense of his own horse too, pricked at Jamie's conscience. But he had a bone to pick with him and maybe now was the time to do it. 'Malcolm, can we talk somewhere?'

'Of course.'

'I mean, about the crash. Our crash.'

Malcolm looked him in the eye. 'Sure. What are you doing at the moment?'

'I was just going to see if there was room for me in the horse box. Pippa's gone off and I need a lift.'

'I'm about to leave. Come with me and we'll talk on the way.'

Why not? It made perfect sense.

'I can't believe you were just going to take off back to London without speaking to me.'

Pippa was giving Dave a hard time and he couldn't blame her. They were in the Land Rover parked outside the station and there were only twenty minutes to go before his train. But it was going to be a tough twenty minutes.

'Look at me, Dave, and just tell me why.'

He shrugged and said nothing.

'We've just had our first bit of success together and you want to leave – why?'

They'd been over and over the same ground since they'd left the racecourse.

'No more, please, Pippa. I can't explain.'

'That's because you won't. What have I done?'

'Nothing, honestly. You're great and I've loved the experience and everything but it's time for me to do something else.'

'Like what? You say you've got plans but what are they? Give me one decent answer and I'll say goodbye and good luck.'

He stared mutely out of the window.

'See?' she cried. 'You're giving up on something you've hardly started. You're just running away and I don't understand it. For God's sake, Dave, you owe me an answer. Why?'

Seventeen minutes to go now. It was agony but he could do it.

He wasn't going to tell her that he was leaving because of her. That once the notion that her marriage might be over had lodged itself in his head it had grown into something that he couldn't contain. He knew that if he carried on working by her side he'd soon be hopelessly in love – and what was the point of that? None, since she was committed to that slime-ball Malcolm.

What's more, if he stayed, he knew he'd end up telling Pippa what he'd seen Malcolm doing with Beverley, God rest her. And he definitely couldn't tell her that. In his experience, the messenger always got shot.

Fifteen minutes to go. It seemed like an eternity.

Malcolm and Jamie pushed through the crowd assembling in front of the Jubilee Stand for the next race. Malcolm vaguely noted the action in the betting ring, his thoughts racing ahead.

It was a stroke of luck, Jamie needing a lift. It couldn't have been better if he'd planned it himself, given the circumstances. But something would have come up – it always did.

299

He noted the preoccupied expression on Jamie's face. It wasn't the look of a lad who'd just ridden a 10–1 winner in great style. It was the expression of a man preparing some awkward questions.

Malcolm just needed to get Jamie away from the course with as few people seeing them as possible – people who might remember seeing them go, that is. For the moment they were OK, the crowd around them was thick. There was nothing like being in a crowd to be invisible.

Joyce was disturbed by the greyness in Clem's pallor. He was taking forever to catch his breath. She had found him a seat near to the first-aid post so, if things got desperate, maybe they could give him some oxygen.

He was mumbling something.

'I can't hear you.' She put her ear close to his mouth.

'I fluffed it, Joyce.'

'What do you mean?'

'He came right by me. I could have got him but I couldn't do it. I'm sorry.'

Joyce was sorry too. More than that, she felt cheated. So that was that. She stared miserably ahead. And saw, appearing out of the crowd away to their left by the betting ring, two men walking towards them. One was tall and broad with sandy hair, the other was shorter, carrying a hold-all. As they passed in front of her, she made the connection. It was Jamie Sullivan and one of the others who'd been in the car, Malcolm Priest. They were heading for the trackside car park. In a few minutes Jamie Sullivan would be gone and their only chance of justice gone with them.

Her brother was still mumbling apologies. A man with the means to take vengeance but broken by his own failings.

'Clem,' she said in a voice that commanded attention. 'There's something I haven't told you about our Marie. She's been seeing Jamie Sullivan.'

That woke him up. 'What do you mean "seeing"?'

'He writes to her. They meet. Use your imagination.'

His face began to redden and his eyes bulged, all trace of weary self-reproach banished in an instant. He was imagining things all right.

'Sullivan's just over there with his brother-in-law. They're going into the car park.'

Clem didn't waste breath on words. He was on his feet, moving slowly but steadily in the right direction.

Joyce took his arm. By crikey she'd push him all the way there if she had to.

Once they were away from the crowd Jamie started, as Malcolm knew he would. He'd had that look on his face, as if he couldn't contain himself any longer.

'I don't know how to put this, Mal, but you know I've been having dreams about the crash?'

Malcolm knew all right.

'They're screwing me up. They won't stop. And I'm not sure if they're what really happened. The doctor said my memory might come back. Suppose it has?'

'What's in your dreams then, Jamie?' He needed to know.

'Don't take offence, Mal, but I picture us all in the car – you, me and Rich. Only I'm not driving. *You* are.'

They were in the car park now, walking along a row of vehicles, Jamie still talking urgently.

'Then I dream about the smash, and you and Rich pulling me out. You both think I'm dead.'

'You did look like a goner for a while.' *And it's a damn shame you weren't – it would have saved a load of hassle.*

'Because you and Rich think I'm dead, you decide you'll say I was driving.'

Malcolm forced a laugh. They'd reached his BMW and he unlocked the boot. 'Chuck your bag in the car.'

If he could get Jamie out of here and off the main road he'd be able to deal with him. They'd take the scenic route over the high fells. There were a few places up there where a body would never be discovered. They'd stop for a breath of fresh air and he'd take Jamie while he was unaware. The man was such a trusting fool – how had he survived in prison?

Malcolm opened the driver's door. Jamie was on the other side of the car, still talking.

'I feel terrible bringing this up. You've always been great to me, Mal. Visiting me inside, giving me a home. And that money you lent me.'

301

'You'll have me in tears in a moment. Just shut up and get in the car.'
Please.

As a rule, police officers do not witness crimes – they are just called upon to solve them. But there are exceptions to any rule.

Jane and Simon had reached the racecourse eventually and had spent half an hour engaging in that well-known pastime of looking for a needle in a haystack.

'I never thought there'd be such a crowd on a weekday,' said Simon. 'Haven't these people got jobs to go to?'

'I except they're all schoolteachers up from Lancashire,' remarked Jane drily.

They were not helped by never having seen Malcolm Priest in the flesh. Armed only with the football photograph ('OK,' admitted Simon, 'it does look like a bruise') and the internet-generated image of Malcolm and Jamie going to court, it was not a simple task.

Jane rang Colin Stewart and asked him if he knew what kind of car Priest would be driving. He called back after a couple of minutes with the information – a black BMW. What's more he supplied the registration number. Jane reckoned she owed the young detective a drink or two.

'If we can spot his vehicle,' she said to Simon, 'then at least we'll know he's at the course.'

Simon regarded her sardonically. 'There's a few car parks here, you know. We'd be better off watching the exits. Or the men's bogs.'

Jane ignored him and caught the attention of a passing steward. A few moments later she was hustling Simon past the bookies in the ring, away from the stands. Ahead could be seen lines of cars parked alongside the track.

'That's where the owners and trainers park, apparently. I bet that's where he's put his car.'

They looked across the vista of stationary vehicles.

'Bloody hell, Jane!' Simon cried. 'That's him!'

She saw him at the same time – a tall, square-shouldered figure standing at the open door of a black saloon, facing another man across the roof of the car. Jamie Sullivan.

Then her view of the jockey was blocked out by a large bulky man, moving awkwardly, supported by a broad-beamed middle-aged woman.

The pair moved slowly along the path, heading directly towards the BMW.

Jane's attention was on Malcolm Priest. 'Quick, Simon,' she said, striding forward, 'before he gets away.'

Clem's breath whistled and spluttered in his ruined chest, the sound of it deafening in his ears. Surely Sullivan could hear him puffing like a steam train?

He was close now, just the width of a car away. Near enough. His limbs were as heavy as lead and he raised the gun in slow motion.

He held it at arm's length in both hands, like he'd seen in the movies, and aimed at the back of the jockey's head. The gun-sight wobbled in his shaky grasp.

He had to be quick.

He forced his hands to be still.

'Get in, mate. I want to beat the traffic.' Malcolm sounded impatient.

Jamie opened the car door. He supposed he had been yakking on a bit. There was plenty of time to talk on the journey.

As he ducked to step inside there was an almighty bang in his ear and he pitched forward. A bomb, he thought stupidly.

There were more bangs and the sound of shattering glass. Jamie crouched in the well of the car, his face pressing against the rubber footmat. He was aware of shouts and scuffling close by.

A voice cried, 'Police! Don't move!' but he scarcely registered the words. His attention was fixed straight ahead as he looked through the car and out of the open door on the driver's side. Lying on the ground, his brother-in-law and good friend Malcolm stared sightlessly up at the sky, a wet red hole in his neck.

The train was pulling in, thank God. All Dave had to do was give Pippa a quick peck on the cheek and hop on board, out of her life. Despite what he'd said about keeping in touch, he knew he wouldn't. Best not to, all things considered.

She'd stopped haranguing him five minutes back but she'd refused to go. Instead she'd accompanied him onto the platform, a hurt and reproachful presence by his side.

'This is it then,' he said, turning to her.

Her mobile rang and she glanced at the incoming number. 'It's Jamie,' she said. 'Probably wondering where I've got to.'

Dave hoisted his pack. 'Tell him cheerio from me.'

She had the phone to her ear. 'Tell him yourself. He wants to talk to you.'

Dave took the little instrument with reluctance. He'd been through all this with Jamie. Carlisle passengers were alighting from the train, taking their time with cases and bags. Their southern-bound replacements hefted their luggage impatiently. Dave still had time.

'Yes, Jamie?'

He listened with increasing concentration. And disbelief. The passengers rearranged themselves on the train and doors began to slam shut.

Pippa jostled his arm. 'You're going to miss it.'

He cut off the call and pointed to a bench. 'Sit down, Pippa.'

'But what about the train?'

'Forget the train. Just sit down.'

'He changed your mind? You're not going after all?'

He nodded and her face lit up.

This was going to be hard. They watched the train depart. And after all the noise and activity had died away, he told her about Malcolm.

Epilogue

4 May, 2002

It was a pity, Jane thought, that you couldn't put the dead on trial. Even though Malcolm Priest was no longer among the living, natural justice surely demanded a public airing of his crimes.

But though it wasn't possible to try a corpse, it was necessary to mount a case against a man who was half dead. Clem Kirkstall had suffered a heart attack on the day after he'd tried to kill Jamie Sullivan and had been in hospital, under police surveillance, ever since. According to the doctors, he was unlikely to live long enough to take his place in the dock.

Jane had been busy since the shooting at Carlisle Racecourse. With three murder enquiries spread across three regional police forces, she was much in demand.

'I'm thinking of retiring and writing a book,' she said to Simon as he entered the bedroom with a breakfast tray. He was wearing a pair of Calvin Klein boxer shorts. Whereas she herself – as she had pointed out to him the night before – preferred to sleep à la Marilyn Monroe, dressed in just a dab of perfume.

'What kind of book?' he asked, as he set about arranging coffee cups and plates on the bedside table. He seemed to have magicked fresh orange juice and croissants out of the air as well. She could get used to this.

'True crime. The wicked deeds of Malcolm Priest. I've got tons of stuff on him now. Did you know he was discharged from the Army after an accident in an armoured car? Malcolm ran over one of his own men. He never was the safest driver.'

Simon reclaimed his place on the other side of the bed.

'Will I get a mention in this epic?' he asked.

'You are the sceptical Mr Plod who refused to listen to the brilliant insights of your colleague and superior i.e. me. However, you do redeem yourself in the end.'

And that he had. Jane's theories about Malcolm would have remained wild speculation but for Simon, who had reminded Jane that certain items from the original crime scene had been preserved in the hope of yielding a DNA match with the perpetrators of the crime. These included cigarette ends, used paper tissues and soft drink cans, most of which had been discarded by the firefighters and spectators who had gathered to rubberneck the blaze.

But Simon had been remorseless in chivvying the laboratory for a test on everything, and they had finally matched Malcolm's DNA with that on a cud of chewing-gum picked off the pavement outside the cottage. It was the link that had turned Jane's pie-in-the sky theories about the Bonfire Night Murders into something more earthbound.

Confirmation of Malcolm's culpability in Alan Kirkstall's death had been easier to prove. Unable to stand up to some probing police interrogation, Richard Priest had admitted that his brother had been driving and that he'd lied to protect him. He'd failed to shield his father, who had supported the brothers after the event, and the pair of them now faced a charge of conspiring to pervert the course of justice. It was a pity that Malcom wasn't able to stand trial alongside them. In a funny way, Jane felt sorry for Richard. With a father and brother like that, she imagined it would have been hard for him not to swim with the tide.

The person Jane felt most sympathy for, however, was Clem. She gathered from her Cumbrian colleagues that, when the doctors had finally allowed them to interview him, he had been consumed with remorse. He was convinced that he'd murdered the wrong man.

It had given her great pleasure to visit the dying man and reveal that he had avenged his son after all – even if it had only been by accident.

'Marie told me Jamie didn't do it,' Clem had whispered, so softly that she'd had to lean close to his bedside to catch his words. 'I didn't believe her.'

'But you must, she's telling the truth.'

'What a great fool I am,' he'd said but she didn't agree. She thought he was a bit of a hero.

She turned now to Simon, who was sitting up in bed by her side. 'Aren't you eating?'

'It's more fun watching you,' he said, leering as the crumbs from her croissant settled on the slopes of her breasts.

She blushed under his gaze. Things were turning out better than she'd thought possible.

The day before, she'd finally met Colin Stewart who told her the Coroner was scheduling an inquest into Beverley Harris's death.

'I'm sure Malcolm killed her,' he said as they sat down. 'Just like you said straight off. Very impressive, ma'am.'

She accepted his praise gracefully. He looked even younger than she had imagined. But there was no denying he was competent.

'We turned up a witness who saw a man get out of a black BMW near Beverley's cottage on the evening she died. An old lady who lived round the corner. A bit of a curtain-twitcher obviously but worth her weight in gold, I reckon.'

Jane agreed. 'Nosy old ladies are often a better bet than a CCTV camera.'

'This one, Mrs Thomson, can't remember much about the man but she does recall he was carrying a big display of flowers. Roses and carnations, she says, scarlet and white. Jamie Sullivan says that when his brother-in-law came home that night he had a large flower display which he said was a peace-offering for his wife, with whom he'd had a row. Mrs Priest confirms the flowers – red roses and white carnations – and also the row. Guess what it was about?'

He didn't wait for her answer. 'Beverley Harris. She'd rung Mrs Priest and claimed Malcolm had been propositioning her. Of course, he'd been doing more than that. Apart from Karen Robinson's testimony, we found Malcolm's DNA and prints all over the bedroom.'

'Well done, Colin. You've convinced me.'

'Wait. That's not all.' He was anxious to give her the whole picture. 'We took away some of his clothes for examination and found a key in a trouser pocket. The key to Beverley Harris's bathroom. I reckon he pocketed it just before she went into the bathroom, in case she got all modest and locked him out. Then he forgot to put it back.'

'The fatal mistake. Murderers usually make one. Though I suppose he might have got away with it.'

307

Colin shook his head. 'Never. I was after him. I'd have nailed him too if he hadn't been daft enough to get himself shot.'

'You sound quite keen on this Colin,' Simon had remarked the evening before as she'd recounted their meeting.

'I am,' she said, sitting at the place he'd laid for her at the dinner-table.

'Should I be jealous?' He was lifting something aromatic out of the oven – her oven, which she used only to warm plates and bake ready meals.

'Dreadfully,' she said, sipping the wine he had poured her. 'Any virile young man is a temptation for me. So you'd better not let your standards slip.'

He'd stood behind her and placed his hands on her shoulders, pressing his thumbs into the flesh at the base of her neck. She shivered with pleasure.

'Yes, boss,' he growled in her ear.

They were at the beginning of something good and both of them knew it. They were trying to keep their feet on the ground but it was hard.

'Jesus, Mum,' Robbie had complained when she'd spent an hour on the phone with Simon. 'You're in love with him, aren't you? Admit it.'

But she wouldn't admit that to herself.

And Tanya, so Jane had gathered, was giving Simon an equally hard time.

Now they'd spent a whole night together and it had taken a bit of arranging. Jane and Simon had not only had to synchronise their own calendars but had to make sure their offspring were otherwise taken care of.

Tanya and Robbie seemed to have a more mature friendship than their parents. Jane had yet to catch them snogging on the doorstep. They listened to impenetrable music. Robbie was teaching Tanya to play a better class of chess. And, at Tanya's instigation, the pair of them went on trips to see his grandmother at The Palm Tree.

Jane was delighted, and mightily surprised. 'I got the impression from you,' she said to Simon, 'that your daughter was a party girl. Now it turns out she's Mother Teresa.'

He'd just shrugged – he didn't understand either.

So, as they lay side by side in bed, wearing little but their own happiness, it was with alarm that they heard the front door open down the hall.

'Oh God, Robbie's back,' cried Jane, leaping out of bed and grabbing her dressing-gown. 'You'll have to stay in here, Simon.'

But it was too late.

'Mum?' The knock was an accompaniment to the door swinging wide open. By Robbie's side stood Tanya.

Caught red-handed.

Jamie sat on the step of Dave's caravan, scratching Matilda's ears. She wanted him to take her for a walk but he wasn't budging just yet, he was waiting for someone. Besides, it was a peaceful spot. He could see why Dave was so attached to it.

Malcolm's death had been a complete bombshell, to be followed by even bigger explosions. Even now, after the information that the police had laid before him, Jamie found it hard to believe that Malcolm had been anything other than the benign and generous brother-in-law whom a man could trust with his life.

'It's extremely fortunate for you,' the sympathetic policewoman had said, 'that you did not leave the rececourse with Malcolm once you had revealed to him that your memory had returned. He might well have decided to dispose of you on the way home.'

Jamie had found that hard to believe.

'Think about it,' she'd said. 'He'd already got rid of three other people who were inconvenient to him. And you were the most inconvenient of all. I suspect if his brother had not been present he would have ensured that you didn't survive the car crash.'

Jamie had said nothing to that.

'Of course, this is just my supposition. I couldn't prove it.'

But they'd proved plenty of other things and Jamie had hardly known how to handle it. It had been even worse for Pippa, realising she'd been sharing her life with a murderer.

Fortunately Dave was still on hand – no more had been said about his threat to return south – and, of course, there were the horses. Pippa had spent a day in bed, sedated against shock, then got up for first lot the next morning. The life of a training yard couldn't come to a halt just because of a seismic human drama. The animals came first.

309

So they'd just worked their way through it. While the police trawled through the house, examining Malcolm's possessions, demanding lengthy interviews from all of them about what had happened when, the three of them and the yard staff had just mucked in and done the best they could. The funny thing was, they'd done pretty well. It had been the best beginning to the Flat season Pippa had had and she was turning owners down. It was funny how things worked out.

The day after Malcolm was killed, when Jamie had no idea whether he was coming or going, he'd taken a phone call from Bertie Brooks. At last his former agent had got round to getting in touch. Thinking about it, Bertie's timing had never been that good.

Jamie had been polite but the decision was suddenly clear-cut. He wasn't going to hand his riding career over to someone he didn't trust. Where was Bertie when he'd stumbled out of Garstone unsure if he even had a future in racing? He'd rather be represented by a rank amateur who'd walk through fire for him.

'Dave,' he'd said. 'Would you like to be my agent?'

'What would I have to do?'

'Ring round trainers and get me rides. Be in there quick when someone else drops out. Big me up and say I'm the greatest jockey on the circuit.'

'But you are, mate. I can do that easy.'

So that had solved that.

Matilda wuffed excitedly and Jamie looked up. Was that a fox slinking across the corner of the field? At any rate, it wasn't who he was expecting.

Matilda calmed down and put her head on his knee.

Vanessa had left. Today would have been her wedding day but that prospect had gone up in smoke. Following Richard's disgrace, no one had been surprised. But Jamie knew that wasn't the real reason. Vanessa had told him Richard had called the wedding off the night before Malcolm was shot. He knew why too and, had it not been for other events, he would have felt guilty. But he was done with guilt.

'You're better off without him,' he said to her. 'Why on earth be jealous of what you got up to with me a few years ago?'

'You're right,' she said. 'I might go back to Australia for a bit. No offence, Jamie, but the guys there have got real balls.'

He looked at his watch. Marie was late. He knew it was hard for her to fit everything in. It was a long trip to hospital to see her father and she spent a lot of time with her Aunt Joyce. The woman had come within a whisker of being charged with being an accessory to murder but it looked as if she'd escaped. Since the intended murder victim had been himself, that made the situation difficult. Particularly for Marie.

Matilda lifted her head and then bolted for the gate. As she careered out of sight he heard a familiar voice welcoming the dog.

A few seconds passed and he fought the urge to run after Matilda. He liked this moment best of all, when Marie came through the gate and walked towards him, a shy smile on her lips and the sunlight catching her thick fair hair.

Just as it did now.